Tox County Teach

A Novel by

John Banks

819 Publishing

Copyright © 2020 by John Banks
All rights reserved. No part of this work may be reproduced or transmitted in any form or by any means, except by reviewers who wish to quote brief passages.
Published by 819 Publishing
3404 Old Acre Ct.
Greensboro, NC 27410
Cover Design by BespokeBookCovers
Printed in the United States of America
ISBN: 978-0-9833334-2-5

Also by John Banks

W – A Novel

Tox County Teach

1

ONE SUMMER SATURDAY when I was eight, my mom decided she wanted to spend the afternoon visiting with her friend, Mary, who lived about a mile from our house. We lived out in the country, with houses far apart and sitting on large tracts of land within the desolate remains of pine forests. My dad was on the road.

"It's *Saturday!* Can I just stay here?" I said. Normally, I would spend most of Saturday with Charles, but he was at the beach.

"I'm not leaving you here alone all afternoon. You and Robbie go put on your shoes."

"I don't want to!"

"I don't care if you don't want to. You two go pick out a couple of games to take with you. You can watch TV."

As we were getting ready to leave, our Chihuahua, Señor Perro, came running up to us, tail wagging, mouth panting and yapping. Any collective movement within the household would set him off. Mom bent over and vigorously rubbed the dog along both flanks. As was her habit, she started babbling in baby talk. (She had another habit, more unusual – if Señor Perro misbehaved, she would inexplicably translate the dog's name into English – Mister Dog! Bad Mister Dog!) Although technically belonging to me and Robbie, Señor Perro was most loved by our mom. He, true to his nature, had a tendency to snap at us if we got too rough, which we, true to our natures, usually did.

Robbie and I selected the games we wanted. I chose *Monopoly* because it had a car as a game piece. Robbie, four years my junior, chose one of his silly kid games called *Horsefeathers!,* which involved putting strange animal body parts together to create even more unusual creatures.

Mary was an older woman who lived alone, and there wasn't anything in her house for a kid to get excited about. Robbie and I spent an hour playing *Monopoly* and arguing incessantly. Robbie's math skills left a lot to be desired when it came to counting money, dots on the dice, or moves along the game board. At one point, increasingly frustrated by the whole affair, he threw all the Community Chest cards at me, and the game was stopped peremptorily by Mom when I lunged at Robbie, grabbed his neck, and tried to make him eat a hotel.

Robbie had a more sedentary disposition than I and seemed satisfied to spend the rest of the afternoon lying on Mary's living room carpet watching cartoons. But soon after the *Monopoly* debacle I was desperate to be outside.

My persistent badgering finally paid off.

"All right, Tommy," my mom relented. "I'm going to leave in a few minutes anyway. I guess you'll be okay at home by yourself for a little while. You can go on two conditions. Number one, don't walk in the road. Stay on the grass. Do you hear me?"

"Yeah, yeah."

"Repeat what I just said."

"Don'twalkintheroad. Stayinthegrass."

"Okay. And when you get home, stay in the yard. Don't go into the woods. Now what did I just say?"

"Stayoutofthewoods. Stayoutofthewoods. CanIgonow? CanIgonow?"

Even though Mom had to drive over, it was easy for me to run the distance back home. I stayed on the road all the way. The idea of running on the grass was ridiculous. The ground was uneven and rutted in places; I was much more likely to fall and hurt myself if I followed my mom's instructions.

The reason I was so eager to leave Mary's house was because I was excited about practicing my pitching. Dad, a few months ago, had put up a tire swing in the backyard. Though it had been installed for its traditional purpose, it didn't take me long to discover that the swing was also the perfect device to improve my pitching. The tire's inside circumference was an excellent approximation of the Little League strike zone, and its height off the ground matched the height of most batters my age. Making this development even more exciting, I had finally been able to convince my dad to "ruin" the backyard by building a pretty convincing pitcher's mound. So far, I had collected five baseballs from various places, which I carried in a toy bucket brought home from the beach. After throwing my five pitches, I would run to the chain-link fence to retrieve them. It was a good set-up, though I did wish I had more than five balls to pitch.

When I got back home, after a nearly mile-long sprint, I wasn't even breathing very hard. I walked around to the side of the house, to where the spare door key was hidden, and let myself in.

Señor Perro was at the door to greet me. In my haste to get my glove and bucket of balls, I ignored the Chihuahua. I tended to ignore the dog anyway, though there were certainly times when both of us were in playful moods and I would wrestle Señor Perro and roll with him on the floor – until bad Mister Dog would emerge, turn nasty and snap at me. I had not yet developed a habit of cursing, but would damn the dog in my own little-boy way.

Back outside, I ran to my pitcher's mound in the backyard. My windup featured a very high left-leg-kick, which allowed me to balance on my right foot and lean my body backward to the point where I felt almost in danger of toppling over. In this way, I assumed, I would be giving myself the greatest amount of forward momentum possible as I threw the ball toward home plate. My pitches, more often than not, made it through the center hole of the tire, and sometimes a ball would ricochet off the inside rubber of the tire before being called a strike by the imaginary umpire.

After a half hour of pitch practice and ball retrieval, I heard Señor Perro barking from inside the house. He was impatient and inconsistent when he needed to go outside, so I knew I needed to postpone my fun for a few minutes to attend to Señor Perro and to prevent him from being transformed into Mister Dog when Mom returned and discovered a dog mess in the kitchen.

I opened the back door and the dog immediately scampered outside. We had a high concrete deck with steps leading into the backyard. This side of the deck, facing the backyard, created a formidable concrete wall. And against this wall, which was about as high as I was tall, was Señor Perro's favorite spot to cock his leg – which he now did.

Having done my duty, I was in no mood to play with the dog. I wanted to pick it up and carry it back into the house so I could continue to pitch and to see how many consecutive strikes I could throw. Señor Perro, however, was unwilling to cooperate. He ran away when I tried to pick him up. He ran over the top of my pitcher's mound, under the tire swing and then began running along the perimeter of the fence – with me in full chase. After two laps around the backyard, Mister Dog ran once again under the swing and came to a sudden stop on top of my pitcher's mound. It was here that the dog started doing the unthinkable. Furious and not believing my eyes, I ran to the dog and picked it up, even though the animal was in full squat, with a long, segmented turd hanging halfway to the ground. Mister Dog growled furiously and snapped his jaws at my arms, which were stretched out to full length, as it continued to defecate. In my anger, I threw the dog to the ground. Señor Perro once again took off running, this time toward the front of the house.

I wanted to forget about the dog and to return to my soiled pitcher's mound, which would require a bit of excavation before play could resume. But I knew how fearful Mom was about her dog being in the front yard, where there was no protective fence making it safe from traffic and a dog's natural wanderlust. So once again I was forced to postpone my play in order to be a good son. Señor Perro, however, did not run up the short bank to the front yard. He stopped once again at the bottom of the concrete deck-wall and once more cocked his leg. I took this opportunity to seize the little bandit, and this time I was not going to let go. Still angry at him for desecrating my pitcher's mound, I started to squeeze Señor Perro tightly, holding him the way a running back holds a football. The more I squeezed the dog the harder I wanted to squeeze. I felt my arms squeezing more tightly, and more tightly still, as my teeth clenched and my arms started to tremble. The dog yelped loudly and struggled to free itself. Using my thumbs and forefingers, I garroted its neck to prevent its head from moving side to side to bite me. Its helpless yelping was muffled somewhat beneath my arms.

My anger slowly subsided and I loosened my grip on the dog. I felt badly about having perhaps hurt him and probably would have given him an extra dog treat upon returning him to the kitchen; however, Señor Perro snapped viciously at me, grazing my arm with one of his fangs. I yelled out in pain and all of my anger returned in full force. Señor Perro leaped from my arms, but before the dog could escape, I jumped on it, picked it up with both hands, and with all my strength hurled the dog toward the concrete wall. Señor Perro howled when he hit the wall and started yelping as he hit the ground. Señor Perro's pathetic yelps were continuous, metronomic and piercing. Panicked, I could see I had broken the dog's leg badly. I had no idea what to do. Señor Perro's yelping was incessant. I reached down toward the dog, but it snapped at me again, with foam flecking from its mouth. I started running aimlessly around the yard. The dog's yelping only seemed to be intensifying. I reached the fence at the far end of the yard, put my fingers through the chain links and began to shake and rattle the fence, to what purpose I have no idea, except perhaps to drown out the noise of the dog. As I stood shaking the fence, I suddenly thought about Mom and became terrified that she had heard Señor Perro from Mary's house. I became sure of it. Even more panicked now, I started crying. I released the fence and started walking slowly back toward the dog, which continued to yelp steadily. As I gazed around the yard, I saw a shovel propped against the back of the house – the shovel my dad had used to build my pitcher's mound. I grabbed the shovel and continued walking toward the dog.

When I got to within a few feet of Señor Perro, his yelping was unbearably loud.

"Shut up!"

The dog continued its crazed yelping.

"Shut up! Shut up!"

I raised the heavy shovel shoulder-high and brought it down on the dog's head. There was a metallic clang against the skull, but the dog continued to yelp, now with an even faster cadence.

Desperate, I raised the shovel again – this time to a full height with my arms fully extended upward – and slammed it down against the dog's head.

The yelping immediately ceased. Once again, I was struck dumb with indecision and fright. I stared down at the dog and threw the shovel far behind me; perhaps I was trying to disassociate myself from what I had done. I sat on the ground, cross-legged, still staring at Señor Perro, who lay motionless, a small spot of blood visible on his brown scalp, one hind leg angled grotesquely away from the other three.

The sudden sound of a passing car brought on another wave of panic as I thought for a moment that it was my mom. I quickly jumped to my feet and ran to retrieve the shovel.

The Chihuahua fit almost perfectly into the blade of the shovel, with only his front leg dangling. It was surprisingly heavy as I carried it across the yard. I slowly lay the shovel aside before I lifted the latch on the gate. When I picked the shovel up again, I was careful to keep all the weight properly balanced – especially as I carried the dog along uncertain footing up into the woods. I trudged deeper, deeper, across a soft bed of pine needles, not knowing when to stop – perhaps not wanting to stop, wishing I could continue on forever into a never-ending forest.

Eventually, however, I did stop, and I carefully dropped Señor Perro's limp body from the shovel's blade onto the ground. I slowly began digging through the moist undergrowth until I hit solid dirt. The soil was rocky and the digging became difficult. The grave wasn't very large, but Señor Perro fit into it well enough. Before beginning to cover the dog, I bowed my head and asked God forgiveness. I had stopped crying.

As I finished my short prayer, I was startled to hear my mom shouting my name. The voice was too close to be carrying from the back deck of our house. Once again, I was helpless about what I should do. Mom continued to shout my name, her voice coming closer. I doubted I could finish burying the dog before she discovered me. I heard my name called once again, much closer now. I wanted to run away, deeper into the woods, but I must have realized how futile that would have been. Instead, I reached down, picked up the dog and began walking slowly toward the sound of my mom's voice.

As soon as she saw me, and what I was carrying, she ran to me.

"Jesus God."
I didn't say anything. She quickly took the dog into her arms.

"Let's go, Tommy. We're gonna have to run. We have to get him to the vet."

"He's dead, Mama."

We were running, sticks crunching underfoot.

"No, baby, he's not dead. He's not dead. I can feel his heartbeat."

Robbie started bawling immediately when he saw Señor Perro.

On the way to the vet, Señor Perro started to regain consciousness.

"What happened, son?"

"I don't know."

"Did you leave the gate open?"

"What?"

"I've told you a thousand times to make sure that gate stays closed."

"I'm sorry, mama."

"Well, I know, son, but as soon as we get back you have to be punished for this."

"Is Señor Pewwo gonna be okay?" Robbie asked, his tears dried now that the dog's eyes were open again. Señor Perro was, I imagine, in shock, strangely silent considering the agony he had been in.

"He'll be fine, sweetie. The vet will fix his leg."

"What happened to him?"

"I don't know, sweetie. He must have fallen down a hill or into a hole. Tommy, where was he when you picked him up?"

"In a hole."

Which was the only true statement I have ever made about the incident.

I KILLED CHARLES when we were fourteen years old. He was my best friend, my constant companion, and in many ways more of a little brother to me than Robbie. I had known Charles almost as long. Robbie came along when I was four; I met Charles in kindergarten when I was five. So much of a relationship with a younger brother is adversarial as you fight over shared time, shared space, shared possessions. As we got older, Robbie and I spent most of our time just staying out of each other's way. I suppose I would have been protective of Robbie if he had ever needed my protection; I felt much more protective of Charles, even though we were the same age. It was not just that he was smaller than I – everyone was – but he had a fragile quality to him that was apparent to anyone who knew him.

When we were ten years old Charles got his first girlfriend – thanks to me. The fact that Charles had never had a girlfriend never bothered him very much. Ten-year-old boys have many other things to get excited about besides soft skin and ponytails. But even so, he couldn't help but become infatuated with one girl or another from time to time. This time it was Darlene. Charles confided in me one day how much he liked her, but, of course, he was unwilling to do anything whatsoever about it. "Have you talked to her?" I asked. "No," he said. "Have you even *tried* to talk to her?" "No." "Why not?" He wouldn't say anything else, but he looked down at the ground and contorted his face, which had reddened. He twisted his legs around and looked so uncomfortable that I felt compelled to change the subject.

Charles's shyness around girls was just one small part of his personality, which was otherwise joyous, adventurous, and fun-loving. As I said, girls didn't take up much of our time. In the past, I had humored Charles's truculence toward girls and respected his panicked, desperate pleas that I do nothing to intervene in his inevitable fate of having yet another cute little thing pass unbidden through his fingers.

("Panicked" and "desperate" were not hyperbole. The one and only time previously I had intervened on Charles's behalf was a couple of years earlier, when we were eight. Outside, during a play period, I told him I was going to go up to his latest crush – I forget her name – and tell her that Charles was madly in love with her. I wasn't bluffing, and I guess Charles knew it, for he immediately grabbed my arm and yelled "No!" I truly thought I was doing him a favor, even if he was afraid of the result, so I remained undaunted. I was so much bigger than Charles and he was helpless to stop me. I pulled him along behind me, my pace slowed quite a bit by his tugging. When he realized I was undeterred, he fell down to the ground and wrapped both arms around one of my calves. He was begging by this point and starting to cry. Luckily, all the other kids on the playground, including my intended interlocutor, were too involved in their own antics to notice Charles's increasing hysterics, and thus he was spared any further embarrassment. I was literally dragging Charles along behind me, taking one normal step followed by a lurching, slow pull. Only at a point a few yards from the girl, when Charles's shrieking reached such a pitch and volume that it was beginning to attract the attention of the teachers and kids, did I decide my efforts to help Charles were probably not worth the trauma they were causing. Charles stopped his bawling and blew his nose into his hands [a funny little habit he had]. I expected him to be grateful to me at least for the concern I was showing for him, but instead he became furious and started pounding his snot-filled fists into my stomach. This in turn made me furious; so what had begun as my sincere attempt to get for Charles what he was powerless to get for himself devolved into full-throttle fisticuffs.)

Now, two years after the above incident, I was becoming impatient again with Charles's shyness. I was eager for him to share in some of the pleasures I enjoyed. I had certain advantages over most other boys in that my height and athletic prowess served to make me automatically attractive to girls, which meant I didn't really have to try that hard or worry too much about rejection. Even at that young age – actually, *only* at that young age, for my genetic advantages didn't last much past puberty – I took girlfriends for granted and never allowed a hand-holding relationship to survive a summer break. It was always wonderful to have a beautiful sweet girl look me in the eyes and tell me she would love me forever; wonderful to sneak kisses on the bus or behind a building; wonderful, frankly, to see the jealous stares of others; but once the school year had ended and I no longer saw my sweetheart daily, I found myself inevitably enjoying my freedom from having to deal with girls and everything girlish. When my ostensible steady called, as she of course would, I would be resentful at having my summer interrupted and I would tell her, in the rudely frank way of children, that I had much better things to do. So when the new school year started, last year's love seemed like a wonderful dream a long time ago, and I was eager to start a new dream.

And so I was eager for Charles to experience some of this, too. I knew better than to include Charles in my plan. If he was too fearful to initiate a conversation with a girl, then if I served as a proxy and initiated it for him, perhaps he would appreciate my efforts and accept their happy results. My "plan" was beyond simple. I was going to wait for an appropriate time when I could corner Darlene for a couple of minutes, and then deliver the good news to her – that I had a boyfriend for her if she wanted one. But the plan was more difficult to carry out than I supposed. I never realized how much time Charles and I spent together until I wanted some time away from him. In such a small school, we were in all the same classes, had lunch together, and rode the same bus home.

As it turned out, Charles was soon absent for a day with some ailment probably related to his having snot in his hands half the time.

During recess, I walked over to Darlene, who was with three of her friends. She seemed terrified to be standing beside me, which pleased me to no end. I asked her if she liked Charles. She made an ugly face and said, "No!" Her friends giggled. "Well, you know, he really likes you – a lot." Her friends laughed louder. "He's too shy to talk to you, though. . . . Why don't you talk to him tomorrow? Just walk up to him and say hi – that's all you have to do – I'll take care of the rest." Darlene's friends were laughing it up, but Darlene was mortified. She looked just like Charles did two years ago when I had tried to help him out. I thought she was going to cry. She turned and ran away, her little dress fluttering behind her. Her friends followed, looking back at me and laughing.

With my plan not working out as I had expected, I needed to try something else. Since persuasion had not worked, the only other option I was aware of was coercion. As we were all lined up at the end of the day to wait for the buses to arrive, I went up to Darlene. "Are you gonna talk to Charles. . . *Darlene*?" I fairly snarled her name back at her. Her eyes got as big as baseballs. That had probably done the trick, but just for insurance, I said in a fierce stage whisper, "You better!"

"Leave her alone, Tommy!" one of her girlfriends said.

"I'll leave her alone as soon as she talks to Charles." I started strutting back to my place in line. "And be nice to him!" I added over my shoulder.

Charles was back at school the next day, and I gave Darlene a mean look every chance I got. At lunch, Charles and I sat across from each other, as usual. By this point, I really wasn't expecting to see Darlene, but yet, here she came, walking up slowly behind Charles – as slowly as was humanly possible. Her lunch tray was trembling in both hands. She came along beside Charles and stood there, unable to speak, tray still trembling, spoon and fork rattling. Charles was startled to see her and was struck dumb as well. So they both stared at each other, silent, motionless – two silly statuettes. I couldn't help but laugh. "Well, hey Darlene," I said, very pleasantly. "You wanna sit down with us?" I motioned for the guys sitting beside Charles to skootch over. They weren't happy about it, but they did it.

There weren't many words spoken between Charles and Darlene throughout lunch, but the ice had been broken and I could tell just by studying his lips and cheeks and eyes how deliriously happy Charles was.

So, thanks to me, Charles embarked on the first romance of his life. Darlene became a fixture at our lunch table, and Charles spoke often of their impending nuptials. I think he called her every night. By contrast, I never called my girlfriends, even if there was nothing good on TV and I didn't feel like reading. In those cases, I would lie on my bed, stare at the ceiling and dream of baseball.

This state of bliss between Charles and Darlene lasted for a month, until she decided to tell him about the origins of that first lunchroom encounter.

He tried not to talk to me for about a week, although his task was made difficult by the fact that we were so academically joined at the hip. The only thing he wanted to say on the topic was, "Why do you have to keep buttin' into my business?" "Somebody needs to!" I retorted. We came very close, first, to fighting and then, to crying.

He and Darlene stayed together, but I noticed they didn't talk as much during lunch. We didn't talk about it, but my guess is Charles was no longer sure whether their relationship existed because she loved him forever, or because she was afraid I would beat her up. The latter possibility became more plausible in light of what soon happened.

She officially broke up with Charles and was then spotted on the playground holding hands with a big, freckled kid named Dexter. I had never liked Dexter, and now I positively hated him. (On the playground, it doesn't take much to become fast friends; it takes even less to become sworn enemies – a life-condition that doesn't change substantially as one ages.) Dexter was the only kid who could hit a baseball as far, and throw one as hard, as I could, and we had never been Little League teammates, which would have helped soften our rivalry. We were both star pitchers on our respective teams, and whenever he stepped into the batter's box I felt especially proud to strike him out. Charles probably believed that the only reason Darlene had taken up with Dexter was as protection against me.

Our Little League season was in progress as Charles was trying to get over Darlene. It was great to have Charles on my team this year. You were not allowed to choose which team you played on, and with ten teams in our league Charles and I certainly beat the odds in being chosen by the same team.

(Every two years you moved up to a different age division, which meant every two years you were obligated to participate in the Tox County Youth League tryout process – a process which consisted, in its entirety, of fielding three ground balls and making three throws to first. All the volunteer head coaches would be lined up along the third-base line. All the boys would be anxiously bouncing around in the outfield. When your name was called you trotted in and took your place at the shortstop position, regardless of which position you may have played on your previous team. The coaches all had notebooks, in which they jotted God knows what as one boy after another nervously bobbled a grounder or threw wildly to first. And then, within a week, as I imagined the coaches spending every waking hour formulating and tabulating, bartering and haggling, every single boy who had tried out would be given a spot on a roster.)

Charles was a defensive specialist. He had always played the outfield on his previous teams, but he and I had played pitch and catch so much growing up that I asked him if he would like to catch me on the days I pitched. He loved the idea, and the coach saw immediately how good Charles was as a catcher. But he also loved playing centerfield, where he would run with a feline grace and catch any ball he could outrun. As a batter, Charles choked up on the bat and swatted at the ball fairly effectively. Any team would have been lucky to have him. I, as the tallest and strongest kid on the team, was the cleanup hitter and was disappointed each time I didn't get a hit.

I knew, however, that my arm was my greatest asset. I had been obsessed with pitching a baseball since as long as I could remember. When I started watching games on television at age five or six, I recognized immediately who the star of the team was. The pitcher held an elevated place on a team – on the mound, he literally stood above the other players on the field and looked down on the opposing batters. Each play of the game began with the pitcher. He controlled the speed of the game. If he was good enough, he could win a game all by himself as long as his offense could manage to score one run. I practiced constantly, year-round. I threw a ball against our backyard chain-link fence until I had loosened it to the point where Señor Perro would escape from underneath where my pitches had pulled the fence away from the ground. My dad then put up, in front of the repaired fence, a large square heavy board on which I painted a rectangular strike zone. My pitches would slam against the board with a terrifically loud *thwack*, so loud that my mom complained about it. She said that every time she heard that sharp pop from the ball hitting the board it would cause her to flinch. My dad eventually put up the tire swing that I discovered had an even better use, which turned out to be perfect for me. Once it became rote for me to pitch the ball through the center of the tire, I practiced nicking its circumference, inside and out. I practiced hitting the tire in different places, outside the normal strike zone.

The typical ten-year-old Little League hurler was happy to throw strikes. With his undisciplined, unpracticed motion and delivery, any pitch's ultimate location within the strike zone was determined largely by luck. A pitch right down the middle would be considered a perfect pitch, a bull's-eye. Of course, anyone who understood pitching knew that a pitch right down the middle was an awful pitch – worse, and more dangerous for your team, than any ball outside the strike zone. And often, a pitch outside the zone was more effective than a strike. In fact, there was one pitch, wildly outside the strike zone – but not wildly thrown – that served a very useful purpose. It was called the brush-back pitch.

For most other pitchers my age, a pitch near the head was always unplanned and undoubtedly as frightening to them as to the batters. But if you were fearless enough, it was a smart strategy occasionally to throw a pitch near a batter's head. It spooked the hitter and worked to make him tentative and uneasy at the plate. I did it often. It was part of my reputation as a "wild" pitcher – a false characterization that I happily and advantageously allowed to flourish. (Since no responsible Little League coach would ever condone a brush-back pitch, I could never confess that all my "wild" pitches actually were what the big-leaguers called "purpose" pitches.) But no pitcher's control was infallible, so occasionally I would hit a batter on his hip or his thigh, but luckily, I had never lost control of a brush-back pitch.

A couple of months after Charles and Darlene broke up, near the end of Little League season, one of our last games was against Dexter's team. I was going to be pitching, and I told Charles before the game that, if he wanted me to, I would be happy to brush Dexter back a couple of times, just to scare him and let him know how much I hated him. But Charles was adamant against my suggestion. "Don't waste any pitches on him – just strike him out," he said.

The first time Dexter batted, Charles jogged out to the mound as Dexter stepped into the box. I assumed he was coming out to remind me of what he had told me before the game, but he mentioned nothing about that. He only wanted to suggest to me that I pitch Dexter outside so he wouldn't be able to pull the ball. "Not every time – I gotta come inside some just to keep him honest," I said, which was sound strategy, but I also wanted to keep my options open. However, I obeyed Charles's directive, threw pitches to Dexter that mostly were on the outside corner of the plate, and made no attempt to brush him back. I enticed Dexter to swing at a high pitch, and he popped it up. To show my infielders where the ball was, I thrust my right arm up into the bug-filled night sky and held my breath as Dexter's popup was, first, located by the proper infielder, and then, caught cleanly by our third baseman. There were no guarantees in Little League whenever the ball was put into play; errors were as common as clean base hits.

I retired the side and returned to the dugout. I sat beside Charles and watched Dexter pitch. My anger grew. Charles and Darlene had been the perfect little couple, and Charles, unfairly, I thought, had blamed me for their problems. I accepted that he was mad at me for going behind his back and talking to Darlene, but if he couldn't deal with a little uncertainty concerning her motives, then that was all on him. But we never talked about it. The real culprit, I knew, was Dexter. Why he was even interested in Darlene was beyond me. Dexter was a popular guy with the girls, just as I was, and if he wanted to compete over a girl, it should have been against me. But since he couldn't steal my girlfriends away, he did the next best thing and went after Charles's. So the way I saw it, Dexter bullied Darlene into going with him, just as I had (somewhat) bullied her into going with Charles. I knew Charles was still heartbroken over Darlene, but he would never challenge Dexter or woo Darlene. I thought he was being much too stoical about the whole thing. Though I had earlier contemplated breaking Charles's edict against brush-back pitches and whizzing one under Dexter's chin, that thought now gave me no satisfaction whatsoever. All I could visualize was knocking Dexter off his feet with a pitch right into the side of his head. I had never hit a batter on purpose – but that, I decided, was about to change.

As Dexter stepped into the batter's box for the second time, however, my resolve withered. I stood in my usual pre-pitch position on the mound, upright, with my glove up to my face, touching my nose. I peered through the narrow slot between the bill of my cap and the top of my glove. This stance and glare were designed to strike fear into the hearts of the opposition. Charles set up my target on the outside corner, per our pre-arranged strategy, but I was unable to throw a pitch. I couldn't focus on throwing the pitch Charles wanted me to, outside and high, and I couldn't summon the courage I needed to throw at Dexter's head.

Charles lost his patience with me, as I continued to stand on the mound stock-still, so he came running out to see me. As he approached, I walked off the back of the mound. I took off my glove and started rubbing the baseball briskly with both hands, as I saw all the big leaguers do, although I had no idea what effect that was supposed to have on the ball. "What's wrong, man?" Charles asked, holding his mask in his right hand and resting his catcher's mitt on his hip.

"Nothing. I'm just trying to decide how I want to pitch Lochsquatch," I answered. *Lochsquatch* was what I was now calling Dexter – a combination of the Loch Ness Monster and Sasquatch.

"Pitch him just like we pitched him the first time, man. It worked."

"Yeah. But he'll be expecting me to go outside again. I'm gonna go inside on him this time."

"Okay, whatever. Just get him out."

"I will." Charles jogged back to the plate, put his mask on and squatted into position. I slammed the ball into my glove, which fired up my teammates behind me, who all started hooting at Dexter. But I was only furious with myself, for my cowardice. In my frustration I walked Dexter on four straight pitches, all outside.

CHERYL HAD A STANDING APPOINTMENT with her therapist for every other Thursday at four. It was always a struggle for her to get away from school by 3:30. She taught ninth-grade English at Tox County High School. She enjoyed going to her sessions. She had begun therapy seven years ago when she left her philandering husband, David. Dr. Whitaker – now just Francine to Cheryl – had helped her cope with the breakup of her marriage, and when she had finally moved beyond David, and she and Teach were developing a nice relationship, there was still no shortage of things for a somewhat neurotic high school English teacher to discuss. For the past couple of years, her main challenge had been coming to grips with the increasing probability that she would never have kids. Teach obviously was in no hurry to get married or have children ("Children shouldn't have children" was his response that irritated her the most). And now, more recently, well – she didn't know what was going on with him. Conversations about Teach's strange behavior took up more and more of her hour. Cheryl was grateful her therapist was female; she knew she wouldn't be comfortable talking with a man about Teach – especially with the topics she knew she needed to discuss today.

"Cheryl, how have things been?"

"Well, the big news is, Teach is starting his therapy next week."

"Great! Who's he seeing? Do you know?"

"Dr. Carney?"

"Yes, I know him. He's good. He'll help Teach a lot. I'm sure you're very relieved that Teach is going to be talking to someone."

"Yes, definitely – finally. And speaking of Teach, I have two things I want to tell you about, Francine. Two things happened with him that I just don't know what to make of. Just two really weird things. . . . Are we ready to start?"

"Sure, Cheryl, whenever you are."

"Okay." Cheryl took a deep breath. "Okay. So I decided last Friday night – well, you know that thing I've been talking about that Teach has been trying to talk me into? You know – the butt thing."

"Sure. Sure."

"Well, I finally decided to go through with it."

"Okay."

"It hurt!" Cheryl laughed nervously. "Just like I knew it would. I just couldn't relax, you know?"

"I'm sorry."

"It's okay. I'm fine. I'm probably making too big a deal out of it. But I'm mad at Teach about it, though."

"What happened?"

"You know, I was actually kind of excited about trying it – scared, but excited – just because of how excited Teach was about it. He got so happy when I told him I would let him do it. But I was so stupid, Francine. I was thinking this whole time, the whole time he's been begging me to let him do it, you know – that way – that he just wanted to see what it was like. 'Come on, Cheryl,' he kept saying, 'it'll be fun, it'll be fun.' 'How do you know it'll be fun?' I said. 'Because we've never done it before. It'll be something new, something different.' He kept treating it like it would be this big new adventure. . . . So I finally said, 'Okay, why not?' Maybe I will like it, who knows? Or at least maybe Teach will like it. If it'll at least give him something to be happy about, then I'm willing to do it." Cheryl took another deep breath and averted her eyes for a moment from Dr. Whitaker. She began to speak again, but with an angrier edge to her voice. "But he knew exactly what to do, Francine! He knew exactly how to do it! 'Do we have any Vaseline? . . . Just try to relax. . . . I know what I'm doing.' That just really threw me for a loop. I know it probably shouldn't have, but it did."

"Of course it should have, Cheryl, if you thought Teach had misrepresented the whole situation to you, if that was the impression you got—"

"It was! I mean, if he liked it so much, why did he wait all this time to tell me? He has never said *anything*, Francine, anything at all, about wanting to, you know, to do it that way – and then, all of a sudden, that's all he wants to do. It's like he became obsessed with it or something – which I could understand, I guess, if he's unhappy with our sex life and got this wild notion in his head that this would be something that could really spice things up and all, or maybe he'd seen some raunchy video, I don't know. . . . But he's done it before, Francine! Who knows how many times! And that's when I started getting really nervous. I knew I was going to have to try to enjoy it like whoever this other girl was. . . . Or *is*. Why didn't he tell me? It's not like I would have been shocked, or would have cared. I wouldn't have cared! . . . He never tells me anything, Francine. That's what I can't stand. That's what's driving me crazy about all this that's going on right now."

"I know, Cheryl."

"He's cheating on me, Francine, I know he is." Cheryl expected a response, but Dr. Whitaker only stared at her and waited for her to continue. "That's not even the weird part, Francine. You know, I said that something weird happened?"

"Uh-huh. What was the weird part?"

"He started crying."

"I know Teach has been crying a lot lately."

"Yeah, all the time. But it still took me by surprise. Why would he cry while we were having sex?"

"So this was still during the anal intercourse."

"Yeah – I didn't know he was crying at first. I couldn't see him because of the, you know, the position we were in, and – God, I never want to do that again, Francine, I swear – but anyway, he was just making this strange sound. I couldn't even tell if he was enjoying it or not. And it didn't take him long to finish – it really didn't last that long at all, I guess. It just seemed like a long time. . . . He slumped down against me and held me

23

really tight, and that's when I could really tell he was crying. He was bawling his eyes out. He was holding me really tight and he kept saying, 'I'm sorry, I'm so sorry,' over and over again. And I felt terrible about it. I said, 'It's okay, sweetheart. It's okay. It was fine. It didn't hurt that bad. It wasn't that bad.'"

"Do you think that's why he was crying?"

"I don't know what to think. I know there's something else going on, but that's all I was thinking about at the time."

"And I'm guessing that Teach didn't want to talk about it or tell you why he was crying."

"Of course not. What do you think?"

"So what happened?"

"The same thing that always happens. He runs into the bathroom and slams the door. I tried to talk to him. I said, 'Honey, what's wrong? Please tell me what's wrong. Please tell me.' And he just gets furious and starts screaming at me and tells me it's none of my god-damn business. And he's still crying this whole time, yelling at me while he's crying. If I weren't so mad and frustrated with him, it would be really sad seeing him like that. . . . I just wish I could figure out why he's crying so much."

"It's not your job to figure it out, Cheryl. Like we've talked about before. But, unfortunately, there's no way to get Teach to talk to you if he's not willing to. I'm really glad he agreed to see a therapist. Did he seem okay with doing that?"

"Yeah, I guess. He was real sweet and apologetic and said that he knew he was putting me through hell, but that it was just something he didn't want to talk about."

"Will he talk to Dr. Carney? Do you think he'll be willing to open up?"

"I don't know. I hope so. Teach will usually talk to anybody about anything. He'll usually talk your ear off."

"Well, like I said last time, it sounds like Teach is seriously depressed, but I think Dr. Carney will help him as long as Teach is willing to open up and talk."

"But why wouldn't he want to talk to *me* about being depressed?"

"He may not realize he is depressed. He may not understand, any more than you do, why he's crying so much. Or he may just be uncomfortable opening up to you about his emotions. . . . Now keep in mind, Cheryl, we're just speculating here. I really don't know what's going on with Teach. We'll just have to wait and see what changes we see after he sees Dr. Carney a few times."

"Okay, Francine. I appreciate you trying to help me out with Teach. He can be so hard to live with."

"Well sure, Cheryl, of course. We're just here to talk about whatever it is you need to discuss."

"Can I tell you about this other thing that happened just a couple of nights ago? It's so bizarre. Well, it probably won't seem bizarre to you – I'm sure you've heard all kinds of strange things, but it certainly freaked me out."

"Let's hear it, then."

"Well, it involves Teach crying again. Surprise, surprise." Cheryl managed to smile a little. "I woke up a couple of nights ago and Teach wasn't in bed. I didn't think anything of it, you know, I just figured he had to go to the bathroom or something. And I had to pee, too, so I got up. But he wasn't in our bathroom upstairs, so I figured he must be downstairs. I guess I would usually just go back to bed, but since he's been behaving so strangely lately, I thought maybe I should check on him." Cheryl hesitated for a moment. "Do you know what I was really thinking, Francine?"

"What?"

"I remember thinking that maybe Teach was having one of his crying episodes and maybe since it was late at night and all, maybe he would be a little more vulnerable. Maybe he would feel like he needed me more or needed to talk to me. You know?"

"Sure."

"Well, he was crying all right, but. . . . Well, anyway, I went downstairs and saw the bathroom light on and figured he was just using the bathroom, but I thought I should probably tell him I was downstairs so I wouldn't startle him or anything when he came out. So I walked over to the bathroom, and the door wasn't quite shut all the way – like he hadn't even bothered to push it to, you know – it was open maybe an inch, and I could already tell that something kind of weird was going on and I just became very curious. Do you think that was wrong of me, Francine? Would you consider that an invasion of privacy? I feel really bad about what I saw because I know I wasn't supposed to see it."

"Well, I don't know, Cheryl. It's your house, and the door wasn't closed all the way. It doesn't sound like you really went out of your way to see something you weren't supposed to see."

"Okay, well, anyway – this is just so bizarre, Francine. I really couldn't see very much. . . . But I saw enough to know what was going on. Teach was standing up and he had this blanket over his head. I mean it looked like it was completely covering his head, and covering up his shoulders and chest. And he was naked. . . . And he was masturbating."

"I see."

"And I don't know where this blanket came from!" Cheryl laughed, but a bit angrily. "That probably shouldn't have been my first concern, I know, but I'm standing there thinking, 'Where did that blanket come from?' It wasn't one of mine."

"What did you do?"

"I didn't do anything. That might have really freaked him out. And even though he was completely covered up with this blanket, I could still hear him crying. I don't know what to do, Francine. I feel so bad for him that he's going through all this, but he won't let me help him. . . . So, anyway, I'm standing there with my face right up in the doorway and I'm afraid to open it too much more, but I do crack it open just a little bit more, because I figure he can't see me – or hear me, either, because of all his crying, and he's masturbating, and I can tell he's probably getting pretty close to, you know, finishing, and then – you know, that stuff can shoot out a pretty long way sometimes. Anyway, it barely misses me. It goes *splat* right up against the door. So I freak out. . . . Before he takes the blanket off his head, I run back upstairs. I don't think he has any idea I saw him. When I came downstairs that morning – this was just yesterday – there was no sign of that stuff anywhere on the door, so he at least took the time to clean up his mess, which is a lot more than I can usually say for him. . . . What am I supposed to make of all this, Francine? And that blanket? Isn't that just so bizarre?"

"Well, yeah, it's a little strange I suppose. It could be a fetish. A lot of people – men especially – fetishize certain physical objects. Have you ever noticed him doing anything like that before, or getting sexual gratification from something like a blanket?"

"No, not at all, but then again, who knows how often he does this? He could be going downstairs every night for all I know."

"But he was crying, though. That's what makes it odd, I think."

"Do you think he might be cheating on me? You know that's what I worry about."

"I know, Cheryl, but I don't think we should jump to that conclusion."

"Yeah, but I can't help it. He starts crying when we have the – the kinky sex, because that's what I think he likes to do with *her*. . . . Some young thing at the college, no doubt. And he feels guilty about it, so that's why he started crying. I can't help but think that. And where else could that blanket have come from? . . . He'd rather jack off – excuse my language, Francine, I'm sorry – but he'd rather masturbate with some other woman's *blanket* – a freakin' *blanket* – than to have anything to do with me." Cheryl reached for a tissue to dab the tears that had sprung into her eyes.

"I understand why you would feel that way, Cheryl, but I don't want you to jump to any conclusions."

"Okay, Francine, I'll try not to." Cheryl blinked a few times, caught a couple more tears with her Kleenex, sighed and decided she had talked about Teach long enough today. She was ready to change the subject.

IF IT IS REASONABLE TO ASSERT that every human being gets lucky at least once during a lifetime, then perhaps the same assertion holds true for communities as well. If so, then for the citizens of Toxonomonomonee County, their moment of supreme good fortune occurred in 1948 when two young butcher-trained brothers from New York decided that Tox County would be the ideal location to house, slaughter, process, and preserve in tin cans a variety of meats and their by-products. With an audacity equal to their ambition, the siblings, Joel and Jonah Meyerstein, called their little start-up operation Amerimeat, Incorporated. Their confidence was not ill-placed, for they had earlier, in their basement kitchen-laboratory, hit upon a recipe for flavored meat they believed would make them a fortune as long as their taste buds could be trusted to be representative of American taste buds as a whole.

This recipe became one of the great highly-guarded secrets in American popular cuisine – right up there with Coca-Cola and Colonel Sanders. The product that put Tox County on the gastronomical map came to be called *Mmmmm*. (Trivia buffs were aware of the fact that for the first six months of the product's distribution it was named DFM, for Delicious Flavored Meat. This was an acronym-crazy country, so it seemed like a good idea at the time. The first magazine ad for DFM featured the slogan, "It's so good, it should be called DFMmmmm." It didn't take a marketing genius to figure out their next move.) During the post-war economic boom, Mmmmm became a household word (or at least, a household phoneme) and Amerimeat, Inc. became the luckiest thing to ever happen to Tox County, economically speaking. Ecologically speaking, however, critics of the company wondered if perhaps the only reason the Meyersteins chose to build in Tox County was because they looked down upon the area and its inhabitants as the most suitable for being figuratively and literally shit upon, considering the environmental disaster the company created as it became more successful and branched out into other areas of meat processing and production. Today, the Amerimeat brand was found on everything from hotdogs to honey-baked hams.

Toxonomonomonee County was so named in honor of its indigenous inhabitants, in a show of respect much different than that afforded the orignal members of the now-extinct tribe. Though county documents coming from the courthouse were still sealed with "Toxonomonomonee," newspaper editors and linotype operators eventually began abbreviating the county's name in their publications, and most regular folk had stopped wasting time on all its superfluous syllableage long before that.

Toxonomonomonee Community College began in 1962 as the Toxonomonomonee Education Center, with one building, two instructors (a retired mechanic and a radio/television repairman), fifteen students, and an oak sapling planted to commemorate its opening. Thanks to LBJ and the USSR (for it was those communists – the Soviets, not the Johnson administration – who kept the US on its toes and on the ball during its twenty-year postwar victory party), federal money poured into the state and county, and the Tox Education Center quickly expanded its size and educational scope and soon changed its name to Toxonomonomonee Technical College. And in 1988, to underscore its broadening educational mission, it became Toxonomonomonee Community College.

During its first forty years of existence the college grew at a steady rate – just like the commemorative oak sapling – sprouting new buildings and branching out into the county with annexes and extension programs. Only recently had the continued growth of the school become problematic, as competition for decreased state and federal funding became fierce. Economic recessions hit community colleges especially hard, because as a county's unemployment rate soars (Amerimeat began laying off its workers, for the first time in its history, several years ago), so does enrollment in training and certification programs. So during times of belt-tightening for everyone else, TCC was actually expected to increase its services. As a result, it became the policy of the school to do more with less, as its president boasted in speeches that TCC would now be able to serve even more students even better, by jettisoning many of its experienced instructors and administrators, imposing hiring and salary freezes, increasing class size, shortening its hours of operation, and asking its salaried employees to work longer hours for no additional pay. "TCC – We Are Your Future!" its website's homepage proclaimed, with no noticeable irony.

Teach worked as a part-time GED instructor within the Adult Literacy Department at TCC. Of the approximately one hundred fifty pages of the annually published TCC student handbook, information about the Adult Literacy Department took up exactly three pages. Within those three pages, the GED program was summed up nicely in one lengthy paragraph. Teach's name was nowhere to be found within the handbook.

One windowed wall of Teach's second-floor classroom looked out upon several of the reddish-brown brick buildings that comprised the main part of campus. These buildings surrounded a spacious, leafy commons area. The walkways and wide boulevards of the commons were paved with red bricks that didn't quite match the color of the buildings. For as long as anyone could remember, the visual serenity and beauty of the commons had been marred by a budget-starved paving project whose goal eventually was to replace the fifty-year-old brick of the original commons with a new brick surface. By now, everyone had gotten used to stepping around wheelbarrows and sacks of cement mix; detouring around the yellow-taped squares sectioning off portions of the commons where the old brick had been removed but not yet replaced, forming large muddy ponds during heavy rains; and sidestepping the occasional trowel, shovel, rake or stray brick. The large metal-strapped pallets of stacked bricks had turned into makeshift benches for students on break or relaxing between classes. By now most could not remember what the commons area looked like without all the paving materials, or when the project had first started. And certainly no one knew when it would be completed or even resumed.

Teach, never one to let bureaucratic nonsense go unsatirized, had quickly taken to coining sarcastic, alliterative titles for the whole muddy mess. At first, he came up with the relatively straightforward Perpetual Paving Project, which quickly morphed into the Paving Project in Perpetuity. As the delays became more extravagant, so did the titles: the Toxonomonomonee Travesty of Trowels, the Bricklaying Boondoggle of Bora Bora (strangely), and most recently, the Immortal Mortar Mortification, which Teach's colleagues hoped represented the outer limit of his nicknaming endeavors.

Besides offering classes for GED instruction, the Adult Literacy Department also contained two other highly popular programs. ESL – English as a Second Language – served mainly the growing Hispanic community. There were other ethnicities represented in ESL classes, such as Asians of various nationalities (though no one within the department made a distinction between, say, a Laotian and a Vietnamese) and a few fortunate refugees of war-torn East Africa (though no one made a distinction between, say, a Sudanese and a Somali), but it was a good bet that someone who enrolled in English as a Second Language spoke *español* as a first language. And just as the minority Asians and Africans within the program had their nationalities subsumed beneath their skin color, so it was also that no one made any distinctions between Mexicans, Guatemalans or Columbians. ESL classes were always brimming with new students eager, or at least willing, to learn the language of their new country. It was difficult for Randy, the program director, to find enough classroom space and instructors to keep up with demand. Though not an ESL instructor, Teach had a steady stream of more-or-less English-fluent Hispanic students in his class and nothing stuck in his craw worse than the xenophobic horde (including his dad) who palavered about Mexicans who were too lazy to learn how to speak English. This, Teach loved to point out, coming from citizens of the country that led the civilized world in linguistic indolence. It was Freudian projection on a national scale.

But there were big changes on the horizon for the ESL program. Starting next school year, it was getting some new policies implemented, along with a name change. These changes were brought about largely through the influence and efforts of a newly elected school-board member – a Fundamentalist pastor named Robert McAllister, who also could boast of having the TCC president as a regular member of his congregation. Pastor McAllister fervently believed that if the schools were going to insist on wasting taxpayer money educating people who weren't even supposed to be here, then they should at least waste it as efficiently as possible. Therefore, McAllister was able to use his friendship with TCC's president to push for the implementation of rigid new English-language acquisition requirements for ESL program enrollees.

Though it seemed to be a mere matter of semantics, one aspect of the program which Pastor McAllister strongly objected to was the name itself. As he pointed out to the president: "If they're going to live in this country, then why should English be their *second* language?" Therefore, what was now the ESL program was to be called, beginning next August, EFL – English as a First Language. To McAllister, this seemingly insignificant nomenclature issue was actually indicative of the liberal mindset that had been in control of America's educational system for far too long. It was an example of a misguided multiculturalism that rewarded and promoted an attitude among immigrants that said, although I am living in America, building its roads, preparing its food, driving its streets, shopping its stores, dating its women, utilizing its services, enjoying its pleasures, contributing to its success, harvesting its bounty, depleting its resources, enduring its miseries, and accepting everything it has to offer, I still have the audacity to want to call myself a Mexican.

Teach didn't much care for the program's name, either, so he actually agreed with McAllister on this one point – though they would be at odds over what that point signified. Teach had always wondered why everyone assumed that the English classes that were taught to immigrants needed a special name. When he took his compulsory two years of foreign-language study at Tox County High it wasn't called Spanish as a Second Language. Some community colleges had side-stepped this semantic banana peel by rechristening its ESL classes *ESOL* – English for Speakers of Other Languages. Fine, but still – why was there so much emphasis on the *otherness* of the immigrants within our communities? Certainly, your heritage was something you carried with you, along with your shirt and shoes, as you waded the Rio Grande, and it was obviously the source of much mutual alienation, but why were our schools trying so hard to institutionalize this divisiveness?

The new English as a First Language implementation at TCC was going to have a profound impact on everyone involved. McAllister, through the president, was insisting that students achieve the desired English-speaking outcomes within two years; if they didn't, then it was *adios, amigos.* Teach's ESL colleagues were appalled by the upcoming changes, which would put enormous pressure on students and instructors alike; and if a student with a full-time job, family obligations, transportation issues, health problems, a learning disability, a lazy streak, or any combination thereof, couldn't meet the new goals and was forced out of the program, then how was that supposed to benefit anyone?

And how could anyone be expected to become proficient in English within two years? Teach was certainly nowhere near fluent in Spanish after two years of indifferent study in high school. And English seemed damn near impossible to learn anyhow. Teach was amazed anyone could learn it as an adult. He knew first-hand the difficulties that even native English-speaking students could have negotiating all the nonsensical idiosyncrasies of spelling, pronunciation and usage (as one of his former students once asked, "why the hell was *whom* ever put into the dictionary to start with?"). Like America itself, English was a mongrel melting-pot of strangeness. As far as Teach was concerned, the only truly appropriate name for such a program would have to be EFUL – English as a Fucked-Up Language.

The other program within Adult Literacy was Compensatory Education – called Comp. Ed. by everyone. The Comp. Ed. program enrolled adults who suffered developmental challenges due to birth defects or, in some cases, traumatic brain injuries. Comp. Ed. students were the darlings of the campus as they roamed around the commons on breaks being unabashedly friendly to everyone. Teach loved the Comp. Ed. students as much as anyone, but on more than one occasion he had to defend himself against charges of insensitivity, or worse. "I refuse to wallow in the PC feces!" he once shouted through the cafeteria, feigning indignation. Everyone on campus – even Teach – knew better than to use "the R-word" when referring to Comp. Ed. students; but even so, Teach still managed to make everyone uncomfortable, and he got quite a kick out of everyone shooting him ugly looks, when he referred to Comp. Ed. enrollees (not within their earshot, of course) as, for example, "short-bus denizens" or the "developmentally screwed."

And the Comp. Ed. program was huge. For such a small community college in a relatively uninhabited county, the program would hold its own against any large metropolitan county in the state. It was true that Randy had a developmentally disabled sister and put a lot of energy into building support for the program, but still, Teach wondered, had anyone ever looked into why there were so many people eligible for the Comp. Ed. program in this county? Could it have anything to do with the stench and chemicals wafting continuously from the meat factory and all its nearby shit pits?

TEACH WALKED DOWN THE HALLWAY as quickly as he could without running. He entered his classroom with an out-of-breath exhalation and greeted his students. A quick visual roll check confirmed two common occurrences: he had perfect attendance today and, of all the people in his classroom, he was the tardiest. Teach always had good attendance in his class. It would be gratifying to think that was because of his reputation and skill as an instructor, but he knew it was more a function of the quality of person who enrolled in a GED program; as to the other matter, his tardiness was entirely a function of his reluctance to finish his coffee and to stop chatting with everyone in the cafeteria. He had spilled a lot of coffee on the bricks of the commons over the years rushing to class.

Teach had been employed by Toxonomonomonee Community College as a GED instructor for the past fourteen years. It was a job he loved. Teach taxonomized GED instructors into four basic groups: retired teachers who wanted to supplement their social security and to continue their service to the community (a group which, unfortunately, included an instructor named Clara Bellevue, who taught the class across the hall from Teach, and whose idea of community service was to commit herself tirelessly to shaming kids into shaping up); secondly, there were energetic, experienced instructors who were already full-time teachers in the public schools during the day, yet who came to TCC to teach GED two or three nights per week; thirdly, there were former elementary- and secondary-level teachers who still felt a calling to teach but who could no longer tolerate the madness of K – 12; and finally, there were misfits young and old, who either were searching for their places in life or had lost them. Teach belonged in the third category, but in a Venn diagram of the groups, he feared he would fall squarely within the fourth as well. (Teach had been born and raised in Tox County, but when he left home to attend college, two hundred miles away, he thought he had left for good. There had been nothing for him at home except the memory of what he had done to his best friend Charles when they were both fourteen. After his college graduation, however, he had no plan other than to crawl back home to his parents' house, where he rolled himself into a fetal ball for the following two years. When he made his decision to walk out into the world once again, he became a sixth-grade teacher, a job he quickly loathed and which lasted two years until it ended, quite literally, in disaster.)

The fall semester at TCC had gotten underway three weeks ago. Unlike college-level curriculum courses, the GED program at the community college ran on continuous enrollment, which meant new students could register at any time throughout a semester. However, it was at the beginning of the fall semester that most new students came in. Teach's students were enrolled primarily in his morning class; however, he also taught a class in the afternoon, whose main purpose was to serve those who worked night jobs and graveyard shifts. Teach's afternoon class was a delightful breeze for him – sparsely populated with mature adults on whom he had time to lavish inordinate amounts of attention. It was also an opportunity to catch his breath and to recover from his morning class.

Though its enrollment was constantly shifting, Teach's morning class was invariably composed mostly of troubled teens and young adults. This semester, Teach had thus far enrolled six new students in his morning class, with six returnees from the summer semester. Five students from last semester had yet to return, which was not unusual (after all, as Clara across the hall liked to say, "dropouts will be dropouts"). At this early point in the school year, there was a pleasant openness to the room, with three tables up front sporting only one student each.

George Delmar and Oliver North were back again, sitting together at one of the tables at the back of the room. This was their second year in Teach's class. Oliver had lost his license and rode to school with George, so they were always in class as a disruptive pair, a tag-team annoyance to everyone else in the room. Teach, as a student of history and knowledgeable about U.S.-Soviet relations, had eventually settled on a Kennanesque containment policy for these two, realizing a more complete rapprochement was not in the cards. George and Oliver had grown up together and were fairly inseparable. Each had numerous indecipherable tattoos running the length of one arm; for George, it was the left, for Oliver, the right. They both wore baseball caps turned backward.

George and Oliver would probably never get their GEDs. They never did any work in class, spending each morning aimlessly sketching cars and vulvas and punching each other in the arms and legs. For many GED students, class attendance was court-ordered, and as soon as George and Oliver completed their probation (assuming they could stay out of trouble, which was asking a lot), they would most likely leave the program and drop back down through the cracks of society. Of the two, George seemed to Teach to be the one who might choose to reach up out of the sinking societal quicksand he was thrown into at birth, grasp with his fingernails the lifeline Teach was offering him, and slowly pull himself up to the relative safety of a life lived more responsibly, with a GED and a steady job. Oliver seemed to be a lost cause.

As much trouble as these two were, Teach was glad they were in his class, rather than someone else's. Teach's goal was to keep these boys off the streets; for some instructors, such as Clara, the goal would be to return them there. Teach hated Clara and some days his most difficult task was to remain civil to her, a task at which he sometimes failed.

At the table across the aisle from George and Oliver sat Jerry Speziak. Jerry, a new enrollee, was being allowed a table to himself because of his obesity. Jerry was a terrible speller, but luckily spelling didn't count for much on the GED. Jerry was also an artist and was always drawing in class. Teach thought Jerry might suffer a bit from delusions of grandeur; but, Teach knew, that was how lonely kids like Jerry coped – they had nothing but their dreams to lean on.

Teach imagined Jerry had been picked on a lot – he exemplified those students who, rather than endure two more years of public school, enrolled in the GED program, came to class for three hours a day and then devoted the rest of the day to their unique interests; they got their GEDs in a few weeks and enrolled in the college curriculum one or two years sooner than they could have if they had followed the traditional track. Teach never asked students why they had left their previous schools. It was none of his business; besides, they would volunteer that information eventually through their conversations with him or through their practice essays. (Clara, on the other hand, would often request – *demand* – this information from her teen-aged pupils and then publicly berate them, first, for doing whatever stupid things they did, such as getting pregnant or getting into fights, which made their lives more difficult than they had to be, and then secondly, for compounding their troubles by making the ultimate stupid decision to drop out of school. Clara was a witch.)

At the table in front of Jerry Speziak were Pilluz and Steve. They were new enrollees, but Teach was already wary of both. "Pilluz" was the *nom de rap* of one Andre Porter. Teach, who many years ago had chosen his own form of personalized identification, was naturally curious about the origin of "Pilluz." He doubted it had much to do with sleep, since Pilluz was a hyperactive hip-hop machine throughout class. "It means big booty, Teach," Pilluz explained. "That's what I like. Something I can lay my head down on and go to sleep, after we finish up business. Mmm, mmm, big and round, baby, that's how they gotta be." Pilluz was the only African American male in class (except for, perhaps, Huy), which, in this rural county, automatically put him under a suspicious spotlight. But that worried Teach much less than the fact that Pilluz was one of those energy-addled, music-obsessed kids who would quickly become a class irritant.

Teach had already admonished Pilluz more than once to stop rapping in class and to keep his human beatbox turned off. And then there were those hand movements all rappers seem to have been born doing, like a genetic hip-hop meme. If you were sitting beside or behind one of these guys, it was difficult to focus on algebraic expressions when you had someone like Pilluz waving his arms around like a spastic maniac.

Sharing a table with Pilluz was Steve Abking. He was a likable young man, but a bit too much so. Highly gregarious, continuously turning around in his chair, and congenitally unable to whisper, he was tall, fit, obviously athletic. He was of a type you rarely saw in GED classes. Most kids such as Steve want to stay in school to participate in athletics.

Across from Steve and Pilluz were Maria and Julie. Maria Gonzales was Mexican, but, unlike most immigrant students her age, she had been in America long enough to learn just enough English to test out of the ESL program and to enroll directly in a GED class. As with most Hispanic students Teach had had the pleasure to meet, Maria was exceptionally well-mannered, conscientious, and determined to complete her GED. Maria was also pregnant, which was news she couldn't wait to share with everyone. Teach had proffered the obligatory congratulations, but was mostly concerned with how pregnancy and motherhood would affect Maria's enrollment status. How many wonderful, studious girls had he had in class through the years whose midriffs had ripened imperceptibly with each passing class period, but who, as their pregnancies advanced and complications arose, missed more and more classes? After they gave birth, most would soon return to class displaying their joy and their baby pictures; however, many would develop chronic daycare headaches, suffer from sleep- and self-deprivation and begin showing all the effects of stress brought on by the endless demands for succor from their infection-prone infants and man-child boyfriends. For some, these afflictions proved fatal to their educational goals.

Sitting beside Maria was Julie Grace. She had been enrolled for only a week, but seemed to belong to that subset of disaffected youth known as Goth. Julie had jet-black hair, black painted fingernails, and wore black eye makeup. She favored black attire, needless to say – usually t-shirts and long black skirts. Despite her macabre appearance, Julie was polite in attitude, if somewhat prone to sullenness. When did all this morbidity get started? Teach wondered. He had been out of high school for twenty-odd years, but he didn't remember knowing any kids like this in Tox County. Just another costume to try on, he supposed.

At the table in front of Maria and Julie were Lillian Baye and Charlotte Gaston. Lillian was another new student – one Teach already could tell he was going to love. Teach's criteria for student admiration consisted of only two qualities: the student showing an interest in learning and showing no interest in disrupting the learning of others. As long as they had goals and weren't offered too many distractions, most of them satisfied Teach's criteria most of the time. In Lillian's case, she had already professed to Teach her love of writing and, in fact, had said she wanted to be a professional writer. Physically, she was fat by today's standard, but voluptuous by any other. She wore black high-top Chucks every day. The only thing Teach regretted about students such as Lillian was the brief amount of time he would know them. Lillian needed to brush up on her math, but she probably would be out of his class and out of his life within a few short weeks.

Charlotte Gaston was another student who passed Teach's beloved-student test with flying colors. But unlike Lillian, she was destined to remain under Teach's tutelage for the foreseeable future. Teach had known Charlotte now for three years – or was it four? Charlotte was the class's elder statesman – a title for which anyone older than Maria Gonzales' age of twenty-six would qualify – but in Ms. Gaston's case, she was sixty-nine and thus had fully earned the honor.

As with many older GED students, Charlotte had a hard time with math. She had a lifetime's experience doing grocery-store and K-Mart math, and, since her husband's illness and death, crash courses in bill-paying and Medicaid-math, but geometry and anything algebraic left her befuddled, and when she asked Teach why she needed to learn these things he had absolutely no answer for her. Once, she asked him, "Why do they mix these letters in with the numbers?" and Teach just smiled, put his hand on her shoulder and said, "I know, Charlotte – whoever invented algebra needs to be buggy whipped, don't they?"

Teach had nothing but the highest respect for any student who came back to school not for some type of certification or credential, but just because it was something she felt she needed to do, to finally take care of some unfinished business – to redeem herself in some way in her own eyes. The only thing that concerned Teach about students such as Charlotte was his fear that they would lose heart and come to the conclusion the GED was beyond them. He had seen it happen so many times. It was usually the math that did it, and often the Writing test. The other three tests in the GED battery – Language Arts/Literature, Social Studies, and Science – were multiple choice and not too hard to muddle your way through by guessing a few correctly, but you couldn't pull one over on Pythagoras or trick an essay reader into thinking you knew how to achieve unity and clarity.

Teach was always very careful not to criticize Charlotte. No matter how poorly she did on a practice math test, he always found something positive to say about her effort. You didn't have to tell students they were horrible at math; they were already painfully aware of it. This was another example of why instructors such as Clara Bellevue infuriated him. Clara would get frustrated with a student's inability to pick up on a concept she was teaching, and, if Teach's classroom door were open, his whole class could hear her say loudly, "I can't believe you don't know this already. You should have learned this in the second grade." And he had known teachers like this when he had taught at the middle school – teachers who had convinced themselves they were doing a kid a favor by telling him he was dumb as a rock, when the real reason was so they could satisfy some singular malicious craving all their own. There was a special place in Hell for the likes of Clara – a place where she would be stricken with dyslexia (like so many of her students) and forced for eternity to read Chaucer without annotation; a place where she would be stricken with dyscalculia and forced to do long division out to an infinite number of decimal places. But if Charlotte never got her GED, it would never be because Teach gave up on her or gave her a reason to give up on herself.

Huy Miller, who sat across the aisle from Charlotte, was the most mysterious student Teach had ever known. The only thing verifiable about Huy that Teach had gleaned over these past two years was that he had a strong interest in ninjas, knives and nunchucks. He sometimes wore into class a bandana sporting Asian calligraphy and would engage George and Oliver in imaginary kung-fu contests.

Teach did not expect GED students to be highly articulate; but Huy was well-nigh unintelligible. Huy didn't have a foreign accent or an identifiable speech impediment that Teach could discern, but there was certainly something going on orally or orthodontically that prevented Huy from making himself understood – not that Huy seemed to be the least bit bothered by this failure on his part. When he spoke in class, Teach often just nodded, regardless of what Huy may have said, and hoped that he wasn't agreeing with anything too egregious. If Teach did ask him to repeat himself, it was only in the hope that Huy would revise and extend his remarks so that between the two versions Teach could piece together enough to come up with a credible response.

Academically, Huy was also puzzling. The formal, standardized assessments that were given to each student on a semi-regular basis were utterly unhelpful. His test scores were all over the map. In class, on some days, Huy would successfully work basic algebra and geometry problems, but then, on others, seem to forget how to add and subtract. He would write strange, short, oddly punctuated essays, but with flawless spelling. Teach knew it was quite possible Huy was suffering from an undiagnosed or nascent mental illness or learning disability, which the college did not have the resources to test for, or to deal with. Also, Teach was not unaware of the likelihood that Huy's unpredictability was the result of prolonged drug use. He was under no illusions regarding the drug-use habits of his students; however, since, here lately, he found himself wishing they would offer him one of their joints, he felt uniquely unqualified to become these kids' unofficial substance-abuse counselor.

And much of Huy's mystery, at least for Teach, revolved around his variegated ethnicity. Teach was a member of the generation in Tox County that, generally speaking, had become the historical divide between those who thought little about one's racial make-up and those who thought about little else. As a result, he saw himself as being nowhere near as blatantly racist as his dad, and yet Cheryl still had to chastise him for describing Huy as "a genuine Heinz-57 human being" and "the human melting-pot."

Anyone unfamiliar with the history of the county might be surprised to learn that Toxonomonomonee County had a sizable Vietnamese population, and that the college's ESL program had been created primarily to accommodate those refugees, long before its demographics began leaning heavily Hispanic. Armed with this knowledge, Teach could only guess that one of Huy's parents was at least one-half Southeast-Asian and another parent (or the same one) was at least one-half Caucasian – or African American – or Hispanic – which still left one parent genetically unaccounted for. This ethnic admixture produced in Huy a remarkable skin tone that was impossible for Teach to pinpoint on the spectrum and which seemed to be subject to unexpected variability. Last year, during a partial solar eclipse, when everything across campus became shadowy at mid-morning, Teach watched from his classroom window as Huy walked across the commons during a class break, and later told Cheryl, "I swear the man was as green as a Martian." "You're horrible," she responded, only half-jokingly.

Sitting at the table in front of Huy was Roy Payne. Students such as Roy were a dime a dozen at TCC. They were, in fact, the most common species native to Toxonomonomonee County. They drove pickup trucks, wore baseball caps (turned the right way, not backwards), liked to deer hunt and fish, watched wrestling and NASCAR, rarely read or wrote anything voluntarily, worked blue-collar jobs (or no-collar jobs out in the burning sun), and came back to school only because they got laid off from the meat-processing plant or needed a new certification to keep the job they had. In short, they were good ol' boys. Teach liked most of the good ol' boys he had taught. Roy was no exception. Good ol' boys would sometimes, in attitude and circumstances, come within shouting distance of George and Oliver "white-trash" territory, but typically they were friendly, funny, polite, smart. And, Teach realized, with unending admiration, good ol' boys – including Roy – had something within them that made them do unfathomable things such as volunteer for the fire department and willingly risk their lives running into a burning building, without thinking twice about it, in order to save a complete stranger.

This was Roy's second semester in Teach's class and he was being held back by his poor writing skills. But he was not the worst writer in class (George and Oliver shared that dishonor, if it were possible to call two people who never wrote anything, "writers"), and was by no means a poor writer compared to others who had drifted into and out of Teach's class through the years. Teach, as a way of getting reluctant writers more accustomed to pen and paper, taught them to write in a casual, conversational tone – to "write the way you talk." Roy took this suggestion to heart, with mixed results. The use of colloquialisms and double negatives in essays was not a bar to passing the GED Writing test; the bar, as it were, was set low. But Roy took this conversational approach a bit too far in his writing. To use Roy's love of cars and racing as a metaphor, Teach's writing method got Roy down off the cinder blocks in his front yard and onto the highway, but he didn't know how to steer or use the brakes. He didn't seem to know where he was going and he sure as hell wasn't going to stop and ask for directions. Roy composed essays full of sentences that slammed on brakes, turned around, headed off in wrong directions and ended up stalled on dead-end streets. This kind of whiplash-inducing prose was a bit much, even by GED standards.

Sitting at the table closest to Teach's desk and completing his enrollment at this point in the semester, was Heather Nicholas, a new student. The fact that Heather was sitting up front, isolated from the rest of the class, was probably a good thing. She was already rubbing everyone the wrong way. She was outspoken, which was tolerable; but she was most outspoken about her homosexuality, which, in this part of the world, still made some people a bit squeamish. But even if some of his students didn't like Heather, Teach certainly did. She reminded him of him at that age – pugnacious, pissed-off, too snide by half. Teach, though strictly straight, could empathize with Heather because he imagined her attitude had as its source the same endless, bottomless river of psychic pain from which his anger had flowed as a teen, after the death of Charles.

Today was essay day in Teach's class – the first such day of the new semester. Teach didn't want his students, or himself, falling into a rut, so he had no set schedules; but one day every other week, or thereabouts, he would ask everyone to write a practice essay to prepare for the GED Writing test. Teach didn't enjoy reading student essays because most of them were rather – shall we say – uninspired. Yet some were profoundly moving. For many GED students – especially the older ones – putting their thoughts down on paper was a daunting task and something they took very seriously. For some, a student essay represented the only time they had ever been asked to express themselves creatively – what for Teach was merely another paper to grade was for the student a memoir, a grand accomplishment, something to be reread over and over and cherished forever. (One of many ridiculous rules eagerly flouted by Teach stated that practice GED essays were never to be returned permanently to their authors. Once the essay was discussed with the student, it was to be put in a file cabinet, locked away, and shredded after five years. The purpose of this rule was to prevent essays from floating around where they could be copied and resubmitted by the program's more Muse-challenged students. Teach, however, loved when students asked to keep their essays; he even made surreptitious copies for friends and family, upon request.)

When making essay assignments, Teach always gave students a choice of topics – a benefit they would not receive on the official Writing portion of the GED test. Perhaps Teach's students would be better served if he prepared them for what they would see on exam day by giving them only a single topic on which to write, but Teach's decision to offer multiple topics was as much for his sake as for his students'. Despite the occasional gem, nothing was more tedious than having to grade a stack of identically themed essays.

Today, Teach had his class choose between two themes – Courage or Forgiveness. From his returning students he knew what to expect: George and Oliver would not write anything except maybe their names at the top of their papers; Huy would write a little something, but God knew what; Maria would write in her tortured English; Charlotte's essay would be short, but sweet; Roy's would be a NASCAR pileup. But what should Teach expect from his new students? He had an eclectic bunch so far this semester. He assumed Jerry, the artist, would have something interesting to say, unless his wayward spelling made reading his essay not worth the effort. Pilluz, the "playa" – what approach did rapmeisters take to expository writing? From Steve, the talkative jock – something about having the courage to compete, or forgiving a teammate for committing a fateful error, no doubt; from Julie – something creepy, no doubt; from Lillian – she said she wanted to be a writer, so here was her chance to put her money where her mouth was; and, speaking of mouths, there was Heather – Teach had to admit he was excited, perhaps inappropriately so, in anticipation of reading about her adventures in lesbianism.

Some took nearly the entire three-hour class period to complete their essays; others took much less time. Again, Teach probably was not doing his students any favors by not watching the clock with them (after all, the

GED test was strictly timed), but Teach wanted to give his students the opportunity to express themselves fully and to write the best essays they possibly could – GED regulations be damned.

Near the end of class, as Teach walked around the room collecting the essays, he was asked by Steve Abking, "Hey Teach – what does G-E-D mean anyway?"

"You mean, what do the letters stand for?"

"Yeah."

One thing Teach had learned quickly as a teacher was never to answer a question himself that a student could answer just as easily. This strategy increased student participation and often gave much-needed positive reinforcement to students who rarely got it from anyone else.

"I'm glad you asked that question, Steve. Let's find out. . . . Class, who knows what the letters G-E-D stand for?" Not unexpectedly, Maria's hand shot up into the air. "Maria?"

"Heneral Educational Development, a-Mr. Teach."

"That's right. Very good. Did anyone else know that?" No one else raised their hand or appeared to be paying any attention, but Teach suddenly got an idea. Effective classroom teachers are good at thinking on their feet and are always on the lookout for interesting teaching opportunities when they present themselves. And this was just such a moment. "Okay. I'm going to do something I normally don't do. I'm going to give you all a homework assignment."

That perked the class up.

"Homework! Man, you ain't supposed to give us no homework," Oliver said from the back row.

"Fuck this shit," George added, under his breath.

"All right. Hold on. This is what I want all of you to do tonight. I want you to write down for me what you think the letters G-E-D should stand for."

"What damn letters for," said Huy, perhaps.

"Folks, I want you to look deep inside yourselves and tell me what you think, in your heart of hearts, those three letters should really mean."

"In-a English?" Maria asked, raising her hand.

"Yes, Maria – in English."

"Are a-you gonna do the assignment, too, a-Mr. Teach?"

"Yes, of course, Maria – what kind of teacher would I be if I gave you all an assignment that I wasn't willing to do myself?" (There was nothing Teach hated more than having to do his own ridiculous assignments.)

"Can it be dirty, man?" George asked. Oliver punched him hard on the arm. "Man, what's wrong with you? Cut that shit out. I'm gonna --"

"Guys! That's enough. I want you to take this assignment seriously. Put a lot of thought into it. . . . I think it will show me a true window into your soul."

George smiled and said, "Oh man, you don't want to see into my soul, Teach."

Immediately after class, George and Oliver walked slowly out to George's car. They had no desire to stay on campus; in fact, the only places they hated worse than the campus in general were specific parts of the campus such as the library or their classroom – but their PO was always sniffing up their ass, so they forced themselves to come to class most days. But they had discovered a loophole in the system – the only demand the PO had made was for them to *attend* class. It didn't matter if they did anything. Nobody could do shit to them – not their PO, not that prick Randy who ran the program, not Teach. Certainly not Teach – he didn't give a fuck what they did.

George's car was, without a doubt, the ugliest and perhaps the oldest automobile in the parking lot. It sputtered and smoked as it started and backfired loudly as George gunned the engine. He revved it a few more times before burning rubber out of the parking lot. Neither George nor Oliver was wearing seatbelts. They were barely off campus and on the road before Oliver reached under the seat for their stash of weed. The bag contained only one more joint.

"Shit, man, where's that other bag of shit we had?" Oliver said.

"I think it's at my crib, man."

"Let's go get the motherfucker then."

They couldn't go very far without music, so Oliver pushed the CD they had listened to this morning back into the slot of the souped-up stereo system that had cost more than the car could ever re-sell for. They loved a white rapper named Zero. Zero took his *nom de rap* from his favorite candy bar. "I may be white on the outside, but I'm black where it counts, bitch," was how the superstar himself explained it. The song that was playing was called "No Money, No Cunny" – an ode to Zero's pre-fame past as a gigolo. The music thumped as George and Oliver sped down the road.

George drove fast and took the curves fast as well, slowing only enough to keep the car on the road. Oliver had already lost his license and George, as best he could remember, only had one more point to give. This fact, however, was not taken into account as George careened down the highway. They turned off the two-lane, tar-riddled blacktop onto a sandy road that went back into the pine trees.

George lived in a trailer with his mom. Outside, strewn all about, was all manner of debris, much of it rusted. There was also garbage – mostly soda and beer cans – of more recent vintage. The trailer was in disrepair, with stained siding and damaged underpinning. Inside, the scene was similar. George's mom was asleep – or passed out – on a couch that had its white stuffing coming out in several places.

"Go find the shit," Oliver said, as George headed back to his tiny bedroom. George's bedroom was unkempt, with clothes here and there and a few empty CD cases on the floor – but it seemed almost tidy compared to the rest of the property. While George busied himself looking under the bed and in the bottoms of drawers, Oliver wanted to ransack the refrigerator, but it contained only a few cans of beer and the only thing edible looked to be a half-empty can of Spaghetti-O's. The sink was filled with empty cans and food-encrusted dishes. He opened a cabinet above the sink and had better luck – he peeled open a can of Mmmmm, followed quickly by another.

George came out of his bedroom empty-handed. "It ain't here, man. I think I left it at your crib."

"Motherfuck! You better hope it is, motherfucker. You sure it ain't here?"

"Yeah, man, it ain't here."

"You think she got it?" Oliver asked, nodding at George's mom, who hadn't moved on the couch.

"She might."

"Damn! That bitch'd deal it."

George went into his mom's room and quickly rifled through her drawers as well. Oliver came in. "It ain't here either," George said. "It's at your crib man, like I said. . . . Let's roll."

"You better hope it is, motherfucker."

George and Oliver went back out on the road, cranked up Zero, blasted their last joint and headed toward Oliver's. A few miles down the road, George said, "I'm hungry as shit, man." He was pulling into the Food Lion. "Let's jack some grub."

The Food Lion was not very crowded, which was good, but it wouldn't have mattered. George and Oliver were so practiced at stealing food that they would have been comfortable stuffing something down their pants regardless of crowd size. Rather than risk getting caught outside the store with stolen merchandise – after all, they were on probation – they took turns going into the store's restroom, closing the stall door, and cramming their mouths full of sandwich meat slices snatched from the refrigerated section. They flushed the empty plastic sheaths down the toilet. Three packs of Amerimeat each filled them up nicely.

Back on the road, burping loudly from their wolfed-down lunch, they re-cranked Zero and re-blasted their last joint.

Oliver stayed with his dad in a ramshackle house right beside the road. If it weren't for George's car, now parked in the yard, passersby might assume the house was abandoned or condemned. Then again, George's car may have only added to that impression. This afternoon, Oliver's dad was not at home. He rarely was – which was fine by Oliver. He was welcome to stay with his mom and step-dad, but that dickhead thought he could boss Oliver around like he was his real dad, so it wasn't worth the shit storm just to have a good meal and to see his mom, who wouldn't stand up to the asshole and never took Oliver's side. If she was dumb enough to marry him, then she could have him. Oliver's dad, on the other hand, didn't give a fuck, which Oliver had no problem with.

At Oliver's place, they always popped a porn flick into the DVD player (which George and Oliver had jacked from a house not too far from here, within walking distance through the woods. The owners had been stupid enough to leave their back door unlocked, so what did they expect?), but they didn't pay much attention to it as they rummaged through the house looking for the bag of weed.

"It ain't here either, motherfucker," Oliver said. "I knew it wouldn't be. I'm gonna slice your fuckin' balls off if you don't find our shit, man."

"Fuck you, man. Why do I have to know where it is all the time? Why don't you ever keep up with the shit? . . . Motherfucker."

"You better hope we find it. Keep looking! Son-of-a-bitch!" They resumed their chaotic search, managing to turn a house that was already upside down even further upside down. When Oliver's dad finally stumbled in tonight, or tomorrow night, he would think the place had been robbed.

"Do you think we left it at Tonya's?" George asked.

"What the fuck for? I ain't givin' that bitch none of our shit."

"Well it ain't here! And it ain't at my place!" George was getting desperate. He wasn't afraid of Oliver, but he couldn't stand the thought of losing all that sweet shit. "I'm going over to Tonya's."

"It ain't gonna be there, you stupid motherfucker. . . . I can't believe you lost our whole fuckin' stash."

"Well, I'm going. You can stay here and beat your fuckin' meat if you want to, but I'm going."

Oliver decided to go with George to Tonya's. He didn't think Tonya had their stash, but at least he could get some of what they went there for any other time.

"It's gotta be in here somewhere," Oliver said, scanning the backseat, with his back to the windshield and his knees pressed into the front seat. He shuffled some candy wrappers around and threw a GED book he had stolen from Teach's classroom from one side of the backseat to the other.

He climbed over the back of his seat, accidentally kicking George's head and causing him to run briefly off the road. Oliver lay down in the backseat and ran his arm as far as it would reach up under the front seat. "Check the motherfuckin' glove compartment."

"I did already."

"Check it again!"

George reached over and clicked the glove box open. In doing so, his car swerved over the center line for several seconds, though George was unaware of this, as he had taken his eyes off the road.

There was no pot in the glove box. George drove on in silence. Oliver said nothing from the backseat; even Zero was silent.

"We'll check the trunk again when we get to Tonya's," Oliver eventually said, calmly, his anger apparently having turned into a resigned stoicism. George, however, knew better – this was merely the calm before the storm.

Tonya Gentry lived in a trailer park only a few miles from the county line. Even though her trailer was not a double-wide, which she hoped to have someday, Tonya tried to keep it looking nice for all the visitors she had. She had a small flower garden in the front of her lot surrounded by a miniature white picket fence. That was the dream of every American, right? To have a white picket fence? Tonya had always heard that, even though she didn't really understand what was so special about white picket fences. But anyway, she wanted to be a good American. George and Oliver had met Tonya four years ago at a convenience store. They were in the snack aisle arguing over which bag of potato chips to buy; Tonya intervened by making an alternative suggestion and, eventually, inviting them back to her trailer.

Tonya couldn't have kids of her own, and when she met George and Oliver she could tell they were about the same age her kids would have been, if she had been able to have kids right out of high school as she had dreamed of. Of course, eighteen-year-old boys don't want a mother; they want something else, and Tonya was willing to oblige. She had been obliging boys her whole life. That was what got her into trouble with her dad. Tonya became sexually active at sixteen (well, sexually *more* active – it was when she first had intercourse) and liked it so much she tried to be sexually active as often as possible with as many boys as possible; and when her dad, drunk as hell, found out, he dragged her into the bathroom by her hair, kicked her until she couldn't stand up, yanked her sweatpants down to her ankles and then reached under the sink and grabbed the Clorox. "You ain't gonna be a god-damn whore like your mama!" he yelled as he poured the Clorox up into her. Often during the day, when she worked in her garden or talked on the phone to one of her old girlfriends, she was glad the Clorox didn't kill her; at other times it was a toss-up. "So, Daddy," she often said to herself, "you thought you could keep me from being a whore – well, you always was wrong about everything, you son of a bitch."

George and Oliver pulled into her little gravel driveway. George hopped out of his car quickly; Oliver took his time. They checked the trunk, to no avail. Oliver was ominously silent.

Luckily, Tonya didn't have any other visitors – though she was expecting one any minute now. She had told the boys, over and over again, to always call, or at least text, before coming over. She told them she worked nights at the meat plant, which wasn't a total lie – she had worked there before and would like to get on there again if they ever started hiring. In fact, Roger, the gentleman she was now waiting for, was one of the higher-ups at Amerimeat, so she saw no reason why she couldn't parlay this new relationship into a good job.

She had heard the car doors and met George and Oliver on her little front porch.

"I told you boys to always call. What if I wasn't home? You would've drove all the way out here for nothing," Tonya said.

The three of them went inside. Oliver came straight to the point. "You ain't seen a baggie have you?"

"No, what was in it?"

"Some good shit, that's what was in it."

"Sorry, boys. I ain't seen it. What makes you think I got it?"

"We can't find it. George thought he might've left it here. Stupid motherfucker."

"Shut the fuck up. Why's it always my fault? You don't know where it is, either, motherfucker, so leave me the fuck alone."

"Well, I ain't got it," Tonya said, "and if you two are just gonna fight about it then you can go somewheres else. You don't come into my house and fight, you understand? And if you was my boys you wouldn't be doin' no drugs, neither."

"Well it's a good thing we ain't your boys then, ain't it?" Oliver said. He then remembered why he had come here with George in the first place. He had already given up on finding the weed. Who the fuck knew where it was? Somebody probably broke into their car and jacked it. Fuck it. He tried to make nice with Tonya. "Hey Tonya, since we're here. . . . You busy?"

"You two come stormin' into my house looking for drugs you know I ain't got, and then you turn around and expect me to put out for you? You two need to grow up. . . . You all get on out of here now and come back when you're ready to treat me a little nicer. . . . And make sure you call me

46

first – you don't just pop in on somebody unexpected. . . . Go on – you heard me – get on out of here. I got a friend of mine comin' over in a minute anyhow."

Oliver's short fuse was already half-way lit, and Tonya's rebuff was the spark he needed to set it off. "It wasn't my fuckin' idea to come here in the fuckin' first place," he yelled. "What makes you think you're so special? What you tryin' to get rid of us for? Ain't we good enough for you?"

"With that filthy mouth you got, I ain't sure if you're good enough for anybody."

"You fuckin' bitch!" He lunged for Tonya. George grabbed Oliver's tattooed forearm, but Oliver jerked his arm away. He grabbed Tonya and pushed her down to the floor. He jumped on top of her and restrained her with both hands pressing down hard on her shoulders. He remained in this position, his arms pushing down so hard on Tonya they were trembling.

George grabbed Oliver's arm again and tried to pull him away from Tonya. "C'mon, man – leave her alone."

Oliver relented, but gave Tonya another angry shove as he stood up. He looked at George. "Fuck, man, what are you stickin' up for this bitch for?" Tonya was still on the floor, but sitting up now, rubbing her shoulder. "Shit. Fuck this shit," Oliver said. "Let's get the fuck out of here," he said to George as he headed to the door. They left Tonya's door swinging open as they left.

"Where do you want to go?" George asked, as his car started with a smoky rumble.

"I don't give a shit. Just go."

After George and Oliver sped away, Tonya stood, staggered a moment, went into her bedroom, and, still massaging her shoulder, removed the plastic baggie from her dresser. She had already rolled its contents into several joints. She needed to calm down before Roger arrived. "I know stealing ain't right," she said to herself, "but I deserve this. After all those boys put me through, and they never show no appreciation for all I do for them, and the way they treat me sometimes – I think I deserve this."

THE NEXT MORNING, TEACH BEGAN his school day, as always, with a stroll to the cafeteria for some coffee and conversation. He hoped his eyes weren't still red from the short bout of bawling he had endured on his drive into campus. He crossed the commons, skirted some yellow caution tape and sidestepped a wheelbarrow. He almost tripped over a rogue brick lying on its side. As he approached the cafeteria, a commotion arrested his attention. He recognized Huy's unmistakable voice. He was yelling loudly at another man, who yelled in turn. As usual, Teach could decipher nothing of what Huy was yelling. He thought he should probably break up the shouting match, but, he reasoned, it would most likely defuse itself after both parties got their grievances off their chests. Besides, Teach knew from experience, it often made matters worse when school personnel intervened. These high-strung kids were paranoid about authority figures and didn't always take kindly to having their disputes mediated. But as he reached for the cafeteria door, Teach saw Huy pull something out of a pocket and then, as quickly as a blink, he was brandishing a startlingly long knife. Huy held it under the other person's chin with its point straight up. The other young man immediately backed away from Huy, who then folded the knife back into its scabbard. Teach could not get into the cafeteria fast enough.

After too many talkative minutes in the cafeteria, he hustled to his class where, once again, he was the last arrival. Huy was sitting at his table, slowly pantomiming martial-arts moves with his arms, seemingly oblivious to everyone else. There was, however, a familiar face waiting for Teach at his desk.

James Henry had enrolled in Teach's class last year but had made no noticeable progress toward his GED. James was sullen, slow-paced, noncommunicative, and not a little scary. He always wore a heavy jacket, regardless of the weather, and combat-fatigue pants. He had sat in the front of the classroom, not, as is often the case, because he was an eager student who wanted easy access to the instructor, but, it seemed, simply because he didn't have the energy or motivation to walk any further back. Teach welcomed him back graciously and extended an arm to shake his hand. James took Teach's hand but didn't shake it. As Teach pumped his own arm up and down, James's arm merely went along for the ride. It was nothing more than a puppet's arm, marionetted by Teach. Teach had assumed, since meeting him last year, that James was on a heavy dose of Ritalin or some other prescribed zombie-maker. Or maybe his brain had been fried in a less socially acceptable manner. In any case, Teach was happy to have him back.

New students, upon first enrollment, were given a prescription-drug and medical history sheet to complete, but James had left his sheet blank, along with most of his other paperwork. In his own way, James was as mysterious as Huy – not academically or verbally mysterious (except that he rarely did any work or said anything), but a mystery as to what was going on inside that brain of his. Teach had tried to talk to James last year, but received in return stares that seemed to contain something more than blank emptiness – not the zonked-out stares Teach would get from his heavily medicated students indicating that there was no one at home; in

48

James's case, he gave off a signal that, though he might be at home, he had the deadbolt secured and definitely didn't want to be disturbed. James was not combative with Teach, but his answers to Teach's questions were generally monosyllabic. Everyone else just left him alone. It was a bit worrisome that this semester Heather, the confrontational smarty-pants, was sitting at the table which James, last year and now, again, indolently claimed as his own. But, Teach hoped, perhaps the outspoken intelligence of Heather would spark something in James to bring him a little further out into the real world.

To begin class, Teach took up last night's rarely-given homework assignment. Maria called his bluff and made him disclose to the class his own preferred meaning of "G-E-D" – a saccharine homily suitable for a Hallmark card and the truth of which – though desperately wished for – he seriously doubted, quickly composed this morning as he drove to work through a rain of tears. His attempts to blink his tears away worked about as well as worn-out windshield wipers. As he walked through class collecting the assignment, he persuaded George and Oliver to scribble something down by assuring them there was nothing they could write that would get them into trouble. George wrote "Gigantic Elephant Dicks" as the true meaning of "G-E-D" while Oliver submitted "George Eats Dookie." Oh well, Teach thought, at least he would have something to put into the two guy's work portfolios. On his return to the front of the classroom, he described the assignment to James, though he expected James to be even less interested in participating than were George and Oliver.

To Teach's surprise, however, almost three hours later, as class was dismissing, James handed him a sheet of paper, ripped from his notebook, containing his own personal definition of G-E-D. James didn't say anything to Teach about what he had written. He merely handed him the page, made momentary eye contact with Teach – which he rarely did – and then resumed his slow-as-molasses pace out the door.

As soon as he read what James had written, Teach regretted that he had ever dreamed up the damn assignment. Jesus – first, Huy before class, and now this.

Over a late-evening snack of cereal, Teach told Cheryl what had happened with Huy. "I'm surprised there's not a knife fight at school every day," she said. "It's ridiculous."

"What do you think I should do? I suppose it's my duty to turn him in."

"Are you serious? You didn't turn him in?"

"Not yet."

"Are you crazy? What's wrong with you?"

49

"Cheryl – don't get me started."

"I'm sorry, honey. I'm not going to argue with you, but I can't believe you're asking me what you should do. First of all, he had a knife on campus. That by itself is enough to get him expelled. But then he actually pulled it on a student? My God, you should have called security and had him arrested on the spot. . . . Why didn't you?"

"I don't want to turn him in."

"You have to. You have to turn him in, honey – if for no other reason than to cover your own rear end. What if this Huey – or whatever his name is – what if he stabs somebody, and then they find out that you knew he had a knife but didn't say anything?"

"Yeah, I know. . . . But it's different for me. You can kick a kid out of class just for farting too loud, and say, 'You can still go get your GED' – but this is last call for alcohol for Huy. What's he going to do? He's already unemployed. Without his GED he'll be unemployable. If he gets kicked out of my class, he might as well take that big Bowie knife he has and slit his wrist with it."

Cheryl reached out and rubbed Teach's arm. "I know, honey. You're in a tough situation. You're right – you have a bunch of dead-end kids and it's so admirable that you want to protect them. . . . But you can't save everybody. It's not your fault that thug attacked somebody with a knife –"

"Huy's not a thug."

"I'm sorry, sweetheart – I'm sure he's not, but he still needs to face the consequences of his actions." Cheryl slid her hands down Teach's arms, removed the cereal bowl from his hands and set it on the coffee table, and then held his hands firmly in hers. "Honey, you have got to turn him in – first thing tomorrow morning. Promise me you will. You can't save everybody, Teach, and it's not your responsibility to. Promise me you'll turn him in to Randy."

"I promise, honey. I'll go talk to Randy first thing before class tomorrow."

"Thank you, baby. I know you don't want to do this, but I really appreciate you seeing it from my viewpoint."

"Okay." Teach picked up his cereal bowl. "So enough about me and Huy. . . . What are you going to be doing tomorrow? What's in the ol' lesson plan?"

"Ugh – don't remind me. . . . 'The Lottery.' Shirley Jackson. Did you ever have to read that?" Teach didn't say anything and turned his face back down toward his cereal. "What gets me about teaching that story," Cheryl continued, "is how differently the boys react to it, compared to all the girls. It's always the same. The girls practically recoil in horror; but the boys love it. It's the only story I teach that the boys take the least bit of interest in –

and that's only at the end. They're bored to death until the rocks start flying. Why are boys like that, Teach?"

Teach shrugged but did not respond as he wiped milk from his around his mouth.

"Are you okay, honey?"

"Oh yeah. Sure. Why are boys like that? I hope that was a rhetorical question. I hope you don't actually expect me to explain fourteen-year-old boys to you. . . . I mean, ninth grade is the absolute worst time for boys – the hormones have kicked in, you're pizza-faced and horny, and there's not much you can do about either condition. I just wanted that whole year to hurry up and get the hell over with."

It was sometimes awkward for Teach to be living with a ninth-grade teacher. He had been in the ninth grade when he killed Charles, but Cheryl liked to reminisce about high school and to solicit anecdotes from Teach. He would try to dredge up something comical or innocent for her benefit, but mostly all he came up with were grumpy dodges such as this. But he remembered "The Lottery" very clearly. He had killed Charles just a few weeks prior to the story assignment. He didn't bother reading it, but his teacher had rolled a television into the classroom and his class viewed an old film adaptation of the story. Cheryl was correct – Teach's male classmates shouted encouragement at the TV screen as his teacher told them to pipe down and pay attention; however, Teach had felt suddenly nauseous and fled to the boy's room, where he vomited.

Teach quickly finished up his cereal. "I'm gonna go brush my teeth and get ready for bed."

"Okay, sweetheart – but just a reminder – don't forget about that Huey guy tomorrow morning. You have to tell Randy. You promised."

"Jawohl, Herr Kommandant." Teach went upstairs.

Considering how Cheryl had reacted to his situation with Huy, there was no way he was going to mention to her what James had written on that sheet of paper. Instead, mindful of her admonition about covering his own rear end, Teach went into their bedroom, retrieved the pants he had worn that morning, took the folded paper from the back pocket, and quickly and thoroughly tore it into shreds.

Teach decided on his way to school not to honor his promise to Cheryl. She was right, of course, but he couldn't bring himself to turn Huy in.

He walked past Randy's office on his way to his classroom, holding a cup of coffee. "Hey Teach, come here a minute," he heard Randy call after he had passed by his door.

"What's up, big guy – I gotta get to class."

"Don't worry. I've got Roscoe covering your class till you get there."

"What's wrong?"

"I need to see Huy. Did you see him yesterday before class, on the commons?"

"Can't say that I did."

"Well, I had five students come in here yesterday afternoon telling me that Huy had a knife and that he pulled it on someone. . . . And all five of them said they saw you when it happened, going into the cafeteria."

"I'm sorry, Randy. . . . I tend to zone out when I'm walking across campus. I almost ran into a wheelbarrow."

"So you're saying you didn't see anything."

"Yes, Randy. If I had seen Huy waving a knife around, I think I would remember it. And of course I would have reported it to you, obviously."

"Well, I was hoping you could help corroborate these kids' story."

"Do you believe 'em? . . . I think it sounds kind of fishy. Do these five kids know each other?"

"C'mon, Teach. On this campus? Everybody knows everybody – except for our Adult-Ed. students. Nobody knows they even exist. This is off the subject, but we've got to do something to increase our program visibility."

"We could give everybody a knife."

"Ha ha. Very funny. . . . So you're sure you didn't see anything."

"Randy, for crying out loud. A knife-wielding Huy would be very hard not to notice, believe me."

"Well, I've got to do something. I've got five witnesses who say they saw him."

"Did all these people come in together?"

"Yeah."

"And they didn't come in until when? Didn't you say this alleged knife fight happened before class?"

"Yeah."

Teach smiled and nodded his head. "Do you believe in conspiracy theories, Randy?"

"I can't just ignore what these people are telling me, Teach."

"Have you had a chance to talk to Huy? Not that you'll understand a damn thing he's telling you."

"No, but Roscoe frisked him as soon as he showed up this morning. He didn't have a knife on him. He probably knew better than to bring it back to school today."

"Huy? Do you know who we're discussing, Randy? I don't know if Huy has the wherewithal to know he's supposed to zip up his pants after he pisses."

"Good Lord, Teach. He's not in Comp. Ed. You don't think he's capable of doing something like this?"

"I don't know, Randy. I think people are capable of almost anything. . . . It just sounds to me like these guys got together after class and they're trying to gin something up against Huy. Who knows why. Huy is no saint. I'll only stick up for him so far. Who knows what kind of chicanery he's up to outside of class. . . . And the fact that they're trying to implicate me somehow – that just makes me think they all cooked it up beforehand. They probably know I'm his teacher and they thought that by dragging me into it, it would somehow give their story more credibility."

"Okay, Teach – you need to get to your class. I need to see Huy. Make sure Roscoe is with him. I've got to have him in here with me when I give Huy the news."

"What are you going to do?"

"I think I can get away with a two-week suspension. I really ought to expel him, but since we don't have the knife, and there's no school personnel who can corroborate what happened, I think he got off lucky this time. At least I'll be sending him a message – that we're watching him and that he'd better not bring anything like that back on campus again."

"I don't think you should suspend him, Randy. I know you're perfectly justified in doing so – and I know you're doing him a big favor by not expelling him if he did what they said he did, but you know what usually happens to these kids when they're out of school for a while."

"Not my problem, Teach. Not your problem, either."

"I know, but if you suspend him we'll probably never see him back here again. You know that. We're just The Man trying to keep him down."

"I know, Teach. I appreciate your concern. . . . Is he anywhere near being ready to get his GED? We could go ahead and sign him up for all the tests."

"That's worth a shot. I really don't know how he'll do. He could be the first person at TCC to get every question right, or the only person ever to get every question wrong. . . . He's the sole inhabitant of Planet Huy, Randy. He's a strange dude. . . . But I would really appreciate anything you can do for him."

A few minutes after Roscoe, the SRO, had escorted Huy to Randy's office, Teach could hear, from inside his classroom, Huy shouting unintelligibly down the hall. The meeting with Randy apparently had not gone well.

Randy had told Huy that even though he was officially suspended for two weeks, he was welcome to stop by the receptionist's desk, as he was being escorted out, and sign up for all five GED tests, which would be administered at various times throughout the next two weeks. He was ordered to arrive on campus no more than fifteen minutes before each test was scheduled to begin and would be escorted off campus immediately after completing each test. If all went well, Randy said, Huy would have his GED by the end of his suspension and would be eligible to enroll in curriculum classes beginning next semester.

To Teach's dismay, as he found out after class, Huy failed to sign up for even one test.

That afternoon, back home, Cheryl asked Teach how things had gone with Randy and Huy.

"Congratulations, darling," Teach said. "The threat against humanity has been neutralized. Randy suspended Huy for two weeks – but I doubt if we'll ever see him again."

"Only a two-week suspension? Really? I can't believe that. But I guess it's good that you and Randy care so much about those kids. You have to take a different approach, I guess." Cheryl came closer to Teach, smiled, and put her arms around him. "I know that was not an easy thing for you to do, honey – but it was the right thing to do. I'm very proud of you, sweetheart. I love you very much."

You and Cait are lying together on top of her blanket on her small dorm-room bed. You are both nude. Her roommate has gone home for the weekend. It's dark outside and you can hear the rain. Two candles are flickering on opposite sides of the room. If you lie still you notice how your heartbeat is at times synchronized with the pulsing candlelight. You are both smiling and laughing as you take turns caressing each other while playing a game she devised.

"Gerald Ford."

You softly rub the length of her arm, her skin smooth until you pass her elbow and you feel the fine hair on her forearm, almost invisible in daylight unless the sun hits it just right. As you gently run your fingers slowly up and down along her forearm you can feel the hairs moving underneath your fingertips.

"Made everybody bored. . . . Richard Nixon."

As your fingers continue moving steadily along her arm, you stare along the length of her body. You are up on one elbow, as she lies flat. You exchange these positions often. You trace with a finger straight down, from her neck, along the hardness of her chest, between her breasts, all the way to her navel.

"Put the fix in. . . . Jimmy Carter."

You think about how wonderful it all is, that you are here with Cait, in this room, on this night. And there will be many other nights just like this one. You are aware, even while you are thinking it, of how happy you are, of how long it has been since you have felt happy, of how you could never be any happier than you are, on this night, in this room.

"Those peanuts made him quite the farter."

"No! That's too easy! You only get half-credit for that one."

"Okay. . . . Jimmy Carter. . . . was Khomeini's martyr."

"Okay, that's better."

"Franklin Roosevelt."

You stare at her pubic mound. You harden and your erection tingles. It's tempting to move your hand down and spread your fingers throughout the luxurious hair. But that might take the night somewhere else, back to where you were earlier tonight and where you will go again later. But right now, you want to do nothing that will disrupt this mood, this lazy love.

"He knew how we felt."

"He didn't need to wear a belt."

"Oh, that's low. That's bad. Shame on you. . . . Teddy Roosevelt."

Is it possible your grief is gone? Does Cait's love have that much power? To kill your grief as easily as you killed Charles?

"He went to trap a pelt."

You study Cait's face.

"He was so very svelte."

You have known her long enough to recognize any small part of her face: an ear, her eyes, her teeth.

"He took a long time to melt."

"Okay. Let's move along, please."

"Have we done George Bush?"

You put your palm down gently against the crown of her head and lightly brush your fingers through her hair. Electrified strands cling to your fingers as you raise your hand and return to the top of her head.

"What a dush. . . bag."

"Ha! Good one."

"Abe Lincoln."

"How did you get from George Bush to Abraham Lincoln?"

"Opposites attract."

You close your eyes, as you continue to stroke her hair. You slide your hand behind her neck and put your fingers through her hair from underneath. You gently work your way through a mild tangle.

"He drove Jeff Davis to drinkin'. . . . James Garfield."

It is now raining harder. You turn over on your back as Cait moves her hand along your torso. Your erection is back and you wonder what she's going to do with it. But you are not going to ask any favors or make any demands. You want her to maintain control of the mood. However, you find it nearly impossible to continue paying attention to the game; but it was her idea. . . . You play on.

"He got shot and killed."

"You tell it like it is."

"Keep going."

"What? The game. . . or what I'm doing?"

"Well, of course what you're doing. . . . But keep the game going, too. Lots of presidents left."

"Whose turn is it?"

"Mine, I think. . . . James Knox Polk."

She moves her hand slowly toward your erection.

"Manifest Destiny was such a joke. . . . Harry Truman."

She is combing her fingers through your pubic hair, but she doesn't touch anything else. This is killing you.

"Dropping the bomb was inhuman. . . . Ronald Reagan."

She is rubbing the inside of your leg with just the tips of her fingers. Now she begins using her palm and the underside of her fingers, rubbing more swiftly. Both her hands are moving without pattern, quickly now, over your chest, stomach, pelvis. Cait rises up to her knees as her hands continue to swirl unpredictably along the length of your body.

"Sucked off Menachem Begin."

You rise slightly and begin to writhe slowly. As she kneels over you and takes you in her mouth, you close your eyes, sigh deeply, and think of nothing, absolutely nothing, else.

2

GONNAREA ENFECTED DEBUTONTS

Practice Essay
By Jerry Speziak

The Possum is a very courajous comic-book superhero I have created. I love to draw and come up with story ideas. I hope someday soon The Possum will be sold worldwide, and maybe even made into a movie. Let me tell you how I got the idea for The Possum and then I'll tell you about the character.

I can really idintify with the possum or any other creature that is hated and dispised. This is a world run by rich and beautiful people. There is no place in this world for people like me. When I go to the mall and walk around, all I see in the stores are pictures of athleets and supermodels with perfect bodies. Even the rock stars who are supposed to be famous because of their musical abillity look like movie stars and models. It makes me sick and very angry. Why is it only the beautiful people who get to be succesful? Are ugly people less tallented? I don't think so!

I really shouldn't be so angry at beautiful people. Is it there fault ugly people like me spend millions of dollars buying all their crap, just because they're beautiful? If you give people a choice between buying something from a beautiful person, or buying the same thing from an ugly person, which one do you think they will buy? What would happen if we just stopped buying stuff from beautiful people? Then there beauty wouldn't matter.

And what makes me just as angry are the people who aren't beautiful, but try to be, with plastic sergery and Botox, or just by wearing a lot of makeup or stylish looking clothes. That's just jeallousy. I'm not jeallous of beautiful people. I don't want to be like them. I hate them with a passion. Maybe it's not fair I hate them just because they were born beautiful, but I can't help it. They only care about other beautiful people. They don't care about people like me, unless we're going to buy some of their crap. When your fat and ugly like me, you have two choices in life. You can either be dispised by society, or totaly ignored. Its not fair those are my only two choices. But I'm not a violent person, so I created The Possum so he could take revenge on all the beautiful people in the world.

The really unusual thing about the possum (or opossum, as it is really called) is there instink to pretend their dead whenever their scared. I can relate so much to that. On most days when I was in high school all I wanted to do was stay in bed and play dead. Predators will ignore the possum when it is playing dead, which is also how I felt most of the time – ignored. People just pass you by like your not even there. Or they look at you like your diskusting – which is how most people react when they see a possum.

But the thing about a possum, which I can also really relate to, is that they are totally misunderstood. People think of possums as being diskusting and nasty, causing diseases and being vishious. Possums are not nasty creatures. Possums are actualy very clean animals. They clean themselves very often, just like cats. Most people are diskusted by possums – they think they are nothing but big overgrown rats. But possums are not rats at all. They are marsoupials, just like kangaroos and those cuddly kowalla bears everyone loves. Imagine that! How different would people treat possums if they knew they were closer to kowalla bears than rats? And unlike most wild animals, they cause very few diseases. They hardly ever cause rabies, unlike dogs. And they are not vishious. They play dead when they are in danger and will only bite out of nesessity. That's what makes me the most angry. How people only judge you by your looks, or by what there own prejudice tells them to think.

So I created this superhero called The Possum because I could relate so much to any animal that is ugly and misunderstood. And I think it will be a very poplar comic because even though I am lonley and I feel like there is no one else in the world like me, the fact is I think there are a lot of people like me who will read The Possum and really idintify with him.

So let me discribe for you The Possum, my superhero. Before he became The Possum his name was

Bernie Baxter. Bernie Baxter was a nobody. He was fat and ugly and didn't have any freinds. He had the worst job in the world. He lived in Toxic City and worked for the Toxic City sewer department as a sewer enspector. He spent all day every day in the sewers underneath the city checking for leaks and monitering for gasses. There were a lot of rats and possums in the sewers, as well as snakes and alligators. So it was a dangerus job. He had to wear a HAZMAT suit because of all the gasses that would build up and because of all the crap people would dump in the sewers.

A lot of the dangerus chemicals in the sewer come from the big endustrial plant in the city called Toxic Chemical Mannufacturing. The plant is owned by the richest man in the city. His name is Bill O'Nair. He is one of the supervillians The Possum ends up always fighting.

One day, Bill O'Nair's plant dumps a particulerly deadly combanation of poisons into the sewer. Bernie Baxter is wearing his HAZMAT suit, so this shouldn't be a problem, but he surprizes and scares a mama possum who is nursing her baby possums. Since she is scared and trying to protect her young, she attacks Bernie and bites him in several places on his body. He is bleeding badly and in pain, but most importently, his HAZMAT suit now has several holes in it. As he is leaving the sewers to go to the hospital, he incounters the lethal combanation of gasses dumped by Bill O'Nair's chemical plant. The gasses pass through the holes in his suit and mix with the possum DNA that is in all of the bite marks on his body and with his blood.

Over the next seviral days Bernie notices a lot of changes when he looks in a mirror. He starts growing fur all over his body. He starts to grow a tail. He starts to find it easier to walk on all fours instead of upright. Most importently, he realises he likes being a possum. He quits his job and begins living in the sewers with the possums. Just like a person who feels like he is a woman trapped in a man's body, or vise-versa, Bernie now feels like he was always meant to be a possum, like he had been forced to live his life as a civilised human and now he was finally free to be himself.

Instead of having to work all day and pay bills and be lonley every night because he's not married and is too fat and ugly to get a girlfreind, he is excepted as a member of

61

the passel (that's what a group of possums is called). And best of all, he gets to mate with as many female possums as he wants to. He just walks around the sewers all day eating whatever he finds that smells good to a possum and if he sees something that makes him scared, he just rolls over and plays dead. He wakes up a couple of hours later and everything is all right again.

Unlike a lot of superheroes, like Batman and Spiderman, The Possum does not have a good-looking altar-ego. There is no Bruce Wayne or Peter Parker in The Possum. Once Bernie Baxter becomes The Possum he is always The Possum. He is what he is. He's fat and ugly 24-7. But he's okay with that now that he's The Possum.

However, there is still a human side to The Possum. He is still half a man, who has just desided to live like a possum. And he still remembers what it was like for him to be a man. And those memories make him angry and make him want revenge.

There are two other supervillians besides Bill O'Nair that The Possum is always fighting against. One is a beautiful woman named Deb U. Tont who tortures men to death. If your a man, she pretends to like you just so you'll do things for her and buy her things, and then when she gets what she wants from you, she tortures you to death. And what Deb U. Tont always wants from the men of Toxic City is to kill her enimies and steel there wealth.

Another villian The Possum faces is named Cort Auerbach, who is a famous football player. He is good-looking and rich and wants everyone to like him, but inside he's a cold-blooded killer. He's also a bully who picks on every guy who's not good-looking or rich like him. He always leads the city's football team, the Toxic City Spillers, to victory, but then goes out after each game and murders someone he thinks is ugly and deserves to die. And because he is a football hero he always gets away with it.

Every superhero has to have a superpower. A special abillity that every possum has is to emitt a green fluid from its anus (that's right – its anus!) when it is playing dead that convinces other animals they are dead. The powerful chemicals which went into Bernie Baxter's body and coalessed with the possum DNA gave him the abillity to squirt out a trully lethal fluid. He has learned how to control it over time so that he releeses only as much as he needs to make someone unconchuss. (Its a lot of fun for me to draw The Possum squirting this deadly green slime out of his anus!)

The Possum began his carreer as a crime fighter by patrolling the streets and helping the police nab bank robbers, purse snatchers, rappists, ect. He would patrol the city through the sewer system, come up through storm drains and manholes and, incogneeto, slink along the streets as long as he could. But whenever he was spotted by a human, they would scream because he looked so vishious, ugly and fat. People would try to kill him just because he was a possum and was ugly. But whenever he saw a crime in progress, and Toxic City has a lot of crimes, he would squirt his powerful liqid and knock the criminal unconchuss until the cops arrived.

Eventually, the police came to appreshiate the Possum and all he was doing for the city. Instead of screaming and trying to kill him, the citizens would cheer and take his picture and treat him like a hero. This made it difficult to fight crime because it's hard to sneak up on a criminal when everyone cheers and calls out "Hey look – its The Possum!" every time you emurge from the sewer. But what he hated the most was the fact he was now being treated just like all the beautiful, famous people he hated. He was asked to be on TV shows and to make public appearances. One day people were screaming at him and trying to run him over with cars, and the next day he's a hero. People are such hippocrits, he thought.

He decided to give up crime-fighting and live like a regular possum in the sewers. But Toxic City saw its crime rate sore without The Possum patrolling the streets. This is when Deb U. Tont and Cort Auerbach go on there crime spree. Almost every day their is a murder, and the police are helpless to stop it. The Possum knows what he must do. He returns to patrolling the streets at night and it doesn't take long for him to have his first incounter with the two supervillians. Just like with all the other criminals, Cort and Deb are no match for The Possum's toxic anal juice, which knocks them unconchuss. But when The Possum calls the police and tells them what happened, they don't believe two beautiful people like them would be murderers. They accuse The Possum of turning to the Dark Side and trying to kill Cort and Deb. So now The Possum becomes a fujitive and must hide from the police while also continuing to save innocent people from Cort and Deb.

That is the story so far of The Possum. I think he is a courajus superhero because he does not try to be one of the beautiful people. He has the couraje to be himself, and I think he can be a hero to a lot of people like me who don't have anyone else who looks like them to look up to.

You and Cait are on one of the outside basketball courts, beside the gymnasium. Cait is wearing a pair of tight-fitting, cottony warm-up pants – a garment she describes as "come-hither casual." It is early March, and cold. Cait complains that you both were too sedentary this winter and she determines that she must lose the weight she has allegedly gained. You don't see it. If she gained any weight, you think, it must be in brain cells. Cait, of course, insists that you are just too chickenshit to tell her the truth, which is that she is turning into a cow. You tell her that it just so happens you love cows – especially to eat them. And to drive your point home, you inform her that you probably know her body better now than she does; you have seen more of it up close than she has and you know for a fact that your tongue *has gone over more of her body than her eyes ever will.*

So, though the existence of Cait's weight gain is still unproven, you are out here in the cold, nonetheless.

You are playing HORSE as only you two would play it. You won the closely contested first game with PENI. Switching to a new word, Cait is well ahead of the second game. She only has V, while you already have VAGI. What she doesn't know is that you have been missing a lot of shots intentionally. As with the first game, you've given her a nice cushion so that this game will go down to the last letter also.

Cait never jumps as she shoots, but she has a unique habit of lifting one of her legs each time she launches a shot. She's a study in concentration as she attempts a shot from the foul line. To your minor consternation, she swishes it as she returns her right foot to the ground. She makes catcalls and other strange noises, trying to distract you as you study the rim and bounce the ball. You miss the shot, unintentionally, and blame it on your cold hands. You are one letter from defeat. Cait watches the ball as she slap-dribbles and shoots a one-legged layup. You should make this shot easily. Cait stands under the basket, turns her back to you and wiggles her fanny. To your great surprise, you miss the shot. She rebounds the ball, smiles over to you, and says, "that's what you get for missing all those shots on purpose."

THE *TOX COUNTY CHANTICLEER*, the local newspaper, had been the voice of the county for nearly one hundred years. The paper, up until a few years ago, had been in the same family since it was founded. But newspapers had hit hard times, and the *Chanticleer* was not spared. But it was also not giving up. Its editor had come up with an innovative idea for keeping the paper afloat, which, though controversial, was proving to be quite successful.

The *Chanticleer*, though never *The New York Times*, had, up until the previous decade, been a thriving enterprise. Fifteen years ago, they had a reporting staff consisting of four eager beavers just out of college, willing to do the most mundane tasks and cover the most uninteresting events without complaint, and one veteran of fifty years, Sophie Bellagio, who, though jaded and ready to retire, enjoyed her role as mentor to all the young pups who passed through the newsroom over the years on their way to better jobs at bigger papers. Now, there was no money to hire young pups and the ones who had been here most recently had been laid off, so that the only full-time reporter left on staff was the seventy-three-year-old Sophie.

As the reporting corps dwindled, Sophie's job had become impossibly exhausting. Though the *Chanticleer* had been her life and love (she had gotten her first-ever real job there straight out of college), she threatened retirement daily and announced almost as often that she was headed to an early grave (though "early" would need to be viewed in a relative light when you're already seventy-three). Realizing the Grand Dame of the Tox County intelligentsia perhaps was indeed on her way to a relatively premature death if something wasn't done, the paper's publisher delivered an ultimatum to its new editor – find a better way to publish before Sophie perished.

When this directive was handed down, the editorial "department" – that is, two men sharing one desk – was in the throes of a leadership crisis of its own, similar to the predicament Sophie found herself in, but further advanced. The paper's editor of thirty years had just quit, in order to spend more time with his grandchildren and less time with chest pains. That left the day-to-day editorial decisions in the hands of the erstwhile assistant editor, a young man with more ideas than knowledge and more ambition than experience.

As it turned out, however, that combination was just what the day demanded.

Every paper in the country had established online versions of its product, but these websites certainly weren't pulling the newspaper industry out of its tailspin. The innovative new *Chanticleer* editor, however, hit upon the notion that perhaps the paper was choosing to emulate the wrong aspect of online journalism. Rather than following its business model and relying on e-subscribers, why not imitate instead its reporting model? Professional journalists were being laid off by the trainload, yet never in the history of information dissemination had there been more journalists, in one form or another. With social media, everyone was a reporter. It was, in reality, the antiquated, elitist print-publishing ethos that was responsible for the downfall of newspapers, the new editor believed. What was needed for the *Chanticleer* was not an online version of its print edition, but rather a print version of what was being done online by ordinary people the world over: ordinary people, well-educated and professional, now seized with the spirit of journalism – the thirst for gathering knowledge, combined with the ability to give creative expression – a thirst and ability many people had, but which had until now been kept secreted by an elitist, self-serving cabal who had convinced everyone else that it was the only group qualified to gather and report information, when, it was now being shown, almost anyone could do it. It was as if a secret society of pedaling enthusiasts had managed to convince the rest of the world that only its members, and only they, had enough training and talent to ride a bicycle.

The editor penned an op-ed admitting that the paper was in dire financial straits and unveiling his plan to save it. House ads were placed prominently within the *Chanticleer* calling for qualified amateur reporters. The response was immediate. Doctors, lawyers, business people, teachers, artists – people of every professional stripe wanted to help write the county daily. These were people, most of whom had been born here, who had an enormous interest in, and knowledge of, this community (two things that, regardless of whatever skills or enthusiasm they brought with them from journalism school, could never be said of the young itinerant reporters who worked at the *Chanticleer* for a couple of years before moving on). They were also people who cared very deeply about the *Chanticleer.* This was their newspaper; they had read it every morning, ever since they were old enough to care about what was going on around them. And they were saddened and frustrated by what had happened to their newspaper. No, it wasn't the reporters' fault, or the editor's, or anybody else's, but the paper just wasn't very good anymore. And now they'd been given a chance to save something that meant a lot to them.

This journalism-by-community may not have met strict professional standards of objectivity, but then again, could a young kid with a fresh journalism degree have learned enough about how to recognize his own biases and the obfuscations of others to ensure a high level of objectivity on his part? And anyway, that's what Sophie was for. Relieved now of her burden as the sole reporter on staff, she no longer had to rush off to every car crash or grand opening or school board meeting, and instead, she was now – in effect, if not title – the editor of the *Chanticleer*. Every evening she would pore over all the copy submitted by her legion of DIY newshounds. Sophie knew most of these reporters personally, and so she also knew their proclivities. She knew who always voted Democratic and who Republican; she knew who had had affairs or had once been arrested; she knew who donated to which organizations; she knew who had what axes to grind and what causes to promote. And she had been around the business long enough to know a tilted story when she saw one; so she would make whatever editorial changes were needed to correct some obvious bias or novice's error and then, with her night's work done, she would put yet another edition of the *Chanticleer* proudly to bed.

So, under Sophie's watchful eye and with a brigade of motivated, idealistic professionals, who, though without any training in journalism, nonetheless had adequate writing skills, the *Tox County Chanticleer* was able not only to satisfy its loyal readership, but gain many new subscribers.

And here's the kicker, the rim-shot, the punch line, the too-good-to-be-true part of this whole idea – these people would do all of these things *for free*.

Since the whole reporting staff was now happily working *pro bono*, the entire paid news and editorial staff consisted of two persons – Sophie and the young genius of an editor who had engineered the paper's salvation. You would think such a boon would have satisfied the publisher and his executive board, but that's not how the corporate brain thinks. The corporate brain doesn't think about what it can be *satisfied* with; it thinks only about what it can *get away* with. So when the publisher saw the bottom line going higher than it had been for a long time, his only thought was to see what else he could come up with to keep the train rolling. He turned to his boy genius and told him to pull one more rabbit out of his hat.

The greatest deficit newspapers had to overcome was the loss of ad revenue. As wonderful as it was to have a squadron of dedicated amateur reporters doing its job for free (and with no insurance costs or paid leave), the real ground that needed to be made up was in advertising.

The inspiration for the editor's next big idea did not come from the internet. It came from the other great entertainment revolution of the twentieth century – television. The editor noticed that sitcoms loved to use product placement in their episodes. Movies did it too, of course. And in one sense, product placement had always been the very essence of newspaper advertising. Put as many ads as possible right under the nose of the reader. Wherever there wasn't a story, stick an ad; or actually, wherever there wasn't an ad, stick a story. First things first. But there was one place within the folds of a newspaper where a reader could still go to escape all the ads clamoring for his attention: the news story itself.

This was the editor's new plan: wherever a news story occurred out in the field, the reporter needed to pay attention not just to the particulars that were normally associated with the reporting of an event, but with anything in the vicinity that was, in any way, shape, or form, an advertising opportunity, which could then be incorporated into the story. For example, a brief about a car crash might be described thus:

> Yesterday evening at dusk, a Dodge Ram pickup rammed into the rear of a Chevy Suburban. The accident occurred in front of Crosley's Grocery. The driver of the Suburban barely missed hitting a sign in front of the grocery, which read, "Pepsi Products – Buy One Get One Free. Sale Ends Sunday." No injuries were reported.

Automobile companies were used to having makes and models of their vehicles used as descriptive matter in news stories, so it might be a tough sell to convince local dealerships to fork out extra money to have their products mentioned in a story that would have likely mentioned them anyway. However, what if you threatened to *not* mention them? The editor of the *Chanticleer* (not Sophie, who was the real editor, but the boy genius) was not above using advertising-by-extortion to prove how effective his latest idea could be. So, the car dealerships would pony up just to ensure that they would receive a mention. And the Mom and Pop establishment mentioned in the story may not have deep pockets for extra (or any) advertising, but the editor's new policy was to haggle as much as necessary to make sure at least a smidgen of ad revenue was generated by each story. To make his plan as profitable as possible, the editor even convinced the tight-fisted publisher to bring on a slew of new hires to man the phones in advertising.

Any news item submitted to Sophie was now expected to have at least one mention of a business or product, whose owner or distributor could be contacted before deadline and an ad-hoc advertising deal struck. If this requirement couldn't be met through the mention of an article of merchandise noticed at the scene, then, the editor instructed, make sure you get something mentioned in quotes. Were you interviewing a school board member about the new budget? Ask him which products the school was looking to purchase. Computers? Which brand? Interviewing the local sports hero? My, those were some snazzy uniforms. Which company did you buy those from? If you were a resourceful reporter, there was always a commercial angle you could work.

The one thing the editor wasn't counting on, however, was the old-school idealism of his new squad of reporters. He had been counting on their vanity – their enthusiasm for seeing their names in a by-line and being able to tell all their friends and family about their new hobbies as writers – to vanquish any consideration they might give to journalistic integrity. And besides, it wasn't as if they were being told to do *less* reporting to get a story; he still wanted all the essential facts which would normally appear in a story – he actually wanted them to do *more* reporting, *more* fact-finding, to be *more* thorough in their digging; just make sure it had an advertising-related component they could sell, that's all he was asking.

But these new volunteer reporters were appalled by what he was now asking them to do, and they rebelled. They hadn't gotten excited about producing the county paper just so they could become shills for the Chamber of Commerce – even though some of them sat on the Chamber's board. For these business leaders, the part of the editor's new reporting policy that was too hard for them to accept was the fact that they were now being asked to promote businesses that were in direct competition with their own enterprises: "I own the Coke distributorship here, and you expect me to write ad copy for Pepsi?"

Sophie was also fit to be tied. Fifty years as a journalist, and now she's supposed to get excited about a car that ran off the highway and slammed into a billboard carrying McDonald's signage – just because McDonald's would pay good money to have the *Chanticleer* casually mention that the McRib is back?

So, the new policy the publisher had been so excited about was now threatening to put him back in the same bind he had just escaped from – the loss of all his reporters and the angry resignation of Tox County's most beloved and well-respected woman. The new editor was not backing down, however. Just give him a few more weeks to talk to the reporters and to Sophie and he would have them back safely in the fold, he demanded. But the publisher recognized that this bold attempt to squeeze even more blood out of the advertising turnip was doomed to failure. The brash new editor resigned – either in disgrace or on principle, take your pick – and was soon working for the local Fox television affiliate, where he argued, quite successfully, with the news director – asking, why on Earth should that on-air reporter be standing in front of that McDonald's restaurant *for free?*

Meanwhile, Sophie, now the only paid employee in the *Chanticleer* newsroom, was promoted by the publisher and given the fancy title of Editor-in-Chief.

This was the situation at the *Chanticleer* when Teach, and many others, answered the call for guest columnists from within the community to submit as many opinionated editorials as they could write.

We live in a world blessed by God. His bountiful blessings are all around us. It is undeniable, and true. And Heaven awaits all those who accept into their hearts His Son, Our Lord and Savior Jesus Christ.

I am a newly elected member of the Toxonomonomonee County School Board. I ran for this position because I understand two things very well. One, nothing is more important than the proper education of our children; and two, our children have not been receiving the proper education which is their due because of the failure of the public school system, not only here in Toxonomonomonee County, but throughout our great state and our great nation.

This failure has not been caused by our hard-working and highly competent teachers and administrators. They deserve, and will receive, our fullest support. This failure has not been caused by our children, who are eager to learn, who have always shown great resilience in facing the challenges that confront them, and who strive daily to meet their academic goals. This failure has not been caused by the parents of these children, who continue to generously support our schools through their tax dollars and their volunteerism.

So, then, who or what is to blame for all the ills that continue to plague our great public-school system? It is not because of a failure to adequately fund our schools – we as citizens of Toxonomonomonee County are already overburdened with taxation. Throwing more money into the system will not solve our problems. It is not a failure of heart or effort. As I stated above, blame cannot be placed on the tireless efforts of everyone within our communities who struggle to make the system work.

My fellow citizens, it is not a problem of who, or when, or how, or where our system failed. It is a problem of what. What are our children, God's children, being taught in our schools? Are they being taught righteousness? Are they being taught Goodness? Are they being taught Truth? Throughout the years, many highly educated "experts" from our elite universities have tried to answer the question, "What should we teach?" And no one has been able to come up with a satisfactory answer. Why? I believe it is because the so-called experts have been asking the wrong question. I think the only proper question that we, as a Christian nation and as a Christian county, should be asking is, "What would Jesus teach?"

When I was a child, I loved nothing more than Sunday School. It made no sense to me that we had to go to our regular school five days a week but were only in Sunday School for one morning per week. It made no sense to me, as a child, that the most important Book and the most important subject in the world would only be taught to us on Sunday. The Bible was, and is, an enormous, wondrous Book full of enriching stories and wisdom – enough to fulfill a lifetime of study. And why did we have to study all those relatively uninteresting and unimportant subjects such as math, grammar, and science for five days a week?

As I matured, I learned to appreciate the importance of these core subjects, without forgetting the primacy of the teachings of Christianity. If we are to save our schools, I sincerely believe it is imperative that we integrate the Gospel of Christ into the core curriculum of our public schools.

For several decades there has been an ongoing, highly publicized debate occurring over the teaching of evolution in our science classrooms. I need not belabor the importance of that debate here, since it is well known. The only question I wish to ask concerning this controversy is this: Why do we debate the centrality of Christian Truth only in our biology classrooms? (And I will add this question: Why are the good Christians who are fighting to kill the scourge of Darwinism hiding behind the guise of scientific creationism and Intelligent Design? They are attempting to fight fire with fire – but this fire can only be quenched with the Holy Water of Christ.)

It is not only in the origin of species that we see the hand of a loving Creator. Throughout our K-12 science curriculum we need to stress that every atom, every molecule, the laws of gravity, electromagnetism and chemistry were all created by Almighty God. And that we, as God's chosen creatures, have been blessed with the ability to observe, study and understand all of His natural wonders.

When we study mathematics, we are learning about complex numerical relationships and formulas that have existed for eternity. How did these relationships come to exist? Nothing can exist without first being created. We take for granted that $1+1=2$, just as we take for granted that trees are made from wood. But we know that trees were created just so, to fulfill a purpose on Earth designed by God; so too were numbers and their relationships created, just so, to fulfill God's purpose of guiding the planets in their orbits and stars through the galaxies. We must teach our children this.

Turning to the study of history, isn't it clear to all that everything that has happened, has happened for a reason? That history is not simply one random accident occurring after another? We know we were not created through random happenstance; therefore, our history is no accident, either. So what reason can we give to justify all that has occurred in human history? That reason must be to glorify, each day, God's Holy Creation. When we teach about the great events of history, why shouldn't we also teach about the greater purpose behind these Earthly events? Why isn't Chapter One of every World History book the story of the world's creation? That is surely where History begins.

King John signing the Magna Carta; our Founding Fathers signing the Declaration of Independence; the Allied victory over the forces of Evil in World War II; the fall of the Berlin Wall – victories for Freedom and God's justice, all. Don't be fooled by all the grotesque atrocities which we witness in the world on a daily basis – these are merely brief, momentary victories of Satan on the world's stage. Anyone who does not see the hand of God in the eternal patterns of history is living with his eyes closed. And there is no justifiable reason why this central Truth should not be taught, not only in our history classrooms, but in every classroom throughout the public-school curriculum.

TOMMY IS ON HIS FIRST DATE with Angie. He had first met Angie in the library after school. She teaches seventh-grade Language Arts. He's been at Toxonomonomonee Middle School for a month, after two years of being holed-up in his childhood bedroom. (When he crawled back home after graduation, Tommy thought he could keep up with Cait's whereabouts in Europe as she progressed through the itinerary they had come up with together. He tried not to imagine whom she might be with. He assumed everything went well on her travels and she enrolled as planned at Stanford. She was in her second year now, presumably, and knowing her, near the top of her class.)

If Tommy is surprised by anything tonight, it's how much he's enjoying himself. Some things had always come easily to him, and, apparently, seduction is one of them. He and Angie are dining at the OK Corral, the county's most popular restaurant – one of those human feed troughs that's a good deal for a newly hired public-school teacher still trying to save up enough to rent his own place. The restaurant's big marquee, standing beside the highway, might display on any given day, in large black plastic letters, a special entrée recommendation, a patriotic slogan for holidays, or a birthday greeting to a lucky local. For the time being, the marquee had reverted to its default setting: the restaurant's motto, which had been used in newspaper ads for years – OUR FOOD IS AOK. However, to Tommy's great amusement, the big capital A had gone suddenly missing, due either to a strong wind gust or to teen-aged mischief. So now, the motto had changed to something less than a ringing endorsement – OUR FOOD IS OK. On this particular night, but also on any other night, the food selection is obscene: fried chicken (mostly dark – the white meat is quickly preyed upon); thick slices of ham floating under pineapple slices which are largely ignored and just get in the way; a full roast beef, bleeding red, with a carving knife stabbed into it, setting on its own throne-like stand, proclaiming itself the King of Meats; a tomatoey meatloaf; chicken pie; thick turkey slices submerged in broth. Those are the meat choices; the variety extends to every other food group. The dessert selections, especially, are scandalous.

"These food bars are a fascinating American phenomenon," Tommy says, slicing some ham. He had never traveled abroad, but he couldn't imagine eating like this anywhere else. "I don't know if it says more about our democratic insistence on having a multitude of choices, or our greedy need for conspicuous consumption."

Angie smiles. "Yeah, I really like it here."

The waitress stops by their table at least once every fifteen minutes carrying a large red-tinted pitcher in each hand to refill their large plastic tumblers. Angie volunteers a lot of information about her alcoholic ex-boyfriend, her decision to break up with him, which was followed by six months of stalking, a threatened restraining order, a stint in rehab and his tearful plea for reconciliation, which, Angie insists, will not be forthcoming. Tommy, however, has no plans to recount any of his time with Cait. Fortunately, Angie politely demurs from poking into Tommy's recent past.

"You said you had a little brother?" Angie asks.

Tommy has a hard time talking with his mouth full. "Yes. . . . Robbie. Good kid. . . . Salt of the earth." Tommy takes a swig of Coke through his straw.

"What does he do?"

"Works at Home Depot. . . . Assistant floor manager. . . . Working his way up pretty fast. Gonna be a big wheel someday." Tommy smiles a lips-only grin, in order to conceal a mouthful of mashed potatoes and cornbread.

"What about your dad?"

"What about him? What would you like to know?" Before allowing Angie a chance to answer his question, he pushes away from the table to return to the food bar for a second plate. "Would you like anything while I'm up?"

"I think I'm good for now. Thank you, though."

Tommy returns with a plate brimming with meat and vegetables, yet containing entirely different contents from his first plate. He digs in.

"So tell me about your dad," Angie says. "What's he like?"

"Ornery old cuss. Tough as nails. . . . He used to be a truck driver."

"What does he do now?" Angie daintily picks up a small slab of ham with her fingertips.

"Well, not much. . . . He's in a wheelchair."

Angie halts the movement of the ham toward her mouth and gives Tommy a look of concern. "Really?"

"He had a little accident." Tommy bites into a plump, butter-covered dinner roll and then licks his fingers.

"Oh my God. . . . I would never want to be a truck driver. That's such a dangerous job."

"No – it wasn't work-related. . . . It was stupidity-related."

"What happened?"

"Well. . . . He fell down, you could say."

"He fell down? He fell down some stairs or something?"

"No, but he definitely fell. He was definitely victimized by gravity."

"How did he fall?"

"Well, how does one usually fall? He put one foot in front of the other expecting to move forward – except he was in for a little surprise this time."

"Tommy – tell me! You said your dad's in a wheelchair. That's not funny!"

"Okay, okay – I'm sorry. He didn't just fall down. He actually fell from a great height. Four stories, to be exact."

"Oh my God – poor man. He fell off a building?"

"Off a building? Well, more like *through* a building. . . . Or *throughout* a building."

"Tommy! Why won't you tell me?"

"Okay. I'm sorry. What happened was – my dad somehow managed to fall down a damn elevator shaft." Tommy laughs heartily, indiscreetly exposing a mouthful of food.

"Oh my God! I can't imagine how he could even survive something like that. . . . He must be really tough, like you said."

"Well, don't give him too much credit. It wasn't actually four stories – not really. He was standing on the fourth floor, but the elevator was on the first floor, which he fell on top of, so technically he only fell two stories – the first floor and the fourth floor don't really count."

"What happened? How did he fall down an elevator shaft?"

"Good question. How *does* a grown man manage to find himself in that predicament?" Tommy puts on a British accent: "Hmmm. . . . I say old chap, I seem to be falling down a bloody elevator shaft!"

Angie laughs despite herself. "You don't know how he fell?"

"Because he's a bumbling idiot, that's how. How else would he do it?"

TOMMY FIRST BECAME TEACH during his first semester at Toxonomonomonee Middle School. He was the new sixth-grade Language Arts/Social Studies teacher. During his first two months in class, he had followed the advice given to him by every veteran teacher he had talked to: be mean as hell; brook no resistance; give no quarter. The other teachers he observed rarely smiled, were gruff to the point of nastiness and tolerated nothing that could be construed as a challenge to their authority. If he had to treat children like hardened criminals to be a good teacher, then he would at least try. But it was an extremely difficult performance to pull off, all day, every day. It was never his natural inclination to treat these kids as anything other than his friends.

This implacable façade crumbled one October morning. It had become his routine, after he had dismissed his homeroom and his first-period class filed in under his stern supervision and everyone silently took their seats, to address the class with a not unfriendly, yet unenthusiastic, "Good morning." The class then dutifully echoed back his greeting in unison. This morning, a young man named Arthur decided to upset the status quo. After a sufficient interval of silence, but before Tommy began speaking, Arthur said loudly from the back row, "Mornin', Teach!" Arthur's compadres laughed, but cautiously. The other students glared at him, stunned and no doubt fearful his reckless gambit would result in punishment for all (this being the standard form of classroom management recommended to Tommy – atonement in reverse: all must suffer to expiate the sins of one). Tommy, indeed, did seem to be on the verge of a Talmudic meting of justice; but as he glowered at Arthur he slowly softened his gaze and said, after much tense silence, "I like that."

Two months of military order-barking, stern task-mastering, insincere sullenness and false, soul-straining misanthropy evaporated with those three words. The class was awestruck, as if they had just witnessed some sort of miracle or religious conversion. Tommy smiled in front of his class, probably for the first time. "I tell you what, Arthur. If you can go the rest of the month without my having to call you down for disrupting class; if you turn in all your homework assignments; and if you pass all of your tests – not just in here, but in all of your classes – if you can do all of that, Arthur, for the rest of this month – then you can continue to call me Teach. No more Mr. Morrison. Do you think you can do that?" The class was incredulous. They started murmuring and turning around in their seats, smiling across the classroom to their friends. "And that goes for the rest of you, too. Everybody who does everything that's expected of you – everything I just explained to Arthur – will have my permission to call me Teach."

"For how long?" one forward-thinking student asked.

"For as long as you continue to meet expectations. If not, then I will revoke the privilege and you'll be the only person who has to call me Mr. Morrison. . . . Is that a deal?"

The class erupted into a brief celebration.

Sadly and predictably, Arthur and several others were soon unable to hold up their end of the bargain, but Tommy's students were good kids and he didn't have the heart, or the resolve, to revoke anyone's "Teach" privileges (even Arthur's, who was undoubtedly proud to have pulled one over on his teacher).

His name change earned him immediate comradery within his classes. During the first day of the new Teach era, his students ran excitedly to their friends in the lunchroom or at the bus lineup and said, "We get to call our teacher *Teach!*"

The other teachers and the administration, however, saw this development in a different light.

His more traditional colleagues – that is to say, everyone else – were aghast that Tommy would not only condone such behavior, but accept – nay, endorse, *embrace* – it. And after a couple of weeks of Tommy's perversion of the conventional teacher-student relationship, his principal said, "I'm sorry, Mr. Morrison, but the policy of the school is that all faculty and staff members must be called by the proper salutation – either Mr. or Ms. – followed by your last name. First names – or nicknames, especially – are not appropriate. Especially derogatory nicknames."

"I don't think it's derogatory at all," Tommy responded. "It's a wonderful action verb, a call to duty, the imperative of our chosen profession – *Teach.*"

"Well, at any rate, you will not be allowed to be addressed in that manner. Is that understood?"

Today, Teach would have been more inclined to stand on principle and to defy authority, but as someone coming off two years of self-imposed exile, without teaching experience, needing a job to pay off student loans, and more than a little unsure of himself, he was willing to stand down. Most people became more accommodating and less idealistic with age; however, Teach's life was playing out in the opposite direction.

Putting this particular genie back into its bottle resulted in one of the worst months he ever had as a teacher – perhaps even worse than the month in which he was fired. Sixth graders, the same as adults, do not like to return gifts. Tommy explained to them patiently, in detail, why they now had to call him Mr. Morrison again. Not having children himself, and not having taught before, he saw no reason why they wouldn't calmly accept his explanations and return to the pre-Teach state of affairs. When many continued to call him Teach, he was flummoxed. He didn't want to punish them for not complying with a policy change he didn't agree with any more than they, but after a few days of gently reminding them of the name re-change, he was left with no choice. He wrote up and sent to detention several students who stubbornly continued to call him by a name he had recently given them full license to use.

He found himself retreating into the bunker mentality he abhorred, of treating children like inmates and displaying an attitude of distrust and menace. It was his first lesson in the perverseness of both sixth graders and public-school administrators.

So he reverted to the role of Mr. Morrison while at the middle school – but as soon as he accepted the job as a GED instructor and realized to his enormous pleasure how much freedom he would have to teach in the manner he wanted, it signaled the triumphant return of Teach. His more elderly students balked at the idea of being so informal with a man of such high authority, but he insisted that anyone else he came into contact with call him Teach. His mom and Robbie were willing to make an effort at the name change (though their success rate was about fifty-fifty – twenty-five years of *Tommy* was hard to overcome). Only his dad, in his usual stubbornness, refused to call him by his chosen name.

You and Cait are at the Wash-A-Rama – it's laundry day. It's intensely hot, especially inside with all the driers running, but outside too, more like July than September. Cait is wearing loose flip-flops, which are doing their eponymous thing during each loud step she takes on the concrete floor. As beautiful as Cait is at all other times, nothing quite compares to seeing her sweltering and sweaty, with her hair back, wearing the absolute minimum she would ever wear in public. Cait is wearing a tank-top that is clinging to her and which features black bra straps that keep peeking out along the front and back of her shoulders. There is a lot of humid waiting and watching as you sit in plastic bucket seats and stare at the driers tumbling. There is a pen which doesn't belong to you on one of the washers and an old, half-emptied wire-ringed notebook on the folding table next to you. You have been studying the history of American westward expansion. You take the pen and notebook and write the following for Cait to finish:

> It's 1836. The Battle of the Alamo is raging. . . .
> Meanwhile. . . .

Cait takes the notebook, smiles, and thinks for a few minutes before writing her answer and returning the notebook to you:

Meanwhile, Davy Crockett says, "Don't lose heart, men! We'll win this fight, and this'll be the last time any damn Mexicans will come into Texas again!"

GREEN EGGS AND DA HAM

Practice Essay
By Pilluz

Forgive and forget – it ain't time yet. For what they did when I was a kid – I hid, they didn't see where I was layin', sayin' that muthafucka think we playin', but I heard every word they said – hidin' under my bed and Daddy's full of lead, yeah he dead, and for just a little more cred, I reckon, they go upside Mama's head with they pistol butt, that cut ain't gonna stop bleedin' – I was just in my room readin', now I'm needin' more than my shirt to soak up this hurt – It feel like a noose, Dr. Seuss, ain't no Mutha Goose gonna cut me loose – Mama gone to meet her Maka, ain't no Quaka in this hood, understood, we worship the gun, like father, like son – here's the deal – when they print our dollah bill, ain't what they mint on no Capitol Hill – In Glock We Trust, E Pluribus Uzi, how you think I got this Jacuzzi? I be dead soon, ain't even seen my first poon, but I'll see my mama, omit the comma, ain't nothin' comin' between us now.

I was sent to my aunt, in Bedford Stuyvesant, old cop on crack say you betta drop back and punt, don't pull no stunt, we watchin' you like Allen fuckin' Funt, but this ain't no Candid Cam'ra, God damn ya, he told me to spread 'em, get 'em wide, Kentucky Fried. I can take a hint, Clint – put me in yo database, make yo case, don't waste yo time, lemon lime, you only gonna see me puttin' down rhymes. That ain't no crime – at least not yet. I ain't no Met, ain't no Yankee, I was born in Philly, call me hillbilly I'll knock yo ass silly, just leave me alone, wanna go back home, but ain't nothing there but dried up bones.

Got a call from my sistah, down south of Mason-Dixah, I really missed her, she got a new mistah, they married, she buried the past, at last – She has fifteen years on Pilluz, didn't shed no tears when those killaz busted in and put an end to my best friends – she was twenty years old, half-way cold in the ground, truth be told, goin' down on guys to buy a high, they ain't nuthin' dory and they ain't nuthin' hunky 'bout bein' a pimped-up crack-ho junkie. But now she clean, she seen the light, she knew my plight, so she put me on a flight. She said where I'm goin' it ain't snowin' all winter, but sinner, get yo ass front and center, gonna take off my Bible belt, leave a welt, like the slave felt when he sassed the massa, gonna take NASA to get me far enough away from this place.

TEACH'S BOSS AT TCC was Randy Forrester, the Director of the Adult Literacy program. Upon first meeting him, anyone who paid attention to such things might assume Randy was gay, based on his noticeably effeminate manner. But as you got to know him, or just looked at all the photos on his desk, you learned he was married, twice divorced, and had four kids divvied up among his three marriages. These facts, while not conclusive of anything, provided enough evidence of Randy's essential manliness to prevent the morally conservative elements within the administration from having to feel too uncomfortable around him. Teach, of course, couldn't care less. In fact, he was one of Teach's favorite persons at the college, though Randy would have no way of knowing this. Randy was thoroughly professional and cared deeply about his programs and his department. The fact that Randy gave a damn about these kids that few others cared about earned him the unflagging support of Teach. So, Teach respected Randy immensely; he just had an unorthodox way of showing it: since Randy was unfailingly professional and sincere around his subordinates, Teach made sure he was as unprofessional and insincere as possible around his superior.

At the beginning of each fall semester, Randy would unveil his new department-wide Literacy theme. Randy had an Art degree and took pride in his graphic designs. Last year, the departmental theme was *Ready! Set! Read!* This exhortation was accompanied by a poster depicting a straight running track, with several running lanes delineated. The track was drawn absurdly not-to-scale – there were five square signs spaced evenly along the poster which read: "Mile 1," "Mile 2," "Mile 3," "Mile 4," and "Finish Line." These five signs represented the five GED tests that had to be passed in order to receive a GED certificate, with the Finish Line also representing graduation from the program. Several copies of this poster were put up along walls throughout the Adult Literacy department. Each classroom got one poster. In addition to coming up with the theme and designing the poster, Randy also produced small-scale cardboard runners, identified with each student's name, to be push-pinned onto the poster at the appropriate mile marker for each test passed.

If Teach had a favorite theme, it was the one from four or five years ago. The theme had been called *Scaling the Heights to Literacy*, with a craggy, yet perfectly symmetrical Everest depicted. At the foot of the mountain was "Base Camp," with the requisite five attainment markers representing the five GED tests spaced equally up the rocky slope. The goal, of course, was to reach the pointy summit where, Teach joked, the students would, with their last oxygen-deprived breath, reach out with weak, trembling hands to grasp the ice-covered GED certificate, before collapsing onto a pile made up of the bones of all the other lucky achievers.

To Teach, these themes seemed childish and insulting; most of Teach's teen-aged students agreed. But these silly slogans and gimmicks were surprisingly effective motivators for many of the older students – probably because many of them had never gotten as far as high school, so this bulletin-board art represented for them how school was supposed to be, or how it was nostalgically remembered to be.

This year's theme was *Throwing the Book at Illiteracy*, which Teach thought showed a serious lapse in judgment for Randy, considering how many GED students have a history of incarceration. Luckily, Randy did not continue the law-enforcement angle when designing the poster. The drawing showed five open books, with the verso for each book leaf featuring an Old English typeface with the words "Chapter One," "Chapter Two," etc., for each GED test. The recto for each leaf was blank. The names of students would be written with erasable markers to indicate their progress toward "Chapter Five" and their GED. Originally, Randy's idea was to have the last page read "The End" – which would make perfect sense normally, but made terrible sense, Randy realized, for a GED program: Randy continually preached to everyone that getting a GED should represent the beginning of a student's educational journey, not the end. And it would have been rather bizarre to have the last page read "The Beginning." So, however anticlimactic it might have sounded, "Chapter Five" was what students were striving for this year.

Teach's class was on break, so he had a few minutes to kill. Teach could not endure any down-time – especially lately. He knocked on Randy's open door.

"Hey Randy, do you have a minute?"

"Okay, Teach, but make it short."

"Okay – short and sweet. I think I've come up with a good idea for next year's Literacy theme."

"It's a little early for that, isn't it? We just finished putting up this year's."

"You can't control when inspiration strikes, Randy. You, of all people, should know that."

"Okay, Teach. Let's hear it."

"Can you draw a pirate ship?"

"Sure. I could manage that."

"Okay, draw a pirate ship – a really elaborate ship, with all the sails and masts and jibs and starboards and whatever else goes on one of those big-ass ships. And you'll draw a really long plank, with each GED test being another step closer to the end of the plank. Test Four will be right on the edge of the plank. Then for Test Five, that'll be down in the water, showing the names of students who got their GEDs. You could even draw a couple of shark fins sticking up out of the water. I think the slogan should be, 'Read, Damn Ye.'"

There was a long pause before Randy said anything. "Well, I don't know, Teach. Isn't walking the plank a *bad* thing? And I don't think we want to show our GED graduates being eaten by sharks."

"You know, Randy, you might be right. I hadn't looked at it that way. I guess that's why they pay you the big bucks – to see things that everyone else misses. . . . But here's another idea you might like. This one wouldn't be as elaborate as a pirate ship. You would just have to draw a straight line, really. . . . I'm thinking of a tightrope walker."

"Okay."

"I like this for the title: 'Reading – Do It Without a Net.'"

"I like that. Not bad."

"Thanks, Randy. I'm glad I finally came up with an idea that you like. So you have the tightrope divided into four different sections – for the first four tests. And then when the student passes the last test and gets his GED, we put him on that little high-rise podium where they jump off the tightrope at the end of their walk. Are you following me? . . . When you make your little cut-out people, you could give them one of those long balancing poles to hold."

"You know, Teach, I really do like that idea. Of all the crazy ideas you've given me through the years, that is actually one I think I can work with. . . . You'll just need to remind me of it again next year."

"Well, hang on, I'm not quite finished. . . . Don't you get really frustrated with students when they don't do as well on their tests as they should? I know I do. They stay out all night and then they come in and fall asleep

84

during the test, or they just get lazy and guess at half the answers, or they don't take their meds – we have so many kids who fail GED tests when there's really no excuse for it." Randy knitted his brow and had a confused, worried look on his face. "Now Randy, you know I'm a big believer in positive reinforcement. I always pat everybody on the back and tell them that they're the greatest thing since sliced bread and all that, but you and I both know that what some of these kids need more than anything is a good swift kick in the pants."

"Are we still talking about the tightrope, or are we talking about something else now?"

"I'm sorry, Randy. I'm taking the scenic route on this, aren't I? Positive reinforcement is great, but I think we need to introduce at least a little bit of negative reinforcement for some of our slackers."

The knitted brow returned to Randy's forehead, even more prominently now. "You've lost me, Teach."

"On the tightrope, if a student fails a GED test that his instructor believes he could have passed if he had only tried a little harder, then we should depict him falling off the tightrope, and then *splat!* on the ground. When you're doing your cut-outs, make some that look like mangled corpses, all bloody and with their arms and legs twisted in all different directions. . . . Don't you think that'll help motivate some of our kids to try harder? I mean, who wants to see their name printed in large letters on a twisted, grotesque heap of bloody flesh?"

"Get out of my office, Teach." Randy wasn't raising his voice, but he didn't seem to be kidding, either. "Go on, get out of here. . . . If you weren't such a good instructor, I'd fire your ass. You're a sick man, Morrison. You need help."

ANGIE IS MEETING TOMMY'S FAMILY for the first time. They've been dating for a couple of months. He still misses Cait terribly, though it's been two years. Tommy enjoys being with Angie, but he can tell it just isn't the same. Nothing will ever be the same as it was with Cait.

Tommy never gave Cait a chance to meet his family.

Tommy's childhood home is rather small to begin with, but it is made to seem smaller by the long, gradually sloping wheelchair ramp that starts well out into the front yard, ascends slowly along half the length of the house and then makes a turn and comes back the same length before ending on the front porch. Tommy's dad likes to complain that he has to travel a "god-damn half-mile just to get inside the god-damn house."

Barry Morrison has been in his wheelchair for six years now. He propels himself quickly and steadily through the house, never bumping anything. Tommy's mom, Beth, out of deference to Barry's limited mobility, has not moved the living room or kitchen furniture around since Barry's accident. And she has learned to keep the floor clear of random shoes and chew toys belonging to Señor Perro Segundo. Nothing is worse for Barry than to be tooling through the house only to be nearly thrown from his chair when something he didn't see suddenly chocks one of his wheels.

It was hard for everyone to adjust to Barry's wheelchair when he came home from the hospital, but no one had a harder time than Señor Perro Segundo. At the time, SP II was five, so he was very much set in his ways. The Chihuahua yapped incessantly at the big-wheeled intruder. At first, he barked at the mere presence of the chair. He soon enough learned to tolerate the chair so long as it was idle, but Barry was unable to go anywhere in the house for two solid weeks without the dog yapping at his wheels. It drove Barry nuts. More than once, if Beth wasn't around to see it, Barry konked the dog over the head with a rolled-up National Geographic. Now, SP II, aging gracefully, quietly ignores the chair as Barry rolls it through the house. Beth had asked Barry if he would prefer a motorized wheelchair, but he was insulted by the offer. "As long as I have my arms, I'm gonna use 'em," he responded. "They're the only damn things that still work."

Tonight, Angie is a big hit with everyone, of course. Why wouldn't she be? Pretty, smart, well-mannered, properly gregarious with everyone. A lot of talk at the supper table centers on Tommy's aborted and – according to most – foolhardy attempt to have his students call him Teach. By this time, he had been ordered by the principal to cease and desist, but his sixth graders were having none of it. "Angie, would you ever try to do something like that?" Beth asks.

"No, ma'am, I doubt if I would, but Tommy's trying real hard to connect with these kids. I think maybe he's trying to do too much too soon, but you only learn these things through experience. I think it's real sweet what he did." She smiles at him and grabs his hand.

Tommy fairly explodes – not at Angie, but at the stupidity of it all. "There was nothing wrong with what I did! Everything was just fine until Der Fuhrer had to get involved. And now everything is ten times worse." He calms down quickly, however, and says, "I still want you all to call me Teach, by the way. I'm trying to get Angie used to it."

"Jackass," Barry joins in. "I'm sorry, Angie. I don't mean to badmouth your boyfriend, but Jesus Christ, what an imbecile you've got yourself involved with. I hope you know that. If you don't now, you will. . . . When I was coming up, if we so much as adjusted our balls in our pants, our teacher would let us have it. If I had called any of my teachers some smart-aleck name like Teach, they would have beat me until I was nothing but two feet tall."

"And don't you miss those days, Dad? Those wonderful days down at the ol' gulag? Boy, those were the days, weren't they?"

"Smartass."

The one question Angie most wants to ask Tommy's dad is about the accident that put him in his wheelchair, but she figures that is a touchy subject, and Barry Morrison didn't strike her, upon first impression, as someone who would willingly discuss touchy subjects. But after supper, as everyone relaxes around the television, he makes it easier for her to ask by starting to describe his injuries and everything he had had to go through – two broken legs, broken back, and all the useless physical therapy he endured – for what? – just so he could be a more limber and agile paraplegic? He laughed about most of it, though, as he was talking.

"Do you mind if I ask you about your accident? I'm not trying to be nosy, but I'm just really curious."

"Didn't Tommy tell you all about it?"

"No. He said he didn't know how it happened."

"Of course he knows how it happened. He was right there with me, the dumbass." Barry adjusts himself in his chair, as best as he can, making sure he doesn't slide too far forward. "I had to go somewhere, to the bank or to the store, I don't remember exactly where, and I ask chucklehead here if he wants to ride with me. He was back from college, I guess, on a break or something – or maybe he hadn't started college yet – hell if I know. But anyway, I know this guy who works for Nationwide, and we were passing right by where his office is – in the Tollinger Building, up on the fourth floor. So I thought it would be good to drop in and see how ol' Frank was doing. So we go in and I notice there's a sign on one of the elevator doors that says Out of Service or Out of Order or something like that. But there's one elevator that's still working.

"So we go on up and I ask the secretary, or the receptionist, or whatever the hell you're supposed to call them nowdays, if Frank McCoy is in. And Frank wasn't even in that day – or maybe he was at lunch, I don't remember – but we ended up just wasting our time for nothing, going up to see Frank." Barry laughs.

"So we turn around and walk back to where the elevator was, and there are these two little boys, little Mexicans, just running around, no sign of their mama anywhere.

"So we're standing there waiting for the elevator. Right beside us there's this guy clanking away, working on the other elevator. He had the door open and it looked like he was doing something with the cables. . . . And then he just left! He just walked away and left that elevator door standing wide open. I don't know what the hell he was thinking. So anyway, we're just standing there, and these two kids – they couldn't have been no more than five or six years old – little kids, I mean" – Barry's hands go out, palms down, indicating a height no taller than the armrests of his wheelchair – "no supervision whatsoever. They're just running around, carrying on like crazy, yelling in Spanish. . . . And then they started running around backwards."

"Backwards?" Angie says, hanging on his every word.

"Yeah, like they were racing each other, but running backwards. Just being little boys, I reckon. But they weren't no more watching where they were going than Jiminy Cricket. Then the elevator comes and the door opens and Tommy gets on and I go ahead and get on, too, thinking, you know, these boys ain't my responsibility. If their mama wants to let 'em run around in front of elevator shafts, then that's her problem, you know, not mine. But as soon as we get on the elevator, here they come barreling down the hall again, ass-backwards, and I didn't have much time to think about it. Right before the door started to close I flew out and jumped in front of 'em as quick as I could. Well, they caught me off balance I guess and bowled me over and so I went ass over teakettle right down that shaft. Next thing I remember I wake up in the hospital with this sorry bastard" – indicating Tommy – "standing there over me with a big shit-eating grin on his face."

"Oh my God," Angie whispers, as if in awe. She then says, a little more loudly, "But you saved those two little boys' lives."

"Well, I don't know. Maybe. I didn't see this myself, of course, but what I was told later was that as soon as I fell down the shaft and got everybody's attention, so to speak, everybody came running out of Nationwide and there was those two little wetbacks just a-swinging on those cables like a couple of little orangutangs! . . . They told me they were crying, though, so they couldn't have been having too much fun."

Angie looks over at her boyfriend. "What did you do when all this was happening?"

"That son of a bitch?" Barry butts in. "I reckon he just went ahead and let the door close back behind me and rode on down to the first floor. . . . But I bet I got down there before you did, you sorry sack of shit."

As Tommy drives Angie back to her apartment, she asks, "Why didn't you tell me about your dad's accident?"

"When?"

"When I asked you. On our first date."

Tommy looks annoyed. "That's why, Angie. I didn't want to talk about Dad's accident on a first date. . . . Not exactly fun subject matter."

"You sure thought it was funny at the time. You were cracking yourself up."

"I was *trying* to be funny. That was the point. I was trying to impress you with my sardonic wit. . . . Obviously, it didn't work."

"I just wish you had told me when I asked about it. That way I wouldn't have had to embarrass your dad by making him tell that whole story over again."

"Don't worry, you're not going to embarrass that man. He gets about as embarrassed as a bear shitting in the woods. . . . That didn't make you mad, did it – having to ask my dad?"

"It's okay. Don't worry about it."

It's okay. Don't worry about it. It's been two years since Cait said that to him. Why hadn't he listened to her? He suddenly starts to well up. Tommy is trying to drive but the tears are making the road nothing but a blur, and he doesn't want to wipe his eyes where Angie can see that he's crying – but he has to do something, so he lifts an arm to his face.

"What's wrong? Are you okay?"

"Oh yeah, I'm fine. Just got something in my eye, that's all."

It's okay. Don't worry about it. Well, this time he's going to learn his lesson. If Angie tells him not to worry about it, then, by God, he's not going to worry about it – ever again.

As part of your work-study financial aid package, you have gotten a job manning the information desk in the student union. You love this job. You believe you've had a chance to see everyone who's enrolled on campus as they scurry to and fro between classes. Then one morning you're proven wrong in that belief. You know for a fact you have never seen this girl before, for there would have been no forgetting her. You can't take your eyes off her, and here she is walking directly toward you. You actually get nervous as she approaches. She smiles at you and your eyes briefly meet. She asks to check out Foreign Affairs *magazine. You know for another fact that she is the only person during your tenure at the desk who has ever requested* Foreign Affairs *– one of several magazines arranged vertically on the rack behind you. As part of protocol, you ask her to sign the magazine out. Unlike every other name on the checkout list, which are all first name, last name, she writes only "Cait." Of course, you think – anyone that beautiful would only need one name.*

She walks over with the magazine and sits on a couch directly in front of you. You stare at her as much as you feel you can without being discovered. Your current girlfriend, if you want to call her that, is named Jenny. Jenny has been very nice to you, though you haven't always been nice to her. You're glad, however, that you have gotten to know Jenny. But you also know that if you get half a chance to talk to this "Cait," and if she shows any interest in you whatsoever, then Jenny is history.

Cait reads – reads, not simply flips through or scans – the Foreign Affairs *for fifteen minutes. You spend most of that time thinking of what you can say to her when she returns it to you. But the hallway becomes packed as classes let out and Cait hurriedly tosses the magazine on the counter and rushes away. But the campus is only so large, and you will never allow yourself not to see her again.*

GIVE EVERYTHING DAILY

Practice Essay
By Steve Abking

I want to write about forgiveness, but I don't know if I'll ever be able to forgive the guy who got me kicked out of school. His name is Bobby and he was my backup on the football team. I know he did it, even if I don't have any proof. What happened is, the principal pulled me out of class one day and one of the SRO's was with him. I didn't know what was going on. I got scared because I thought something bad had happened to my mom or dad. I was almost afraid to ask them anything about why they wanted me, and when I did ask, all the principal said was that we needed to go out to my car. I was scared to death by now. When I got to my car I didn't see anything at first but as soon as I opened the door and looked in the passenger floorboard – wa lah – there it was – a plastic baggie of marijuana.

I know Bobby planted it. He broke into my car, and he put it where it could be seen, but not too easy. Knowing Bobby, he's probably had a lot of practice breaking into cars. His dad is a preacher, but you wouldn't know it. The reason Bobby did it is that he knew he would never be a starter. Now he's the starting quarterback this year, and the team is getting whooped by every team they play. He only knows how to throw two kinds of passes – incomplete and intercepted. I try to look on the bright side and remember that my life isn't completely over. I can get my GED and still go to college. But I won't be able to get a scholarship and I'll have to go here for 2 years before I can transfer, and then I'll only have 2 years of eligibility left. That really sucks. And I have Mr. Bobby McAllister to thank for it. I will never be able to forgive that son of a biscuit.

Since I'm supposed to write about forgiveness, I guess I should mention someone that I have been able to forgive. My big brother Cory got killed in a car crash four years ago. He was 17 years old – the same age I am now. It was hard for me to forgive him because he was acting stupid and he got himself killed and he caused our family a whole lot of grief. He was going way too fast and he wasn't wearing a seatbelt. When he died I was more angry than anything else. You would probably think I would be sad, but I was really mad. If he had been hit by somebody else, then I could have been mad at the other driver. But since it was a single car accident, who am I supposed to be mad at? My mom and dad haven't been the same since Cory died, as you would expect. I'm not sure how it's affected me. I know I felt a lot of anger toward him because he had been so stupid. I had always thought of Cory as being so smart, but then he turned around and did something really really stupid and it made me feel almost like he betrayed me, like I trusted him when I shouldn't have or like I thought I knew him when I really didn't. And I think it's been hard to forgive him because – and this may sound funny, but it's true – I was afraid to lose my anger. Because if I lost my anger then all I would have left was sadness. I think I preferred to be angry than to be sad. If you're a guy it's OK to be angry, but you're not supposed to be sad.

But I realized that wasn't right. Cory didn't deserve to be mad at. He deserved my sadness but not my anger. My parents didn't seem to be mad at him, so why should I be? It took a long time and I guess I'm still not over it, but whenever I start feeling angry at Cory I try to stop for a minute and tell myself that Cory wouldn't want me to be mad at him and that its OK for me to be sad.

TEACH HAD PROMISED CHERYL that he would seek professional help for all the episodes of crying he refused to talk to her about. He didn't know if it would do any good; he didn't know if he wanted it to do any good, but the least he could do for Cheryl was to look online and find a shrink. He met Dr. Carney a couple of weeks later.

After all the preliminary paperwork, Dr. Carney said, "So, Teach, tell me what prompted you to seek out therapy."

"My girlfriend, Cheryl. I wasn't opposed to it, you understand, but I doubt if I would have sought it out. She's real big on therapy and thought it would do me good. She thinks I'm depressed, or wigged out, or both –

which I can't really blame her for. . . . But I can tell you exactly what the problem is, Doc. I'll save us both a lot of time. I'm going to be the easiest patient you've ever had. You'll have no need to plumb the depths of my psyche for answers. We'll make this short and sweet. What Cheryl sees are the tears. I cry a lot. But I don't tell her why I'm crying because I don't want her to know, so she's left with nothing but guesswork and a temperamental boyfriend who won't tell her what's going on, so she's hoping I can come in here and unburden myself and stop crying all the time."

"Do you feel comfortable talking to me about what makes you cry?"

"Sure, I would love to. I would love to talk about Cait. I could talk about Cait all day. But I'll start crying, so get the Kleenex ready. . . . Cait was my girlfriend for the last two years of college, and she was – well, she was everything I could have ever wanted. But she broke up with me right before graduation and, not to put too fine a point on it, I just can't get over her. No other girl I've known has been able to match up to her and I doubt anyone will. . . . And that's my problem, Doc. That's what's brought me into therapy. . . . I miss Cait so damn much." Teach was already starting to cry. "My memories just come up and overwhelm me. And it just gets worse the older I get. None of the old adages seem to apply. 'Time heals all wounds;' 'memories fade.' My wounds aren't healing, Doc – they're metastasizing."

"It must have been a very painful break-up for you."

"It was all my fault, Doc. I have no one to blame but myself. I was immature and I didn't handle things well, and she knew that I probably wasn't going to grow up anytime soon. We were planning on going to Europe for the summer after graduation, and I don't think she enjoyed the prospect of having to change my diapers all the time."

"How long has it been since this happened?"

"Eighteen years. But it seems like yesterday."

"It sounds like you really need some closure to that part of your life."

"Oh, there was closure all right. Plenty of closure. It was closure city. What I need is a re-opening – a grand re-opening, under new management."

"Well, who knows? Eighteen years may seem like a long time, but in the grand scheme of things, it may not be at all. Lots of people manage to rekindle old flames, if the situation is right – but I'm not necessarily saying that's the right situation in your case."

"That would be the most wonderful thing in the world, Doc, but I don't think it's going to happen. I really have no idea where she is. I haven't been able to find her on Facebook, and even if I could track her down, I doubt if she would still want to have anything to do with me. . . . I wasn't exactly the best of boyfriends."

"In that case, Teach, what we have to do is move forward. We need to think of some ways, some strategies, which will help you control these memories of your past and keep you focused on the present. . . . The thing about memories – there's been a lot of very interesting research the past few years on the nature of memory and so forth, if you're interested in such things. I would recommend you do some reading on some of the latest research. It's very interesting. What the neuroscientists seem to be figuring out is how memory is processed in the brain and how memories actually change over time. Our memory of an event next year won't be the same as our memory of it now."

"I know what you're saying, Doc. Memories are not trustworthy. Even short-term memories are highly suspect. I understand the power of nostalgia and the dangers of nostalgic thinking. I understand that, Doc. I'm a student of history, okay? I know that the past is impossible to unravel with any great degree of certitude. So I can appreciate what you want to do – knock Cait down a few notches. 'Maybe things weren't so ideal after all; nothing is really that perfect; you did have a really big fight before she broke up with you, so everything couldn't have been all peachy keen.' Isn't that right, Doc? Isn't that one of the *strategies* –" Teach put air-quotes around that word – "that you're proposing?"

"No, Teach, not at all. I'm not going to try to characterize the nature of your memories. I don't think that would be very productive. I'm sorry I digressed on that point. I just think the literature has some very interesting insights into our understanding of memory, that's all. But you seem to agree that our memories may not always be what they appear to be."

"Yeah, well, like you said, eighteen years isn't all that much time. My memories have not deteriorated one iota, okay? Let me explain something to you, Doc. . . . I remember how her hair smelled. I remember what her skin smelled like when I kissed her. I remember what –"

Here came the tears again, unbidden, unwanted, unstoppable. Teach reached over to the end table and pulled a tissue from its box; then another one. "Put it this way, Doc – I remember what every inch of her body smelled like, okay? And if some neuroscientist wants to tell me that these memories are somehow wrong or deceptive or fallible in some way, then I'll kick his ass real good and we'll just see how well he remembers it."

"Teach, I apologize that I upset you. Do you want to take a little break?"

"No, I'm fine. I'm sorry I flew off the handle. I'm okay now."

"How often would you say you think about Cait? Several times a day?"

"Oh yeah. Easy."

"How often do you find yourself crying?"

"I don't know. It's not like I break down every time I think about her. Sometimes I laugh out loud – God, she was funny. We had these funny little word games and riddles we would give each other." Teach smiled and his gaze looked distant.

"How do these episodes affect what you're doing? Do they affect you at work? Do they last a long time? I just want to find out how these episodes are affecting your day-to-day life."

"I'm okay at work. I stay busy and keep my mind on other things. It's just when I'm alone, or with Cheryl – which is the only real problem. I don't mind thinking about Cait when I'm alone – well, no, I do mind, because it's excruciating. It's an excruciating pain in my brain. But I just wish I could take Cheryl out of the equation. It's not fair to her that she has to feel pain because of my pain from years ago. But I can't help it. If I do something with Cheryl that I used to do with Cait, then the memory of Cait just takes over – it's become more powerful than the reality of what's right in front of me."

"I think one thing we need to try to do – and this isn't something that's accomplished overnight, okay? – we need to put Cait in a box." Dr. Carney smiled thinly. "What I mean by that is. . . . What Cait is to you, Teach – her memory needs to become like an heirloom – a priceless, wonderful heirloom that you will treasure forever – but something that you can decide when to take it out of its box and when to put it back in. . . . Does that make sense to you?"

"Sure – compartmentalize her. Just bring her out on special occasions, for birthdays and weddings."

"Okay, right. You'll want to work on having a certain time – maybe every day, or several times a day, but eventually less and less, when you can control your memories and not have them be so disruptive and damaging to your present relationship. . . . But it takes a lot of conscious effort and work on your part to be able to do this. It's not how your neurons are used to operating right now."

"Right. I think that's a good plan, Doc. I really do. It's definitely something I can work at."

"Good. Do you want me to outline another strategy we can work on, or do you want to talk about something else for a while? We're doing well on time."

"Let's keep on keeping on, Doc. Cheryl sent me here to deal with this problem, so let's deal with it."

"Okay, good. So far we've just been talking about Cait and the memories of Cait that you have, but I think we need to spend some time talking about Cheryl – she's an important part of this problem, too." Teach nodded his head in agreement. His tears were starting to dry. "Teach, it's absolutely imperative that you not compare Cheryl to Cait. And I'm sure you understand the reason why – Cheryl is the relationship you have now. How you relate to her is all that matters. How she compares to someone you knew ten years ago, fifteen or twenty years ago – none of that matters. . . . This is a knife that can cut both ways, too. There are a lot of people who will stay in an unhealthy relationship just because it is perceived to be better than the one they were in before. Okay? But just because a current relationship may be marginally better in some way than the last one is still not necessarily a good reason to stay in it. And in your case, if you insist on comparing what you have with Cheryl to what you had with Cait, then – well, what do you think is going to happen?"

"Your point is well taken, Doc."

"Okay, so what do we need to do to make sure Cheryl remains the focus of your relationship?"

"Keep Cait in her box. Only let her out for national holidays and certain sporting events."

Dr. Carney laughed softly. "That's right. Keep Cait in her box. But there is more to it than that – you're still thinking of Cheryl in terms of Cait. That's going to be your big challenge, Teach – to think about Cheryl in terms that don't involve Cait. When you look at Cheryl, are you thinking about how she looks compared to Cait? When she responds to something you say, are you thinking about how Cait would have responded?"

"Most likely. . . . I'm even comparing you to Cait right now, Doc, and I must say, you're not stacking up very favorably." Teach smiled.

"That's okay, Teach. I wouldn't expect to. So, tell me a little bit about Cheryl."

"Oh – she's a knockout. She's school-marm beautiful."

"What's school-marm beautiful? I've never heard that before."

"That's because I just made it up. A lot of teachers are school-marm beautiful. When you first meet them, you aren't that impressed. You might think they're cute, or pretty, or maybe even a couple of notches below that, but then they really grow on you. Maybe it's the way they dress, or wear their hair, or carry themselves, I don't know. But it just takes a while for their beauty to shine through. . . . But when it does, you're hooked. The only reason I asked Cheryl out, honestly, was because I was just very lonely at the time. And we dated for several weeks, or maybe even months, and then one day I looked at her and I thought, Jesus Christ, Cheryl's gorgeous. . . . She's got a great body, too, by the way – once you get underneath all that tartan. I think she believes she needs to wear three of four layers of clothes every day so she doesn't turn all those horny pubescent boys on."

"Do you think maybe you were falling in love with her at that point – when you started thinking of her as gorgeous? That's what it sounds like to me."

"Nah, I don't think so. To be honest with you, Doc, I don't think I've ever been in love with Cheryl – not when I think about what I felt for Cait."

Carney was silent for several seconds. "Do you realize what you just did, Teach?"

"Hmmm." Teach shook his head.

"That last thing you said."

Teach thought for a moment. "Oops, I let Cait out of her box, didn't I? Little ol' Cait-in-the-box. Pops up when you least expect her."

"That's okay. That's going to continue to happen for a while. What's important to do right now isn't so much to prevent it from happening, but just to recognize it when it does. You see, you had no idea that you had done it."

"But how can I not do it? Why shouldn't I do it?" Teach's voice was raised noticeably. "How can you make any kind of personal decision if you don't base it on past experiences? 'Live and learn,' right? You learn from past mistakes. 'Those who do not remember the past are condemned to repeat it.' How am I supposed to know if someone is the right person for me if I don't compare and contrast them to other people? How does that work, Doc? Please tell me."

Carney began speaking more slowly than usual. "It's perfectly normal to compare and contrast, as you say. It's perfectly normal for you to compare Cheryl to Cait, Teach. But the problem is, it sounds like your relationship with Cait, at least the way you've described it, was not a normal relationship. It sounds like you two had something really special. But unfortunately, it didn't end well, so, as a result, I think you may need to think about some special measures to try to deal with the difficult consequences of that. 'Drastic times call for drastic measures.' Isn't that how that saying goes?"

"No, but close enough."

"This is what you're going to have to do, Teach. Just think about Cheryl in terms of Cheryl. How does she make you feel? Does she make you feel happy when you're around her? You should be able to answer that question without having to compare her to anyone else. You know what it feels like to be happy."

"Don't jump to conclusions, Doc – most people don't have any fucking idea what it feels like to be happy."

"Okay. Fair enough. But you know what it feels like to be happy, right?"

"Yes, Doctor, I do. As a matter of fact, I know exactly what it feels like to be happy. I was happy for almost two whole years of my life. Would you like to know which two years those were? Would you like to know where my definition of happiness comes from? Would you like to hear about my Cait-happiness or my non-Cait happiness, Herr Doktor? There is quite a difference, actually. In fact, I would be hard-pressed to use the same word to describe them. I don't think the word *happiness* can stretch that far, but if that's what you want to insist on calling it, then so be it." Teach's anger was now threatening to dissolve into tears as memories of all that Cait-happiness came bubbling up.

"Okay, Teach. Fair enough. I'm sorry. I was jumping to conclusions, and I apologize. I think we've covered a lot of good ground today, and made a nice foundation for you to build on. . . . We'll stop for today. Maybe this is the wrong time for me to ask, but I would like to get your feedback. Do you feel that this was a profitable session for you today?"

"Yeah, sure, Doc. Very profitable. I got a nice pretty box to keep Cait in. I hope she likes it."

"Okay. . . . For next time, Teach, I just want you to continue to try to be cognizant of when you're comparing Cheryl to Cait, and think about whether you're being fair to Cheryl when you do that."

"I know I'm not being fair to Cheryl, Doc. I don't have to think about it. . . . I've never been fair to a single girl in my life."

GOD ES DEVINE
GOD ES DEVOTION

(*Note from Maria:* Mr. Teach, I can not deside which one es more better.)

Practice Essay
By Maria Gonzales

When I was 17 years of old I was raped. I was raped by a man that I thout was en love with me. He was 20 years of old and he sayed he loves me and he wants to marry me. This es when I am still living en Mexico. I told him we would have sex when we got married. But he did'nt marry me. He raped me. It es very dificil now to still talk about but he came to my house when I was alone. I could smell a lot of alcoholl en his breth. He called me names I never want to hear again – but I do hear them on TV and sometime at school and I think about when he raped me. I hated that man for many years and I sayed I could never forgive him. Why should you forgive the man that raped you?

I tried to understand why I was raped. I did'nt deserve to be raped by a man that sayed he loves me. But then I understand. I am lucky that I did'nt get pregnet from the raper. I think God was watching me and sayed Maria, I will let this man rape you for all your sins. We are all siners and we must be punished for our sins. But because God knows that I am a good girl most of the times, God sayed, Maria I will not get you pregnet with the man who es raping you. And now I am pregnet with a man who realy do love me and married me and makes me very happy. This es prove that God is watching and that he loves me too. God did'nt get me pregnet when I was raped because he new that I would meet the man who realy do love me and who wants to marry me. My baby en my belly es prove that God loves me and I am en his plans. And when I understood

99

that my raper was part of Gods' plan for me too, then I could finaly forgive the man that raped me.

You and Cait are in the computer lab, typing term papers. Cait is a fast typist; you, through the years, have improved from two-finger typing to using four fingers and the occasional thumb on the space bar. From time to time you reach over and sabotage Cait's typing by randomly and repeatedly hitting a key. She retaliates in kind. Your progress is slowed not only by your typing ineptitude, but by your inability to keep your eyes off Cait. You watch her eyes move from the computer monitor to her handwritten rough draft, her hands never lifting from the keyboard. "Get to work, slowpoke," she tells you, "I don't want to be here all night." Despite her admonition, and knowing she will be finished well before you, you take the time to write to her the following:

> *It's 1876, and Alexander Graham Bell has just invented the telephone.*
> *Later that same week. . . .*

Cait does finish soon and walks over to the printer to retrieve her final draft. She proofs it one more time while you continue to peck away. Soon, she's typing again and printing out the results. When you finally finish your paper and have gotten everything stowed in your book bag, she hands you her reply:

> *Later that same week, Bell is once again testing his device. He speaks through the primitive mouthpiece to his trusty assistant: "Watson, what are you hearing? I'm not hearing anything." Watson, through enormous static, thinks he hears, "Watson, what are you wearing? I'm not wearing anything," thus inadvertently receiving the world's first obscene phone call.*

TEACH'S VISITS HOME to see his folks were, taken as a whole, routine and predictable. Since he lived with Cheryl only a few miles away, he dropped by often. His dad spent most of his time in front of the TV. His mom liked to stay busy piddling around the house. He and Cheryl tended to stay longer on Sundays, often all afternoon. It was also predictable that Teach and his dad would get into at least one verbal jousting match each

Sunday, arguments that were passionate (at least on Barry's side) and bizarre (courtesy of Teach).

The arguments between Teach and Barry were usually precipitated by whatever current news controversies were being discussed on the cable channels Barry was continually clicking through. Today, the big story in the news cycle was the shooting death of an alleged abortion provider. The shooter had been arrested at the scene and then videoed while handcuffed outside a police station, shouting anti-abortion epithets. The shooting victim, however, was a pediatrician, about whom it was not yet known for certain whether he had ever performed any such controversial procedures.

"Another baby killer, biting the dust," Barry said, as he and Teach, joined soon by Robbie, came back into the living room after Sunday lunch and resumed watching television. The ladies were cleaning up in the kitchen.

"Baby killer? Why do you call him that?" Teach said. "I thought they said he was a pediatrician. How do you go from being a pediatrician, where you dedicate yourself to saving babies' lives, to being a baby killer? I mean, even if he did do an abortion every now and then, the poor guy probably spent 99.9 percent of his time healing babies, and now you're calling him a baby killer?"

"So how many babies do you have to kill before you're a baby killer, jackass?"

"Seriously, does it really bother you that this doctor, every once in a blue moon, maybe took a few minutes out of his day to help out some poor sixteen-year-old girl who got knocked-up by her no-count boyfriend?"

"I'm not defending what that nut did, if that's what you're trying to get me to do – nobody deserves to be shot down in cold blood."

"Yeah, but I know you. There's a part of you saying, 'That guy just got what was coming to him.'"

"No – get the wax out of your ears, peckerhead. What did I just say? Nobody deserves to be murdered. . . . Are you deaf or just dumb as shit?"

Robbie, at this point, did what he usually did when Teach and his dad started their crazy conversations – he stood up, and, without saying a word, made his escape. He went into the kitchen to help his wife and mom and to check on his two little girls to make sure they weren't going to be exposed to any of the filth that was surely forthcoming from his dad and his brother.

"So, what you're saying is, when all these pro-life people come on TV today and start in with all of their *yes, buts* and *no, howevers* you're going to call them on it, right? You're going to call them what they really are, right? A bunch of equivocating, lying cowards, right?"

"You don't have to agree with what somebody does, even if you agree with what they're saying, idiot. . . . You're the only lying coward I know around here."

"Okay – here's what I'm talking about." Teach grabbed the remote and turned the volume up. On the screen was a spokesman for a pro-life organization, condemning the murder first, but then also launching into an anti-abortion political message at the end of his prepared statement. "Why is the abortion issue even being dragged into this? Can you tell me that? Why is the word *abortion* even being used? And, for God sakes, why are they asking anti-abortion people to comment on it? Why is that, Dad?"

"Because they think he was an abortion doctor, shithead."

"Well, what if he had been a podiatrist?"

"Then we wouldn't be having this asinine conversation. I would be taking a nap."

"No, if he'd been a podiatrist or any other person in any other walk of life, all that the media would be talking about would be what a nut job the killer was – if they even mentioned it at all. Why would it even be on the news? But since the victim was a doctor who may have coincidentally performed a handful of abortions – *legal* abortions, I might add – then all of a sudden a lunatic's opinion on something matters."

"But he wasn't a podiatrist, dipshit. Grow up. Why can't you see the difference? You think you're so damn smart, but you make the stupidest-ass arguments I've ever heard."

"Okay, now this is what really pisses me off." On the TV screen was someone identified as an abortion-rights advocate, condemning the murder in no uncertain terms. "Why does someone who supports abortion rights have to jump out of bed on a Sunday, rush down to a TV studio and comment on why an insane lunatic killed an innocent person? It's absolutely ridiculous. It doesn't matter if the killer says he hates abortion. That has nothing to do with it. It's irrelevant."

"It has everything to do with it! It's the only reason he was killed!"

"You don't know that. Nobody knows that for sure. Maybe he didn't even know the guy was a doctor. He may go around shouting 'Death to abortionists' everywhere he goes, for all we know. He may go up to the cashier at the supermarket every week and yell at her, 'Abortion is murder! Abortion is murder!' Maybe this was just some crazy guy who went off his meds, and he just happened to be strolling through the neighborhood and just happened to see the good doctor putting his garbage out on the curb, and maybe he just happened to notice a can of green beans in his garbage. And, who knows, maybe he had been forced to eat green beans every day growing up because his mom was some crazy health-food nut, so seeing this can of green beans in the doctor's garbage made him snap and he just went psycho and shot him. Okay? That sounds plausible enough to me. So should the media start questioning what possible role the over-consumption of green beans had in this terrible tragedy? Does the president of the National Green Bean Association have to go to Capitol Hill and testify about what possible liability his organization might have regarding this murder? . . . I'm just asking."

"What in the name of God have you been smoking?"

"No, Dad, I'm asking you a serious, simple question – Should the president of the National Green Bean Association have to go to Capitol Hill to testify about his organization's possible liability in this great national tragedy? Yes or no? It's a very simple question."

"Give me that," Barry said, reaching for the remote. "I used to think your mother probably dropped you on your head once or twice when you were a baby. But I swear to God, I think she must have dribbled it like a fucking basketball."

Teach threw his head back with laughter. "I love you, Dad."

TEACH AND CHERYL ARE on their first date. They are at the pizza buffet. When it comes to food, Teach believes that quantity trumps quality every time. The pizzas brought out to the buffet have dry, often burnt crusts, and sparse toppings, yet here's Teach going back to get a clean plate and another stack of slices.

He thinks he might like Cheryl. She's smart – someone with a little more intellectual heft. Nothing like Cait, of course, whom he saw as his intellectual superior – but he's given up on finding anyone like Cait in Toxonomonomonee County. Cheryl is a ninth-grade English teacher at Tox County High. He had met her, however, at TCC, as he subbed for another GED instructor who had a night class. After her divorce, Cheryl moonlighted for a couple of years at TCC as a part-time freshman English instructor, bumping heads again with many of the same students she had bumped heads with four or five years earlier.

Another first date for Teach. His time to shine. He's had only a couple of these since Angie. (He and Cait didn't really have a first date. There didn't seem to be that process of getting-to-know-you – there was so much immediate shared joy in each other's presence that it eclipsed the fact that they were still strangers to one another.) He went with Angie for a couple of years – the same amount of time he had known Cait – yet after their breakup he didn't lie awake every night thinking about Angie. He didn't have cars honking at him at stoplights because he was in the middle of some Angie-dream when the light changed. He never stopped in the middle of whatever he was doing and burst out laughing at the memory of something Angie had said. And remembering Angie didn't make him cry.

It had been good for him to get out of his parents' house and start dating again, so his two years with Angie had been time well spent, but, in the end, the continued presence of Cait looming over his life had not only overpowered him, but it had been too much for Angie as well. As their relationship reached the point where Teach was even contemplating proposing to her somewhere down the line, he decided that he should be honest with Angie about Cait. It seemed like the mature thing to do. Well, he was determined not to make that same mistake again.

He had really wanted things to work out with Angie. He knew he had to commit to someone if there was going to be any hope for him getting over Cait – someone with whom he could build up a stockpile of pleasant memories to compete with all the Cait-memories currently occupying all his brain cells. But how could he get over her if he couldn't stop thinking about her? And, if Teach were honest with himself, how much did he really want to get over Cait? The fact was, the whole time he had been with Angie he never stopped waiting for his phone to ring, with Cait on the other end. He had promised himself after he and Cait broke up that he would leave her alone. If she wanted to get back together, she knew where to find him. But after six months without Cait, keeping an arbitrary promise he had made to himself in an effort to be heroic didn't seem to make much sense, not when everything could be put back together with a simple phone call. He called her home number during what would be her Christmas break, hoping to catch her at home and not in California. Whether she had been there or not he would never know. Cait's mom had answered. Yes, she said, of course she remembered Tommy. She was polite to him, but firm; she said Cait had explained the circumstances of their breakup; had told her that Tommy would almost certainly try to contact her; and when he did, Cait had given instructions for her to be polite, but firm, and to tell Tommy to please understand that what they had together had been very special but that it was over and they both needed to try to get on with their lives without one another. But dreams die hard, and even after starting up with Angie, two whole years after that phone call, he was still waiting for Cait to call him.

After Angie, Teach retreated romantically for a while – now knowing how difficult it would be to abandon Cait. But then there was Sharon. Man, she was wild – a Waffle House waitress he had struck up a double-entendre'd conversation with, but who was walking such an emotional tightrope that she soon had Teach running for the hills. One incident involving Sharon – and there were others – began with her picking Teach up in her pick-up truck to take him out somewhere special to eat, and ended with an automobile inferno blazing somewhere in the next county over. It was wintertime, already dark outside, and en route to the restaurant Sharon decided to pay her ex-husband a visit. Supper could wait. Sharon drove out of Tox County, for what seemed like an hour, with her bright beams on and country music blaring, then turned off onto a dirt road and drove for another fifteen minutes. Eventually, she stopped outside a small farmhouse, killed her headlights, jumped down from the cab, retrieved something from the bed of her truck which was most likely a gallon of gasoline, and the next thing Teach knew a car, no more than twenty-five feet from where he was sitting, was lighting up the night sky. At least Sharon had had enough sense not to stand there watching it burn until either the car exploded, the cops arrived, or her ex-husband intervened with a rifle.

Teach then dated Yolanda. She had been his GED student, but was exactly his age, and since student-teacher romances were considered to be bad form, he was fortunate that Yolanda was a smart, motivated student who quickly passed through the program. But it was not Teach who had made the first move. Yolanda had been a bit flirty in class, but more so on breaks, often choosing to hang out with Teach in the classroom or the hallway rather than joining her classmates as they mingled elsewhere. Teach was sad when she graduated from the GED program, for he enjoyed her company and had been smitten by her smile. She enrolled in the college curriculum and surprised Teach one morning by showing up outside his classroom door, just to say hello. She continued to swing by his class regularly and soon asked him if he would like to escort her to a party she had been invited to.

When she was still his flirtatious student, he had found it exciting to be the hunter's quarry for once, but still he held back, coy, reluctant to return too much of her affection. If the situation had been reversed and Teach had found himself in his usual role of suitor, then he would have accused the young lady of playing hard-to-get. Teach's unusual reserve may have been a result, in part, of the teacher-student status they shared at the time, but it was mostly because he had no idea how to react to the fact that an African American woman was coming on to him. He had never dated beyond the confines of his race and had never felt the inclination to do so; yet he also told himself that it shouldn't make a bit of difference one way or another.

But it did. Yolanda's mom never gave her blessing to their relationship. She was welcoming to Teach, in person, but Yolanda told a different story privately. And for his part, Teach had to wonder, why was he always so eager to bring Yolanda around to see his folks? What were the chances that dating Yolanda was, as much as anything else, just another means of messing with his dad? If you were a white Southern male dating a black woman, there was still something in the air that turned everything you did together into a sociological experiment. And, he had to admit, he couldn't help but view their relationship in the same light. Teach surmised – after eight months with Yolanda – that for an interracial relationship to work, at least in Tox County, the couple needed to be as closely bonded as he and Cait. With Cait he could have withstood anything.

Tonight, at the pizza parlor with Cheryl, Teach slides back into his side of the booth with his plate piled high with six different varieties of pizza.

There's nothing teachers enjoy more than swapping war stories, so after listening to Teach describe the wonderful life of a GED instructor, Cheryl is eager to find out what sort of horrific experiences led to Teach's decision to abandon the public schools in favor of the community college – the underlying assumption being that teaching within a contemporary school system is so harrowing that anyone who leaves for other pastures – greener or otherwise – must have been traumatized by their experiences. Teach did not contradict that assumption.

"So, Teach, what was sixth grade like? I've never taught below high school."

"Probably no different than teaching ninth grade, I suspect, except that the forces of evil arrayed against you are shorter and need to blow their noses a lot more often. . . . No, I'm just kidding – the kids were fine for the most part. It was the grown-ups who caused most of the problems. The chain of command was a chain of fools. The principal was an idiot; the administrators were idiots; the parents were idiots; the other teachers were idiots – no offense, Cheryl – I'm talking about middle school teachers here, not high school teachers." Teach smiles; so does Cheryl. "But the kids almost made it worthwhile, actually. They were the smartest people I dealt with. . . . Which is ironic, to say the least. When I first started, it was having to deal with all those children that I really dreaded, but then they turn out to be the best part – which goes to show you, I guess, just how incredibly untenable our positions really are, when you consider how plum slap-crazy some of these kids are. . . . Jesus. . . . Let's just say I'm content to no longer be associated with that particular peculiar institution."

"Yeah, I know what you mean – I think about quitting all the time. I think everybody does. But what else am I going to do? It's kind of hard to change horses in midstream."

"I had my horse shot right out from under me."

"What do you mean?"

"I was asked to vacate the premises and never to return."

"You were fired?"

"Yep."

"What on Earth for? I'm sure you were a wonderful teacher."

"Thank you, Cheryl. I think I was a darn good teacher, if they had just let me teach. So what was I fired for? That's a very good question. I never was given an official explanation. I'm not sure what grounds they had, really. . . . Being politically and metaphysically incorrect, maybe? Do you want to hear the whole story about what happened?"

"Sure. Of course."

Teach puts his pizza down, so his hands will be free to gesticulate. "I was teaching a unit on the Salem witch trials. And knowing how kids love to dress up and pretend, I thought it would be great to let the girls dress up as witches for one day – you can probably tell already where this story is headed. But I went out and found a costume store and bought a black pointy hat and some green makeup. And, of course, every self-respecting witch has to have a wart on the end of her nose, right? – so I bought some little round stickers, all shiny and colorful. They didn't look anything at all like warts, but the kids didn't care. And I bought a fright-wig – the whole works. I already had an old ratty coat that looked like something a witch might wear, way too big for those little girls, but they loved it. Oh man, the kids were so excited. I knew this was going to be a good lesson."

"I bet it was."

"We had a wooden coat rack in the room that we used for the stake. And after I bought all the costume stuff, I stopped by Home Depot to see if I could buy some kind of straw or hay. They only sold it by the bale, so I bought this big bale of hay, even though it was a lot more than I would ever need. I planned to spread a little of it along the floor, around the coat rack, just to add some verisimilitude to the *mise en scene*, as it were.

"I didn't have enough for the guys to do, unfortunately. I think that was my big mistake. I couldn't find any of those big pilgrim hats. So what we did, I asked all the girls in class how many wanted to be witches. And of course they all threw their hands up in the air and started wiggling in their seats. Well, we only had one witch costume and I had fifteen girls who wanted to be witches."

"Good Lord."

"Yeah, well, I panicked for just a second. I thought, maybe I should have spent less time shopping for a costume and more time actually planning the lesson." Teach and Cheryl both laugh. "But sixth-grade teachers – and ninth-grade teachers, too, I'm sure – have to be really good at thinking on their feet, so it didn't take me too long to figure out what to do. I figured we would only have time for maybe four or five girls to get dressed up, and my classroom had four rows of desks. So I went over to the hay bale and picked out some straws and let the girls on each row draw straws. The longest straw on each row got to be a witch."

"Good thinking."

"Young girls are so much more agreeable about things like that. Good God, if I had tried something like that with the boys, they would have started bitching about how the winner cheated because he saw how I arranged the straws or how they saw one boy tip off another boy – it would have been a disaster. . . . And I had this one boy, a little kid named Martin, who was a drag queen in the making, who said he wanted to be a witch –"

"I bet I know who you're talking about – Martin Bellagio. I had him, too."

"That's him all right. . . . How many Bellagios do you reckon there are in Tox County?"

"I know his grandmother works at the paper."

"Well anyway, thank God he didn't draw one of the long straws. My plan was, I had printed out copies of the actual trial transcripts, with the questions that the judges asked the accused witches, with the witches' replies. The boys took turns reading the questions and the witch would read each reply. That turned out to be problematic, though. So many of these kids were such shitty readers, it was a struggle to get them through all of that arcane language. It was fun, though. The girls all helped each other get into the witch costume. I had the witch just stand up against the stake. There was no way I would have actually tied her up – even I wasn't that stupid. That alone would have gotten me fired quicker than anything else that happened."

"Oh, I don't know. It all sounds pretty innocent to me."

"You would think so, wouldn't you? Well, just wait till you hear what happened and you'll see just how innocent everybody thought it was. Jesus Christ. . . . So while the witch was standing up at the stake and the boys were struggling with the questions, all the other girls were laughing and giggling and the boys were hootin' and hollerin' and yelling, 'burn the accursed witch, burn the accursed witch' – they had fallen in love with the word *accursed* while we were studying the vocabulary. . . . For a few days there everything was *accursed* this and *accursed* that – 'where's my accursed pencil?' or 'I'm gonna kick your accursed butt.' It was funny."

"You're lucky. They actually took an interest in what you were teaching them. By the time they get to the ninth grade they could care less about any new vocabulary words."

"Yeah, it was fun. And I remember how the classroom next door started getting out of hand, too, because you know that no sixth-grade class wants to hear another class having more fun than they are. . . . Okay, so everything was going fine until near the end. But then the boys started getting restless and when I had my back turned, somebody – who just so happened to have a cigarette lighter illegally in his possession – I don't know who it was, but somebody set some of the hay on fire that I had scattered on the floor around the stake."

"Oh my God."

"Well, you can imagine. Holy hell broke loose. . . . Smoke was everywhere. The kids were screaming. The fire alarm went off. . . . They never did find out who set the fire. These kids have a code of silence like the Mafia."

"Wow."

"Wow is right, but the fire wasn't why I lost my job. . . . It wasn't my fault one of my students was a junior arsonist. But the principal got a call from the mom of the girl who was standing up at the stake when the fire started. She had hired a lawyer and was all set to sue me, the school, the county, and whoever else she could get her hands on. It turned out she was one of those Kooks for Christ who want to ban Halloween and arrest you for saying Happy Holidays. She said I was demonic. . . . Then the TV stations found out about it. I was watching TV and one of those news teasers came on. The anchorwoman said, 'Is a local six-grade teacher promoting witchcraft? Story at eleven.' – "

"Oh my God, Teach, that was you? I remember that! We were all talking about it at school. About how crazy it all was. . . . I can't believe that was you!"

"It was unbelievable, all right. So that's when I got fired. The principal did a complete one-eighty and completely caved in to the whackos. So in the end, I was the one who got burned at the stake. . . . I was the human sacrifice – martyred on the altar of political expediency and superstitious stupidity." And with that, Teach raises his arms in the air like a Roman orator and leans back in the booth with a satisfied smile.

God's Eternal Damnation

Practice Essay
By Julie Grace

It takes tremendous courage to commit suicide. More, apparently, than I have. I have thought about killing myself since I was thirteen years old. I have only tried to once, to no avail (obviously). I have often heard people say, "Suicide is the coward's way out." THESE PEOPLE ARE FULL OF SHIT. It is the people like me, who make these half-assed attempts to kill themselves, who are the cowards.

There are so many ways to kill yourself – all of which I'm too scared to do. Some people jump off of buildings or high bridges. Can you imagine the terror they must feel as they plummet, fully conscious, knowing they only have maybe five more seconds to live? What goes through your mind when you know you have only five more seconds to live? I don't know, but I do know what goes through your mind when you're standing on the railing of a bridge at 3:00 in the morning and your best friend is pulling on your arm, crying and screaming, trying to talk you down.

They say that right before you die, you see your whole life flashing in front of your eyes. I must have known I wasn't going to die because the only thing I experienced was the same loop, like a hip-hop sample, going over and over in my head – JUST FALL FORWARD, JUST FALL FORWARD, JUST FALL FORWARD.

But I couldn't do it. It would be much easier for me to write an essay on cowardice. I have no idea what courage is, but cowardice I understand. Cowardice is fear, this invisible force holding you back, preventing you from doing what you know you want to do.

Another way to kill yourself is by slitting your wrist. I could never do this. The idea of lying in a pool of my own blood sickens me. I know people who own guns. I could put a gun to my head and blow my brains out. But I know I couldn't do it. First of all, it would be a bloody mess, but it would also take too much courage for me to pull the trigger. It would be just like when I was standing on that bridge and all I had to do was let myself fall forward. Somehow, the simple act of putting my finger on the trigger and then just moving my finger an inch backward seems like it would take as much strength as that Greek god who has to keep rolling the boulder up the hill.

I think what makes these simple acts so difficult to do is the fact that they *are* so simple. It doesn't seem possible that something so simple as moving a finger one inch backward, or letting your body fall a few inches forward, or moving a knife one inch across your skin is all it takes to end a life. As I was standing on top of that bridge I was paralyzed by the idea that everything I have experienced, terrible as it was, and everything I had ever thought, depressing as it was, and all the memories I had, as bad as they were, would be gone forever with just a simple body movement forward; a movement that is so common and so easy we don't even have to think about how to do it. If committing suicide was as difficult as rolling that huge boulder up a steep hill, then maybe I could do it. It would take a lot of time, and great effort, and when I finally got to the top I would feel like I had made an effort that was worthy of the goal. After all, anything worth doing in life has to be earned through hard work, right?

I think that people who have a lot of suicidal ideation actually have a better understanding than most people about just how precious and delicate life on Earth is. Ironic, isn't it? I remember a few years ago having a fight with my mom. I ran out into the front yard screaming at her. I was so mad at her – I don't even remember now what it was about – but I really wanted to do some damage. She had just planted some flowers around a big tree in the yard. It would have been so easy for me to have uprooted every one of her precious little flowers, and I definitely thought about doing it, but something stopped me. Even in my anger, there was something unbearably sad about killing such innocent, vulnerable flowers. I couldn't do it. So I kicked the tree instead and almost broke my damn foot in the process.

So why do I sometimes want to kill myself? People have asked me that question like I was crazy to even think about it. THESE PEOPLE DISGUST ME. They act so wise like they understand life and how wonderful it is, when in reality the only thing keeping them from jumping off the nearest bridge are all the lies that they have convinced themselves are true. My psychiatrist thinks my suicidal thoughts are all caused by a chemical imbalance in my brain, and if he can only find the right drug, then all of a sudden my life will become a big bowl of delicious cherries. Well, excuse me if I'm insulted by that. Is it my brain chemistry that caused all the senseless violence and starvation and misery in the world? Is it my brain chemistry that caused my parents to go from loving each other to hating each other? That caused certain other people to go from loving me to hating me? That caused my boyfriend to take off his condom and to get me pregnant? That caused me to eventually decide to have an abortion after I realized I couldn't force myself to fall forward off a bridge?

If it is just a chemical imbalance, then I know the name of another drug my psychiatrist hasn't prescribed yet that will straighten out my brain chemistry and keep me from having such terrible thoughts. IT'S CALLED HEROIN. What do people say to all those poor, misguided people who think that heroin, or some other drug, is the only thing that will keep them from falling forward off a bridge? They tell them the drugs are only giving them an illusion, a fantasy, and that the only way to live a truly meaningful life is to embrace reality, even with all its problems. To face life drug-free. Then they fill me full of the latest drug-of-the-day so I can live an illusion that life is hunky-dory. CAN YOU SAY HYPOCRITE? I'm not stupid enough to do heroin. I don't want to be addicted to something that will make me die a slow, painful death. The idea is to do just the opposite – to die a quick, painless death.

So, here is how pathetic I am as a suicide victim. The one time when I thought I had taken the necessary actions to kill myself, and was happy about what I had done, I still managed to chicken out. I take 90 mg of Nardil every day. I thought an overdose would be the one way to kill myself that I could actually go through with, and that wouldn't be bloody and disgusting. I would just drift off to sleep and never have to wake up. But I also knew a botched overdose could become really disgusting. I didn't want to embarrass myself by drowning in my own vomit. I may have low self-esteem, but I do have my dignity.

It had been exactly one year since my best friend had screamed and cried enough to convince me not to fall forward off that bridge, and a little less than a year since my abortion. Was I grateful to her for saving my life? Was I happier now because of what she had done? Sadly, the answer to both questions was no. Could I imagine myself feeling differently this time next year? Again, the sad answer was no. Based on these facts, I decided that that night was finally going to be THE NIGHT. I wanted to spend time with my friends one last time, but I didn't tell them my intentions for fear that, once again, I would be screamed and cried out of what little courage I had.

So I came back home later and still felt courageous enough to swallow what I thought would be enough Nardil to go to sleep permanently and not humiliate myself for eternity. I thought about waking up my mom and saying goodnight to her just so she could hear my voice one last time, but that would have been so out of character for me that I decided instead to let her sleep and to make sure I said something nice to her in my final letter to the world. I wrote my suicide note and laid it on my bed beside me. I spent the first half of it apologizing to everyone I didn't blame for anything. I spent the second half damning everybody else to hell. But then I thought better of that and wrote a long P.S. where I apologized to all those I had just damned to hell. I realized nobody is really to blame for the way the world is, except maybe God, but then again it may be all beyond His control, too.

I was really proud of myself for finally doing what I had been too afraid to do for so long. I thought I had finally done the right thing. It had been a very difficult decision to have the abortion. You have no way of really knowing if you are making the right decision. And it's not like you are just unsure about which dress to buy or what food to order. It's not even like being unsure whether or not to break up with a boyfriend or to have sex for the first time. It's even more serious than that. What you're unsure about is whether or not you should kill something that might be the best thing to ever happen to you – or the worst thing. But as difficult as making that decision was, it was even harder dealing with the uncertainty afterwards.

Before you make the decision, you are still hopeful you will make the right decision, and that you'll know you made the right decision and you will be happy and proud of yourself when you realize you made the right decision. But afterward, you realize you will never know whether you made the right decision – no matter how many kids you decide to have or how many you decide not to have – you will simply never know.

So maybe the reason I couldn't bring myself to fall forward off that bridge when I was pregnant was because I still had that little glimmer of hope that I could actually make the right decision about one thing in my life. But that hope went away after the abortion. All I had was the feeling that no matter how long I lived I would never really know what I had done. Had I killed the best thing to ever happen to me? Or had I killed the worst thing to ever happen to me?

So I actually had the courage to swallow a whole bunch of pills, and I'm lying in bed feeling proud of myself, and I have my suicide note forgiving everyone laying on the blanket beside me, and a warm feeling of happiness comes over me. And what I think about is how ironic it is that what is finally bringing me happiness is the knowledge that I'm getting ready to die.

I start to feel dizzy, but I haven't gone to sleep yet, and I'm still thinking, and I start to think more deeply about this unfamiliar sense of happiness and calm that I'm feeling. And it occurs to me that the reason I'm suddenly feeling so happy isn't necessarily because I'm finally getting close to death, but that it could have something to do with finally being at peace with everyone since I wrote my suicide note.

I panicked. I was no longer sure I wanted to die. I jumped out of bed and fell. My legs were very wobbly. I made it into the bathroom and started gulping water. But I wasn't sure if that would be enough. So, even though it's probably the most disgusting thing I've ever done, I stuck my finger in my mouth and down into my throat until I threw up.

All this commotion woke up my mom. She ran into the bathroom. I told her I was sick, but she didn't believe me. She said my speech was slurred. She smelled my breath and realized I wasn't drunk. So the only other explanation my genius mom could come up with was that somebody had slipped me a roofie. "No, Mom, nobody – slipped – me – a roofie."

"How do you know? You wouldn't know it if they did."

"These – were – my – friends." My speech really was slurred. I sounded like I had a mouth full of peanut butter.

"I know what kind of friends you have."

"Screw – you – Mom."

So that is how my pathetic suicide attempt ended, with me arguing with my mom, with disgusting puke drooling down my chin, trying to convince her that drugs played no part in my present condition.

She wanted to take me to the hospital to have my stomach pumped, but I refused to go. First of all, I didn't want her to see what would come out of my stomach, and secondly, the only thing I can think of more disgusting than induced vomiting is getting your stomach pumped. My refusal to go to the hospital made my mom furious. We started screaming at each other. It was not a good night. She followed me into my room and picked up my suicide note on my bed. I snatched it away from her before she realized what it was. I finally managed to kick her out of my room, but I was afraid to go back to sleep – even if I could have at that point.

The brief feelings of tranquility I had that night are now long gone. But I'm still able to bring them back somewhat when I read over my suicide note, especially the last paragraph. I carry it with me everywhere I go, so whenever I'm feeling overcome with thoughts of suicide I can read over it and feel a little better. It's not heroin, but it'll have to do. Here is the last paragraph:

P.S. I don't really believe what I just wrote. Justin, you were a jerk, but being mad at you has brought me nothing but pain. The pain is about to end for good, but I don't want to die mad. And that goes for everybody else I've been mad at. And not just the people I know. I've been mad at the whole world, for good reasons. Anybody with half a brain should be able to see that the world is a miserable place to be most of the time. But I guess that means the world is miserable for everybody, so maybe I should cut the whole world some slack. And that goes for you too, God, who created this unholy mess. Everybody is always asking you for forgiveness, but maybe it's you that needs to get down on your holy knees and beg us to forgive you, since this is all your fault to begin with. So, Almighty Asshole, I forgive you. Since I'm forgiving everybody, there's one person I haven't forgiven yet – me. I guess that's the hardest person for me to forgive. But it wasn't my fault I was born into this horrible world. It wasn't my fault I have the parents I have, and I've already forgiven them anyway. And for all the things that were my fault, it wasn't because I wanted to hurt anyone, or that I didn't try to make the right decisions. I guess everything I screwed up can be blamed on either my ignorance, my weakness, or my fear. But can I really blame myself for these things? I've always tried to be smart and to learn as much as possible. I've always tried to be strong. I've always tried not to be afraid. I can honestly say I did try very hard to make the right decisions every time. I'll never know if I made the right decision about my abortion, but I should forgive myself because I know I tried to make the right decision. I have no reason to blame myself for a decision that was impossible to make from the start. There was no way to make a decision I could be happy with. Damned if I did, damned if I didn't. So how could it be my fault? And I know I never wanted to hurt anyone, unless I got pissed off, and I've already forgiven everyone who has pissed me off. So what is there left to feel bad about? So, Julie Grace, I forgive thee. Now I can die at peace.

LAST YEAR, THE PRESIDENT had instituted a campus-wide smoking ban at TCC. Over the past thirty years, helpless nicotine addicts had been herded into designated smoking areas – first, onto lonely, out-of-the-way hallways, where the pure-of-lung were forced to inhale and hold their breath as they scurried to pulmonary safety, and then gradually further and further outdoors into the rain and cold. Despite complaints regarding the new policy last year, the administration's totalitarian instincts had prevailed, and so one-third of the school's enrollment was transformed, overnight, from mere second-class citizens into full-fledged outlaws.

The students affected by the ban coped in various ways. Most chose to remain in cars until classtime – often joining with friends to create cramped, portable cigarette klatches. Before class, many cars that were parked along the fringes of the campus parking lots sported gray, smoked-over windows – and witnessing a car door being opened was very much like watching a magic trick being performed, as an impossibly large group of people suddenly emerged from within a billowing cloud of smoke.

Others attempted to avoid detection by taking to the trees. The campus had no shortage of strong-limbed maples and sturdy oaks – and no shortage of young, athletic students willing to climb them. On any given morning, throughout summer classes and well into autumn, as Teach pulled into his usual parking spot and strolled to the cafeteria, he could see two or three trees smoking, with small wisps of smoke swirling in and around the leaves, emanating somewhere from within the trees' leafy centers. Those with lesser climbing skills realized they could gain access to the roofs of the many single-storied campus buildings by scaling ladders rather than tree trunks; so every morning there would be someone hauling out an extendable aluminum ladder from the back of a pickup, running with it to the least exposed side of a building, and shimmying up with several of his friends right on his heels. The last one on the roof was responsible for quickly pulling the ladder up behind him. Roscoe, the SRO – who also was forced to fight a daily battle with nicotine withdrawal – sympathized with and adopted an attitude of benign neglect toward the tree climbers, roof shimmiers and car stuffers.

There was a lot of commotion on the commons this morning. A work crew with chainsaws and a man high up in a bucket lift were sawing down a large oak tree. Teach, so he wouldn't have to be alone with his memories, went into Randy's office during his class break. "Why are they cutting down that tree, boss?"

"Some guy was hiding up in it last night, smoking. He fell and broke his neck."

"Jesus. Did it kill him?"

"No, thank goodness. He might be paralyzed, though."

"I guess they're going to have to add another warning to the label, now. 'Smoking has been shown to cause paralysis in people falling out of trees.'

– So they're sawing down a beautiful old oak tree just to keep somebody else from falling out of it?"

"That's what it looks like."

"Unbelievable. . . . Chopping off their nose to spite their face. . . . Well, the reason I dropped by is, I just wanted to run another idea by you. I know how strapped for cash we always are, and I think I've come up with a great fund-raising idea. . . . Have you noticed how hot a lot of our young female students are?"

"Excuse me?"

"Well, actually, you may not have noticed, Randy, but man, we always have some really hot babes coming through this program."

"This is not appropriate, Teach –"

"No, no, hear me out. I always have at least two or three girls every year – at least – who tell me they want to go to New York and become models. Why don't we give them a chance to gain some experience while we have them? Why don't we get together with the photography department and do a photo shoot, and put out a calendar with pictures of our students?"

"What kind of pictures?"

"Nothing really racy, of course. Maybe bikinis, maybe one of the girls wearing those Daisy Duke shorts. Maybe a little lingerie. . . . Nothing too provocative. I wouldn't want to do anything exploitative. We could even let the girls decide. They could wear whatever they were willing to wear. If a girl wanted to – I don't know, I'm just spitballing here, Randy. . . . A little booby here, a little butt cheek there – that would be entirely up to her. We wouldn't tell her she had to do it; we wouldn't even suggest it. Let the girls take total ownership of the project. It could be a really valuable learning experience for them. . . . But think about how many of these puppies we would sell. Even in other counties. We could put other GED programs out of business. . . . I'm thinking we could call it something like, 'The Girls of the GED – We Ain't Too Smart, But We Sure Are Hot!'"

"You're kidding, right? Are you serious? I never know when to take you seriously."

"I'm serious as a heart attack. We're talking big bucks here."

"Well, I'll need to think about it."

"Sure, sure. Just think about it. What I could do in the meantime is mention it to some of the girls – try to generate some interest."

"No! Don't do that. Don't mention it to anybody, Teach."

"Really? Okay, then. You're the boss. . . . Oh, I get it. I see where you're coming from. You're thinking it would be a more effective marketing tool if we kept the whole thing under wraps until we can have the Great Unveiling, right? That's how they promote all the big new products now. Keep everything a big secret, plant a couple of strategic leaks just to pique everyone's interest, build the suspense, and then – *pow!* – initial sales go through the roof. That's pretty canny, Randy. I gotta hand it to you. You're not the director of this program for nothing."

"I said I would think about it, Teach. Don't get carried away. . . . Is there anything else you wanted to talk about?"

"No, I think I've taken up enough of your time. But I bet you're seeing dollar signs right about now, aren't you? . . . Oh yeah, we should also do a guy's calendar as well. I don't want to be sexist. You could be in charge of that one. . . . See you around, buddy."

There were no dismissal bells in the Adult Literacy Department, so instructors (and students) kept a diligent eye on the clock. The departmental budget being what it was, the clocks in each classroom were inexpensive, double-A-battery-operated, and – every student's nightmare – prone to elongating class time.

As Teach's students watched the clock, approximately five minutes before dismissal they would begin slamming books closed and rustling through book bags to retrieve their cell phones. (For teachers in classrooms, the proliferation of cell phones had quickly become the equivalent of staphylococcus in the O.R. for surgeons.) The last five minutes of class were always the hardest for Teach. He sympathized with his students, who, for the most part, had been working hard (or hard enough) for three hours, so he felt it was unfair to give them a hard time at the very tail-end of class. What made these last five minutes especially difficult to navigate were students such as Maria and Charlotte, who valued every minute of study time, who needed a quiet environment and had a right to expect it. So for the benefit of these super-students, Teach felt obligated to clamp down on the chaos as much as possible until he officially dismissed class. He often found himself resenting, during the final five minutes, the very students he had so dearly loved during the previous 175.

Today, as Teach endured the last five minutes of class and dismissed it at noon, sharp, Jerry Speziak was more animated than usual. Teach had given him the good news that he had passed his first two GED tests, which he had taken yesterday. As he zipped his book bag at the rear of the room, he said loudly, "I'm glad I came here, Teach. I'm glad I left that crappy school." Teach replied, also loudly, "I'm glad you left your crappy school and came here too, Jerry. . . . Make sure you tell all your friends."

As soon as Teach said this, he turned his head and saw Randy, who liked to walk the halls as classes were dismissing. Randy was standing in the open doorway with a disapproving look on his face. After all of Teach's students had left, Randy said, "I need to see you in my office."

As Teach entered Randy's office, Randy said, "You shouldn't have said that, Teach."

"What?"

"'Make sure you tell all your friends. I'm glad you dropped out of school.' I don't know how much you know about our relationship with the public schools, but let me just tell you one thing. You should never try to recruit students into our program if they're still enrolled somewhere else. You have no idea how much grief I get from the superintendents, who think we're trying to steal their students."

"That's ridiculous."

"I know it is."

"That's like saying the U.S. is trying to steal Mexicans."

"We have a very important program here, Teach, and I want people to know about it – the people who need it. I ran an ad in the paper last month, and I was very careful how I worded it. It said, 'Have you recently lost your job? Is your lack of a high school diploma holding you back in the job market?' I mean, it was clearly aimed at adults. But Superintendent Carlton raised hell about it. . . . They seem to think that their students have no idea that we even exist, and if they ever find out then there will be a mass exodus."

"Interesting. I wonder why they would think that."

"I don't know, but what I do know is that they wish that we didn't."

"Didn't what?"

"Exist. You know, a lot of counties in this state don't allow sixteen- and seventeen-year-olds to enroll in a GED class. And this is the reason why – recruitment. How do you think it's going to look if this kid you were talking to goes around telling all his friends—"

"I don't think Jerry Speziak has any friends. But you don't think that happens all the time anyway? These kids are in constant communication with each other. They're always recruiting their friends – if for no other reason, just so they can hang out together."

"But they don't usually have their teacher egging them on. . . . What do you think is going to happen if one of those kids tells his principal that – what's the kid's name? Jerry?" Teach nodded. "That Jerry has a teacher who's telling him and his buddies to drop out of school?"

Teach laughed. "They don't listen to anything we tell them. How much money is spent on ad campaigns telling kids not to drop out of school? Does it do any good? . . . Maybe we *should* start telling kids to drop out. They're just going to do the opposite of what we tell them anyway."

"As I was saying, the principal finds out; he gets pissed off and calls the superintendent, and then guess who the superintendent calls?" Teach points his finger at Randy. "Me? No, I'm just middle management, Teach.

He calls the guy he plays golf with – the president of the college. And he tells the president his side of the story, about how he's fighting tooth and nail every day trying to educate kids and keep them in school so they're better equipped to succeed when they come here to enroll. And the president, he's standing over his putt thinking about all of this. . . . How much time do you think he spends thinking about the GED program? It may mean the world to you and me, but to him? How many pages does the GED program take up in the college handbook? . . . Now don't get me wrong – he knows we generate a lot of FTE. But he's going to be looking at the big picture. What's best for the college as a whole? A small number of sixteen-year-olds getting their GEDs and enrolling early in Curriculum? Or the continued goodwill of the public-school system? As these administrators get more and more desperate to retain students – I tell you, Teach, it's going to get ugly."

"And all because of little ol' me and Jerry Speziak?"

Randy stared at Teach for quite a while before responding.

"No, Teach. This is always an ongoing battle, all the time. . . . I just need you to understand what role you play, to make sure you hold yourself accountable and act responsibly. It's a very delicate political dance that goes on every year, every semester, at every Board of Trustees meeting – and all it really boils down to is just an old-fashioned turf war."

"Turf war, huh. . . . Are we the Bloods or the Crips?"

Randy took off his glasses, rubbed his eyes, and sighed deeply.

"Teach, I just need you to stop telling these kids they're doing the right thing by dropping out of school."

"Even if they are doing the right thing."

"Yes. Even if they are."

You and Cait have decided to take in a little culture and attend a ballet recital in the music building. You both know, however, what will end up happening. There is no way either of you will ever sit straight-faced through a ballet. As far as you're concerned, you're looking at it as an evening of comedy.

The ballerina is on stage, all twinkle-toed and lacey. "What are those costumes called?" you ask. "Is it a tutu or a muumuu? I can never remember."

"It's a tutu, dummy." Cait tries to whisper over the music. "Believe me, if she were wearing a muumuu she wouldn't be a ballet dancer."

"Why is that?"

"You really don't know what a muumuu is?"

"I'm not well versed in feminine fashion, Cait. The only thing I know about what you wear is how sexy it all is."

"Well, it's just a big, loose-fitting dress. Women who are big fat cows wear them."

"So that's why they're called moo-moos? Because cows wear them?"

Cait splutters out a laugh. Two elderly ladies sitting in front of you who have been visibly annoyed during this whole conversation finally decide to do something about it. One of them turns her head around and shushes you loudly.

"I'm sorry," Cait apologizes, leaning forward and touching one of them on the shoulder.

For you, the highlight of any ballet – the only reason to watch one, actually – is to marvel at the sight of a man prancing around with the largest scrotum wad you've ever seen. "Is that a requirement to be a male ballet dancer?"

"What's that?" Cait asks.

"To be hung like a horse. . . . My God, look at that thing. It should get a separate billing in the program. How do they get up the nerve to do that, anyway? To go on stage in that getup?"

"Tommy – shhh. Be quiet," Cait says, pointing at the ladies sitting directly in front of you. But she's laughing as she does it.

"They must be exhibitionists or something. Maybe it turns them on. That would explain why it's so big."

Cait's suppressed laughter takes the form of a series of snorts. The ladies in front of you look at each other and shake their heads. You lean forward and tap the shoulder of one of them. "Excuse me, ladies, I apologize for bothering you, but I don't know much about ballet. Do you mind if I ask you a question?" Cait's head is bowed and her hand is up on her forehead like the bill of a cap, shielding her face as she tries desperately not to laugh. "When you're watching that guy dance, are you able to concentrate on anything at all besides the enormous amount of genitalia he has? Now be honest. . . . I just find it to be a huge distraction – no pun intended."

"Young man!" the old lady snapped. "You need to leave this theatre right now if this is how you intend to behave. . . . The only huge distraction is you."

"Well, I'm sorry ladies, but I just happen to be highly offended by this blatant exhibitionism. Aren't there laws against this kind of public indecency? And if you don't mind my saying so, what does it say about you if you enjoy all this voyeurism? No offense, of course."

One of the ladies stands up and leaves. When she returns she is accompanied by someone who appears to be in charge. You and Cait are asked to leave. You have made it through only twenty minutes of the performance. You both laugh all the way back to Cait's dorm, where you spend the rest of the evening participating in much more worthwhile activities.

"TEACH, LAST TIME WHEN WE STOPPED we were discussing ways to think about Cheryl that didn't involve unfair comparisons to Cait. Did you have a chance to think much about this? Were you aware of any times when you made judgments about Cheryl based on how you felt about Cait?"

"Well, like you said last time, Doc, this is going to take a long time. I'm trying to look at Cheryl differently; I'm trying to do what you're asking of me, Doc. . . . I've got Cait here in her box. Would you like to see her? I bought her something special to wear just so she would look nice for you."

Carney tried to smile at Teach but couldn't quite pull it off. "Okay, Teach, we kind of ended on the wrong foot last time, talking about happiness, and, again, I apologize for that. But I do feel it's important for us to continue in that vein, if you don't mind. . . . Let me put the question to you this way – how does Cheryl make you feel? I won't use the word *happy* or any other word. I just want you to describe to me, in your own words, how Cheryl makes you feel. . . . Just make sure Cait stays in her box, that's all." Dr. Carney smiled.

"She's still in her box, Doc. I think she's taking a nap, so let's keep our voices down." Teach thought for a long time before answering Dr. Carney's question. "Cheryl makes me feel a lot of different ways. . . . That's the problem, Doc. There's just so much ambiguity – so much uncertainty. With Cait, there was always. . . . Oops, I'm sorry." Teach pretended to open the lid of a small box. "I'm sorry, sweetheart. I didn't mean to disturb you. Go on back to sleep now. . . . I'm sorry, Doc."

"But see – that's good. That's great, Teach. You recognized what was going on there. The first step is recognition. That was actually a very important thing that just happened, Teach, although you like to joke about it."

"If you say so, Doc." Teach remained silent for another moment. "Do you know what the major problem with Cheryl is, Doc? And this is really true of every woman I've ever known – hell, every *person* I've ever known – except for you-know-who, of course, she-whose-name-we-must-not-mention. The problem is, nobody seems to have a sense of humor. I love to laugh, Doc, as you have probably figured out, and I apologize to you, sincerely, if I sometimes laugh at your expense, but the laugh is more important to me than the consequences of the laugh, and that gets me in trouble sometimes, but the way I look at the world is, you can either laugh, or cry, or go numb. So I choose laughter. It's very important to me. And any woman I'm involved with needs to have a good sense of humor. Cheryl just doesn't laugh very much. She doesn't seem to find very many things funny. It didn't bother me so much at first. She was just so sweet and pretty and smart – but after a while, this chronic, terminal seriousness she has just starts to wear you down. And it isn't so much that she isn't funny herself – there are lots of outlets for laughter; I can find lots of different ways to laugh; so I can live with that – I can live with Cheryl being a serious person. I can respect that about her. But what I really have a hard time with is when she doesn't laugh at me, when I'm trying to be funny. It's like I'm hitting my head against a wall, I swear. My jokes just bounce right off her. It's like she's surrounded by comedic kryptonite. Or some kind of anti-funny force field. I tell a joke and she raises her humor deflector shield. It's brutal, Doc. It really is. Nothing is worse for a comedian than having someone not laughing at their jokes. And it seems to me it would be brutal for her, too. Like trying to sit through a movie that thinks it's funny, but isn't. You have to walk out of it. Nothing is more brutal than failed comedy. So I don't know how Cheryl can stand living with me. I'll say to her, 'that was a joke, honey,' and she'll say, 'well, I just didn't think it was all that funny.' Well, baby cakes, if you don't like baseball, then don't buy season tickets. . . . But I don't see how she can stand it. She must say to herself, 'Why won't he stop with the lame jokes! He's not funny! I can't stand this anymore!' If I were in her shoes, I'd certainly –" Teach suddenly stopped speaking, his unfinished thought left floating in the air.

"Are you okay, Teach? You were saying?"

"That's okay, Doc. I really doubt if I understand Cheryl all that well. I shouldn't be putting words in her mouth. I'm sure there must be some reason why she stays with me, some reason known only to her."

"Do you ever talk about these things with her?"

"What things? Her insufficient sense of humor?"

"Well, no, not that necessarily, but what reasons she might have for wanting to be with you. I'm sure she must have a lot of reasons why she likes you, Teach."

"And I have lots of reasons to like Cheryl – it's just that. . . . Never mind, Doc. I almost opened up Caitdora's Box again. We don't want that to happen. We don't know what that might unleash."

"That's okay, Teach. That's good. . . . You're getting good at recognizing when that happens. . . . But let's go back to what we were just talking about. About talking with Cheryl. Have you ever talked to Cheryl about your feelings for Cait?"

"Good God no. . . . Is this something you're actually recommending to me? Are you sure you're a licensed practitioner? Do you carry malpractice insurance? Have you ever been in any type of relationship with any type of woman? . . . I'm sorry, Dr. Carney. . . . Just another example of my insensitivity – always making jokes at someone else's expense. I do apologize."

"That's quite all right, Teach. No harm done. But I am serious about talking to Cheryl about this. Or at least think about it. It's your decision, but I would at least think about it. What do you think would happen if you talked to Cheryl about Cait?"

"Well, let's see here. I'm obviously no expert on the feminine psyche, but let me hazard a guess. I sit Cheryl down, and I say, 'Honey, there's something I really need to tell you. There's this woman that I went to college with, my college sweetheart – my soul mate, actually. This is a woman that I love ten times more than I'll ever love you. This is a woman who is at least ten times more fun, and I would say one hundred times funnier than you will ever be. I just wanted to make you aware of her existence, that's all – oh, and one more thing – she's all I ever think about, morning, noon and night. And all this crying I keep doing? Well, that's just because I'm with you right now instead of her – so, sweetie, what's for dinner?' . . . Do you really think this plan of yours will work, Doc?"

"Well, not if you say it like that, no. But keep in mind the whole reason you're here with me is because Cheryl doesn't know what's going on with you emotionally right now. It was her idea for you to see me, right? So she's confused, frustrated, and probably more than a little bit hurt that you won't tell her what's causing you so much emotional turmoil. So you know that none of this has been easy on her. So please don't take this the wrong way, Teach, but if you decide to continue keeping Cheryl in the dark, then maybe I should be asking you, 'How well is this plan of *yours* working?'"

"Well, let me just tell you about another plan I once had. Several years ago, I decided to be upfront and honest with a previous girlfriend. Do you want to know how well that plan worked? Here's a clue for you – she is a *previous* girlfriend. I told her all about Cait, and you know what? She reacted not unlike how I imagine any normal human-being-type person would react. She said, 'if you're still that much in love with Cait, then I think we're finished here. I'll see myself out.' Or words to that effect. So I don't know, Doc. I just don't see anything good coming from Cheryl finding out about Cait."

"That would be for Cheryl to decide. She would decide what to do with the information. I understand your concern, but it might not be as bad as you fear. She might actually be relieved, Teach. It might be better for her to know, rather than have to continue not knowing. And she might be relieved that it's all based on things that happened eighteen, nineteen, twenty years ago and not just last week. I know that Cait is still very much a part of your life, or at least her memory is, but to me and Cheryl and anybody else, this is all stuff that happened a long time ago. Plus the fact that you no longer have any contact with her, and, most importantly, you're in therapy to learn how to deal with those memories. . . . Tell Cheryl, Teach. You need to tell her. . . . It's okay. It'll be okay. She'll be okay."

When Dr. Carney said these last words, the memory of Cait, so apparently harmless to everyone else, caused Teach to quickly dissolve into a pool of tears. He leaned forward and put his head in his hands and sobbed, his body shaking. "I'm sorry," he spluttered.

"It's okay, Teach. No need to apologize. Go ahead and let it all out."

Teach continued to sob. "I'm so sorry." He reached for a tissue.

"It's okay." Dr. Carney sat in respectful silence, his head bowed, looking down into the notes on his lap, as his patient continued to sob. After three or four minutes, with no end in sight, he stood silently and left his office.

"I'm sorry. Please forgive me," Teach sobbed one more time as Dr. Carney closed the door behind him.

Teach continued to cry, and he continued to mutter, "Please forgive me. I'm so sorry. . . . I'm sorry. . . . Please forgive me. . . ." But after the doctor left the room, Teach added one more word to his sobbing mantra – a name – the name belonging to the girl in the box.

JAMES HENRY WAS TWENTY MINUTES LATE arriving to class, but at the pace he walked Teach doubted James could arrive anywhere on schedule. Tardiness was not unusual for young GED students. For many of them, the inability or refusal to follow simple regulations and procedures accounted for their estrangement (either voluntary or enforced) from the public schools. When students were late for only the first or second time, Teach would let it slide. However, he would also let it slide after the third, fourth, and every subsequent time as well, even though that flew in the face of one of the policy sheets all students signed upon enrollment, which stated that after a third incidence of tardiness the offending student would be sent home and counted absent for the day; after four tardies the student would be suspended for the semester.

The hardest thing for Teach to do was to tell a student to leave his class; he knew that for these at-risk kids, his classroom was the best, safest place for them to be. Perhaps Teach would have been willing to enforce stringent disciplinary policies if he saw any evidence they worked. But in his experience, kids who were suspended never – never – returned to class with a more mature attitude, chastened, with a new understanding of the importance of following rules; in fact, they often never returned at all. Which fact, Teach knew, was the sole purpose of suspension policies – they were there not to ensure that students came to class, but to ensure that a certain type of student didn't.

This morning, at first break, with too much time to kill – time that would turn into Cait-time – Teach retreated to the breakroom. He made the mistake of mentioning James Henry's chronic tardiness to the other instructors gathered there, including Clara. "You let these kids run all over you," Clara said. "First of all, by asking them to call you Teach. That's the craziest thing I've ever heard of. You're just inviting discipline problems."

Teach turned around and showed Clara his back. "Do you see anything back there, Clara?"

"No."

"No tread marks? I thought you said they were running all over me."

"You can joke about it if you want to, but it's your other students who suffer – the ones who actually want to learn. Having to put up with kids coming in late, talking all the time, being disruptive – you may not see it, but that's the effect it has on your classroom. The bozos who don't want to learn anything end up making all the rules, and the good kids –"

"Bozos!" Teach roared, enraged. "Would you like to tell me which one of my students is a bozo? Or maybe you can take me into your class and point out all of your bozos. Go right up to one and say, 'here is one of my bozos right here – one of many.' But you'd probably get a big kick out of that, wouldn't you – you pestiferous old hag."

"How dare you speak to her like that!" another teacher said. Teach ignored her.

"Or why don't you go to Randy and tell him about all the bozos he's letting into the program? I'm sure he'll appreciate that."

"You can insult me all you want to – Teach – or whatever your real name is – but I've been doing this for a whole lot longer than you have. You could learn a lot from me, if you weren't too hard-headed to listen. These kids need discipline. They crave it, and they definitely benefit from it."

"I tell you what, Miss Clara. I'll make a deal with you. When the day arrives when you have more kids getting their GEDs than I do, then at that point I'll start paying attention to whatever slime happens to be oozing out of your mouth. But until then, shut your damn hole."

Teach stomped out of the breakroom and returned to his class, where Charlotte and Maria and Lillian and Jerry and Julie and Heather and Roy helped to return him quickly to his happy Clara-less world. He did, however, have to shut down George and Oliver's farting contest. Those two, he had to admit, were certainly a bit bozo-like.

Teach had no interest in returning to the breakroom an hour later, during his students' second break, to continue his discussion with Clara. Instead, he thought he would have some fun with Randy.

"Hey, Randy – got a minute?"

"Come on in, Teach."

"I've been thinking a lot about what you said during our staff meeting – about how our students never feel like they're a real part of the campus life, and we need to come up with ways to increase their participation in student activities. You mentioned Fall Fest in particular."

"Yeah, Teach. You walk around during Fall Fest and you don't see any of our students. They have zero visibility on campus. . . . Zero. . . . They come to class, mill around outside during breaks, and then they go home. They're a part of this campus community, too. They may not realize that – they still think of themselves as high school students, but they have just as much right to participate in whatever's going on as the Curriculum students."

"That's always been my philosophy, too, Randy. Kids who don't have a high school diploma have just as much right to be in college as anybody."

"That's exactly right. Our job is to increase their awareness and to let them know that this is their college, too."

"So as I was saying, I've been giving this Fall Fest thing a lot of thought. I agree with everything you've said, and I couldn't have said it any better, but I think the biggest reason why our kids don't participate is that we don't offer them anything they would want to participate in. . . . What kinds of activities do we have at Fall Fest?"

"Well, there's always a DJ, and karaoke's been really popular the last couple of years."

"Kids don't need a DJ – they have their headphones and they can throw a party at their house and do karaoke all night if they want to. . . . What else is there?"

"The dunking booth is always a lot of fun."

"Randy. I think the only way you're going to get these kids within fifty feet of a dunking booth is if you sit a girl in a wet T-shirt up there, which is something I would suggest, but something tells me you wouldn't go for it so I won't even bring it up."

"But what about the girls? They would probably get a kick out of the dunking booth – especially if you volunteered to do it."

"I *was* talking about the girls, Randy. Have you seen some of my girls this semester? The girls I have in class now have a better chance of getting a good piece of pussy than Jerry Speziak. Have you met Heather? My God."

"Okay, Teach. That's enough. Cut to the chase. What do you have in mind?"

"We have to offer them some activities that they could really get excited about. Bobbing for apples just ain't gonna get it done."

"Like what?"

"I'm thinking drag races. . . . These kids love race cars. I guarantee you they would feel like a part of this school if they knew it was a place they could come to for drag racing."

"Once again, Teach, I can't help but think you're trying to pull my leg."

"No, Randy. This would work. We've got a huge parking lot. Plenty of room to accelerate. We can line up some hay bales at the end so they don't crash into the Vocat Building. . . . You wouldn't happen to know how much those little parachutes cost, would you? The ones that pop out the back end of the car?"

"Well, I'm sorry to burst your bubble, but drag racing is out of the question. It's much too dangerous."

"Yes, there is an element of danger. Agreed. But I know we have an EMT program that's growing by leaps and bounds. I guess they must be planning to see a big upswing in traffic accidents, with everyone texting now instead of watching the road. But anyway, we have all these EMT students just dying for some on-the-job training. They could all be there beside the track, you know, just in case."

"I can't believe you're being serious."

"Okay, Randy, if you don't think the drag racing idea will fly, how about this. . . . Target shooting."

"What kind of target shooting?"

"What do you mean, 'what kind?' What other kind is there? . . . With guns."

"With real guns?"

"Of course real guns."

"You do realize, don't you, that we have a strict policy banning all firearms on campus."

"But couldn't we waive that, just for that one day?"

"No. Of course not."

"Well, they wouldn't be *our* guns. We would tell all the kids to make sure they leave all their own guns at home. We could ask the Sheriff's Department or the Police Department to bring the guns. They would be fired only under the strictest supervision imaginable. . . . Or they could take turns shooting Roscoe's gun."

"No, Teach."

"Will you at least think about it? . . . The strictest supervision imaginable."

129

"No, Teach."

"Just one bullet at a time – like Barney Fife. Just give them one bullet apiece."

"Teach – no. End of subject."

"Okay, Randy. You're a tough sell. I'll let you get back to work now – but don't come crying to me if none of our kids show up at Fall Fest. It's on your head, not mine."

GREAT EMOTIONAL DISTRESS

Practice Essay
By Lillian Baye

I was asked to choose between two topics to write about – either Forgiveness or Courage. But I would like to write about both and juxtapose the two topics into one long essay. I would like to write about the Courage to Forgive.

Like untold millions of young women throughout the world, I was the victim of parental abuse from a very early age. The abuse I suffered at the hands of my father was psychological, physical, and sexual. The agony of the abuse and the equal agony of the memories and the sleepless nights of contemplation about the abuse have utterly and completely controlled my life. It has touched every part of my life and I know it will always be a part of my existence. My ambition in life, through research and autobiography, and perhaps poetry, is to understand as completely as possible all of the effects of abuse on me and others like me, who I hope to meet through my writings. And I want to understand the man who did this to me.

I don't know if I can remember a time before my father had abused me. But I can never forget the first time he did sexually abuse me. He stuck his finger into my still-virginal vagina. [Note to Teach – I apologize for the graphicness of my descriptions. I hope you understand – that as a writer it is necessary for me to be as truthful as possible. If you think that it may affect my grade on the GED Writing test, then I will be glad to be less graphic on the test when describing my abuse.] I was seven years old. I remember how badly it hurt and that I started crying. I bled and started screaming. My father apologized and put his hand over my mouth. He said he was only trying to show me how much he loved me. He said that that was what he did to Mommy to show her how much he loved her, and that was all he was trying to do with me. I believed him

131

because he was my daddy. He made me promise not to tell my mother because she would be mad at him for hurting me. I promised.

But I didn't keep my promise. At first I did, because I didn't want to get my father into trouble. I remember praying to God that He wouldn't let my daddy put his finger inside of me again because it had hurt so much. My father did continue to abuse me. He would say, "Do you know how much I love you, little Lillian?" After a while it didn't hurt anymore. Or perhaps I just got used to the pain. I forgot about the promise I had made to him, so one day I said to my mother, "I know Daddy loves me. Do you know how I know?"

My mother's reaction was exactly what you would expect. But my father cried and begged us to forgive him, so she didn't leave him. I will explore in my future writings how a woman can possibly stay with a man whom she knows has abused her daughter. Life is incredibly complicated, isn't it? I have never spoken to my mother again about my father's abuse, for reasons which I am attempting to explain in another essay I'm currently writing.

But in short, the reason I never mentioned it to my mom again is because the only time I did mention it, it made the abuse so much worse. I blamed myself for this. I told myself at night, lying alone in bed, "If I had not said anything to Mommy, then everything would be all right." Of course it wasn't my fault, but you don't know that as a child. I even started thinking of the times my father had abused me, before I had told my mom, with nostalgia, "the good ol' days," when all he did was put a finger (or two) inside me and tell me how much he loved me.

I understood why my mom was angry at my dad, but I didn't understand why she seemed to be so angry at me as well. "Never let him do that to you again!" she yelled, as though I had the power to stop him. I hoped the abuse would stop, now that Mom knew about it. No such luck. He continued his habit of abuse, but now he always threatened to hurt me if I said anything to anyone about it. The threats were totally unnecessary, since I wasn't about to open my mouth about it ever again, for as long as I lived.

Around this time, his abuse escalated. He said to me, "Do you want to know what your mommy does to show how much she loves me?" The sight of my father's penis was the most frightening thing I had ever seen in my life. It is still the most frightening thing I have ever seen. I didn't understand how a human body part could be so terrifying. [Note to Teach – I will spare you the graphic details of my father's forced fellatio, but that is not a cop-out. I just don't think that a GED practice essay is an appropriate place for such graphicness. In my other writings, it has been helpful for me to confront all the gruesome details of the abuse I have suffered.]

I was twelve the first time my father raped me through intercourse. It was the single most terrifying thing I have ever experienced. Try to imagine, if you can, the crushing weight of your father's body pounding down on top of your little pubescent body, coupled with the angry, murderous look on his face as he does it. I always closed my eyes after the first time. I was afraid to open them. I would hear him grunting like a wild animal in my ear. There was no longer any talk of how much he "loved" me. It was just anger and threats and physical domination.

Then he started hurting me in different ways. There had always been the threats of violence, in order to keep me quiet, but now he would come into my room and really hurt me. He would cover my mouth and pinch me in unusual places (which I won't detail here – see note above, please) or hit me on top of my head, but never on my face. I doubt if I thought about it at the time, but I eventually realized he was choosing ways to hurt me that didn't leave behind any physical evidence, like blood or cuts or bruises. I have spent hours upon hours ruminating on the reasons he would have for wanting to hurt me. Perhaps he wanted to show me that his threats were not just threats. That he would actually do to me exactly what he said he would do. Perhaps he started to enjoy this new violence against me more than the rape. Perhaps the violence he directed at me was really intended for someone else, someone he didn't have as much power over. I hope someday to have the courage to speak to him about this. Until that time, if it ever comes, I hope to interview other abusers so that I can better understand the roots of their evil. It is a goal of mine to write an entire book on the subject of why men abuse the girls they profess to love.

Now we finally come to the topic of this essay: the courage to forgive. [Note to Teach – I understand that I will need to improve the structure of my essays. I prefer to write in a less formal, more "stream of consciousness" style, but I know I need to write in a more conventional manner for the GED test, and will do so on the actual test. Sorry.] I have failed to mention how often my father made seemingly sincere apologies after his brutal attacks. He would buy me flowers, about which I had to lie to my mom and tell her they were from a boyfriend at school. (In reality, it is impossible for me to have a boyfriend. I also hope to have the courage in the future to trust a man enough to love him.) He bought me boxes of candy, which certainly contributed to the eating disorders I have struggled with. He begged me for forgiveness. He cried.

I was afraid to tell him that I could not forgive him. I was so powerless against him. What I wanted to do was to physically attack him as he had done to me so many times. He definitely would have deserved it. But I knew better than to actually try to hurt him. I was afraid to even raise my voice to him. Can you imagine, dear reader, what it is like to be so angry with someone that you want to kill him, yet so afraid that you can barely speak to him? So it is with victims of abuse.

So I would tell him that he was forgiven. It didn't take me very long to understand that his apologies were worthless. It is possible they were even part of his abuse. Wouldn't the next attack be made even worse if you thought they had come to an end? After several meaningless apologies, I stopped the charade of telling him he was forgiven. I would stay silent and just stare into space as he cried and held my hand. I would nod my head a little, finally, just to make him shut up.

I moved out of my house and into a trailer with a couple of friends when I was sixteen. I quit school. This caused a lot of pain and problems for my mom. I couldn't tell her the real reason I was moving out, so now there is a lot of tragic and unnecessary mistrust between her and me. Abuse can cause so many problems with your relationships with other people (I haven't even mentioned my older brother – there's so much I could write, and will write, about our difficult relationship).

So I was finally able to escape my father's abuse. When he came to see me I would lock the door and pretend to be away. He would yell and tell me to open the door, but would eventually walk angrily away. He would leave phone messages I never returned. I could not avoid him completely, of course. As much as I may have wanted to, I couldn't cancel Thanksgiving and Christmas. (I had to buy this man Christmas presents!) But I was safe from him as long as I wasn't alone with him. Abuse is a private killer.

When I turned eighteen, however, I made the most difficult decision of my life – to try to forgive my father. Why would I want to forgive the man who had caused me so much incredible pain? That is a valid question I will attempt to answer.

I can't take all the credit for making that decision. I think with most major decisions in life, you need a little help – someone to push you in the right direction. One of the girls I live with – her name is Valerie – had broken up with a very abusive boyfriend a few months earlier. (What is it with guys – are there any men out there who aren't violent?) She said there was no way she would ever get back together with him, but she needed to forgive him. I asked her why.

She said, "Because all this anger is fucking up my life." [Note to Teach - Obviously, I know better than to use profanity on the GED test.]

At first, what she said didn't make any sense. It wasn't *her* fault that her life was messed up. Why should it be her job to deal with an anger caused by someone else? But then, a few days later, I had what writers call an "epiphany." In one brilliant flash of insight I realized exactly what she meant. I had been out of my father's abusive grasp for almost two years. How should I feel about that? Shouldn't I be elated? Shouldn't I be the happiest person in the world, knowing I never had to be victimized by him again? Instead, I was absolutely miserable – and angry. Really angry. And instead of the anger subsiding over time, it was becoming more intense. I was still allowing this man to destroy my life, without him even laying a hand on me. So only by releasing the anger could I finally be free of his control over me. And only through forgiveness could I be rid of the anger.

Why does it take so much courage to forgive? First of all, dear readers, this is a man who threatened to kill me countless times and who physically assaulted me on a regular basis. To understand what it is like to forgive this man, imagine yourself holding a gun to the head of someone who has killed a member of your family. Perhaps he has been captured and is tied up; perhaps he is injured and is at your mercy. Would you pull the trigger if you knew that no one would blame you for doing so? (It is easy for me to imagine this, because I had this fantasy every day of my life – and I always pulled the trigger.) Forgiving him would mean throwing down the gun and walking away, letting him go free. But the anger, you see, comes from living in this fantasy world, where justice and vengeance are actually possible. In reality, I was powerless to do anything to this man – victimized into silence. Anger is the emotional expression of the frustration you feel when the justice you desire is thwarted by the helpless reality you are forced to live in.

I find it interesting that the word "forgive" also contains the word "give." I don't think that is a coincidence. To forgive someone is to give them something, as in a gift. Most people deserve the gifts they receive; some do not.

So the question became, Do I want to give this man a gift he could never deserve? Why would I ever want to do that? To forgive him seemed like I was once again succumbing to him, letting him victimize me once again.

In the end, my decision to forgive my father was a purely selfish one. It had nothing to do with wanting to give him anything; i.e., it was not done out of the goodness of my heart. It was only done to get rid of all my anger. It was a selfish gift – if that makes any sense. I've discovered that if you want to get rid of your anger, you have to have the courage to give it away.

You and Cait want to picnic on the quad. You walk over to Cait's dorm on a late Saturday morning to begin yor adventure. There is a shortcut you can take that goes through a woodsy area that cuts through the campus. An unauthorized trail has been carved through the woods down through the years. To discourage the use of this path, however, the school annually refuses to build a footbridge over the small stream which must be crossed. You have no trouble leaping over the creek, but the sound of the water trickling over the rocks always makes you think of Charles. You only go this way if you're in a hurry.

You and Cait hold hands and walk down to the little grocery store on the edge of campus to buy some bread and sliced ham, mayo, potato chips, cookies, and a couple of sodas. You are all set.

You find a nice spot on the quad. You and Cait spread out the blanket from Cait's room, the one from her bed. She is laughing. Her laughter and the fact that you can make her laugh mean more to you than anything. There are others all around you throwing Frisbee, playing hacky sack, walking, running, kicking a soccer ball back and forth. Music is blaring from an open dorm window. The weather is perfect. Cait is smiling. You are smiling, all the time. You are barely aware of everyone around you. You sit as closely together as possible on Cait's blanket. When you aren't smiling and laughing, you are gazing at Cait with love and wonderment. You lean over occasionally to kiss her.

You are ready to eat, but realize you don't have a knife to spread the mayo. You sigh, frustrated, and resign yourself to eating dry sandwiches. Cait says, No, just do this. She puts her finger into the small jar, brings out a dollop and runs her whitened finger all along your bread. She wipes as much mayo as she can on the bread slice and then brings her finger slowly up toward your mouth. You suck her finger clean, and without letting go of her hand you return her finger to the jar for another dollop of mayo. You spread the mayo on the other slice, slowly, and clean her finger with your lips. You then enjoy the most delicious sandwich you've ever eaten.

LESS THAN A WEEK before I killed Charles, I once again felt the irresistible urge to help him out with girls. We were in ninth grade now. It was no longer a given I would have a steady girlfriend. If I took an interest in a girl, I sometimes had to compete for her. But I discovered another girl, who had a specialized talent no one had to compete for. All you had to do was ask. Her name was Tonya Gentry, and Tonya liked to give hand jobs.

I made what I suppose would be called an appointment with Tonya, a time when we would rendezvous during class, in the woods behind the bus parking lot. This wooded area was a haven for every sort of illicit activity before, during, and after school. To enter the woods, you had to slide or side-step down a steep embankment. This lower elevation gave you even more cover than the trees.

I chose to cut my third-period class so that after Tonya and I had concluded our activities I could go directly to the cafeteria. Rules were looser for lunch period with no tardy bells to worry about or roll calls to answer. I rarely cut class, so I was by no means expert at it. In fact, I probably had cut class fewer times than I had had my cock fondled by a female, so this escape from school grounds was the real adventure for me. I remained in the restroom until the tardy bell sounded, then I ran headlong down the hall as if I were late for class. I was particularly proud of this maneuver. Most guys, I assumed, sneaked around corners and tried to escape by stealth. But I was utterly brazen as I ran down the hall and straight out the back entrance, followed by another sprint to the bus lot.

I bounded down the steep slope and into the woods. I noticed Coke cans and plastic snack wrappers strewn here and there, and if I had looked more closely I undoubtedly could have found more than one used condom, as well as countless cigarette butts. And, although there was no evidence left behind to prove it, pot was just as likely to have been present down here as tobacco. I saw Tonya. It was awkward at first. Even though we had one class together, I had never spoken to her, except for the short chat we had as we arranged our tryst. But we both knew what to do, so the awkwardness didn't last long. I had no interest in kissing her, and she was really only interested in one thing as well, so we groped each other cursorily for a few minutes as my young erection quickly hardened.

Although Tonya fit almost any definition you could give for *easy,* she apparently defined herself in more demure terms. "I ain't puttin' this thing in my mouth, you can forget about that," she said, holding my prick, as I explored how far she was willing to go. At any rate, it was a highly pleasurable experience, swiftly concluded. Tonya and I had very little to say to each other as we lay on the embankment and listened for the dismissal bell to ring beyond the buses.

Two weeks later, Tonya and I were at it again and at some point between coming and going, as I lay silently on the bank leading into the woods, I thought about Charles and decided to offer myself as intermediary between him and horny-handed Tonya. I assumed he would say no, but was surprised at lunch when he agreed, albeit rather squeamishly. He had finally decided to take his first baby steps toward manhood.

Of course, agreeing to something in principle is easier than seeing it through, so a week later, at the appointed hour, I had nothing but doubts about Charles's resolve. But when he failed to arrive for our third-period algebra class I was proud of him. But he had never cut class in his life, so I worried for the whole hour about his escape attempt. If he did make it into the woods, however, I had asked Tonya to make sure Charles thoroughly enjoyed his first carnal experience.

I did not see Charles at lunch, nor for the rest of the day. My heart sank. I assumed he had gotten nabbed trying to cut class. I had told him to follow my escape plan, but he obviously didn't have the chutzpah to pull it off. I called him as soon as I got home. He said he didn't want to talk about it, but I persisted. "C'mon, man, tell me what happened. Did you run straight down the hallway like I told you to?"

"I said I'm not gonna talk about it. Leave me the fuck alone."

"I'm gonna beat the shit out of you if you don't tell me what happened."

"Then beat the shit out of me, you asshole – it won't be the first time."

"Did you get suspended?"

"No, I didn't get fuckin' suspended."

"Well, that's good. . . . So you'll be able to come back to school tomorrow?"

"Yeah."

"You know, if you feel like trying it again, I'll talk to Tonya for you."

"Forget about it, man. . . . I'll see you tomorrow." With that, he hung up.

Charles and I, as well as Tonya, had first-period Science together. Charles was in a slightly better mood, just quieter than usual. I had decided not to harass him anymore about yesterday. I also needed to apologize to Tonya for Charles not showing up and to make sure she was willing to accept a rain check if Charles changed his mind about meeting her again. I would do that after class.

Midway through class a commotion broke out at the table across the room, where Tonya was sitting. She yelled out, "Don't! Stop it!" and reached, half-standing, across the lab table, with its sink and surrounding gas valves. On the other side of the table was Kenny, who was known for his artistic ability. He drew constantly during class, and he was, indeed, a superb artist. He excelled at those thirty-second caricature drawings you can sit for at the carnival, with the large faces and perhaps one or two body parts exaggerated for comic effect. Apparently, today, Kenny was drawing something Tonya disapproved of. It wasn't hard for me to imagine what it might be. I figured Kenny had found out about her and me (for Tonya's extracurricular activities, though unadvertised, weren't exactly a secret – and I wasn't exactly tight-lipped) and that he was drawing some hilarious picture of me squirting off with her assistance, my face most likely contorted in cartoon ecstasy and with an enormous pecker in her hand. "Hey, Kenny," I called out across the room, "if she doesn't want that picture, I'll take it!"

"Kenny! Don't you dare!" Tonya screamed again. She was not laughing, or even smiling. Our teacher reprimanded us, uselessly. Kenny was laughing hysterically. He stood up and started to walk over to the table across from me and Charles. Tonya lunged at him and grabbed him. There was true hysteria in her voice. "Kenny!" she wailed. Kenny held the picture over his head, where she couldn't reach it.

Our teacher bellowed, "Tonya! Kenny! Sit – down – right – now! And don't get up for the rest of the period! If you do, you're both going to the principal. Sit down!" Tonya released her grip on Kenny's arm, and he relaxed and started back toward his table. But he wheeled around and reversed direction suddenly, handing the picture off to a guy sitting one table over. I couldn't hear what Tonya hissed at Kenny at this point, but she was clearly infuriated.

The drawing slowly made its way around the classroom, with everyone careful not to let the teacher see it. For the next fifteen minutes, Tonya, forbidden to leave her seat, motioned frantically and stage-whispered to whoever received the picture next, trying to get it passed back to her. As it was passed around, the reactions were restrained, as everyone tried not to draw attention to themselves. The guys chuckled and made funny faces; the girls either rolled their eyes, looked disgusted, or shot a mean look in Kenny's direction. Strangely, I thought, no one looked over at me. Finally, it reached our table, to Felipe, who sat across from me and next to Charles. Tonya flew up off of her stool, but took only a couple of running steps before Kenny grabbed her arm and jerked her toward him. Felipe looked at it, smiled, and passed it on to Charles. "Charles!" Tonya cried. She seemed to be crying, I noticed.

Throughout this whole incident, I had noticed Charles slowly melting away. We were usually cutting up throughout class, as much as we could get away with. But as soon as the trouble erupted at Tonya's table, Charles lost all interest in clowning around. He seemed to start shrinking inward. Whenever I looked his way, he was staring blankly at whoever was handling the drawing at that moment. His posture became hunched on his stool, his arms pressed into his sides and his hands disappeared into his lap. He sat perfectly still. As the drawing circulated closer to us, I noticed a slight tremble throughout his body. "Don't worry, man," I told him, "I don't think that has anything to do with you." Why would it? I was eager to see the drawing, even if it turned out not to be about me. I certainly wasn't the only guy, and perhaps not even the most recent, to sneak into the woods with Tonya. I became annoyed at Charles's peculiar behavior. "What the fuck's wrong with you, man?" I pushed him on the arm only half-playfully, causing him to lose his balance for a moment on his stool. He ignored me, utterly. His attention remained transfixed on the circuit of that drawing around the class.

I wondered if maybe I was missing something. Did Charles actually see Tonya yesterday? Did he manage to elude capture and make it into the woods? Then why was he sent home early? Another scenario took hold in my mind. The woods were not regularly patrolled by anyone at the school, but occasionally one of the SROs would wander around. That would make a funny picture for Kenny – Tonya, with a big hard dong in her hand, being discovered by an SRO. No wonder she was so upset. I asked Charles, "Did you get caught in the woods?" He made no attempt to answer. I said, "Don't worry, man, whatever's in that picture, I don't think anybody will know it's you."

Felipe handed the drawing to Charles as Tonya cried his name. He studied it for a moment. He dropped it on the table and darted for the classroom exit. I saw his face as he disappeared through the door. He was crying. I snatched up the drawing and jumped away from the table to go running after Charles. He had always been faster than I, and he had had a head start, so there was no way I could catch up to him. I yelled his name. He didn't stop. He didn't look back. He was running through the student parking lot. He soon disappeared.

From the direction he was running, I figured Charles was headed home. He lived, I would guess, five miles from school. I decided I might as well walk to his house, too, and try to cheer him up, since I was probably already in trouble with my science teacher for running out of class. I walked along the road that led to the main school entrance. I was clutching the drawing in my left hand. I stopped and looked at it for the first time.

As I had expected, it was one of Kenny's elaborate caricature drawings. There was a girl drawn with the typical oversized head and greatly reduced body size. It was clearly Tonya. Her tiny shrunken arms and hands were up in the air. There was a word bubble above her head. "What did I do wrong?" it said. The other person in the drawing was easily recognizable as Charles. As with Tonya, the head was comically oversized, but my eyes were drawn to the other exaggerated feature of the picture. Kenny had drawn a grotesquely long penis, which went down past Charles's shoes and then snaked along the ground. In fact, it looked more like a snake than anything else, except for the penis head on the end. Kenny had drawn big tears shooting from Charles's eyes into the air. His word balloon said, "I'm so scared!"

The drawing confused me. Where was the SRO? Obviously, I realized, Kenny had not had time to draw the third figure before being harassed by Tonya. That was the only explanation that made sense. Tonya's arms were in the air as if she were being arrested, and she was trying to play innocent with the cop. Charles, of course, was scared by having been discovered with his pants down. I ached for Charles's embarrassment, but I had to admit it was a funny drawing. It would have been funnier, however, I thought, if Kenny had drawn the penis reaching high up into the air, fully erect, like Tonya's arms, as if the penis, too, were being arrested. I chuckled at my own cleverness.

And now Charles, who had always been a good boy and who had never been in trouble, was running home in shame because the whole world now knew what he had been doing yesterday. My plan was to walk to Charles's house to cheer him up and try to convince him that what happened yesterday with the SRO was much more likely to turn him into a hero than a pariah.

It took well over an hour for me to walk to Charles's house. I rang the doorbell. His parents were at work, I knew, but Charles should have answered. I knew there was nowhere else he would be. I went around behind his house. His bedroom light was off. I called his name, but he did not respond. I honestly didn't understand why he was so upset, but there was nothing I could do at this point. I walked to my house and called him. He did not answer.

He wasn't at school for the rest of the week, and I didn't hear from him for three days, when he called Friday afternoon and said he wanted me to go on an overnight camping trip with him and his dad. I was very relieved to hear from him.

By noon on Saturday, Charles was dead, killed by my own hand.

GRANDCHILDREN EVERYONE DESERVES
GOD'S ELEGANT DESIGN

(Note from Charlotte: Mr. Morrison, thank you for such a wonderful and inspirational assignment. Just like you said, I think this has been a window to my soul. I spent a long time coming up with these two answers to your question – What should GED really stand for? These two answers can show everyone the two things that are most important in my life. God Bless You, Mr. Morrison.)

Practice Essay
By Charlotte Gaston

The most courageous person I know is my husband Horace, who went home to be with the Lord four years ago next May. He is my hero. He died of lung cancer. He was 67 years old. He is my hero for many reasons. Cancer is a terrible disease, but Horace never let it get him down. He always had a smile on his face, and it was Horace who would be the one to cheer me up when I got sad. His cancer seemed to make me a lot sadder than it did him. I don't know how he did it. He stayed in a good mood, even when he started coughing up blood every morning. Horace would always say to me, "You've got to enjoy your life while you've still got one." Truer words were never spoken.

Horace had a very strong faith in Our Lord Jesus Christ. That is another reason why he is my hero. The love of Jesus sustained him and me both throughout his illness and throughout our lives. Jesus should be everybody's hero. Horace went to church every week, except for when he was too sick to leave the house. Then Preacher Stokes would come to our house and pray with Horace. One of the last things Horace said to me was, "I can hear Jesus calling my name, Charlotte." It made me cry to hear him say that.

Another reason why my husband Horace is courageous is the way he lived his whole life. He grew up poor, just like everybody else. He had seven brothers and sisters and he worked hard his whole life. He didn't get very far in school. He didn't have a GED, but he didn't really need one. He always had a job to go to, even if it was just fixing a door for somebody or mowing a yard. Sometimes I did have to read something for him, if it was something he got in the mail that he didn't understand. But he got through life just fine. But I know he would be really proud of me for going back to school to get my GED. One reason I did it was because I got very lonely at the house all day without my Horace.

The other reason why Horace is courageous is because he and I both grew up during segregation times. It won't be too long before all of us who remember what that was like are dead and gone. But I remember what it was like as a little girl to have to drink out of the colored fountain. And Horace lived through those times with enormous courage. We all had to have courage back then.

My husband Horace is my hero. He was a very courageous man. He was a good man who loved me, who loved Jesus and who loved life. And I miss him very much.

TEACH AND DR. CARNEY were chatting at the beginning of their session about, among other things, the difficulty of keeping the increasingly restless Cait in her box.

"By the way, Doc, I apologize for that little meltdown last time."

"That's quite all right, Teach. I do want to ask you though – did you think about what we were discussing at the end of our last session? About telling Cheryl?"

"I thought about it, sure. But I haven't put your plan into action yet, Doc. It may take me a while to marshal all my resources and to muster all my troops. It's a big operation we're planning. Lots of contingencies."

"Don't let it fall by the wayside, Teach. I think it can be a very important part of your therapy. Okay?"

"Okay, Doc."

"Well, I thought maybe this week we could take a little break from our discussion about Cait and Cheryl and see if maybe there are some other issues you would like to talk about. You've learned a couple of strategies for coping with these painful memories and you're working on being less judgmental about Cheryl, in relation to Cait, so unless you want to continue talking about that today – which would be perfectly okay with me – then maybe we could see if there's anything else we need to discuss. Are there any other problem areas between you and Cheryl? Or any other personal issues you're having?"

"No, Doc, I think the whole Cheryl-Cait thing is the big enchilada. As long as we can make progress on that, then I'm happy."

"How are things at work?"

"Great. Couldn't be better. I've got the best job in the world."

"You said you teach GED classes, right? I've had a few patients down through the years who said they dropped out of school and got their GED."

"But never tell a GED student that they've dropped out of school. You'll never hear GED students refer to themselves as dropouts – at least not the young kids I teach. And they get really offended if you call them dropouts, or ask them why they dropped out."

"Why is that?"

"Because in their view – and they're absolutely right – they haven't dropped out of anything. They're coming to my class every day of the week, aren't they? What they've done instead is to make a very important decision about their future. They've decided to leave a bad situation in the public schools and try to make the situation better. The only people who call them dropouts are the thoughtless bureaucrats who run the schools. You would think, wouldn't you, that the state and local administrators would much rather call these kids *transfers* – because that's exactly what they are – because that way they wouldn't show up on the statistics as dropouts and the actual dropout rate would go down and you could get a more accurate picture of what's really going on. That would make sense, wouldn't it?" Teach didn't wait for Dr. Carney to answer before continuing. "So why do the pencil pushers continue to insist on calling these kids dropouts when they know good and well they're coming into my class and succeeding? . . . Because all they're really interested in is covering their own asses and not having to be held accountable for all their failed programs. They just shift all the blame for failure onto the kids. If all these kids from Tox County High were seen as transfers to the GED program, then people in the community might legitimately ask, 'What is making all these kids want to transfer?' But if they *drop out*, well, that still looks bad for the school to a certain extent, but it's still a good deal for them because now they can get money for dropout prevention programs and bitch and moan about 'How do we keep kids in school?' and 'What's wrong with kids nowadays?'. . . It becomes more of a social issue instead of having to deal with how shitty the schools are."

"This is obviously something you're very passionate about, Teach. What is it about the GED that makes you so passionate about it?"

"For me, Doc, the GED is all about second chances. A kid screws up, makes a big mistake and gets kicked out of school – what would he do without the GED program? And the older students I get – I mean, some of them are in their sixties, or even seventies – but every single one, Doc – they all tell me how much they regret not getting their diploma when they were young. And they are all so grateful that this program exists for them to come back and redeem themselves. That's really what it's all about, Doc, for me and them both – redemption."

"Why do you feel you need redemption?"

Teach laughed. "Not for me, Doc. I'm beyond redemption. There's no hope for me. I meant that's the reason I teach – to provide redemption. I'm the redeem*er*, not the redeem*ee*."

"Why do you feel there's no hope for you, Teach?"

"Jeez, I was just kidding, Doc. Just another joke in a long line of jokes. Don't take me so seriously, okay? I can't be serious for very long without cracking wise. It's really difficult for me to come in here and stay serious with you for an hour. I have SDD – Seriousness Deficit Disorder."

"Okay, Teach, I'll try, but that kind of goes against my grain. I'm trained to take people's problems seriously. . . . Well, let's see here. I haven't asked you anything much about your family. Any family issues? Anything there you want to discuss?"

"No, not really. I like my mom and dad. . . . I drive my dad crazy, though."

"There's nothing unusual about that." Carney smiled.

"Yeah, but on purpose?"

"You drive your dad crazy on purpose."

"Oh yeah. It's one of my favorite pastimes. It's my way of showing affection. I do it to my boss at work, too. It drives him nuts."

"So you and your dad get along okay?"

"Oh sure. Now at least. It didn't used to be that way, of course. I was rather humorless in high school."

"Really? That surprises me. You weren't the class clown?"

"Pagliacci, maybe."

"Any particular reason for that? The sadness?"

"Nah, Doc. Just the usual adolescent melodrama. Nothing worth talking about."

"Are you sure?"

"Quite sure. Once I got away from home and met Cait, then all my problems went away – until Cait went away." Teach felt his eyes start to burn. He couldn't even say her name anymore without welling up.

146

"Okay then. In that case, let me go back and ask you about your dad, if you don't mind. Fathers are always interesting subjects to talk about. What can you tell me about him?"

"He's a pretty tough customer. Really rough and tumble. . . . Actually, though, I think I'm a lot more like him than he realizes. Our relationship is complicated by the fact that I'm always fucking with his mind."

"That's twice now you've mentioned that, Teach. You just said a minute ago that you drove your dad crazy on purpose. I would take that as a sign of some hidden hostility. A passive-aggressive behavior. What do you think about that? Any thoughts?"

"Hostility toward one's father. What a concept, Doc. You could win the Nobel for that, you know."

"What I would find more interesting is the passive-aggressive part. Do you ever get outwardly hostile with your dad?"

"No, not really. And I don't think I'm being passive-aggressive, either. My dad's a great guy – I just like to take the air out of people's balloons, that's all."

"How did your dad treat you growing up?"

"Okay, here we go. Now it's time for the did-your-dad-take-you-outside-behind-the-woodshed-and-show-you-his-thingy type of questions, isn't it? Well, there was none of that, Doc."

"I wasn't trying to suggest there was, Teach. I'm sorry if I gave you that impression. I was just trying to find out a little more about your dad, that's all. But I am wondering if there's any reason for any hostility that you're aware of."

"I don't think I am hostile toward my dad. I love my dad. He's a great guy."

"People feel hostility toward the ones they love. At least occasionally. It happens in every relationship. It's happened in every relationship that's ever existed. Wouldn't you agree?"

"I can't argue with that, Doc."

"Good. So we're in agreement that there's at least a certain degree of hostility there. And you know, Teach, it may not even be worth exploring. You seem to be on good terms with your dad, so. . . . I just thought it might be helpful for me to know a little bit about your family dynamic growing up, that's all."

"Well, I think my family dynamic was pretty normal. My dad wasn't home a lot, actually. He was a long-haul trucker. He would be gone for days at a time. My mom was pretty much in charge of things most of the time."

"So what did you think of your dad being gone so much? Did you miss him?"

"No, actually. . . . I was kind of glad when he left." Teach chuckled. "It saved me some wear and tear on my gonads."

"Pardon me?"

"Never mind. I shouldn't have said that. . . . But I can tell by your face that you're not gonna let that one slide, are you?"

"What did you mean by that?"

"Well, along with his many fine qualities, my dad sometimes utilized rather unorthodox methods of disciplining me."

"Do you mind explaining to me exactly what he did?"

"Now, Doc, I know what you're going to think. But I don't want you painting a picture of my dad as some kind of sadistic child abuser."

"I understand, Teach. But you're the one painting the picture, not me, and if you don't mind talking about it, I would like for you to paint that picture for me."

"But isn't every kid abused in some way? Seriously, have you ever had a patient come in here who didn't have some bizarre story of parental malfeasance?"

"A lot of people – my patients included – are lucky to have had a non-abusive upbringing."

"Well, okay – but my guess is they're just not telling you the whole story."

"I would certainly hope that's not the case, wouldn't you?"

Teach reflected for a moment. "It's really strange how society sets up its standards. . . . My mom would spank the living hell out of me – in the standard textbook fashion. . . . She would bend me over her knee, 'this hurts me more than it hurts you' – just like they teach you in corporal punishment class. No one would ever accuse her of abuse."

"Spanking is certainly frowned upon more and more now."

"As it should be. I'm not condoning it. It hurt like hell. . . . But the point I wanted to make was that my mom's form of abuse is traditionally accepted, but my dad's – let's just say, his more unconventional methods of behavior modification – would probably be frowned upon by the medical establishment – not to mention the DSS and maybe the local law enforcement authorities as well."

"What would your dad do, Teach?"

"Keep in mind, he was never the primary enforcer in the family. Mom was. He was gone all the time. . . . Mom would build the suspense, which was almost as bad as the spanking, but Dad would just react. He was a reactionary. He had what you would diagnose today as anger management issues."

Dr. Carney sat emotionless, but nodded his head slowly, repeatedly.

"He would just haul off and slap the holy shit out of me if I pissed him off – which was often. . . . But the point I keep returning to is that I didn't see my dad's punishment as being any more abusive than my mom's."

"So he hit you?"

"Just with his open palm. He never cold-cocked me."

"Did he ever do anything else besides slap you?"

Teach laughed. "Yeah, I should say so. . . . One time, he burnt my arm with his cigarette."

"He burnt your arm with his cigarette."

"Yeah – not a pleasant experience. . . . I howled. . . . It only happened once, though."

"How old were you?"

"Eight."

"But he only did it once?"

"Yeah – my mom made sure of that. She noticed my arm. . . . I didn't want to say anything. I figured he would go to Def-Com One if I ratted him out. I think I probably tried to lie my way out of the situation, knowing me, but I think it must have been pretty obvious to my mom. Cigarette burns are rather distinctive, I imagine. It's hard for an eight-year-old to explain something like that away. . . . She hit the roof. . . . I heard her screaming at him. 'I'll take the boys and you'll never see them again!' My dad learned his lesson. . . . Well, he learned *a* lesson, just not the one I think my mom intended." Dr. Carney continued to nod up and down with an elbow on the arm of his chair and with his hand playing thoughtfully around his mouth. "The lesson he learned was that he needed to find another way to voice his displeasure. . . . One that left no visible scars."

"What did he do?"

"It was ingenious, really. I don't know why every father doesn't think of it. The most primal, visceral form of punishment that it is possible to inflict – and with no physical evidence left at the scene."

"Tell me what he did, Teach."

"He started kicking me in the balls."

"I see."

"Hard and often."

"How often?"

"Doc, really, I'm giving you the wrong impression of my dad. He was not some psycho who would come home off the road and decide to kick his kid in the nuts just as his way of saying hello. . . . He would just respond instantaneously to my, shall we say, negative stimuli. He didn't exactly think things through."

"So you don't characterize your dad as abusive."

"Well sure, in hindsight. Jesus Christ, I'm making him sound like a monster. But from a child's perspective. . . . Like I keep saying, I don't think I made a distinction between my mom's socially acceptable form of abuse and my dad's more unorthodox methods. I would be scared to death waiting for my mom to deliver up her punishment. She would schedule a spanking like it was a hair appointment – I'm surprised she didn't write it on the calendar. I think I rather preferred my dad's spontaneity. . . . Just get it over with. I would be doubled over on the floor for two or three minutes, and then everything would return to normal."

"Were you frightened of your dad?"

"Just when I was alone with him. That was the only time he would hit me. . . . My mom was like a buffer. When the family was together he would defer to her. . . . She was either a calming influence on him or he would just relinquish his authority, I don't know which, but I felt safe from him with Mom around."

"But you say your mom was the primary disciplinarian."

"Oh yeah, definitely."

"Did she spank you a lot?"

Teach sighed and gathered his thoughts. "I think she met her quota, yes. She would say, 'You're gonna have to be punished for that,' or 'You're gonna pay for that in a minute,' and I would hope she would forget or if I was extra good maybe she would commute my sentence." Teach laughed. "But I doubt if she ever did. . . . And then when the appointed time came she would go full-bore apeshit for about thirty seconds. You could tell she wasn't holding anything back – it was concentrated fury. Every injustice she had ever suffered, every frustration she had endured, anybody else she was mad at – it all came down on a little white pair of quivering buttocks." Teach burst into laughter. "I got to see her in action a few times, from a safe distance – with Robbie. Robbie was a better kid than I was. He was more amenable to swallowing the party line. In fact, it's hard for me to imagine him doing anything to warrant my mom's wrath – most likely, it was a miscarriage of justice. I could be pretty persuasive. But my mom – her mouth would tighten, her eyes would bulge, her face would redden. . . . She would bring her arm all the way back –" Teach demonstrated for Dr. Carney – "She had excellent spanking technique – no wasted motion."

"So what were you doing to get into so much trouble all the time?"

"I don't know, but I definitely had a way of doing the wrong thing. I think it was just me. Like I said, Robbie steered clear of trouble most of the time. But me, if I wanted to go up into the woods – we had a nice patch of forest right behind our house – so if I wanted to go into the woods, I went into the woods. If I wanted to watch TV when we had company, I watched TV. If I wanted to beat the shit out of my little brother, then – but is that really abnormal? Aren't big brothers supposed to whoop up on their little brothers? Aren't rambunctious, mischievous boys like me supposed to spend most of their time either getting into trouble or trying to get out of it?"

Carney grinned weakly. Teach continued: "I just don't want to give you the wrong impression. I know you're just doing your job – you have to poke around my memories and make sure I wasn't diddled by my big hairy uncle. I understand that. But then I tell you that one time my dad – *one time* – burnt me with a cigarette and I'm afraid you're sitting over there wondering if that turned me into little Charlie Manson. . . . To be honest, today's the first time I've even thought about my parents and how they raised me, vis-à-vis, you know, how abusive they may have been. I've never looked at it that way. I've always thought of myself as having a pretty normal upbringing."

"I can appreciate that, Teach. I'm sure this whole conversation has been very uncomfortable for you – and I really appreciate your willingness to be open with me."

"That's okay. Sure. So, how much time do we have left?"

"About fifteen minutes."

"Okay. . . . Hey Doc, let me ask you a question. This is completely off the subject, I know, but – what do you do when you get a patient who comes in and the minute you see him, or from the minute he opens his mouth you just lose it?"

"What do you mean?"

"I mean, they have some crazy twitch, or a nose shaped like a banana, or a head like an eggplant, or pointy ears like Spock or they have the funniest god-damn accent you've ever heard, or a stutter like Porky Pig. And you have to sit here and try to keep a straight face for an hour. I couldn't do it. . . . I had this guy come into my class last year – he looked pretty comical to be sure, but here's what cracked the whole class up. He had some kind of sinus condition and he would blow his nose about every five minutes, and when he blew his nose, I swear to God, it sounded just like one of those air horns or one of those bicycle horns that a clown carries around – *honk!* And the more I saw him the more I realized how much he actually looked like a clown. He was bald on top but he still had hair around the side of his head, and he still wore it in this crazy 1970s curly-perm style. Can you picture this guy? And he was pretty roly-poly with a big round face. All he was missing really was the big bow tie with the water that squirts out. And then every five minutes – *honk!* It was brutal. Everyone in class – I have a lot of sixteen- and seventeen-year-olds, but they're good kids. They don't want to embarrass anyone, but after a while. . . . Everybody had their own way of trying not to laugh. They would have their cheeks puffed out, their fingers in their mouth, biting on their pencils. I'd see people with their heads down on the table, hiding their face, but their whole body would be shaking with laughter. I have these two guys, George and Oliver, sitting in the back – they would fall out of their chairs and roll on the floor. And this guy – he was oblivious to what was going on. . . . Oblivious. It amazes me how people can be so oblivious to their own inherent hilarity. I had to leave the classroom. I would see the guy pull out his handkerchief and I knew what was coming next – *honk!* I would go out into the hallway and I know the guy must have heard me cracking up. I just felt so bad for my students – they didn't have the option of going outside. . . . Thank God this guy got his GED. I don't know what we would have done. . . . I guess I would have had to transfer him to another class. Let some other class suffer like we suffered. . . . Oh, and then I had this other guy three or four years ago – he only had this one snaggly tooth in the very front of his mouth, and whenever –"

"Teach – Teach. Sorry to interrupt you, but we need to start wrapping this session up. I want to quickly review some things and maybe give you something to think about for next time."

"Okay, Doc, but you haven't answered my question. How do you deal with people like that?"

"Well, Teach, I think I can honestly tell you that I've never had a patient that I've wanted to laugh at."

"No – not that you *wanted* to laugh at, but somebody you couldn't *help* but laugh at. . . . It's okay, Dr. Carney. I'm not trying to impugn your profession or put you on the spot. I believe that the patient-doctor confidentiality thing should go both ways. I promise not to tell anyone about anything you tell me while we're in here. You can trust me."

"I appreciate that, Teach, but what I want you to think about –"

"So how many years have you been in practice?"

"I've had this practice for twenty-five years."

"Twenty-five years? And you say in all that time you've never had some odd-voiced, queer-shaped, inadvertently hilarious, real-life cartoon character come in here for therapy? I find that impossible to believe."

"Well, I'm sorry, Teach. I'm sorry to disappoint you."

"You know what I think it is? I think you're holding things back from me because I'm a new patient and you don't know me very well. I bet once you become more comfortable, you'll be more willing to open up and tell me some of your funny patient stories. We just need to be patient and take it one week at a time. Right, Doc?"

Teach made an appointment to see Dr. Carney again in two weeks, but by the time he was in his car and on his way home he knew he wouldn't be coming back. He was through with Carney – that dream-destroyer, that Cait-hater, that foul maker of boxes. There were two things Teach knew he deserved to have more than anything else in his life – his guilt over Charles and his love for Cait. He wasn't going to talk about Charles with anyone – there were some things you didn't tell anybody, not even your shrink. He had killed Charles in cold blood, so if there was any justice left in the world then it was only proper that Teach be tormented by his actions for the rest of his life. And as for Cait – Carney wanted to keep Cait locked away and wanted Teach to stop living in the past. But dammit, thought Teach, I'm a historian – where the hell else am I supposed to live?

In the final analysis, what had these three sessions of therapy accomplished? Cheryl had gotten her way and had persuaded Teach to roll up the blinds a little to let in a bit of much-needed sunlight – sunlight that had exposed just how disenchanted Teach was with Cheryl; so, as a result, Cheryl had now qualified as the latest grand-prize winner in the be-careful-what-you-wish-for sweepstakes. Therefore, where did this leave his relationship with Cheryl? At the mercy of Cait, it seemed. She was more powerful than Cheryl's love, more powerful than Cheryl's desire to save their relationship; more powerful than Carney and his army of neuroscientists and neo-Skinnerites; and certainly more powerful than Teach's less-than-Herculean efforts to diffuse her sway over him. Cait had saved Teach once – her love had been strong enough to combat his grief over Charles; but Cait wasn't trying to save him now. Quite the contrary. This Cait was out to kill him.

3

Hi Baby,

Wow, that was quite a remarkable use of technology last night. Enough to convince even the most hardened Luddite of the telephone's beneficial applications. I'm just so fortunate and thankful that I live in the modern era of telephone communications. Writing a letter such as this is fun and rewarding, but how did the lonely Victorian lady who missed her lover so terribly much ever get her rocks off? Somehow, epistle sex just wouldn't be the same. And I could tell how much you enjoyed it too, baby. Hey-Zeus Christ. When you came, it sounded like your little Tommyknockers (or Tommy-knock-me-uppers, if we're not careful) were flying all the way to Boston just to be with me.

Speaking of which, only ten more days! (How's that for a segue?) And less than that by the time you're reading this. But I'm sure we'll talk about it a lot tonight, so I'll use my epistle-space for other things. I'll also just mention briefly, as part of my role as nagging bitch girlfriend, that I wish you would let me come down to beautiful Toxomommamommamia (whatever) County to meet your folks. It'll be great, honey. We don't have to do anything. I'm not going to be bored. Please? Pretty please? With my cherry on top? But I understand. I just wish you would reconsider. I miss you so much. This has been the longest summer of my life.

I just returned from the mall with my mom. I spent all my time browsing in the bookstore while she stimulated the local economy. I found myself looking at this silly little book called Handlebars and Muttonchops, *which was about the history of facial hair. (Yes, I know. Fascinating, isn't it?) But what struck me was what I realized about why I was reading it. I realized that the only reason I was looking through it was because I knew how much fun you would have with it. I just started imagining you and me looking through the book together and cracking each other up. Here I was, all by myself, laughing my damn fool head off because in my mind you were standing right there beside me cracking jokes. I find myself doing that a lot.*

Of course, the most fascinating moustache in history has to be Hitler's. What was up with that thing? Just this little swath of evil right under his nose (A swathstika?). I cracked myself up thinking about (or was it me thinking about you thinking about?) – anyway, I started thinking about the effect of Hitler's moustache on the history of the war. I mean, that was one scary-ass moustache. I think that's how he got Czechoslovakia. It's like, 'Man, you don't want to mess with that dude with the crazy moustache – just give him what he wants.' But what if, instead, Adolph had had a handlebar moustache or one of those gay little Hercule Poirot jobs? Can you imagine Adolph Hitler with a handlebar moustache? All greased up like Snidely Whiplash? Chamberlain would have laughed his ass all the way back from Munich. It would have changed the course of history. The Moustache That Saved Europe. But instead, he had his evil little swathstika and it freaked everybody out. So that's what happens now when I go into a bookstore. I go in with my invisible Tommy and we entertain each other all afternoon. But in ten days you won't be invisible! We'll go back and look at the book together.

I think the fact that I would go into a bookstore and spend an hour looking at a book on facial hair is an indication that perhaps I'm getting a little burned out on historical scholarship. I'm glad I'm going to law school. I don't think I have what it takes to be a history scholar. I somehow doubt that John Hope Franklin would have spent his time this morning reading what I did. I've actually given this some serious thought lately.

The problem with studying history is, there's no end to it. You get interested in a particular time period and read several books. Then at the end of each of those books there is a fifty-page bibliography of other books that you absolutely must read if you want to dare think of yourself as any kind of authority; and then, of course, all of those hundreds of books have bibliographies at the end of them. And to really understand any period of history it is imperative that you study all the events and circumstances leading up to that time, that helped create that era. And you must learn all about the subsequent eras as well to get a perspective on what the consequences and lessons of that era were for future generations. So, just to keep your brain from exploding, you specialize, and specialize, and specialize some more, until eventually you spend your whole life becoming the world's foremost expert on the Concordat of Worms. I just don't have the time and patience needed for serious scholarship.

I think that's all I'm going to write for now, sweetie. I've given you something funny to laugh about and something serious (but not too serious) to think about. But the only thing I want you to think seriously about is how much serious fun we're going to have in a few days.

I hope we have a repeat performance tonight of last night's extravaganza. My loins are anxiously awaiting your call, sir.

I love you!
Cait

TOMMY, OF COURSE, HAS a blast in Boston with Cait and her family. It had been his first plane ride and he was somewhat embarrassed that Cait had insisted on buying his round-trip ticket ("I'm the one who invited you up here; it's only fair that I pay for it," she had said, sweetly.). He meets her lawyer dad and her history-professor mom. His mouth gapes at the size of their house (mansion is more like it). Cait spends every day of his week-long visit giving him the Fodor's treatment, hitting all the highlights of historic Boston. At night, he and Cait and her family eat at restaurants that are as far removed from anything he had grown up with as, well, Tox County is from Boston. Her parents, being the Massachusetts liberals that they are, don't mind – assume, actually – that they will be sleeping together in her bedroom (an attitude also far removed from Tox County). They make love each night on the floor, however, as a preventive measure to keep Cait's antique four-poster bed from squeaking (or breaking).

As glorious as that week in Boston is, during their first and final summer together, Tommy's mood of exultation also contains more than a hint of its opposite. He feels so out of place here in upper-crust Boston. But what concerns him most isn't that he knows he's a fish out of water, but that perhaps Cait doesn't know it – perhaps she doesn't have the experience outside her caste to understand just how different their backgrounds are. Over their dinners, Tommy plays up his ambition to be a college history professor like Cait's mom, an idea he had never given much thought to until Cait's mom had started asking questions. He plays up his dad's heroism in saving the lives of those two little boys, but doesn't mention his own cowardly role in that same episode; he even plays up the importance of Amerimeat to the economy of not just the Southeast, but of the entire U.S., in his attempt to make Tox County seem, at least in one respect, as vital as Boston.

Cait wants to come to Tox County to visit and had been pestering Tommy every night over the telephone. He had been on the verge of relenting, the gravitational pull of Cait being so strong, but he realizes in Boston the wisdom of his decision to keep Cait away from Tox County. The reasons he gave her were legitimate, more or less: "What are we going to do when we're not screwing? Take a daily tour of the potted meat factory?"; "You'll be disgusted by the smell of the shit pits"; "You'll be disgusted by everything about my dad." But the real reasons are the ones he can't confess to Cait. He thinks of Tox County as a great poisonous psychic swamp. He doesn't want to contaminate Cait with the noxious pall of memory that hangs over the place: "Here, darling, let me show you my back yard, where I practiced pitching through a tire swing – and incidentally, over here is the spot where I tried to club my poor dog to death"; "Would you like to go for a ride, my sweet? I'll take you down to the river where I murdered my best friend just seven short years ago. Won't that be fun!"; "And if you look over to the right, sweetheart, there's the building where my dad, just a couple of years ago, almost plunged to his death while I calmly rode the other elevator down to meet him. The elevator door opened on the first floor to the sound of screams"; "While we're at it, love, let me drive you over to my high school, where I skulked the halls like a ghost, the halls that echoed with the sound of Charles's high-pitched joyful laugh." No, as much as he misses Cait, he must protect her at all costs from the deadly poisons permeating this place.

In high school, Tommy's grief took the form of a hair-trigger temper and a general apathy concerning most things. He continued to play baseball, but not very effectively. His baseball career was ruined by his inability to control his curveball. Pre-teen boys were strictly forbidden from trying to throw breaking pitches. Their growing skeleton and musculature were deemed too fragile to risk permanent injury, so Tommy had made his reputation solely on the power of his fastball. When he learned how to throw a breaking pitch, it was difficult to throw for strikes. This problem could have been overcome with the kind of energy and eagerness for sustained practice that Tommy had demonstrated throughout childhood as he pitched daily in his backyard; but he no longer cared to practice his pitching. He became frustrated easily and would quit after only a few off-target pitches. Anything baseball-related also reminded him of Charles. Sometimes, in his backyard, he would break down and cry as a summer sound or a summer scent brought back an unwanted memory.

Everything he did in high school mirrored his experience playing baseball. Things he once did with enthusiasm and skill, he now did carelessly and halfheartedly. Tox County High wasn't academically rigorous, so he had no trouble making good grades, but his straight A's sometimes slipped to B's or C's. He lacked friends and didn't care. He tried to seduce girls on occasion but had no relationships. Previously boisterous, but generally well-mannered and well-liked by teachers and peers, he now would get into shouting matches with boys who crossed him and would become surly with teachers. His guilt produced a paranoid feeling that people were looking at him oddly – he knew what he had done to Charles, even if everyone else believed his lies about freak accidents and slippery river rocks. Tommy was inconsolable for days after Charles's death and received everyone's sympathy – even his dad's, up to a point. Barry was on the road when it happened and then gave Tommy a wide berth upon his return, which Tommy at first appreciated as silent commiseration – but then he overheard the end of an early-morning argument in which his mom had yelled at his dad, "How can you even think such a thing – of course it was an accident!" A son naturally assumes that his father understands him better than anyone else, and now Tommy had his proof.

The general feeling Tommy had through high school was a desire to escape. College was the only thing he vaguely looked forward to – a possibility to put everything else behind him and perhaps to start over, with a new home away from home, new goals, new activities, hopefully a new life altogether. He thought very little about love. It was nice to dream about as an abstract concept, but he had no idea someone like Cait actually existed in flesh and blood.

The one significant change in his habits during high school that could be seen as positive – though it had its roots in the same grief which colored every other aspect of his life – was his discovery of history. He had always been a warm-weather scholar, becoming easily engaged with any book that interested him but rarely reading steadily over an extended period of time. But now he became absorbed in one historical era after another, in no particular order. This unforeseen, intense interest in history served two purposes during this traumatic period of Tommy's life. It provided an immediate means of escape; he couldn't physically leave Tox County now, but at least he had somewhere else to go in his mind. It also gave him a new world of people and lives to keep him company at a time when his own world was becoming increasingly lonely. His study of history, through college and into adulthood, was always about, first and foremost, all the interesting people it allowed him to meet and get to know.

TEACH AND BARRY WERE SITTING in front of the TV in the living room after Sunday lunch, Teach in the recliner, his dad in his wheelchair. Robbie was in the kitchen with the lady-folk. The story everyone was talking – and laughing – about today was the Congressional candidate from

Texas, who had just admitted in an interview that, as a teenager, he had once had sexual intercourse with a horse, "just to see what it was like."

"I guess he's going after the lonely-cowhand demographic," Teach said. Though a few commentators praised the candidate for his courageous honesty, the Fundamentalist talking heads were taking this opportunity to preach about moral perversity, the exposure of our children to such filth, and how this was yet another example of the inherent dangers of the slippery slope of same-sex marriage. These comments were followed by rebuttals from those supporting gay marriage, who were outraged that any connection should be made between the matrimonial aspirations of two human beings in love and the vile bestial ruttings of the gentleman from Texas.

"Hey Dad, do you think there's much of a difference?"

"You mean between two guys screwin' and that guy screwin' a horse? You wanna know what the difference is? The difference is, one of 'em has four legs and a three-foot *shlong*!" Barry cracked himself up and Teach faked a half-laugh.

"So you're implying that he was not only screwing a horse, but that he was, in fact, screwing a *gay* horse."

"Shit, man – you even have to go and ruin a good joke, don't you?"

"Whatever you say, Dad – whatever you say. . . . But seriously, I think the gay-marriage folks are making a big mistake. They could really use this to their advantage if they would come out in full support of bestiality instead of trying so hard to distance themselves from it. . . . I say they need to stand behind their fellow perverts."

Barry started coughing with laughter. "Yeah, they'll stand behind them all right!"

Teach's mom came out from the kitchen, followed closely by Señor Perro Tercero. "What in the world are you two in here talking about?"

"We're talking about the one thing Dad and I can agree upon – that politicians who have sex with horses are funny as hell."

"You two either need to grow up or quiet down – preferably both." Teach and Barry laughed and ignored Beth. She retreated back into the kitchen.

Teach continued, "The gay-marriage people think they're getting brownie points with everybody –"

"Or fudge points, in their case!" Barry laughed through another cough.

"As I was saying, before I was so crudely interrupted. . . . They think they're getting brownie points with everybody by lambasting this guy, but when they go on TV and say they're just as disgusted by bestiality as everybody else, then they're just playing into the hands of all the homophobes out there who think that AIDS is God's gift to Christianity."

"Hey, jerkoff, don't bring Christianity into this. There ain't nothing we're talking about has the least god-damn thing to do with Jesus."

"All right, all right. All I'm saying is, when gay-marriage supporters say that bestiality is disgusting and unnatural and gross and it shouldn't be tolerated in our national leaders, then that gives every homophobe out there the perfect chance to say, 'Well, now you know how *we* feel.'"

"Damn straight. . . . Bunch of fudge packers. . . . Corn-holers."

"Okay, Dad, you've made your point. You've done a magnificent job standing up for good old-fashioned American heterosexuality."

"Well, what the hell kind of point are you trying to make? That gays are supposed to go around telling us it's okay to screw anything with four legs? Man, that'll really help their cause, won't it? Dipshit."

"Ah, but you're not looking at this the right way. This could defuse the whole gay-marriage issue. . . . It's all about getting what you want by asking for more than you want. Social negotiation. . . . What do you do when you're trying to sell a used car? You haggle. You negotiate. You ask for a higher price than you're willing to accept. You see where I'm going with this?"

"Of course not. . . . At least you're not talking about the god-damn green beans again. . . . I don't know about you, but I think I'm about ready for a nap – why don't you help me out of my chair, so I don't have to bother your mother. . . . Make yourself useful for a change." Barry rolled himself into position alongside the couch. Teach, as he had done so many times over the years, bent over his father, slid one arm under Barry's lifeless knees and with his other arm reached around behind his dad and grasped him tightly under his shoulder, pulling Barry closer to him. Teach lifted his father out of his wheelchair, and for a moment the two men were face to face. Teach laid his dad gently on the couch. Whenever Teach performed this little act of charity for Barry, he always thought of the Tollinger Building, those two little boys, what his dad had done and what he hadn't.

As Teach returned to his recliner he picked up where he had left off. "Okay, let me make it simple for you. The gay-marriage groups need to encourage all those people out there – and we know they're out there – encourage them to come out of the – well, not the closet in this case – the stall, or the barn, or whatever – encourage them to stand up for their rights and to insist on being treated with dignity. . . . They need to come up with a name for themselves. Every social movement has to have a name. They need to be called something that captures the essence of those unique pleasures they feel – like homosexuals co-opted the word *gay*. What can we call them, Dad? Help me out here."

Barry slowly shook his head but said nothing.

"For this to work, they need to associate themselves with all the gay-marriage people, but make sure they maintain their own identity as well." Teach rubbed his chin; Barry rubbed his eyes and yawned. Suddenly, Teach erupted with laughter. "They'll be the *neighs*! Instead of *gays*, they'll be *neighs* – get it?" Barry had closed his eyes. "They can form the Neigh Brigade. All the prominent gay leaders who have experience with protests and whatnot could lead it. They could help organize another march on Washington and all the Neighs could bring all their lovely horse-brides with them, with their pretty manes all curry-combed out all nice and shiny – Norman Rockwell couldn't paint a sweeter picture. . . . And they'll need a catchy little slogan they can chant, like 'Hey, hey, I'm a Neigh. . . . Kiss my ass and hear it bray!' Maybe this guy from Texas can stand up in front of Abraham Lincoln and give a big I Have a Dream-type speech. . . . 'Give me your Palominos, yearning to run free! Give me your spotted Appaloosas! Your majestic Clydesdales! Neighs of the world, unite!'" Teach chuckled at himself. "People will be so fed up and disgusted by the whole Neigh thing that gay marriage will seem quaint and harmless by comparison. The Fundamentalists will be more than happy to let gay people go skipping down the aisle if they'll just shut up about the damn horses. . . . You see what I'm getting at now, Dad? What do you think?"

"I think you're full of shit up to your eyeballs, that's what I think. Shut up so I can go to sleep."

"But that's the best way to get any kind of social change in this country. You get everybody riled up about some extremist fringe group, and then that makes you look like a moderate by comparison. . . . Look at the civil rights movement. People thought Martin Luther King was nothing but a Communist agitator until Malcolm X and the Black Panthers came along and really scared the bejesus out of everybody – then Martin Luther King became the voice of reason all of a sudden."

"Yeah, and you see where that got him."

"Yeah, well. . . . That reminds me of something I was thinking about the other day. Why is it that all the successful assassins in this country are Republicans?" Teach heard his dad give out a heavy sigh. "It's true, though. . . . Oswald certainly wasn't a Republican, but he killed Kennedy, so they should at least make him an honorary member of their party, right? But both Kennedys, Martin Luther King, Huey Long. . . . Timothy McVeigh was a registered Republican. . . . When a Republican sets out to kill somebody, man, they know how to get the job done, don't they?"

Teach was essentially talking to himself by this point – but being an audience of one had become more and more preferable to Teach as he studied the alternatives his life was offering. Everyone else was in the kitchen, but being with Cheryl brought with it now so many undesirable

164

sensations – sadness, guilt, resentment; Robbie had become a stranger to him since high school and he had so often mistreated his little brother growing up that he assumed Robbie's feelings toward him were mixed, at best. If Robbie didn't hate him, he probably should. Or, while his dad slept, he could sit here quietly and allow his mind to quickly drift to the one thing it always came back to – which would be excruciating and would quickly send him scurrying into the bathroom on another weeping jag.

Before Barry had set the remote down in preparation for his move to the couch he had switched the television to one of those ubiquitous Sunday-afternoon shark programs. What is this fascination that Americans have with sharks? Teach wondered. We love our cold-blooded killers, apparently. And was it true that sharks die if they stopped swimming? If so, then Teach imagined that went a long way toward explaining their ferocity – angry at the whole aquatic world for the swim-or-die ultimatum they were forced by fate to obey. So, faced with his own beastly choices and afraid to stop swimming, Teach, the Great White Bullshitter, continued on: "And then look at what the Democrats have to offer by way of contrast – it's the gang that couldn't shoot straight. Sara Jane Moore and Squeaky Fromme? Are you serious? Did they even know how to hold a gun? And Arthur Bremer? He shot Wallace at point blank range and emptied the chamber, and still couldn't finish the job. No killer instinct, you see – his heart wasn't really in it. . . . Hinckley? Maybe if he had stopped daydreaming about Jodie Foster and took his hand off his pecker long enough, he could have scored more than one lucky hit on ol' Ronnie. Maybe if the Democrats would join the NRA and take some freakin' target practice, they could actually eliminate some of their enemies. . . . Going all the way back to Teddy Roosevelt, just a pathetic, incompetent parade of futility. The guy who shot Roosevelt, he pumped a bullet in him and couldn't even make Roosevelt stop giving his speech – Jesus, talk about your embarrassing assassination attempts. . . . Now, McKinley, I guess he was the exception that proves the rule, but the guy who shot him – my God, man, what's the use in having your name go down in history if nobody can fuckin' pronounce it –"

"Hey, big mouth," Barry opened his eyes and looked over at his son. "If I pump a bullet into you, will that make you shut the hell up?"

Gɪᴀᴄ ᴠÊ Dᴀᴏ

Practice Essay
By Huy Miller

Yo Teach. It's Huy — I can see you from inside my dream. I want you to know that I forgive yo ass. I don't know what you done but everybody done something. So whatever it was you did dude I forgive you for it. Don't worry about forgiving Huy. I'm in a dream where everything is cool and soft. Like the other side of your pillow bro. Cool and soft. Nothing can bother Huy now. I turn that pillow over and go right on back to sleep. I gotta get back to my dream Teach. It's always a good time to dream Teach. It's never too late to dream Teach.

You and Cait are in her dorm room. Her roommate, Amanda, is gone for the weekend. You are getting ready to play a game. The goal of the game is to remove each other's clothing as slowly as possible. The first one to become erotically ravenous loses.

"On or off?" Cait asks, with a finger on the light switch.

"Doesn't matter. You're going to get fucked either way."

"We'll leave 'em on this time."

"That has its advantages."

The game has begun. You are fully clothed. You are in an embrace. You smell her hair and move your nose slowly along her hairline. You move the side of your head along her forehead, your hair barely brushing her skin. Your strategy is to continue to slide your head slowly down along her body until you can reach her shoelaces, at which point you will remove her shoes. As you begin to move your head downward, however, Cait suddenly sticks her tongue into your ear. You get an immediate erection.

"Hey! That's not fair! You've already unleashed your secret weapon. I might as well surrender if you're going to launch that thing."

"You could retaliate." Cait presses her hands all along the front of your body, from your chest down to your thighs. She lingers over the crotch of your jeans.

166

"Good God Almighty. Are you mad, woman?" You reach around behind her and squeeze her ass slowly with both hands. She's still rubbing the front of your jeans.

"What's wrong? Are you having a missile crisis down there, Fidel?"

"You don't want to do this. It's madness I tell you. Pure madness."

"What are you going to do about it? Blockade me? Ooh, I'm really scared now." She is unzipping your jeans.

"You need to back away from the brink, lady. I can't be held responsible for the consequences." She starts stroking you, slowly and gently. "It's called mutually assured destruction. There are no winners when you play that game."

She continues stroking you for a moment, but then stops, moving her hand back up to your chest. "Okay, Mr. President, you win. . . . Crisis averted." But not really, because even though Cait has taken her hand off your hard-on, she leaves it out, where it will continue to rub against her. Cait raises her arms to remove your sweatshirt.

"So now I'm Kennedy? . . . That would make you Marilyn." You do likewise, pulling off her sweatshirt. Doing so also raises her T-shirt, revealing her navel.

"Not Jackie?"

"Jackie's pretty hot – but no, I see you as more of a Marilyn."

Your shirt is now off and Cait is kissing your chest, slowly, lingering sweetly over each kiss.

"Okay, I'll be Marilyn. Just don't have me killed," Cait whispers into your chest. You pull her T-shirt over her head while she is still kissing your torso. Cait is wearing a pink bra today. You gently caress her arms before reaching behind her to unsnap the hooks.

"I love you, Cait," you say softly into her ear.

"I love you so much, Tommy."

The game ends in a tie as you and Cait are successfully naked with neither of you becoming erotically out of control.

Now, however, you are together on her bed and the situation has changed dramatically. You are both up on your knees, kissing madly. You both now have lost complete erotic control. Suddenly, Cait stops kissing you and looks at you with mischief all over her face. "Hey, you wanna try it in my ass?" she asks, bouncing on her knees.

"What? Really?"

"Yeah." Cait keeps your passion simmering – she is stroking you. "Don't you wanna know what it's like?"

167

"I'm not entirely sure."

"Let's do it."

"Will it hurt you?"

"Now don't go all wobbly on me, George."

You laugh. "God, don't make me visualize Margaret Thatcher at a time like this."

"C'mon, it'll be fun."

"I don't know. . . . I'm thinking maybe there's a reason why God made me a heterosexual – you know, so I could avoid just such situations."

Cait pushes you over backwards. "Stop being such a prude and fuck me in the ass."

So, after much experimental shifting and giggling, and a brief need for focused care, Cait guides you safely into unexplored territory.

She had said, C'mon, it'll be fun. . . .

It is.

YOU ARE IN YOUR DORM ROOM, bored. Your roommate is out, partying. You spend every evening with Cait, but she begged off tonight, citing the need for an emergency level of study for her Poli. Sci. test tomorrow. You saw no need for that to preclude studying together; you are together any time you need to prepare for tests or term papers. It's true that the times when you study together always degenerate (or blossom) into silliness or sex, but you like to think you have enough self-control and maturity to resist those temptations if need be.

She said there would be too much noise in her dorm, so she had gone to the library. You decide to go find her. You'll read a book to distract yourself while she's poring over her notes. At least you'll be with her.

You check all your usual study spots, but no Cait. Maybe she's taken a break and gone to the Union for a snack. You continue searching the library, however. You finally spot her on the second floor, over in a corner, shielded behind a bookcase. She is not alone. There is a guy with her. They appear to be studying, but while you stand perfectly still watching them, hiding behind the bookcase, they break out into hushed laughter. You become furious but decide against a confrontation in the library. You stalk back to your dorm and become lost in a morass of anger, fear, and self-pity. You try to distract your thoughts with television, but it is useless. Cait has promised to come see you tonight as soon as she leaves the library, but you can't envision this night ending well. This will be your first fight – the first time Cait has given you any reason to be mad at her; you have been together for over a year. You lie on your bed, imagining yourself yelling at her with hurt in your voice. Though you try, you can't imagine how she will defend herself. You had a bad feeling about this when she had said she wanted to go to the library alone. And none of her explanations will satisfy you – there is no possible way for her to explain what you saw in the library.

You spend two hours in this miserable state. It makes you almost physically ill. Eventually, the intercom in your room announces to you that you have a visitor in the lobby. To calm yourself before seeing Cait you slam your fists into your mattress several times. When you meet Cait in the lobby you appear happy to see her. You don't want to make a scene here; you will wait until you are back in your room to confront her.

You walk well in front of Cait on your way back to your room. Normally, you would hold her hand. She says, "Why are you walking so fast?"

"I'm anxious to get you back in the room," you say, without looking back at Cait.

"Ooo-la-la."

As soon as Cait enters your room you ask, "How did your studying go?" You close the door behind her.

"Very well. Maybe I'll do okay tomorrow. . . . So where's Rodney?"

"Out."

"Oh yeah?" She says this with a look in her eye that you have seen many times, which usually sends you over the top with desire.

"I went to the library to find you."

"Really? You must not have looked very hard. I was just up on the second floor. . . . Sorry you didn't find me." She rubs your shirt with both hands.

"Oh, I found you all right," you say, your voice rising.

"What's wrong?"

"I saw you with that guy."

"*That guy?*"

"Well, are you going to tell me who that guy was?"

"*That guy? That guy?* Well, why didn't you come over and introduce yourself to *that guy? That guy* was a friend from one of my classes last year."

"What were you doing with him?"

"*What was I doing with him?* What do you mean, what was I doing with him? He saw me and invited me to study with him. . . . You're not gonna make a big deal out of this, are you?"

"I don't know. Should I?"

"Oh my God. You are so *jealous.* What brought all this on?"

"Why didn't you want me to study with you? You said you wanted to be by yourself."

"For your information, mister, I did want to be by myself. But Claudio came over –"

"*Claudio?*"

"Yes, dear. Claudio. He's my Latin lover, darling. He wants to take me away to his chateau on the Riviera. Jesus Christ."

"Who is this guy?"

"*This guy.* There you go again. I'm sorry, Tommy, I'm just having trouble taking this conversation seriously."

"Well, you better take it seriously."

"My God – are you *threatening* me, over something like this? . . . Can we continue this little tete-a-tete tomorrow? I'm tired – and I think we both need to get some sleep. I don't want us to say something stupid to each other just because we're tired and bent out of shape."

"You weren't tired a minute ago."

"Well, that was before you turned into Torquemada." Cait laughs.

"Don't laugh at me."

"Wow – I had no idea you were so insecure. Why are you insisting that I was somehow cheating on you? Why don't you believe me?"

"Why *should* I believe you?"

"Jesus fuckin' Christ, Tommy, you've gone off the deep end. I'm leaving." Cait picks up her book bag and walks quickly out of your room, but, in the hallway, she turns around. "You know what, I'm not gonna let you off this easy. This whole conversation has really pissed me off. . . . What if I really did have something going on with Claudio, or some other guy? Just for argument's sake. . . . Just for argument's sake, Tommy, what if I really were bangin' the hell out of Claudio? What would you do about it? What would that mean? What right would that give you to – to treat me like you fuckin' own me? You can't treat me like this, Tommy – like 'that thar cattle rustler done made off with one of mah steers!'"

"Don't make fun of me!" you yell. Without thinking, you slap Cait. You slap her as hard as you can.

"Oh my God! Oh my God! You hit me. You fuckin' hit me!" As she rubs her jaw she begins to cry. So do you.

"I'm sorry, Cait. I'm so sorry. I don't know what happened." You reach out to touch her.

"Don't touch me!" Cait screams through her tears. She runs out your door, leaving her book bag. You are unable to follow her. You are paralyzed. Your hand is still stinging.

You thought you felt miserable before the fight started. But you had no idea.

You somehow managed to sleep at some point last night, after you had hit Cait. You suppose your body had chosen to shut itself down, like unconsciousness after a severe body trauma. When you awake you have to

170

go see Cait. You are afraid that if you don't you might never see her again. You have no idea what to say to her, but you must persuade her to forgive you.

You ask Stacy, the receptionist at Cait's dorm, to page her. Visitation doesn't start until eleven, so she refuses to page Cait. It's an emergency, you tell her. "I'm sorry Tommy, I can't do it."

"C'mon, Stacy. We had a big fight last night. I need to apologize."

"I can't do it Tommy – I'm sorry."

"Yes you can. What if it was a medical emergency? Or what if Cait's dad came running in here and said that her mom had just died? Would you page her then?"

"Tommy – stop it. You can wait till eleven."

"I'm not gonna wait, Stacy. I'm going up." You turn and walk to the elevator.

"Tommy! You'll lose your visitation privilege!"

"I don't care."

You take the elevator up to Cait's floor. A girl wrapped in a towel walks by you as you exit. She's one of Cait's friends on the hall. "Tommy, what the hell?"

"Have you seen Cait?"

"No – what's wrong?"

"Nothing."

"Then why are you up here?"

You ignore her question and continue toward Cait's door. You knock.

"Who is it?"

"It's Tommy."

"Go away, Tommy."

"I don't want to. I want you to let me in. . . . Please."

"I'm not ready to talk to you, Tommy. Go away, please."

"Cait. Please let me in. You have no idea how sorry I am." The girl in the towel is standing in her doorway, watching and listening.

"Tommy. Leave. If you don't, I'll call downstairs."

"Cait. Please. Why won't you let me in? I just want to apologize, and talk." There is a moment of silence in Cait's room, but then you hear her through the door: "Stacy, this is Cait. I'm okay, but could you please call security?"

"Okay, I'm doing it right now."

"Thanks."

"I can't believe you just did that," you snarl. You regain your composure and try to whisper through the closed door, "I'm leaving now. I love you, honey, and I always will. What happened last night will never happen again. I promise."

"Just go, Tommy. Go."

You walk swiftly down the hall, past the girl in the towel, and make it into the elevator before anyone from security arrives. As you pass the reception desk you say, "I'm leaving, Stacy. You can call off your dogs."

You don't talk to Cait again for one week. You have two classes together, but she avoids you and, though it is difficult, you resist the urge to push the issue. You don't see her in the cafeteria. She must be making a great effort to avoid you. Finally, she leaves a message for you at the front desk of your dorm. She will come by at three so you can talk.

When you see her in the lobby, at three, you almost start crying. You keep yourself together and you and Cait walk back to your room.

"No Rodney?" she asks.

"No Rodney."

Cait takes a deep breath. "All right, Tommy. Let's talk. Do you want to tell me what the hell happened last week?"

"I don't know what happened, Cait. Honestly. I just snapped, I guess."

"Is that supposed to make me feel better? The knowledge that you can just go *snap*, whenever you get pissed off at me?" You remain silent. "We've got a big problem, Tommy, if this is something you can't control – I need to tell you this right now, before we go any further. . . . I will not allow you to hit me again. Or bully me. Or threaten me. I am not going to play that game. I am not going to be a passive victim, for you or anybody else."

"Of course not. You shouldn't be. I don't want you to be."

"This really changes our relationship, Tommy. You realize that, right?"

"Yeah. How can it not?"

"Can we leave the door open?" You always shut it out of habit whenever Cait visits.

"Of course." You respond to her question before realizing its import. "Are you afraid of me? You think I'm going to hit you again?"

"See there, Tommy – that's what we need to be talking about. Your anger. You're already raising your voice. Where did this come from all of a sudden? I've known you for over a year and you've never raised your voice to me. And then you slap the shit out of me. What's going on?"

"You hurt my feelings." You can't help but laugh, realizing how childish you sound. "I'm sorry, baby. I'm so terribly terribly sorry." You lean over on your bed to hug Cait.

"No. No hugging – not yet. We have some serious talking to do. The hugging will have to wait, Tommy. . . . And spare me your apologies. I understand how sorry you are. You damn well should be sorry. Stating the obvious isn't going to get us anywhere."

172

"Yes, ma'am." You smile.

"Just out of curiosity, how exactly did I hurt your feelings? If I'm not mistaken, you were the one accusing me of some sort of infidelity – I'm not sure exactly – what, mentally fucking Claudio in the reference section?"

"Are you trying to make me mad again? Are you trying to gauge my anger?"

"No, not at all. I just don't understand what all the hubbub was about."

This is one question you can answer. You've had all week to think about it. "The reason I acted so immature and insecure, Cait, is because I don't feel like I deserve you. I'm just this redneck from Toxonomonomonee County –"

"I'm sorry, honey, go ahead – I can't help laughing every time you say that."

"You see, that's exactly what I mean. I'm just this country redneck, and you're from Boston, for crying out loud. Every day I wake up and think, how'd I get so lucky? What does she possibly see in me? When is she going to wake up and realize she could do so much better? It's just because I love you so much, Cait, and I'm so afraid I'm going to lose you."

Cait stares at you and appears to be thinking about something. "Okay, Tommy, let's analyze what you just said. First of all, do you really think of yourself as a country redneck? Honestly?"

"Well, compared to you I certainly am."

"Do you think that's the way I see you?"

"I don't know. . . . Hence the insecurity."

"Okay, let me rephrase the question. Do you think that I would ever fall in love with someone who was nothing but a country redneck from Toxo-nono-nono-nono County, wherever the hell it is that you're from?"

"Well, since you put it that way. Probably not."

"Right. And for those other questions you wake up every morning asking–" Very unexpectedly, Cait chokes up and starts crying.

"What's wrong?"

"Those questions you ask," Cait continues, sniffling, trying to stop her tears, "How'd I get so lucky, what do you see in me, when are you going to realize you could do better –" She's lost it now, sobbing uncontrollably. You have no idea what it means. "Did it ever occur to you –" she tries to continue. "Did it ever occur to you that maybe I ask those same questions myself, every god-damn morning, when I wake up and think about you?" You start crying, not quite able to believe the revelation that has just been made to you. You assume it's okay now to hug her. She returns your embrace, but not for long. She pushes you back. "I'm not finished yet. . . . Do you know how insulting it is for you to think that I'm not capable of making a rational, thought-out decision about the person I'm getting involved with? That I must be this foolish, naïve waif who can't see past the end of her nose?" Cait sniffles and runs an index finger underneath her eyes. "Do you really think I'm that stupid, Tommy?"

"Of course not, sweetheart. Just the opposite."

"I just don't know about us, Tommy. I don't know about you. How can you be so sophisticated one minute and then such a – a rube?"

"Well, I am just a redneck from Toxo-nono-nono County."

"Stop making me laugh. I'm trying to be serious."

"I'm sorry."

"What does it say about you? Did you think you were pulling some kind of wool over my eyes? Casting some kind of spell over me? What makes you think I don't see right through you?"

"Do you? See right through me?"

"Obviously not. I didn't see this coming." The tears are drying now. You both can talk without sniffling. "I try to give you credit, Tommy. I say to myself, 'Well, he must see something in me. He must think I'm good-looking. He must think I'm funny, and smart. There must be some reason he loves me so much.' But if you can see me sitting with another guy, just sitting there, studying, and think 'she must not love me – she must love him instead,' I don't know what to make of that, Tommy. I honestly don't know."

"You're the only girl I've ever truly loved, Cait. That's the god's honest truth. All the other girlfriends I've had, I don't know – it's just not the same. . . . With all the other girls – I think I was very arrogant, to be honest with you. All the time I dated them I kind of thought I was doing them a favor. I didn't have to ask myself why they were with me. I figured I knew. You're the first person I've dated where I think it's you doing me the favor. . . . So in that sense, I'm still very naïve."

"But how can you think I must not know you very well? That's what I don't get. You seem to think, 'if she knew the real Tommy Morrison, she wouldn't love me.' Are you hiding something from me? Are you putting up a façade? Or do you think I'm just not observant enough to notice what kind of ignorant jerk you really are? That I've been hoodwinked and swept off my feet by your charm? Which one is it? It has to be one or the other. Either you're hiding your true self from me, or I'm too stupid to see it. So which one is it?"

"Hell if I know, sweetie. I hope it's neither one."

"Well, I want you to try to answer it. It's important."

"I don't know, Cait. You've obviously thought our relationship through a lot more deeply than I have. All I know is, I wake up every morning thanking my lucky stars that you are in my life. . . . And then I see you with another guy, I get jealous, because that's what guys do, they get jealous, and possessive, and then you try to psychoanalyze me and – you know, I could very easily turn this whole conversation around and start asking you the same questions. . . . Do you really think you're stupid? C'mon, Cait, you know you're not stupid. Do you really think you've been hoodwinked by me? Really? Do you actually think that anyone could ever hoodwink you?"

You are both silent. You thought this fight was about to reach a very satisfying conclusion, but now it's right back where it started. "Tommy, we're not even talking about what I came here to talk about. . . . You hit me. Any other problems we have we can work out, but not if you hit me. If you ever hit me again, it's over. I swear."

"I know." You can't look at her.

"What are you going to do about that?"

"What do you mean? What do you want me to do?"

"I mean, what can we do to make sure you never do anything like that again? You're too important to me, Tommy, to let something like this tear us apart without trying to fix it."

"Cait, I swear to God, it's never going to happen again. . . . I will never let it happen again."

"But how can you be sure you won't let it happen again? Is it even something you have any control over? Did you want to hit me the other night?"

"Of course not."

"Then why did you?"

You look at her, right into her eyes. "Because I didn't have any control over it, Cait."

"Have you always been like this?"

You shrug. "I don't know. I guess. Probably." You consider telling Cait about your dad, about what he used to do, but you're not sure whether that would help your cause, or hurt it. You decide not to risk it. You don't dare tell her about Charles.

"What I need to know is, what's going to happen the next time we have a fight?"

"I won't hit you again, Cait. Ever. I promise."

"We've already been over this ground, Tommy. Promises aren't good enough. Every abuser always promises –"

"I'm not an abuser!" Your frustration starts turning to anger, but you manage to reel it back in. "I don't know what else to tell you, Cait. . . . I like to think I have at least a little bit of self-control. I think things are a lot different now, since, you know, the other night. I never imagined in a million years that I would be capable of doing something like that to you. But now that it happened, I think I'll be a lot more self-aware, a lot more diligent in making sure I control myself. There's too much at stake now. I

175

don't want to lose you, Cait, and I know I will lose you if I ever do anything like that again. . . . I got mad just a second ago, when you called me an abuser, and you see how quickly I calmed down."

"I didn't call you an abuser."

"Okay. I'm sorry. I misunderstood. . . . Please, sweetheart, you have to believe me." You start to cry again. "I'll cut off my hands if I have to, if that what it takes. I swear. I'll never lay another hand on you again – not in anger, at least." You smile through your tears. Cait does not smile back, however.

"Oh Tommy. I sure hope you're right." Cait leans across the bed and embraces you. You look deeply into each other's eyes. Cait now has tears too streaming down her cheeks. You are stroking each other's hair and trying to smile.

"I love you, Cait."

"I love you, too, Tommy."

"Things will be okay. I promise."

"I know."

You play sweetly with each other's hair for a moment before you begin kissing, slowly at first, then suddenly passionately. You get up quickly and shut the door, kicking off your shoes as you do so. You lock it as well. If you hear Rodney's key in the lock that will be the signal for you and Cait to duck under the covers.

GLAD EARNHARDT'S DEAD

Practice Essay
By Roy Payne

I will never forgive Dale Earnhardt Junior for what he did to Jeff Gordon at Daytona even if it was a long time ago which it was. With only seven laps to go Jeff was in the lead, he has already won Daytona 3 times and was going for number 4. Dale Junior thinks the world owes him anything he wants since his daddy got killed but I think what happened was he undid his lap belt on the final lap and look what happened to him. Dale Junior is just like his daddy, he thinks he can get away with anything, he came up behind Jeff on Turn 2 and tapped his bumper, it wasn't no accident, I can tell you that much for sure, Dale Junior does that kind of stuff all the time. I don't care when it's somebody else, but not Jeff Gordon, Jeff Gordon has always been my favorite driver, he really knows how to run a race and he don't cheat. Dale Junior tapped Jeff and spun him out and almost sent him into the wall. How would he feel if Jeff went head-first into the wall just like his daddy done? That might make him think twice about what he did. It wouldn't be so bad if he just admitted what he did, but he didn't, he just lied about it, after the race he said that things like that always happen in a tight race. Yeah, right, he won't own up to anything he does, just like his daddy, that's the difference between Jeff Gordon and Dale Junior. In conclusion, I don't like Dale Earnhardt Junior and I don't think I ever will, unless he decides to grow a backbone and starts acting like a man.

P.S. I'm not really glad that Dale Earnhardt is dead, like I said in that other assignment. That was just a joke, nobody deserves to die like that, not even Earnhardt.

You and Cait are in your favorite restaurant, right off campus. You hold hands across the table as you wait for your burgers to arrive. Cait removes her sandals and starts rubbing the inside of your legs, beside your calves. You reach down and grab her foot and start tickling it wildly. She screams and jerks her leg away from your grasp.

You grab her leg again, quickly, but this time you just want to hold it in your hand. You caress her foot and play briefly with her toes. You move your hand easily along her leg, as far as your hand will reach under the table, only up to her knee. Her shin is as smooth and cool as wet glass. You tell Cait that you love her legs and that you will never cheat on her legs with another pair of legs.

You're still caressing her outstretched leg when the server brings your food. You grab the red squirt bottle at the side of the table and apply concentric circles of ketchup to your fries. You ask Cait if she would like some as well. Impulsively, you try to squirt her fries from your side of the table, making a ketchup trail all the way over to her plate. You also overshoot Cait's fries by quite a bit, getting ketchup on her white shirt. You laugh and she screams your name. You are now worried that your joke backfired and Cait is mad at you for ruining her clothes. She angrily grabs a napkin and scrubs at the ketchup stain. Suddenly, she throws the soiled napkin at you and lunges for the mustard bottle. She immediately squirts it and scores a direct hit on your shirt. She is now laughing. You return ketchup fire and she shoots more mustard. The restaurant manager yells at you to stop wasting his condiments. You declare a bi-lateral ceasefire and begin your meal a Technicolor mess.

The Tox County Chanticleer
Guest Columnist
Thomas "Teach" Morrison
Instructor, TCC

Pastor Robert McAllister, our esteemed, newly elected School Board member, has written a guest column that, were I so inclined, could doubtless keep me in the pages of the *Chanticleer* as a guest columnist until one of us – this publication or I – died a slow, painful death brought on by the loss of circulation.

To offer evidence to back my boast, this guest column will be entirely devoted to rebutting one, and only one, sentence of his column – his opening sentence, with the understanding that it would be equally feasible to devote a column next week to sentence number two, and so on, until I have finally aired all the quibbles I have with this undoubtedly fine man.

"We live in a world blessed by God." So begins the Reverend McAllister. And so, perhaps, we do. There are indeed many days when I feel my life, and even the whole world, is blessed by God. But, as I will caution below, it may not be wise to make such a bold assertion without first looking at all the evidence that is available to us.

When we look at our lives and the world around us and come to the conclusion that we are blessed by God, it reminds me of the horse with blinders on who says to the other horse, 'Don't you just love this beautiful tunnel we live in!' In order to make such a statement, Reverend McAllister, there must be many things you aren't seeing.

Let's look at the big picture, shall we? Can anyone deny that the universe is a cold, desolate place? Astronomers won't deny it. Even optimistic ones, who think we may have one or two relatively nearby neighbors that we may one day visit to borrow intergalactic cups of sugar from, are well aware of the basic inhospitality of our gaseous, poisonous universe. And for many Christians, who profess a human

179

exceptionalism which would not coexist easily with extraterrestrials, the universe must be, *ipso facto*, utterly desolate.

So, we start with an immense, perhaps infinite, universe created by a god who wishes for it to remain virtually lifeless. For what purpose? What possible purpose could all these billions of lifeless galaxies, containing billions of lifeless stars, heating billions of lifeless planets serve? Well, our closest lifeless neighbor, the moon, has served us well as an object of exploration and rock collection. Could that be God's purpose in creating such an enormous lifeless universe? To give our space agencies something to do for eternity? I can think of worse things for a god to do.

But if that's the noble purpose God has given to Man for taking advantage of such an enormous lifeless universe, what purpose does it have for God? What is He getting out of it? Had He been waiting billions of years with bated breath to witness the launch of Sputnik? If so, imagine how exciting it must have been for Him when Neil Armstrong finally took that one small step! It must have made Him feel finally vindicated, after billions of years of self-doubt, wondering if perhaps he had set his sights too high by creating just for us a gigantic lifeless universe to explore, only to have His specially created creatures fall short of His misplaced ambitions for us – but no, the Apollo program finally justified the faith He had put in us, after billions of years of waiting and worrying.

As glorious as this possibility is, I can't help but feel that God must have had some other reason for creating such a gargantuan lifeless universe. It just seems as if God would have needed something else to help Him pass the time while He was waiting for the Eisenhower administration to launch NASA. So, what did He create all this lifeless matter to do?

Well, the one thing all these billions of lifeless objects do a lot of is collide. And not just stars colliding, but whole galaxies! Boom! Billions of galaxies all set on a collision course with each other like celestial bumper cars. That is what galaxies do. They collide. Does it make sense to you that the universe was created by God just because He likes to blow stuff up?

While it may be comforting for some to think of God as having the mentality of a Hollywood movie producer, I, personally, cannot buy into this idea. So that leaves us with two possibilities. Either there is some other purpose for a gigantic, virtually lifeless universe, or it was created by someone other than the God we all know and love. Unfortunately, the neocortex of this particular hominid cannot fathom why else such a universe would be created. Why else would something be created that could have no other possible purpose other than as an intergalactic demolition derby? That leaves us with only one other alternative: the universe must have been created by someone else, someone about whom it makes sense to say would want to create a desolate universe chock full of colliding galaxies simply because he likes to watch things get blowed up real good.

We know, of course, the universe is not utterly lifeless. We are all here. But at least for the time being, the assumption we can make is that we are its sole inhabitants. But if all galaxies are doomed to collide, and yet we were created to live within one of them, then the question I would have to ask this Creator is, Why? Or more accurately, Why bother?

Why would we be created to exist on a doomed planet? Well, as before, let's take off our blinders and try to see the big picture. This planet is teeming with life – a seemingly endless variety of life. It's truly wondrous to behold. But what's really going on here? Let's pore over the fine print. Let's read between the lines. While it would seem sensible to say that this planet was put here in order to create life, upon closer inspection I would argue that it was actually put here in order to create death.

You cannot have death without first having life. The opposite claim is not true for life. You can, theoretically, have life without death. But death only exists as the result of taking a life. Most life on this planet, as soon as it comes into existence, gets wiped out. Look at the big picture – or, if you like, the microscopically small picture. One of the basic ingredients that we humans have for life – the noble sperm – is created in a super abundance just so one – *one* – can, if it's very lucky, survive long enough to help create a human life. Most other life forms face similarly long odds. Does this sound like a god who wants life to thrive? Or one who has set up a sadistic game of planetary cutthroat?

So far, my comments have only concerned our physical world. But the Rev. McAllister, I'm sure, is much more concerned about the state and nature of our spiritual world. Therefore, I will devote the balance of my space here to those concerns.

A world blessed by God, I assume, is a happy world. But, just as no one can seriously deny that we live in a universe that is almost entirely uninhabitable, I also propose that no one can seriously claim that this is a happy world. You can put on a happy face, enjoy happy hour, get slap-happy, and celebrate a happy birthday, but this is not, my friends, a happy world. Misery abounds. I don't think I need to go into unnecessary detail here. Misery abounds. Physical, mental, spiritual misery. And the mother of all misery, in theological terms, is Evil. And for Christians, this presents a problem, doesn't it? How to justify the presence of evil in a world blessed by God – the "Problem of Evil," it is called, when the writer wants to sound real serious and use capital letters. And Christian theologians have been tying themselves into knots for two thousand years trying to deal with the P of E. But if the world is so blessed, then why is the P of E such a humdinger of a head-scratcher?

If you spend two thousand years trying to pound a square peg into a round hole, perhaps it would be wise to lay down your hammer and pick up a razor – Occam's razor, to be precise. If your problem is that Evil seems to be everywhere, all the time, with no letup in sight, what would you suggest the simplest, most straightforward answer to the riddle is? Well, if you're honest with yourself, the answer qualifies as a no-brainer: we live in a world created under the aegis of Evil. When you see that Evil abounds in the world – something that nobody denies, though there are myriad ways of explaining it away – it should be obvious who is really running the show.

The Christian will counter, reasonably enough, that if Christians have a Problem of Evil to deal with, then I, and all those like me, have an equally serious Problem of Good to contend with. Isn't there an extraordinary wealth of goodness in the world? Can you really say that Evil is all-pervasive? How can you look a little child in the eye and honestly think she is a product of Evil? Good questions, all. And the answers I would give to them are, respectively, "yes," "no," and "easy."

Of course there is a wealth of goodness in the world. I try my best to be a good person. All of my friends and family are good people. And I am happy to assume the same about you and all of your friends and family. And no, Evil is not all-pervasive. How could it be, with so many good people around? But as for doe-eyed children, if you cannot see their inchoate evil, then you obviously have never set foot inside a sixth-grade classroom.

The rub, as I see it, is a problem of disparities, of relative strengths. Evil has the tanks, the napalm, the nuclear warheads. Goodness is always fighting the uphill battle. Compared to the weaponry of Evil, the forces of Good are merely little angels armed with bows and arrows of happiness, fighting a guerilla war against Evil: freedom fighters for goodness; asymmetric warriors of love; the angelic intifada.

So, how does all this play out in the real world, when Good meets Evil head-on? First, let's decide who the best combatants are that we can put into the ring to face off against each other. What is the worst evil a man can do? Take the life of another? Okay, there's our first contestant. What is the greatest good a man can do? Save the life of another? Fine, that works for me. So how do these two heavyweights compare? Is it the immovable object meeting the irresistible force?

If I save someone's life, do I then have permission to turn around and kill someone? Of course not. That one act of evil, everyone understands, would completely annihilate my one prior act of goodness. Conversely, if I kill a man, but then, the very next day, run into a burning building to save someone, do these two separate acts cancel each other out? Do I, the murderer, say, "It's okay that I killed that man yesterday because I saved someone else's life today"? Our justice system, of course, would not agree to that settlement and I doubt if anyone else would either.

So, what would it take to equal things out? How many lives would I have to save to be exculpated? One hundred? One thousand? That is an open question. Any man who has killed another man, I would assume, understands better than most the powerful sway that Evil holds over the world. But if we all take off our blinders, stand back, and study the big picture, perhaps we can all see that a little more clearly.

I would like to thank the *Chanticleer* for the opportunity to express my views, and, especially, the Rev. McAllister, for the raw material he has provided for numerous future columns.

"TEACH!" RANDY YELLED, as Teach rushed past his office.

"I'm late for class, boss man. Can it wait?"

"No. Get in here right now. Don't worry about your class. Roscoe's in there." Randy held up the morning paper. "What the hell were you thinking? With this article?"

"What's the problem, Randy? Are the Kooks for Christ giving you a hard time?"

"Why did you do this?"

"It was a rebuttal. I was responding in kind. An eye for an eye. An idiocy for an idiocy."

"My phone's already ringing off the hook. It's only nine o'clock."

"What do you want me to do?"

"I want you to keep your god-damn crazy opinions to yourself. Everyone I've talked to this morning wants me to fire you. . . . Some woman just called and said you tried to turn her daughter into a witch. That you tied her to a stake and tried to catch her on fire. What the hell is this crazy woman talking about?"

"How am I supposed to know?"

"Do you ever think about the consequences of your actions, Teach? Or do you always just act on impulse? Or do you just do whatever the hell you want and then expect to always bullshit your way out of it?"

"Yeah, Randy, pretty much. All of the above."

"How do you think your students in there are going to react?"

"Are you kidding? Do you think they ever read a newspaper? They won't know anything about it – or care."

"Oh, they'll know. I guarantee it. News travels fast."

"What do you want me to do?"

"I don't know. I'm just blowing off steam. I don't want to fire you, Teach – I just want you to grow up."

"You couldn't fire me, Randy. On what grounds? I haven't violated any school policies, or any local, state, or maritime laws."

Randy leaned forward in his chair and planted his elbows firmly on his desk. He gestured continuously with his hands as he spoke. "This is a rural county. In the South. A highly religious community. And you've taken on the responsibility of teaching a lot of their children. . . . And now they find out you're a devil worshiper?"

"I'm not a devil worshiper, Randy. It was very tongue-in-cheek. You don't think I really believe all that stuff I wrote, do you? People really need to lighten up."

"I don't care what you believe, Teach. I really don't. All I care about is what your students believe about you, and what the people of this community believe about this program."

"Don't worry about it, man. . . . I'm being serious. It'll all blow over. I pissed everybody off, everybody will write their crazy letters and make their angry phone calls, and then everything will return to normal. It always does."

"What are you going to say when you walk into your classroom?"

"You're blowing this all out of proportion. I'm not going to have to say anything."

"I hope you're right. But what if you're not? I want you to go in there and apologize. Say that you're sorry if you offended anybody, that you don't really believe what you said, that it was all just a joke, whatever. . . . Just tell them that you screwed up and that you're sorry."

"For God sakes, Randy, I don't have anything to apologize for. It's all the idiots out there who need to grow up, not me. All those people who get all bent out of shape whenever they disagree with something they hear somebody else say. Shit, man, I disagree with just about everything I hear on a daily fucking basis, but you don't see me running around trying to get everybody fired. . . . I'm not going to apologize, Randy. I'm sorry, but I'm not."

185

"Well, if that's the case, Teach, then you *are* in violation of school policy. It's called insubordination. . . . You go into that classroom, and if need be, you get down on your knees and beg forgiveness. I'm not going to let you give this department a black eye. I'll fire you if I have to, Teach."

When Teach stepped through the doorway of his classroom, he nearly panicked as he sensed immediately that perhaps Randy was right. There was a strange aura bouncing around the room, from table to table, that caused the normal behaviors of everyone to be just a little out of sync – but maybe that was only the result of Roscoe standing guard at Teach's desk, clearly out of his element; as the SRO quickly departed, Teach got a more reliable read on the situation – though the classroom still felt as if it contained some alien presence floating through the air. Everyone seemed to be either more focused on their activities, or more detached from them – he couldn't determine which. George and Oliver still poked each other in the ribs and slammed their fists into each other, but they seemed to stare at Teach more than usual; Maria still raised her hand and asked for help, but she seemed unable to make eye contact; Pilluz still silently mouthed his rap lyrics, bobbed his head, and did those spastic things with his hands, but he seemed to do it more intently; Jerry still drew his cartoons, but perhaps less attentively; Steve still turned around in his chair every five minutes, but he seemed quieter than usual. However, Charlotte was the only one Teach was truly concerned about. He knew she read the paper every morning. She also went to church every Sunday and most other nights as well. She did not ask for his help all morning.

Was there something that everybody was thinking but that nobody wanted to say? Should Teach say something? Should he, indeed, apologize? Teach struggled through three awkward hours of class, worried mostly about the discomfort he feared he had created for these people he cared about. When Teach dismissed class and his students filed more silently than usual out of the room, Charlotte waited until everyone else had left before she came up to Teach's desk. Teach could see tears shining in her eyes.

She spoke softly. "Mr. Morrison, do you really believe all those things you said in the paper this morning?"

"No, Charlotte, I don't. I was just trying to be funny, that's all."

"Well that's good. I didn't find what you wrote very funny, if you want me to be honest with you, but I'm glad to hear you say you didn't mean it. Satan is an evil, powerful force, but I know, in the end, the Lord will prevail."

Teach didn't say anything, but he nodded with understanding. Charlotte continued: "When I opened up the paper this morning and saw that my teacher had something in it that he wrote, I was so excited to read it – but then it made me so sad I almost wish I hadn't read it. . . . Mr. Morrison, I've been crying all morning. I was hoping I wouldn't start crying during class. I just tried to stay focused on doing my math. . . . I have the utmost respect for you. I really look up to you, if you don't mind my saying that. I know for a fact that you are the smartest man I have ever met – except maybe for my Horace. He was a very smart man, too, but a different kind of smart. You know, he couldn't read or write all that well, but he was still smart. You're book smart – which is very important, don't get me wrong. Book-smart people have made this a much better world to live in since I was a child. All these new medicines they keep coming up with and new machines – but my Horace was really smart too, just the way he could solve any problem that came up or figure out how to do just about anything he needed to do. But anyway, I'm wasting your time up here talking about Horace – you don't want to hear me talk about Horace. But what I wanted to say was that it has caused me a lot of anguish this morning – reading what you said in the paper. Because I believe everything you tell me, Mr. Morrison. Like I said, you're the smartest man I've ever known, and I've always trusted you to teach me what I need to know. You've helped me tremendously with my math, but you've helped me in a lot of other ways too." Charlotte had been speaking in a near whisper, trying to keep her emotions from welling up. But now she nearly started crying again. "What am I supposed to do when the man I've trusted to be so smart and who I always turn to, to explain things to me, what am I supposed to do when you say something that goes against everything I've always known in my heart to be true?"

"Maybe I'm not as smart as you think I am, Charlotte. I don't know everything there is to know."

"Are you sorry you wrote it, knowing how many people it upset? I know a lot of people who were very upset by it, not just me. I would hope that you're at least a little bit sorry about upsetting so many people."

"I am sorry, Charlotte. I'm sorry what I wrote caused you so much grief this morning. I never would have wanted that to happen to you. And if it makes you feel better, I am sorry I wrote it. I don't think it had its desired effect, anyway. I'm not sure what its desired effect was, to be honest with you, but whatever it was, I don't think it worked. So I'm sorry, Charlotte, and I hope you can forgive me."

She immediately smiled and walked around his desk to give him a hug.

"That's all I wanted to hear you say. . . . I know you're a good man, Mr. Morrison. You've helped me tremendously with my math. . . . I don't know why you wrote what you did, but I can always forgive those who are sincere in their desire for it. . . . Ask and ye shall receive, Mr. Morrison. Forgiveness is a blessed thing.

"Yes it is, Charlotte."

"God bless you, Mr. Morrison."

"God bless you, too, Charlotte. . . . I'll see you tomorrow morning. We'll do some more math together."

"Yes, sir. I'm very much looking forward to it."

You are one of the first students to arrive in class. It is the beginning of your junior year. You are excited about all the history courses you have loaded your schedule with. Up till now, you have focused on all your core courses, but now you are starting your major program of study in earnest. You see most of your classmates enter. And then there she is – Cait with no last name. It had occurred to you more than once that Cait, being a fan of Foreign Affairs, *may grace at least one of your classes. She takes a seat on the other side of the classroom, but luckily there is an open desk right beside her. You gather your stuff and walk quickly toward the open desk. You are willing to clock anyone who tries to sit there.*

You nonchalantly say hi, but it is only she you greet, ignoring all the others sitting around you. The professor enters and class begins. You steal as many looks to your left as seem plausible, considering your professor is standing in front of the room and to your right. Cait is always busy taking notes. However, the only class you're attending this morning is Cait 101. Using only your peripheral vision, you admire the way she holds her pen. The hand and wrist of a woman can be extremely alluring, you realize. You must find some way of communicating with her. Waiting until after class is not possible. You loudly tear out a sheet of notebook paper and think briefly of something to write to her. It'll be like high school, or rather, high school as it's supposed to be, since you were never in the mood to write mash notes to girls. On the paper you write:

What did Ben Franklin say when he discovered electricity?

You look over at Cait, affording yourself your first extended glance in her direction. She notices you and offers you a warm smile. You hand her the note and she gives a cute little-girl shrug of the shoulders to go along with her smile. She reads the note and her grin widens. Without even having to think about it, she writes a brief answer to your question. She hands the note back to you with a twinkle in her eye.

You read her answer:

Ouch.

TODAY WAS BARRY'S BIRTHDAY – his sixty-fifth, so now he was officially old. To honor his dad, Teach had spent a couple of hours putting together a little skit he knew his dad would love. He wouldn't tell anyone what the skit was about. He and Barry went into Teach's old bedroom and rehearsed it a couple of times. Cheryl and Beth and Robbie could hear them laughing, even from the living room. Robbie said to his wife, "Why don't you go downstairs and stay with the girls and make sure they don't hear any of this – I'm sure it'll be disgusting."

Barry rolled into the living room with a big grin on his face, with Teach and Señor Perro Tercero behind him.

By way of introduction, Teach said, "All right, ladies and germs – this is Lenny Bruce meets Abbott and Costello. Ready, Dad?" Barry chuckled mischievously as Teach announced, "All right. I get it started." Teach cleared his throat and held his fist up to his mouth as if it were a microphone. He read from his hand-written script:

"Hello, sports fans. It's time for another exciting season for our hometown ball club, the Tox County Stench. I'm here with head coach Barry Morrison, who's going to introduce us to all the exciting new players on this year's roster. It's always great to have you on, Coach Morrison. We can always count on you to tell it like it is."

"Thank you. It's great to be here for another season with the Stench."

"Okay, Coach, let's just go around the horn and talk about your infield. Who's on first?"

"Well, we have Some Asshole that we're gonna try out on first."

"Excuse me – who's on first?"

"Some Asshole."

"I see. You don't like this guy very much?"

"We'll just have to wait and see. He's young and green, but with a lot of potential, so we'll see how it goes. He can hit it a mile."

"What if it doesn't work out for him at first?"

"In that case, we can always stick Some Asshole in right field."

"Then who would play first?"

"Well, we always have A Sorry Son Of A Bitch who can play first. He's our best bench player right now. It's always good to have A Sorry Son Of A Bitch you can bring off the bench."

189

"I see. Who have you got at second this year?"

"Our second baseman is Full Of Shit."

"How did you come to that decision?"

"That our second baseman is Full Of Shit?"

"Yes."

"Well, we tried out a lot of people, and he showed a strong arm and he's good on the pivot when he's turning a double play."

"And I understand he's a lot of fun in the clubhouse. A real character."

"Oh yeah, always clowning around. That's just who he is. He'll always be Full Of Shit no matter what."

"Okay Coach, let's move along. Tell me who's on third this year."

"Fuck You Buddy."

"What did you just say?"

"I said Fuck You Buddy."

"Coach, I would say you're getting really defensive."

"That's right. We have to get more defensive. We made way too many errors last year. We were looking for a good defensive third baseman, and every scout I talked to kept telling me, 'Fuck You Buddy, Fuck You Buddy.' So I'm glad we were able to sign him."

"Okay Coach. Let's move on to short. I was watching him earlier during infield practice. He looks pretty impressive. He doesn't let anything get by him."

"Yeah, that Cocksucker is really good. He really clamps down on any balls that come his way. He's like a vacuum cleaner out there."

"And he's not the only Cocksucker playing in the league this year, right?"

"That's right. He has a couple of brothers, but this is *our* Cocksucker. He may turn out to be the best Cocksucker of them all."

"There always seems to be at least one Cocksucker every year. They go back a long way, and it looks like there'll be many more in the future."

"Yeah, they're a real baseball family, that's for sure. All those Cocksuckers. I used to play with his dad."

"Okay, Coach, who do you have behind the plate this year?"

"Well, our catcher today is The Only Niggro On The Team."

"Yeah, I can see that. I see him down in the bullpen."

"Yeah, he's a good one. I wish we had more just like him. He's very versatile. He can play a lot of positions. As a matter of fact, The Only Niggro On The Team usually doesn't catch. And The Only Niggro On The Team is never the pitcher."

"Why is that?"

"Well, we want to make sure The Only Niggro On The Team is in the lineup every day, obviously. He's our fastest player by far, and our most versatile. Like I said, I wish we had more just like him. Maybe we could clone The Only Niggro On The Team, so we would have a whole team just like him."

"Of course, in that case you'd have a hard time telling them all apart."

"That's right. They would all look alike, wouldn't they? . . . Hey, I want you to check somebody out – that guy running sprints in the outfield. That guy's A God-Damn Fairy."

"What position does he play?"

"We like to always have A God-Damn Fairy in the outfield."

"And why is that?"

"Because A God-Damn Fairy can really fly."

Barry cracked up one last time as he delivered his final line. He looked up from the script and saw three stone-faced adults staring blankly at him and Teach. "Well," he demanded, "wasn't that funny as hell? Tommy finally did something with his time that I can appreciate, and you all are just sittin' there like a, like a bunch of, like the three blind mice or those three blind monkeys – what the hell am I trying to say, Tommy?"

"I don't know, Dad. . . . See no evil, hear no evil, speak no evil?"

"Yeah, that's it! Those three god-damn monkeys."

"Well, honey," Beth said, getting up from the couch, "it was your birthday present from Tommy – I mean, Teach – so as long as you enjoyed it, that's all that matters."

Robbie and Cheryl stood to go with Beth. "Jesus Harry Christ," Barry said, "if you all would just reach around behind you and pull those sticks out of your ass, then maybe I'd have enough kindling to start a nice fire – Jesus Christ!"

GAYS EVOKE DELIGHT

Practice Essay
By Heather Nicholas

I think the most courageous thing a person can do is to be honest about who you are and to speak out about it. It is also the one thing that will keep you from going insane. I know this from experience. I know I get on a lot of people's nerves because I am so outspoken about so many things, but if more people would follow my example, I think they would be less stressed out and could lead happier lives. But speaking out and being honest are not easy things to do. That is why it takes courage. People are afraid to be honest about themselves, and what makes it worse is that so many other people don't want you to be honest. They want you to lie about who you are because the truth makes them uncomfortable.

My favorite quote of all time is the one by Mr. Henry David Thoreau that says, "the mass of men lead lives of quiet desperation." That is so true, and so sad. Why are they desperate? And why are they quiet? It is because they desperately want to speak out, but they feel they can't, so they must remain quiet. And this is the recipe for insanity.

I know I annoy people because I talk a lot about being a lesbian. They say, "I don't care if you're a lesbian, but why can't you just be quiet about it?" Well, I was quiet about it for a long time, and I was miserable. And I know many people today who are quiet about it because they are afraid of what will happen if they come out, and this quiet desperation is driving them crazy, and, in many cases, killing them.

You don't just wake up one morning and suddenly realize you're a lesbian. You would, I suppose, if that was what society considered normal. Because puberty hits you really hard and those feelings you've never had before come washing over you like a flood. But you are so programmed by society to expect certain things, that if you find yourself feeling something different than what you expected, then it takes a long time to sort everything out. First, you go into denial about what you're feeling, and then you start hoping these feelings are temporary and will go away. You just can't accept the fact that you're going to have to go through life so different than everybody else.

All that my girlfriends ever wanted to talk about was boys – so I talked about boys. You just play along. And you wonder how many other girls there are who are just playing along. And how do you find out? It's like you end up playing this really stressful game of chess with every person you know, and everyone you meet. Or it's like walking in a minefield. One wrong step, one miscalculation about what someone else is thinking, and boom! You just blew up a good friendship with someone. It was terrifying. I wanted to be honest and I didn't want to lie. But no matter how much you want to be honest with everyone, there are just so many things always pushing against you – things inside yourself and things outside in society – that you feel like a prisoner inside your own skin.

And as difficult as it is to come out to your peers, it's ten times harder coming out to your parents. Some people never do. I didn't know if there was any way they would ever accept the fact that their little girl was never going to grow up and marry a nice man and have a bunch of kids. But you want them to know. You don't like hiding things from your parents, especially something this important. You fantasize about just coming right out and telling them – walking into the living room and saying, "I have something I have to tell you," and then taking a deep breath, and then it's over. All the stress and fear and uncertainty will be over. But it took a long time before I could bring myself to do that. What is it that holds you back, when you know you would feel so much better if you could just be honest?

It's such a complicated situation. You try to think your way through it and you end up tying yourself in knots. I'm sure all the time I spent thinking and worrying about it was just another way to avoid dealing with it. But you do think about a lot of things. You sincerely don't want to hurt your parents. Even though their attitudes made me angry at

193

them, I guess I still had enough love and respect for them that I didn't want to hurt them. And part of it was an honest assessment of all the possible consequences. All the emotional turmoil it would cause – all the yelling and crying, and the very real possibility I would have to move out. I think there was also just fear of the unknown and a fear of change. Whenever you're contemplating a big decision in your life you try to imagine all the possible results, but the fact is you don't know how it will all turn out. All you know is that it will cause a big change in your life, for better or worse.

So how did I finally deal with it? Well, have you ever tried to tell someone something without actually telling them? Let me tell you, it will drive you nuts. In the past, whenever my mom or dad got on the subject of homosexuality and gay people going to Hell, I wouldn't say anything. I would act like I didn't even know what a gay person was. But now I would try to bring up the subject, just to test their reactions. I would say things like, "I met this new girl at school today and she said she was a lesbian." My dad would tell me, "You probably shouldn't spend too much time with her." My mom would treat it like a sign of the coming apocalypse. "I can't believe what kind of stuff goes on with kids nowadays – who knows where this world is headed." I would try to engage them in conversation about homosexuality. I thought the more I talked about it, the more accustomed to it they would become. They never took the hint and they never changed their views.

I had gotten some brochures from the guidance office about "Growing Up Gay" and "How Do I Tell My Parents?" I thought for sure if I left one or two of these pamphlets strategically placed on the dining room table or on my bed, they would be forced to deal with it. I waited for the bomb to go off. It never did. The brochures just disappeared from wherever I had put them. I found them in the garbage. So I did it again. And again. And again. It turned into this ridiculous battle of wills, where I would put "Was I Born Gay?" on the coffee table and dare my mom to throw it away. Which she would. It really was ridiculous. They just didn't want to deal with it.

But I guess I didn't really want to deal with it, either. Because after dropping all these clues, after all the conversations I started about homosexuality, after defending gay people until I was blue in the face, after all this, when my mom finally gave me the chance to tell her what I had been trying to tell her for two years, do you know what I did? I lied my ass off.

My mom called me into the living room one night, where I had placed "Am I the Only One?" on the sofa for the sixth time. She looked really sad and said, "Do you want to talk about this, Heather?" (Why did I have to put it there *six times* before she decided to say something?) I acted nonchalant and said, "Oh, those are just things they keep handing out at school."

She looked visibly relieved. "This is the kind of stuff they're giving you at school?"

"Yeah, mom. All the time."

"Every day, more and more, I wish we had home-schooled you."

So I stopped putting out the pamphlets, and I stopped talking about gay people, and the quiet desperation just grew and grew.

I felt like such a failure because I wasn't able to come out to my parents. I thought I had felt bad before, but now I felt about ten times worse. I went into a deep depression. You just can't imagine things ever changing in your life for the better. It just seems like a problem that will never go away. How could it? Your parents are never going to change. Society is never really going to change (although it has a little bit, thank God). And you know that you're never going to change. You hope you can just meet one person you feel comfortable enough around to come out to. I guess that's all that kept me going. I don't think I ever seriously considered suicide, although I don't know why. A lot of people in my situation commit suicide every day. The attitudes we have in this society about homosexuality are absolutely unbelievable. And these attitudes kill people every single day. That is why I'm so outspoken now about myself, and gay rights in general. If I can do one small thing to change people's ridiculous attitudes, then I feel like maybe I'm saving someone's life.

195

Anyway, I went into a deep depression and I didn't see any way out. I obviously wasn't ready to come out, or else I wouldn't have lied to my mom like I did. And I knew I didn't want to kill myself, although I didn't know why. So the problem I had now wasn't how to come out, but how can I live my life without coming out? I didn't know how, but I knew I needed to try.

I decided to put my sexuality on hold. After all, a person's sexuality is just one aspect of their life. I would just continue not dealing with it until I felt more like dealing with it. The difference now, I hoped, was that I wouldn't obsess over my sexuality and how different it made me feel. I would just turn that part of me off and worry about it later. So I threw myself into everything I could think of, just to keep from thinking about it. I played sports. I became an even better student than I already was. I ran for student council. I joined clubs. It all sounds quite wonderful, doesn't it?

Well, the problem is, you can't just turn your sexuality off like a faucet. You can't tell your sex drive to go take a vacation. Your sex drive doesn't want a vacation. It doesn't even want to take a day off. The more socially active I became, the more miserable I became. It was like having a dream where you know if you stop running you will be killed. You may not know what's chasing you – all you know is that if you stop or even slow down a little bit, then you will be caught by this monster and killed. This was a different kind of desperation. I was still being quiet, but I was desperately running. Running away from something. I really felt like I was going insane. I had never felt crazy before, like I was losing my mind. I knew what it was like to be incredibly angry and incredibly sad and depressed and frustrated. But this was different. I wasn't depressed any more. I wasn't sad. I wasn't even angry. I was even happy much of the time. But I was running and I couldn't stop. I started hyperventilating a lot, like I couldn't breathe. I had panic attacks and would just take off running. Wherever I happened to be at the time, I would just take off and not stop until the attack stopped. If a shark stops swimming it dies. That's how I felt.

I think what happens is people come to a point where they no longer believe that whatever they're doing now is better than what they're trying to avoid. You can go a long time living in quiet desperation and still feel it's better than the alternative. In my case, for a long time I ran and ran and ran until I started going insane, but at the same time I still thought it was better than coming out and having to deal with everything that entailed. But then the day came when I no longer believed that.

Nothing happened that was any different than the usual craziness I had been experiencing, but I just had a different reaction to it. I thought about that time when my mom had finally asked me about that brochure. Five times before she had thrown it away, thinking that was preferable to dealing with what I might tell her. But then the next time, number six, she reacted differently. She finally realized she couldn't keep throwing those brochures away forever. I think my mom's quiet desperation was that she desperately wanted to talk to me about this, to know the truth one way or another, but she was too afraid of what she might lose if she found out the truth about me. She might lose her daughter. But she got to the point where the not-knowing was worse than the knowing, so that was when she knew she had to talk to me about it.

So I came to that point myself, where I realized all the running away from my lesbianism was no longer preferable to confronting it and coming out about it. I no longer needed brochures sprinkled throughout the house to say what I needed to say. I told my parents myself. My mom started crying. My dad hit the roof. It was pretty much everything I had always feared would happen. My parents couldn't accept it. My mom said she would try to forgive me, which made me madder than if she had said she hated me. After several days where it felt like the house was going to cave in on top of us, I knew that I would have to leave. My parents didn't kick me out like I had always feared, but I made the decision myself to leave. I guess it was another situation where the uncertainty of the future was a better option than the reality of the present.

I was always so afraid that I would be crushed by the rejection of my parents. I had loved them so much as a child and had always wanted to please them. But when I saw firsthand how twisted they had become, how they had let something which was completely out of my control

197

totally control their life and their opinion of me, I realized something very important. None of this was my fault. Their anger and ignorance and intolerance were not my fault. It had nothing to do with me. I had thought it had everything to do with me, but it had nothing to do with me. I had tried to educate them. I had tried to meet them half way. I had tried to live the life they wanted me to live, just to make them happy, and it nearly drove me insane.

I had been so afraid that people's rejection of me would destroy me. What I learned was that it only made me stronger. It wasn't the rejection that made me stronger – I would much rather be accepted than rejected – but just the freedom of knowing now that I'm not responsible for other people's ignorance. I am responsible, I believe, for trying to undo their ignorance, but it's not my fault if I fail. I take it upon myself to try to educate people, to point out the error of their ways – and that pisses people off. Which is why I ended up leaving high school. I lost a lot of friends because of my new attitude. Nobody likes to be told they're ignorant or wrong. But I also believe it's everybody's job to try to improve society as much as they can, and the only way to improve society is to educate it. So I go around pissing people off every day. But it's so much better than being quiet.

You and Cait are in the library, up in the stacks, late in the evening. You came up here to study, but instead, you're playing hide and seek. Cait's hidden herself really good this time. You've looked down each row of stacks and in each study carrel along the back wall. You start back down the stacks, thinking she is being devious and is moving as you move, never letting you get close enough to see her. You start to whisper-call her name, annoying everyone else trying to study. The only other places you haven't looked are two private offices, which are dark inside, and which you didn't try to open, until now, assuming they were locked. There is one, however, which is not locked. You enter and there is a small glow of red light coming from a sensor on the ceiling. You see a shadowy figure, dimly red, in the far corner. The figure says nothing as you approach, but steps around the office desk and into a darker corner. You wonder, just briefly, if you could get expelled for this. You quickly go back and lock the office door from the inside. When you return to Cait, she is taking off her clothes. Neither of you says a word. You allow her to undress you and you lay together on the office carpet. Neither of you has spoken a word. The silence is the excitement.

You leave the office a half hour later, going back to your table to resume studying for your finals.

ON SATURDAY MORNING, after a campfire breakfast, Charles said he wanted us to wade downstream to a good fishing hole he knew about. The river looked especially low and I could see rocks everywhere poking their heads out of the water. We waded into the river and had no trouble walking out into the middle of it. We shouted bye to Charles's father on the riverbank. We walked with the current, the water cool against my calves. I was careful, though – the rocks along the river bottom were slippery, and if I shuffled along and didn't pick up my feet I could easily break a toe against one of them.

To get to Charles's fishing spot we had to walk down a miniature rapid, wildly rock-strewn. More than once the stones shifted under my feet as I almost fell down and my leg muscles strained to stay upright. "Shit. God dammit," I said more than once. Charles laughed in his sweet, high-pitched way and said, "You're crazy, man." It seemed to take a long time to get to where Charles wanted us to go.

At the foot of the mini-rapids was a large, calm pool, with sand now to stand in. This was where we cast our lines – Charles nonchalantly, me with the concentrated effort of a novice. Charles loved to go fishing, but it was far too solitary a pastime for me to enjoy. But I was more than happy to spend the weekend on the river with him.

We held our fishing poles and stared out into the river in a relaxed silence for a long time. I followed Charles's lead and occasionally reeled my line in a little or moved it around in large circles. Charles and I had not talked about what happened at school three days ago, except to imply that that was the whole reason for this fishing trip. He had said he wanted to come down to the river so he could get out of the house and "get all this shit out of my head." It was Charles who first broached the subject, though at the time I didn't realize he was doing so. "Do you ever have any trouble with girls?" he asked, at the same time that I had a different question of my own.

"Does this river even have any fucking fish?" I said, getting tired of holding a fishing pole without any results.

"Sure it does. It takes time to get a bite. . . . See if you can stand your pole up." He demonstrated by stabbing his rod into the sandy bottom of the pool we were standing in, the water up to my waist and up to Charles's shirtless navel.

"Hell yeah, I like standing my pole up," I joked. I jabbed my rod into the river bottom beside his and tried to find a comfortable spot to sit down amongst all the rocks gathered at the foot of the mini-rapids we had descended. I sat, and the cold shallow water didn't even cover my thighs.

"So, do you ever have any trouble. . . with girls?" Charles repeated. He never asked me about girls. This was probably the first time he had ever done so. It was as if the very mention of the subject terrified him.

I didn't know what he meant, but since it was the first time he had asked such a question, I tried my best to answer it. "Yeah, man. I have a lot of trouble with girls. That's why you break up with them. . . . They become a pain in the ass after a while."

"That's not really what I mean."

"Then what the fuck do you mean?"

"I mean – with your dick. With it working."

I burst out laughing. Charles was sitting beside me, staring down into the water. "Trouble with my dick?" I laughed again. Charles was trying to smile, or trying not to cry, his lips pursing a little. "No, man. . . . You don't have to worry about that. . . . Your dick will work just fine." In my still-limited experience, in the throes of puberty, that was how I understood things to be. Erections, and everything that followed, were just natural bodily responses. If you get cold, you shiver. If you get hot, you sweat. I wanted Charles to understand this – that he had nothing to be afraid of. Charles was still staring into the water. I stood up into the pool, looked around behind me and picked up several small rocks to throw out along the length of the river. I was happy he was moving on from the embarrassment of earlier in the week, with everyone who had seen the drawing. His worries now were back to being the typical Charles concerns: he would worry about passing a test – but make an A; he would worry about batting against a hard-throwing pitcher – but get a hit; he would worry about being late for class – but be one of the first in the room. And now he was worried about his dick not working.

I wasn't able to tell him this, but I was very proud of him for overcoming his fear and cutting class and going into the woods with Tonya. "It sucks about what happened," I said.

"Yeah."

"What did happen, anyway?"

Charles pounded the palms of his hands into the water, making two loud splashes. "I don't want to talk about it, man. I didn't come out here to talk about this shit."

Why didn't I return to throwing my rocks silently downriver – throwing them so far I sometimes lost sight of where they landed? Why didn't I lie back against the rocks and let the water flow loudly over my ears and close my eyes against the sun? Why didn't I go for a swim, out beyond where our lines were cast, out as far as the river would let me swim, until the tranquil pond turned back into riverflow? Why didn't I allow ourselves to return to our silence of a few moments ago, when we were listening to birds and the trickling water and whatever thoughts happened to come into our heads? Charles said he didn't want to talk about it. Why didn't I, for once in my life, just let Charles have his way?

"Which one was it?" I asked.

Charles looked at me, puzzled. "Huh?"

"Was it Livingston or Rudley?" We had two SROs. I could see Charles thinking, trying to make sense of my question.

"What?" Charles said, with a sharp edge of annoyance in his voice.

"I was just wondering which one it was. I figured that's what happened." Charles didn't respond. I'm sure he was satisfied to let me think whatever I wanted to think, as long as he didn't have to tell me the truth.

"I can't believe we haven't had a bite yet. . . . We can go on back if you want to," Charles said.

"What I want is for you to tell me what the fuck happened, so I don't have to keep guessing." Charles had seemed so genuinely puzzled when I mentioned the SROs that I concluded I must have been wrong about them. So I continued to try to imagine what could have transpired out in the woods. A much more obvious explanation quickly occurred to me. "You chickened out, didn't you?" Charles was reeling in his line. He didn't say anything. "You fuckin' chickened out again." I picked up another rock and heaved it as far as I could. "You didn't let Tonya do anything, did you? I bet you didn't even unzip your fuckin' pants, did you?" I thought I had it all figured out now. Charles saw Tonya, freaked out, and probably ran out of the woods faster than he had run into them. And rather than coming back to class late, being counted tardy and subjecting himself to my ridicule, he would have gone to the front office and checked himself out for the day, feigning sickness, and then walked all the way home. So that meant for two days in a row he had walked, or run, home, in shame. "You're such a god-damn chickenshit. You're never gonna get laid, man – you're never gonna get fuckin' laid. You're gonna be a god-damn virgin your whole fuckin' life. . . . Man, you need to stop being such a fuckin' chickenshit."

Charles could always surprise me with his quickness. He pounced on me like a cat. He knocked me off my feet and we both went underwater. We found our footing again and he immediately tried to push me back down.

"I hate you!" he screamed. "You don't know fuckin' anything!" His voice sounded as if he was crying, but with all the water dripping from his face, I couldn't tell. It was hard to fight in the waist-deep water. I was angry at being attacked, but I was still fighting defensively. I tried to hold on to Charles, but he was struggling desperately, kicking me underwater, punching blindly, grunting loudly. I had been that way before, and have been since – insane with a rage beyond control, when, after it subsides, you wonder how it's possible the other person is still alive. Were your hands not strong enough to choke the life out of him? Were your fists too weak to pound him to death? Or maybe he was just lucky, because it certainly wasn't because you wanted him to live – not at that moment when your thinking mind had stopped functioning and you were nothing more than a wild, wounded animal. I wasn't at that point, but Charles clearly was. He kicked my leg hard enough so that I lost my balance. He pushed me and I fell. I thrashed about and struggled to regain my footing. I was near panic, because in his unthinking fury if he gained the upper hand and trapped me underwater, I would be in real danger. Charles put all his weight on me and drove my head and chest underwater.

This was that moment for him – when he didn't really give a damn whether I lived or died. I became desperate. Charles was still standing – standing between my legs and holding me underwater by my wrists. I felt my legs kicking in the air above me. Charles had my arms pinned to my sides. I was almost upside down underwater. I was helpless and I couldn't hold my breath much longer. With a desperate adrenaline surge, I wrenched my body sideways and in doing so my leg must have caught the side of Charles's head. He lost his grip on my wrists and I splashed wildly in the water until I felt the sand once again under my feet.

All I wanted to do was escape. I was gasping for air as I struggled to climb out of the pool and onto the rocky footing of the rapids. Charles yelled at me, "You son of a bitch! You fuckin' coward! You're the fuckin' chickenshit! You're the fuckin' chickenshit!" As I started walking away, back up the river but only a few feet from Charles, a rock whizzed past my head. Before I could turn around, a second rock hit me on the neck. I grimaced in pain and reflexively grabbed the back of my neck.

I whirled around, my chest burning, and noticed the rocks lying all around me. This, I know for sure, was not one of those moments of blind, unthinking fury. What I did next may have looked instantaneous, instinctive, but I know I took time – a sufficient second of time – to think about it. The rocks were of different shapes and sizes, and as I leaned down I know I took at least enough time to grasp only the one I wanted. There were much smaller stones all around, but I didn't choose any of them. In that second of decision I knew which one I needed.

202

And I knew exactly where I was throwing it, and I knew I wouldn't miss. I drew my arm back. I still had time. I had plenty of time within my shoulder and within my wrist. Time to stop my arm, to change the trajectory. And I had time to see the strange look on Charles's face. His brow was furrowed and his lips were puckered slightly. Was it a steely look of determination or a pitiable one of surrender? He held out his hands, wrists up, palms outward. As with his expression, I've never known what to make of this. It looked like a gesture of surrender, a begging for mercy; but it also looked like his pose as a catcher, waiting to receive a pitch.

Charles, why didn't you catch it? Why didn't you use those cat-like reflexes to catch it? You were the best catcher I ever had. Nothing got by you. In the outfield, nothing got by you. It would have hurt your hands. The rock would have stung your palms mightily. But you could have caught it. This was your chance to prove, once and for all, that you were better than me in every way, even as an athlete. Why didn't you catch it, Charles?

But my decision had been made and in a flash the rock flew from my fingers, past Charles's hands, and into his suddenly shattered temple. Because of the sound of the water trickling over the stones I didn't hear any thud of impact, and Charles didn't call out or scream or make any noises that I recall, but I saw his head snap back and I saw him wobble slightly and fall forward.

As soon as I had thrown the rock, I lunged toward him in helpless fear as he fell forward. I clutched him as he started sliding down into the pond. I turned him over and was shocked at the mealy flesh and the pulsing blood. I knew I had to get him back upstream. I struggled to pick Charles up and had trouble walking, kicking against the current and stumbling on the unseen rocks underfoot. My only thought was to get him back to his dad.

I had a long way to carry him. I tried to walk fast, but I kept tripping over rocks and my feet kept sliding out from under me. I didn't want to fall and drop him. His blood poured down the side of his face, over my arms and into the water.

Charles's unopening eyes and unexpressive mouth terrified me, but as I neared the bend in the river, beyond which I would be able to see our campsite, the thought of him regaining consciousness suddenly began to frighten me as well. How could he ever forgive me for what I had done? In his shame over what had precipitated our fight, Charles may have chosen to lie or to remain silent about what had happened between him and Tonya, but his dad and many others would insist on knowing what had just transpired between him and me. Would he lie about that as well? Would he lie about it, as I have lied to everyone since – to his father, the authorities, my family, and to everyone else who wanted to know what had happened to Charles that morning? All I knew for certain, from almost ten years spent with him, was that Charles was a much better person than I would ever be.

I was breathing very heavily. I tried to summon the courage to scream for help, to get Charles back to his father, to face whatever consequences awaited me.

But I chose to do something else.

I knew that Charles's father was up ahead, out of view now but just around the river's bend. I remember thinking: *I have to stop the bleeding,* thinking also, that as soon as I stop the bleeding and Charles regains consciousness, we can then talk about what had happened – right here, calmly, with Charles's head resting in my hands, and all could be forgiven. I kneeled into the river and set Charles's body down into the shallow water, cradling his head in my left palm. I pressed my right palm as hard as I could into his wound, which worked for only a moment to staunch the blood flow. I began to panic as Charles's blood continued to flow heavily around my hand and to drip off my fingers into the river. I quickly maneuvered my legs into a crouch and set his head on my thigh. I now used my left hand, as well as my right, to apply more pressure to Charles's wound. I pressed his head hard between my hands and my stomach. The blood flow was slowing, but Charles's eyes remained closed. I began to cry. I was afraid to release my hands' pressure that was holding back the blood. My tears dripped steadily onto Charles's face.

How long did I remain in this position, waiting, expectantly, then hopelessly, for Charles to open his eyes? I don't know, but shaking in terror, I eventually removed my trembling hands from around Charles's lifeless face and used them now to cradle Charles's body and to rock him in my arms like a baby.

Minutes later, my body shivering and convulsing with sobs, I rose slowly and carried Charles to his father.

You and Cait are on the soccer practice field tossing a baseball. She is wearing your baseball cap from high school and your baseball glove. The glove seems almost too heavy for her. You are catching her throws bare-handed. She throws the ball with her right arm with the same motion and ability that you would have throwing it left-handed. You started out tossing the ball to her underhand, but she threw it back to you as hard as she could and told you to throw it like a real man, though you can't bring yourself, even overhand, to throw it any harder. She occasionally drops one of your tosses or misses it altogether. She turns around and runs with a little added skip as she retrieves it.

There have been many times when you were with Cait that you felt tears welling up. Tears of happiness. Tears in recognition of this miraculous gift you have been given – the gift of Cait. After four miserable years of high school, after two numb, listless years here, to meet Cait. It is too good to be true. You don't deserve to have this happening to you. You had no idea it was even possible to be this happy. This time, however, rather than blinking your eyes and clenching your jaws until the tears subsided, you let them go. You look at Cait smiling, wearing your cap and your glove, and you just let the tears go. Cait runs over to you, almost panicked, to ask you what is wrong. You smile as tears fall to the ground and you tell her everything is fine, everything is wonderful. She kisses your tears and tells you that she feels the same way. You kiss her with all your strength and you embrace each other completely. Soon, you unclench your hug, sniffle, smile sheepishly and tell her to go back and get ready to catch one of your fastballs. You're okay now. Everything's okay.

YOU AND CAIT ARE in the cafeteria. Neither of you can stop talking about all the great things you will be doing in Europe together. You have never been so excited in your life. Graduation is only a month away. Cait has known about this trip for four years. Her dad promised to pay for her to travel through Europe after she graduated. However, he didn't promise to pay for two people. But Cait told him last week that she didn't want to go without you and, being daddy's girl, another promise was easily extracted from him. So, the only thing bothering you, and only slightly, is the added expense you will be causing. Two can travel almost as cheaply as one, Cait assured you. Just be sure to thank my dad profusely, she had said, adding, he's really looking forward to seeing you again, Tommy. You try to keep all your excitement focused on the trip, but you can't help but also contemplate your wonderful future together. Cait will be moving to California to attend Stanford Law, and you plan to go with her and do – whatever. You can't afford law school, at least not at California prices, so you assume you'll land some teaching job, teaching something, somewhere. Cait seems as excited as you about the two of you living together. There seems to be nothing but bliss in your future. Neither of you are far-sighted enough to mention marriage, but you see no reason why it won't happen.

"I think I'm looking forward to being in France the most," Cait says. You are holding hands across the table.

"*Oui, oui.*"

"The *Louvre.*"

"*Oui, oui.*"

"The *Champ d'Elysee.*"

"*Oui, oui.*"

Cait, unlike you, has taken French, but you both now begin speaking with comical French accents.

"Your French is excellent, monsieur."

"So, you like my *oui oui,* mademoiselle?"

"Yes, very much."

"*Oui oui.* But it's not *oui oui.* You will see. My *oui oui.* My *oui oui* is not *oui oui* at all. *Oui oui?*"

Cait makes a fist and wiggles her thumb in the air. "Monsieur, do you like my *pouce?*"

You laugh. "Your what?"

"My *pouce.* It is a very nice *pouce,* no? It goes well with monsieur's *oui oui.*"

Someone is coming up to your table. You know her. "What are you two lovebirds over here laughing about? Whenever I see you two you're always laughing about something."

You push back your chair and stand. You retain your faux French accent as you say, "Mademoiselle, the world is but to laugh at. What else is there but to cry?" You take this person's hand and kiss it, as you imagine a French nobleman would.

"Hi, Cait," the girl says, as you start kissing her up and down her bare arm.

"Hi, Jenny."

"Tommy, I think you're embarrassing Cait. . . . Tommy." You put your arm around Jenny's waist.

"Madame Cait may be my bride, but *Jhen-nee,* you are my *mees-tress.*" You dip Jenny at the waist, low to the ground. She shrieks out with surprise. You kiss her fully on her lips. You are standing in front of Cait's chair. You hold the kiss until you and Jenny are again standing erect. Many people sitting around you applaud and catcall your antics. You turn around and bow dramatically, with a flourish of your arms.

"Wow," Jenny says, "where did that come from?"

You drop your silly French accent. "I'm so excited. Cait and I are planning our big overseas trip. . . . You wanna come with us? The more the merrier."

"Uh, I think not," Jenny says. "I better go before you attack me again. How can you put up with this guy, Cait?" Jenny waves to you and Cait as she walks away.

"Are you quite finished?" Cait says. "Can we go now?"

Cait stands to leave.

"What's wrong?" you protest, as you bus your trays. "C'mon, Cait, I'm sorry. I was just having a little fun."

Cait is silent as you two begin the walk back to your dorm. You say, "I got a little carried away, honey. I'm sorry."

"It's okay. Don't worry about it."

"Are you mad at me?"

"No, Tommy, I'm not mad."

"Good. I'm glad I didn't mess anything up. I do really stupid things sometimes, don't I? . . . I'm really sorry about what I did back there, Cait." You clumsily kiss Cait as you are both walking. She accepts your peck on the cheek but gives you nothing in return. "Do you forgive me?"

"You didn't do anything to be forgiven for, Tommy. . . . I said don't worry about it."

"I love you, Cait."

"I love you, too."

"What do you want to do tonight?"

"I don't know. What do you want to do?" Cait says, without any enthusiasm.

"I think that depends a lot on whether Rodney is home."

Cait says nothing.

You walk along in silence for what seems like a long time.

"I thought you said you weren't mad at me."

Cait sighs. "Tommy, for the last time. I'm not mad at you. Can we please just drop it?"

"Then why aren't you talking to me?"

"What do you want to talk about?"

"We could start with this fucking attitude you're giving me."

Cait stops in her tracks. "Don't you say another word to me. Not right now."

Your happiness has evaporated. You've apologized at least twice, yet she won't kiss you. She says she isn't mad, yet she obviously is. She says she loves you, but she isn't showing it. You were ecstatic, joyous, on top of the world, just a few minutes ago. And now Cait's ruined it. Ruined it with her hypersensitivity, her refusal to accept an apology, her determination to rub your face in your mistakes and to make you feel like shit.

All you had wanted to do was to apologize and start having fun again. But Cait wants to fight. Okay, if Cait wants a fight, then she'll get a fight.

You continue to fume as you walk in silence toward your dorm. All you had wanted to do was apologize. But there will be no more apologies now. You prepare yourself for a long night ahead.

You arrive back at your dorm. You both look miserable. You walk slowly. You don't look at each other.

207

You are back in your dorm room. Rodney, as usual, is gone. Cait goes over to your desk and sits in its plastic-backed chair. You shut the door behind you, and then sit on your bed. You push yourself against the wall, and shove two pillows angrily behind your back.

"Okay, Cait. Tell me what I did to fuck up this time. I know you've been waiting to tell me."

"I haven't been waiting to tell you anything. But I know you've been waiting to yell at me."

"I had to wait – you made me. I was under a gag order, remember?"

"Tommy, please don't make a big deal out of this, okay, but I can tell you're not going to give this thing a rest until I tell you what was wrong in the cafeteria. Just promise me you won't make a big deal out of it."

"How can I tell whether it's a big deal or not until I know what it is?"

"Okay, Tommy, whatever. Let's just get this over with. . . . The problem, sweetheart, is that you can be so insensitive sometimes."

"I said I was sorry."

"What were you thinking?"

"I was just so happy, Cait. I do stupid things sometimes without thinking. I was just so damn happy. I was just trying to spread some of the joy I was feeling. . . . Why do you have such a problem with that?"

"You kissed her right in front of me, Tommy."

"I'm really sorry, honey. I wasn't thinking. I know how that must have made you feel. I know if that had been me sitting there – if one of your old boyfriends came over and you planted a big ol' wet kiss on him – my God, there's no telling how I would have reacted. But it wouldn't have been pretty to watch. . . . So I can't blame you for being jealous."

"I wasn't jealous. That's not what this is about."

"Then what the hell is it about? If you're not jealous, then what's the fucking problem?"

"This is the problem, right here, the way you are right now. . . . Clueless. Completely insensitive –"

"I'm not insensitive! I just told you that I knew exactly how you were feeling and how sorry I was for doing that to you. I was putting myself in your shoes, trying to see things from your perspective. How is that being insensitive, for God's sake?"

"You're *trying* to be sensitive, sweetheart, I appreciate that, but you just don't get it."

"Then what is it I'm not getting? Why don't you just tell me what's bothering you and stop trying to make me look like an idiot."

"The problem, Tommy, is that I don't think you have any idea, at any time, what it is that I may be feeling. Your idea of understanding someone is just putting yourself in their shoes – but it's still just you. It's still just you, imagining them having the same emotions you would be having in the same situation – but I'm not going to be having the same emotions as you. . . . The only thing you could possibly imagine being wrong back there was me being jealous – just because that's how you would be feeling. . . . Tommy, I don't care if you were cavorting around a little bit with Jenny. I couldn't care less. But you were doing it *right in front of me*. It was like I wasn't even there."

"So you were jealous. Why don't you just admit it? You just don't want to admit that maybe you do have the same emotions as a troglodyte like me."

"No, Tommy, I wasn't jealous. I wasn't. I was just annoyed. It was just very annoying having to sit there and witness that spectacle. But the point is, it wouldn't have mattered to you one way or another. Whether I was jealous or not – you still would have done the same thing. You didn't think, for one second, about how it might affect me, did you? That's what I mean by you being insensitive, Tommy – it was like I wasn't even there."

"So what am I supposed to do?" You bound off your bed. "Ask your permission before I do anything like that? 'Pardon me, Cait, so sorry to bother you, but I would like to have a spontaneous outburst of emotion right now, if that's all right with you, dear?'. . . This is such bullshit!"

"Tommy. Tommy. You need to calm down, okay? Remember what we talked about last time? You need to control yourself, sweetheart."

"So now I can't even get angry? What am I allowed to do, Cait? You've gotta let me get angry. I've gotta let this shit out."

"But why are you so mad? It's not that big a deal. It's not. I wasn't even mad at you."

"Then why do you say those horrible things about me? Like, I'm insensitive. That I'm clueless. That I can't possibly understand you. You're so complex and sophisticated, and I'm such a dolt. Where do you get off saying those things? It all comes back to what I was worried about last time – you don't think I'm good enough for you."

"Tommy, God dammit. You're the only one who believes that. *You* don't think you're good enough for me. This is just your insecurities coming through. Let's just please stop this ridiculousness, before it gets out of hand."

"Ridiculousness? Out of hand? First of all, who are you to say this is ridiculous? It's only ridiculous to you now because I'm fighting back. It certainly wasn't ridiculous to you when you stormed out of the cafeteria in a huff. It was a high and mighty principle then. . . . And what's getting out of hand? Just because I'm angry, and defending myself, and raising my voice a little bit? This is not out of hand. This is what couples do when they fight. . . . I'm not going to hit you, Cait, if that's what you're worried about. . . . Are you still afraid of me?"

"Yes I'm afraid of you! Look at you! You're stalking around the room like a madman. . . . Tommy, you need to listen to me. Will you please just listen to me for a minute? Will you just sit down, and be quiet, and listen to what I have to say?"

You sit down angrily on the edge of your bed, bouncing hard on it twice. Cait gets up from her chair and sits beside you. She turns her entire body to face you, crossing her legs on the bed. "We've been talking about how much fun we're going to have in Europe and everything, right? Well, we will have a lot of fun, but you know, this will also be a very stressful trip at times. With all the travel and train schedules and looking for cheap places to stay, and having to watch our money and not always being able to take a shower or eat or go to the bathroom when we need to. Are you ready for that?"

"Of course. Of course I'm ready. None of that will be a problem, Cait, as long as we're together, right?"

"Sweetheart, I have to be honest with you. With the way you're acting – Tommy, look at me – Tommy, with the way you act sometimes when we disagree about things, I'm starting to have second thoughts about – about whether it's a good idea for us to go on this trip together."

"What are you saying, Cait?"

"Well, I'm just saying, I'm starting to have second thoughts. I'm worried, that's all."

"Worried about us, or just the trip?"

"Well, just the trip. That's all I was thinking about right now. That's all we have to worry about right now."

You feel dizzy, almost nauseous. "I want to go with you, Cait. Please let me go with you." You feel tears welling in your eyes. You try to control them, but they start running down your cheeks. "Please, Cait, let me go with you. Please."

Cait uncrosses her legs and sits up straight. "Good God, Tommy, don't start this. All I said was that I was having second thoughts. I want us to have a mature discussion about this. . . . Would you please stop all this blubbering? You're overreacting. As usual."

You explode off your bed. You scream, "What do you want from me?" You move quickly toward Cait. You are right up in her face. "In the cafeteria I got too happy! We come back here and I get too angry!" Cait retreats on the bed until her back is against the wall. "Then you make me cry so now I'm too sad!" Your face is red. Spit sprays from your mouth. "I can't be too happy around you! And I can't be too angry! And I can't be too sad!" You grab a textbook from off your desk and throw it heavily against the wall. "What the hell do you want from me!"

"I want you to fuck me."

You look at Cait, stunned.

"I want you to fuck me, baby. Right now. I want you to fuck me as hard as you can."

Your anger disappears. "Are you serious?" Cait is taking off her shirt. As soon as her shirt is off, she removes her bra. You glance to make sure your door is shut. "What about Rodney?"

"Fuck Rodney." Cait is pulling off her panties by the time you are able to get your shoes off.

You take off your pants and underwear. You don't bother taking off your shirt. You fall heavily on top of Cait, causing the bed to squeak. As you writhe on top of Cait, she whispers into your ear, "Tommy, my darling, we don't ever have to fight again. We'll just fuck. Whenever we get angry at each other, we'll just fuck. Whenever you get angry with me, we'll just fuck. Does that sound like a good deal? Is that a deal, baby? Is that a deal?"

Yes, it is.

You and Cait are in Boston, in her bedroom. You have been down on her floor performing, to the complete satisfaction of you both, your favorite sexual maneuver – the wondrous 69. You discover another hair in your mouth. Or maybe it's the same one. It's been at least thirty minutes since you retired to the bed and you're still finding Cait's hairs in your mouth. You're in no hurry to remove it. You play with it with your tongue, rolling it along your teeth, being careful not to lose it again somewhere between your gums. You are sitting up with your back against her headboard; Cait is lying with the top of her head pressed tightly into your side, her cheek high on your thigh, her arms secure around you. She is asleep. You gently stroke her hair. Her nude body is curled beside you. In how many ways can you experience this love? You see Cait: you watch in the dimmed lamplight as her chest rises and falls with each breath; you touch Cait: you softly move your fingertips down her back and over her buttocks, careful not to awaken her; you hear Cait: you close your eyes and listen – in the room's stillness you can hear her gentle breathing. You see Cait, you touch Cait, you hear Cait. You can also still smell her in your nostrils and taste her in your mouth – regardless of what you do, it's all the same: it's all love. The feeling is the same regardless of which sense you use to experience her: it's all love. You realize that for the past ten months you have felt nothing but love around Cait; you have experienced

211

nothing but love with Cait. This can't last forever, can it? Can it? How can you and Cait not last forever? So how will you next experience your love for her? Will you sit here in bed and stroke her hair until you, too, fall asleep? Will you sit here until Cait's beauty arouses you anew and you gently awaken her to make love again? Will she stir and sit up so you can cuddle and talk and laugh until the day breaks? It doesn't matter: it's all love.

On school days, you always meet Cait in the lobby of her dorm about thirty minutes before one of you has to be in class. You then walk together to the cafeteria for breakfast. This morning, however, Cait is late coming down to meet you. You ask Stacy, the receptionist, to buzz Cait. "Cait? Tommy's down here waiting on you."

"I'm not feeling well. Tell him to go on without me." You can hear Cait through the intercom behind Stacy's desk. She does indeed sound sniffly.

You ask Stacy to push the intercom button again. "What's wrong, honey?" you say loudly, to make sure Cait can hear you.

"It's okay, Tommy. Just go on to class and then come back here. I'll see you then."

You eat breakfast alone and make it to class just before the professor enters. You will not hear much of what is discussed in class. You are still mesmerized by Cait – by what she did yesterday, while you were arguing. Did she really mean it? Fuck instead of fighting? Is this girl great, or what?

You have two classes, back to back, so you are not able to see Cait until eleven. Stacy pages Cait upon seeing you, without having to be asked. "Stacy, please let Tommy come on up. I'm still not feeling well." All male guests had to be escorted up the elevator and back down, but exceptions were always being made.

You get off the elevator and walk quickly to Cait's room, worried. When she opens the door, you are somewhat shocked by her appearance. She certainly doesn't look well. Her face is pale and puffy and her eyes are very red. She hugs you as soon as you enter, a long hug, full of affection. She turns her head sideways and buries it in your chest. She rubs your back. You hear her sniffle. Her roommate, whom you haven't acknowledged, says quietly, "I'll leave you two alone – I'll be right next door, Cait, okay?"

Cait lifts her head from your chest and nods. "Okay. Thanks, Amanda." Cait's roommate walks out and leaves the door open. Cait keeps her arms wrapped tightly around you.

"What's wrong, sweetheart? Are you having another allergy attack? Are you sick?"

Cait clings to you, her arms trying to pull you even closer. "I just want to hold you, that's all," she whispers hoarsely into your chest.

"Is everything okay? . . . Are you crying? What's wrong, baby?"

Cait releases her hug and takes you by the hand and leads you to her bed. You both sit down. Cait sighs deeply. "Tommy." She sighs again. "Tommy. . . . Before I say anything. . . . I want us to handle this like adults, okay?"

You are suddenly too afraid to speak.

"Tommy, I'm sorry, but things are not going to work out between us." Cait looks directly into your eyes. "What happened yesterday —" she looks down and sighs again. "It's not going to work out, Tommy. I'm sorry."

"I don't understand. What are you saying? The trip?"

"No, Tommy. Not just the trip. . . . Nothing. Nothing's going to work out."

"Why? What happened? What's wrong? Tell me what's wrong, Cait – I'll fix it. Whatever's wrong, I'll fix it – I swear. . . . We're not breaking up, are we?" You are gripping Cait's hand tightly. You want her to look at you, but her face remains bowed. She is squeezing your hand tightly, also. "We're not breaking up, are we?"

Cait doesn't speak for a moment. She does not look up. "Yes, Tommy. We're breaking up." Cait's face lunges forward, heaving with her sudden crying. Her sobbing is convulsive, uncontrolled, her face heaving forward with every hard, loud sob.

Cait continues crying, with the same intensity. She has buried her head in her hands. Her whole upper body shakes with her sobbing. "What can we do?" you ask. "What can we do, Cait? We can't just break up. . . . We haven't even talked about it. Where is all this coming from?"

Cait is making an effort to stop crying. "Your anger, Tommy. You scare me."

Your anger quickly rises. "How can I scare you, honey? I love you. . . . I love you. I love you more than I can ever tell you. You have no idea how much I love you. How can you possibly say I scare you? I'll never hurt you, Cait. Never. Never. I will never hurt you. . . . Why don't you believe me?"

"You will hurt me, Tommy. At some point, you will. I know you love me. I know you don't want to hurt me. I believe you, Tommy. . . . But you will hurt me. . . . You can't control it."

"I can control it! I'm not going to hurt you. I promised you I wouldn't hurt you. . . . C'mon, Cait. I promised. You said you believed me."

"Tommy, this is very hard for me. And I know it's really hard for you, too. But you have to respect my decision. . . . It's over, Tommy. It's over."

"How can you just say that? *It's over.* How can you just say that? We haven't even discussed it. How come you get to make that decision all by yourself? I come up here worried about you because I think you're sick, and you present me with this – this fait accompli. *It's over.* You don't get to make that decision by yourself, Cait. It's too important."

Cait's roommate peeks her head into the doorway. "Is everything okay, Cait?"

"Yes, Amanda, it's okay. I'll call you if I need you. Thanks."

"Okay. Just checking."

"What the fuck is this? You think you need a bodyguard now? . . . Do you have a security detail in the hallway, Cait? Do you have a sniper posted on the roof?"

"Stop it, Tommy. Don't make things worse than they already are."

"Jesus Christ. . . . What can we do, Cait? What can we do about this?"

"Tommy, I know this has come as a shock to you, but you're just going to have to accept it. I was up all night last night. This has been the hardest thing I've ever had to do –"

"Then you don't sound too sure about it. If it was such a tough decision. Why are you in such a rush to break up? What's the hurry? Let's talk about it some more – we've got a whole month left to go. I don't understand what the big rush is."

"Tommy, listen. We don't need to draw this thing out. That won't do either one of us any good. One more month won't change anything. . . . We just need to end it and try to move on."

"What's the big rush? I don't understand. What's one more month? . . . One month is a long time, Cait. Come on!"

"Tommy, please. I knew this would be hard on you, but you're making it so hard on both of us – harder than it has to be."

"What am I supposed to do? Make it easy for you? Am I supposed to make it easy for you to break up with me? Am I supposed to make it easy for you to break my fucking heart in two –"

"Tommy –"

"You're god-damn right I'm making it hard. You're god-damn right this is going to be the hardest thing you've ever done. I'm gonna make god-damn sure of that. I'm fighting for my life here, Cait. If you think I'm going to break up with the only girl I've ever loved in my whole fucking life, the only girl who's ever meant anything at all to me, the girl who means everything to me – if you think I'm going to break up with you without a fight –"

"Tommy – stop it!"

"No Cait, I'm not gonna stop it. I'm not gonna stop it until you give me a chance to talk to you about this. It's not fair! You can't just make that decision without talking to me. You have to give me a chance to –"

"No, Tommy – there's not gonna be another chance! I should have broken up with you the first time you hit me!" Cait is yelling now as well. "You're immature. You're violent. . . . I'm not gonna give you another chance to hit me."

In desperation, as Cait is yelling at you, you quickly pull off your shirt and unbutton your pants. "Let's fuck, baby. Come on."

"No, Tommy."

"Come on, Cait."

You remove your shoes and take off your pants.

"Come on, baby. This is what you said you wanted from now on."

You take off your underwear. You are naked, except for your socks. The door behind you is open.

Cait tries to leave the room by walking around you, but you grab her.

You are squeezing her arms tightly below her shoulders. She winces and tries to wrench herself away from you. "Come on, Cait, we have to fuck. That's our deal. We made a deal." You move your arms quickly from Cait's arms to her shoulders. You grip her shoulders near her neck and push down on her with all your strength, hoping she'll fall to her knees and take you in her mouth.

"Let go of me! You're hurting me!"

You release one of your arms but maintain your grip on Cait with the other.

Cait struggles to break free. She slaps you hard on the face.

Enraged, you clutch Cait again. You squeeze her arms tightly, so tightly your arms are trembling.

"Please let go!" Cait is crying. "Tommy! . . . Amanda! Amanda!"

You shake Cait. You shake her, you shake her, you shake her, you shake her.

As Amanda runs in you throw Cait backwards. You have no idea how hard you are throwing her, but at this instant you want to throw her as hard as you can. The force of your throw lifts Cait into the air and she hits her head heavily on the corner of her wooden dresser. She crumples to the floor. Blood is flowing from her forehead. Three other girls follow Amanda into Cait's room, running.

You are crying. "Cait, I'm sorry. I'm so sorry –"

"You fucking bastard!" Amanda yells at you.

"Cait, I'm so sorry. Please forgive me." Your tears fall down onto your naked chest.

Amanda yells to her friends, "Call Stacy! Call Stacy! Cait, Cait, can you hear me?"

You are muttering, almost under your breath, "Please forgive me. Please forgive me darling. Please forgive me sweet Cait."

215

"Cait, we're getting help for you. We're going to stop the bleeding for you."

"Please forgive me Cait. I'm sorry. I'm so sorry for everything. Please Cait."

"Megan! Grab some towels! Stacy – call 9-1-1, Cait's hurt. Quick!"

"I love you Cait. I love you darling. Sweet Cait. Please. Please forgive me."

"Cait, don't talk. Don't try to talk. Okay, sweetie, you're gonna be okay. We're gonna stop the bleeding."

As you continue sobbing, one of the girls in the room takes the blanket from Cait's bed and hands it to you. It is the same blanket you and Cait have so often shared. "Please cover yourself up," she says. You wrap Cait's blanket around your waist. You bend down to pick up your pants. You stare at Cait, who is also silently looking at you. You don't want to take your eyes off her. A large towel is wrapped around the top of her head. Your blind sobbing has subsided into a steady stream of tears. You can only see Cait clearly as you blink and clear the tears. "I'm sorry Cait. I'm so sorry. I love you."

"I know Tommy. I know. . . . You need to go now. I'm okay. I'll be okay. You can go now. It's okay."

You turn around and walk slowly away from Cait and past a large group of girls. When you get past everyone, you stop long enough to put your pants on. You keep Cait's blanket wrapped around your chest and back. As you are in the elevator you bring the blanket up to your face.

You inhale deeply.

4

Gun Everybody Down

TEACH WAS COMING OUT of the cafeteria holding a cup of coffee when he spotted James Henry walking slowly toward him across the commons. James had not been in class for two weeks. That amounted to ten straight absences, not to mention the other absences James already had accumulated during the semester. With any other instructor, this long stretch of absences, combined with his chronic tardiness, would have resulted in a suspension for the remainder of the semester for James – but Teach was not any other instructor, and as he watched James coming toward him he congratulated himself on his forbearance. Here was James, Teach assumed, coming back to class after God knows what kind of domestic crisis had precipitated his prolonged absence. Teach had seen this happen too many times with his students not to think it had happened again.

Sometimes they would come to him and say that they had been kicked out of their house by their parents, or maybe they were moving out on their own to escape their parents; or they had lost their license and the person they had been riding with totaled his car; or they had some kind of heavy shit going down they didn't want to tell Teach about, but they knew they needed to tell him something. Teach believed they were telling the truth, or at least their version of the truth. Maybe they were exaggerating how dire things were at home, or how difficult it was going to be to find a ride, but he believed they were telling the truth because he had gotten to know them five days a week for however long they had been in class, and he didn't have to know these kids long to understand how difficult and obstacle-strewn their lives were. And so what if one or two little shysters played him for a fool every now and then? If a kid lied to him, then he probably had a good reason to lie; Teach didn't take being lied to personally.

Then there were other kids, such as James, who didn't inform Teach that they were taking a hiatus. They didn't think they owed anybody any explanations, or didn't think Teach would believe them even if they told him the truth, or didn't have the social wherewithal to even know they were supposed to say something to somebody in charge, or maybe they didn't get out of county lockup until yesterday. But even those like James – who was headed his way now – those who had not cleared their extended absences with Teach beforehand, were granted forgiveness by Teach – simply because they returned. And because they returned, Teach granted forgiveness as well – by Randy. For every time he was admonished by Randy for keeping students on his roll who, by all rights, should have been suspended long ago, Teach could take Randy into his classroom and show him the most recent beneficiary of his mercy – a student who, had he been expelled from, say, Clara's classroom, would have been back on the streets, in jail, dead, or, more likely, at home playing video games all day; but, instead, was now back in class, working hard, his life in better order, and on track to get his GED. And as grateful as these students may have been to Teach, he was just as grateful to them, for justifying his faith in them and for justifying his teaching philosophy to himself and to Randy. And every student who returned, for whom Teach had bucked the system and broken the rules, was a Bronx salute to Clara and every hateful instructor just like her.

So now, as James walked even more slowly and robotically than usual toward him, Teach was feeling justifiably proud of himself. He strolled over to one of the large square pallets of bricks left behind from the Perpetual Paving Project, which also featured a lonesome shovel propped up against it. Teach set his coffee down on one of the bricks, and waited for James, in his methodical pace, to walk past him. He wanted to be the first to welcome him back to TCC.

James didn't acknowledge Teach's presence as he neared; he would have walked right past him if Teach hadn't spoken to him. Even then, Teach had to yell his name twice to get James's attention. James turned around, reluctantly, it seemed. "Mr. Henry! Welcome back. It's good to see you. Go on up to class – I'll be up in a minute."

James turned away from Teach and looked all around him, at the crowded commons, which was always bustling first thing in the morning. After this short pause to acknowledge, somewhat, Teach's presence, James continued on his way, leaving Teach scratching his head and chuckling to himself. As he took a sip of coffee and watched James walking away as slowly as a Hollywood zombie, he realized that although the weather was still October-warm and most everyone was wearing shorts and t-shirts, James was wearing his usual heavy black coat, which also seemed to be fitting a little more tightly than usual. He had a large backpack slung over his shoulder and had on the same camouflage pants he always wore. Teach stopped paying attention to James and checked his watch. He needed to get to class. He decided to finish his coffee first, however, as he took a larger sip than he preferred. He ogled a particularly spectacular blonde wearing a miniskirt as she sashayed across the commons. Teach saw a lot of gorgeous young women strolling across the commons – he saw more of them now than ever. Either young women were becoming more genetically flawless, he thought, or he was becoming more depraved. As he followed her with his eyes, his vision once again fell on James. James had stopped walking, perhaps fifty feet from where he had turned around and deigned to look at Teach.

Suddenly – very suddenly, considering how slowly James moved – James dropped his backpack, kneeled, and unzipped it quickly. As James arose, Teach heard the sounds before he realized where they were coming from. The popping sounds were followed immediately by screams. Since James had his back to Teach, it took him a moment longer than everyone else to figure out what was happening. As James turned slowly, as if in a turret, firing continuously, Teach fell to the ground behind the full pallet of bricks. He heard a sharp ping as one round ricocheted off a brick just above Teach's head. He heard one whiz over his head and another impact with the bricks protecting him. To his right there lay one brick on the ground that was within his easy reach. Teach stretched out and picked up the brick. As the shooting continued, Teach held the brick and moved his hand, wrist, and forearm up and down slightly, trying to acclimate them to its weight. He then started moving the brick up and down in his hand much more quickly, and higher and lower, until it felt lighter in his grasp. Teach stood up, stepped quickly around the pallet, and ran toward James, who continued to spray bullets as he walked away in the direction of the Adult Literacy Department.

People who have sudden, inexplicable, violent urges, and act upon them, often explain them in terms of *snapping*. The word *snap* was used many times during the next few days to help make sense of James's actions. But no one said that Teach snapped. Certainly not Teach. But Teach had always responded to threats and conflict reflexively, so perhaps he did experience a brief psychological break, a kind of reverse-snap, where these violent reflexes, so destructive in the past, were this time put to use in the service of good, rather than evil.

Teach ran until he felt instinctively comfortable with the throwing distance. As it turned out, the distance between Teach and James when Teach released the brick was roughly the same as the distance between Teach's old back-yard pitcher's mound and his tire swing. James's back had been turned to Teach as Teach was approaching him, but he turned around just as Teach prepared to throw the brick. Some combination of adrenaline, instinct, years of practice, muscle memory, and Teach's continual calibrations within his shoulder, arm, wrist, and fingers, as he ran toward James, ensured that the brick flew true to its target. James fired one round in Teach's direction as the brick slammed into his forehead. The bullet grazed Teach's side, a wound he didn't realize he had until several minutes later. James fell to the ground and dropped the gun he had in his hands. He had another one, however, slung over his shoulder, which scraped against the brick surface of the commons as James writhed on the ground with blood trickling from his forehead. Teach looked around as James rolled over and attempted to stand. He spotted the shovel resting up against the near side of the pallet of bricks he had hidden behind. He darted a distance of several yards over to the pallet, grabbed the shovel, and started running back to where James was sliding his auxiliary gun around off his shoulder and into firing position. Teach raised the shovel over his head as he ran, fully exposing his chest just as James squeezed the trigger for what turned out to be the last time. Teach brought the shovel down on top of James's head with a brutal force. James slumped to the ground and appeared to be dead, or at least unconscious, but Teach was taking no chances. He held the shovel high aloft, with his back arched, his arms stretched skyward, and his legs separated, knees slightly bent, as if frozen in mid-stride, ready to pound James again if he showed any signs of life whatsoever.

In the center of the commons, in a sudden silence punctuated by the moans and screams of the wounded, Teach, unmoving, statue-still, stood towering over James with his shovel raised high and poised to strike. Indeed, there were three separate angles of Teach's heroic pose which were cell-phone photographed by three brave persons who came out of hiding in the immediate aftermath of the attack, and of the three angles it would be hard for anyone to decide which one was most majestic, statuesque, and awe-inspiring. Within minutes, those three photographs raced around the internet and, within hours, television, turning Teach into an instant hero the world over.

There were twenty-four people wounded – fourteen seriously, three critically, and six, not counting Teach, who were grazed by bullets and treated and released from the hospital. One person was killed. The fatality was the blonde in the mini-skirt that Teach had eyed lecherously seconds before the attack. She had been at point-blank range when James opened fire. None of Teach's students were among the wounded. In fact, except for Teach (who, had he made it to class that day, would have been late, as usual), no one else associated with the Adult Literacy Department – neither student nor employee – was anywhere near the shooting. For once, the department's total lack of visibility and presence on campus, which Randy habitually bemoaned, could be seen as a blessed thing.

According to the official report on the shooting, using, among other things, all the ballistics information gathered concerning types and numbers of rounds fired and the types of guns used, the entire attack, from first trigger squeeze to last, lasted exactly fifty-eight seconds. A lot can happen in fifty-eight seconds (a Toxonomonomonee Minute, as Teach later called it). Teach's almost-instantly iconic shovel-pose over the fallen James ("Spade of Righteousness!", one tabloid called one of the images) may last forever in the annals of American photographic history (there was really nothing to compare it to – the combination of grace, menace, and coiled calm – but it reminded many of Rosenthal's Iwo Jima photo, though Teach is standing alone; or of Ali towering over Liston; and for many American historians, Curry's mural depicting John Brown in all of his righteous fury came to mind as they saw the three photographs for the first time); however, in reality, Teach was standing over James for much fewer than the fifty-eight seconds it took James to create all of the carnage. When the shooting began, Roscoe, the SRO, was in the cafeteria men's room pulling up his pants after completing the most inopportune bowel movement in recent American history. With the belt of his uniform pants still unbuckled and flapping as he ran, Roscoe got to the cafeteria door in time to witness Teach's heroic spade come crashing down. With gun drawn, he ran out to where Teach was standing vigilantly over James, took possession of James's gun and checked for a pulse. He found one, and had just finished handcuffing James when he regained consciousness. So, quickly relieved of his monolithic guard duty by Roscoe, Teach continued cutting his swath of heroism across the commons by moving around from victim to victim, offering whatever assistance and comfort he could. The police and ambulances soon arrived, quickly taking over the scene. With his adrenaline still pumping, Teach didn't feel the pain of his wound and when a bystander pointed to Teach's blood-soaked shirt, he was surprised to discover it was his own blood and not someone else's.

It wasn't long before the local news cameras were on the scene and Teach began his week-long immersion in celebritydom. Considering how emotion often takes precedence over facts, it was not surprising that the most common type of question asked of Teach was not, *Can you tell us what happened?*, but *Can you tell us how it feels?* Specifically, Teach was asked numerous times how it felt to be a hero. Teach being Teach, he was having no part of the standard aw-shucks, I-was-just-doing-what-anyone-in-my-place-would-have-done claptrap. There were many other potential heroes on the commons that morning, cowering behind pallets of bricks or running into buildings in panic. If he were just doing what anyone else would have done, then why didn't anyone else do it? How many lives did his actions save? How much courage did it take to do what he did? If heroes are so beloved, then why doesn't anybody want to be one? Or at least admit to wanting to be one? As Teach told one journalist, testily, at the end of another long, grueling day of travel and interviews, "Hell yeah I'm a hero. What's wrong with being a hero?"

Teach's irreverence made for good copy and great television, so Teach was even more in demand and more ubiquitous than most American fifteen-minuters. He was flown to New York and LA, put up in the best hotels, appeared as first guest on all the late-night talk shows and early morning news shows. He made a surprise walk-on appearance on Saturday Night Live and received a standing ovation. He met the president. He smashed the big gavel to open the New York Stock Exchange and joked that it was much lighter than a shovel. He was asked to be the guest referee on the popular new show, Celebrity Tag Team, where B-List celebrities were matched with professional wrestlers and participated in showy, choreographed matches. His greatest thrill was throwing out the first pitch at a Yankees game – a playoff game, no less. Unlike many people who are given this honor, Teach did not stand halfway between home plate and the mound. He walked up on the mound, toed the rubber, told the Yankees' catcher to assume his position, went into his old windup, and threw what could judiciously be called a minor-league fastball which was, if not right over the plate, then certainly too close to take with two strikes. For one solid week he was wined and dined, chauffeur'd and coiffeur'd; he rubbed elbows and glad-handed, he schmoozed and mingled.

And then it was over, except for all of the continued local interest and controversy. The school was closed for a week as all the various law enforcement agencies did their investigations, the media prowled around, the community tried to come to grips with what had happened, and clean-up crews scrubbed blood off the commons. The Perpetual Paving Project had been given at least a mention in every news story, often focusing on the irony of what had been a campus joke, inconvenience, and eyesore for longer than anyone could remember turning out to be responsible for saving so many lives. Numerous people on the commons that morning had ducked behind the two other brick-stacked pallets besides the one that had shielded Teach before he reverse-snapped and became a hero to the nation; and, of course, the PPP had provided the materiel for Teach's heroics. As a result of the media attention on the paving boondoggle that had run out of funding, donations began pouring into the college from around the country. A benefit concert was organized called "Rock The Commons" that attracted a handful of well-known performers who otherwise never would have come within driving distance of

Toxonomonomonee County. It was decided that instead of merely finishing the partially completed commons re-paving, all the current bricks would be taken up and new bricks put down; this time, however, with more-than-sufficient funding provided, it could be completed quickly and efficiently. The decision to undertake a complete re-paving was a popular one in no small part because no one enjoyed the thought of walking every day over the same bricks that had soaked up so much blood of so many friends.

With all the donations pouring in, the school's budget was sitting pretty for the upcoming year. Though no one dared to say anything, many folks recognized the uncomfortable irony of how this tragedy had benefited the school and community enormously, perhaps (notwithstanding the death of the blonde girl) to a degree greater than the tragedy itself. The local economy received a boost with the influx of outsiders. Local artisans and entrepreneurs took advantage of the opportunity with the sale of T-shirts and bumper stickers (*God Bless TCC* being the most popular). One local craftsman hit upon the idea of carving little wooden statuettes of Teach in his Spade of Righteousness pose, which made him (the craftsman, not Teach) a small fortune.

The aftermath of the shooting, however, did create its share of controversy – with most of it swirling around Teach. It was inevitable, and appropriate, that part of the windfall would be spent on a memorial, located on the commons. Most wanted a simple, traditional, religious memorial – which certainly would be apt, but, as others argued, nothing special or unique. Those who dissented from the majority by calling for the erection of a monument that was different from the usual run-of-the-mill memorials pointed out that because of the existence of those three already-legendary photographs – taken right here at TCC by TCC students – the school had been handed a golden opportunity to distinguish itself for eternity from all other community colleges in the nation. The money was available – or could be made available – to create a truly stunning sculpture which would memorialize the event and its victims as well as create a tourist draw state-, nation-, or, perhaps even, world-wide. (And there was controversy even among the supporters of this idea. Some thought it was only fitting that a local artist should be selected through a design competition to create the memorial; but others saw the advantage of trying to lure a big-name artist to design and create the sculpture – someone with a national or, better yet, an international reputation to produce something truly magnificent which would attract people from around the world to Toxonomonomonee County.) These dissenters soon came to be called The Shovelers, based upon the assumption that any statue undoubtedly would take as its starting point the most famous image produced by the memorialized event.

The Shoveler contingent, though small in number, had the political and economic advantage over the majority of county residents who, for various reasons, disliked the Shovelers' ideas. Most local business leaders sided with the Shovelers. The politicians, and the president and Board of Trustees of TCC, were in a much more delicate position. They, just as the business leaders, heard the *ka-ching* of cash registers, but they also knew what most of their constituents and students, respectively, thought about the issue in general, and about Teach, specifically. (Teach, to everyone's surprise, wrote a sincere, non-satirical letter to the editor endorsing the traditional ideas of the majority of the community. "This memorial," he wrote, in part, "should not be about the making of money and the seeking of attention, and it should most definitely not be about me.")

Since most residents of the county had admirably humble and reverential reasons for not wanting some grandiose, artsy statue of the Spade of Righteousness carved in granite on their community campus, these artistic preferences also made clear their intense, personal reasons for not wanting a larger-than-life image of Teach Morrison representing this life-altering event, the most significant thing – with the possible exception of the establishment of Amerimeat – ever to occur in Toxonomonomonee County. Most residents remembered that sacrilegious atrocity he had recently published in the *Chanticleer;* some still recalled that he had been the person responsible for the infamous witch-burning incident that nearly incinerated the middle school several years ago; but absolutely everyone knew what he had said only weeks ago on the *Staying up Late with Larry Davidson* show.

Teach's infamous interview on the Davidson show quickly garnered thousands of views on YouTube, including probably every local resident who couldn't stay up that late but wanted to hear Tox County mentioned once again on national television:

> Davidson: How do you pronounce this county where you're from, Teach? I can't even figure out how many syllables it's supposed to have. *(Crowd laughter. Shot of the leader of the house band, Scott Pfeiffer, grinning maniacally. The sound of someone in the crowd whooping loudly.)*
>
> Teach: You pronounce it just like it's spelled, Larry. There's nothing to it. But yeah, Toxonomonomonee County leads the nation in two things – potted meat and vowels. *(Shot of Davidson looking around, grinning. Shot of Pfeiffer,*

226

grinning. Drum roll. Cymbal crash. Crowd laughter. Several people in the audience whoop. Another shot of Davidson, laughing, now apparently finding the remark funnier than when it was first uttered. Another shot of Pfeiffer, doing nothing but grinning. He then doodles something on his keyboard, followed by another drum roll and cymbal crash. Crowd laughter. Shot of Davidson rubbing his eyes, cackling. He moves some papers around on his desk. Another shot of Pfeiffer. This one exchange between Davidson and Teach has now taken up sixty seconds of airtime.)

Davidson: Hey Scott, do we have any openings for staff writer for this guy?

Pfeiffer: I don't know, Larry, I'll have to check. Could be. *(Camera lingers on Pfeiffer, though all he's doing is standing, grinning, and looking over at Davidson. Crowd laughs, for no apparent reason. Shot of Davidson, now also cackling again, for no apparent reason. Shot of Teach, not laughing, but trying to smile as if he's wondering why everyone else is laughing. Davidson continues to cackle. Members of audience whoop loudly. Another shot of Pfeiffer, doing nothing but grinning, his bald head shining under the lights. Another sixty seconds have elapsed.)*

Davidson: Are we having fun, folks? *(Crowd boisterousness.)* Potted meat, huh? So, do you like potted meat, Teach? *(Davidson cackles. Pfeiffer grins.)*

Teach: You bet, Larry. Have you ever tried it? We call it Tox County T-bone.

Davidson: Tox County T-bone, huh. *(Crowd uproariousness. Shot of bass player in the house band, holding his instrument, grinning. Shot of Pfeiffer, grinning. Shot of drummer playing a drum roll followed by a cymbal crash. Camera lingers on the drummer, who is sitting behind his drums, holding his drum sticks and grinning. Shot of Pfeiffer pointing at the drummer and laughing. Shot of Davidson, laughing at either the drummer or Pfeiffer, or perhaps it's the bass player he's laughing at, since the camera now shows the bass player, who's still just standing, holding his bass and grinning. One person in audience whoops loudly.)*

227

Davidson: So, Teach, tell me more about – okay, folks, I'm gonna try to say it – are you ready? . . . Scott, are you ready? *(Shot of Pfeiffer, grinning.)*

Pfeiffer: I'm ready, babe.

Davidson: Okay, I'm gonna try it, Teach, are you ready? . . . So tell me about this Tox-o-no-no-mee County. *(Crowd erupts into wild applause that lasts for thirty seconds, whooping continuously. Pfeiffer plays something funky on his keyboard, joined into briefly by the drummer, until Pfeiffer suddenly stops playing. He stands looking over at Davidson, grinning.)* Did I get it right, Teach? Did I get it right? Did I get it right, folks? *(Crowd whoops loudly.)* Did I get it right, Scott? *(Crowd continues whooping.)*

Pfeiffer: I think you nailed it, Larry. *(Camera stays on Pfeiffer as he stands, grinning.)*

Davidson: What about it, Teach? Did I nail it? *(Crowd whoops one last time.)*

Teach: Well, Larry, not quite. But not bad for a beginner. *(Crowd boos. Shot of Pfeiffer, who is booing, but also smiling. Shot of guitar player, who is sitting on a stool, not doing anything. Camera quickly goes back to Davidson, who is hanging his head in mock shame. Crowd continues to boo.)*

Davidson: I'm sorry, Teach. I tried. I really tried. *(Crowd laughs, and whoops.)*

Teach: That's okay. Was there a question in there somewhere, Larry? Weren't you going to ask me a question?

Davidson: I don't know. Was I? Hey Scott – was I getting ready to ask Teach a question? *(Shot of Pfeiffer, who tries to talk, but can't because the crowd is whooping too loudly. He continues to smile, however, showing no impatience with the unruly audience. Shot of Davidson, smiling at Pfeiffer, apparently amused that Pfeiffer isn't being allowed to speak.)* Speak up, Scott, I can't hear you. *(This causes crowd to become even louder, whooping. Shot of Pfeiffer, smiling, shrugging his shoulders. Davidson laughs for several seconds. Camera alternates between shots of Davidson laughing and Pfeiffer smiling. The crowd slowly calms down enough so that Davidson can speak.)*

Davidson: I think I was probably going to ask you about what life is like in – in – in – in that county you live in. I'm not going to embarrass myself again by trying to pronounce it. *(Crowd whoops, as Teach starts to talk over them.)*

Teach: Do you want to know the truth? Do you really want to know the truth? I'll tell you the truth, Larry. With the odor of the meat refinery, which will take you about a year to get used to, not to mention the *reason* for the odor, which I won't go into, and all the illiteracy and stupidity and bigotry, and all the mental and cultural and intellectual retardation, and all the poverty and abuse and addiction – don't cut me off yet, Larry, I'm on a roll – and all the beat-up, broke-down pickup trucks, and all the overcrowded trailer parks and shanties and hovels where people feel lucky just to have somewhere to live, and just mile after mile of physical, emotional, and psychological squalor, where more and more people are being forced to live just like the swine we slaughter every day at Amerimeat – all in all, Larry, I would say that Toxonomonomonee County would have to qualify as being the putrid, unwiped cornhole of these here United States. *(Crowd breaks into raucous whoops and cheers.)*

Davidson: Well, Teach, we need to go to commercial. I wish we had more time to talk. It was good meetin' you. . . . We're having some fun tonight, folks! *(Everyone in crowd whoops loudly. Music plays. Davidson looks immensely bored as show cuts to commercial.)*

"So," said every resident of Tox County who wasn't more concerned with money and prestige than with common sense and decency, after viewing the Davidson episode, "we're going to build this guy a *monument?*"

Of course, the Shovelers' desire for a historic display for the commons had nothing to do with Teach, per se. In fact, with this latest insult still ringing in their ears, the Shovelers would have preferred any other resident listed on the Tox County tax registry over Teach. It just so happened that it was this apparent devil worshiper and ungrateful son of a bitch who had had the *cojones* to take down an aspiring mass murderer with nothing more than masonry materials. And then who had had the luck to be photographed from not just one, but three majestic angles as he stood waiting heroically for the slightest opportunity to continue pulverizing the sick bastard who had just traumatized this community for perhaps a whole generation. For the Shovelers, it was only about striking while the iron was hot and not missing out on this once-in-a-lifetime opportunity to put Toxonomonomonee County on the world's map for good and always, regardless of who the man was who got chosen by fate to be immortalized in granite.

The Board of Trustees and president of TCC, after a show of much hand wringing and brow knitting, eventually made the decision everyone knew they would make, which was to dive head-first into the deep end of the cesspool of corporate greed with the cabal of local bigwigs known as the Shovelers. This decision was soon derided as a debacle as the project became bogged down with in-fighting and threatened litigation over issues major – such as which competing *artiste* should be awarded the big prize – and minor – such as the exact location on the commons of the proposed statue. (Should it be placed on the spot where Teach had clanged Henry into unconsciousness with his mighty spade, or the spot where the blond girl had fallen?)

As a result, two years later, after Teach and the survivors and everyone touched by the tragedy had made the effort to move forward with their lives, the proposed memorial statue, created by a world-class artist, which was going to draw tourists from hundreds of miles in all directions to spend money in Tox County, had yet to have its first stone shard chipped away.

The battle over the proper way to memorialize the shooting was one controversy involving Teach. Another concerned the actual metaphysical nature of the event itself. As the initial shock of the shooting began to give way to sober reflection during the first few days and weeks afterward, some people in the community began to comment carefully, gingerly, with all due respect to the poor dead girl, that, when you thought about it, considering how many students were on the commons that day, and how many rounds were fired by James Henry, wasn't it really amazing – unbelievably amazing – that only one person (may she rest in peace) had been killed? And with all those seriously and critically wounded victims being ambulanced and air-lifted to far-away ICUs, could it really just be incredible good luck that – notwithstanding life-long limps, occasional blurred vision and blinding headaches, and probable PTSD – they were all on the way to full recoveries? And wasn't it also hard to believe that when Teach Morrison was running toward James Henry – not just once, but twice – with the brick, first, and then with the shovel, Henry could shoot at Morrison at point blank range, with Henry's weapon pointed right at him, and yet Morrison escape with a mere graze wound? At first, *miraculous* was used figuratively by newscasters searching for the right word to describe how relatively fortunate it was that there were not more fatalities, but the more that people thought about it the more convinced they became that there was obviously more to this incident than mere luck and coincidence.

But there were skeptics who believed – for even skeptics have beliefs, the believers pointed out – that there were sound, logical reasons why things played out the way they did. The fact that James Henry was firing randomly, rather than taking careful aim, would actually decrease the likelihood of lethal shots. The skeptics also were quick to point out that there were three large, impregnable pallets stacked with bricks that many people had benefited from. Many were able as well to flee into buildings, and those without refuge were running and scurrying, thus creating moving targets. Still, the Miraclers insisted, the fact that so many people had been hit by the shooter, yet only one killed, showed evidence that the bullets must have been divinely guided away from vital organs. And the poor girl who was killed – well, she was standing right in front of Henry when he first fired, so, obviously, it was her appointed time to go. If you found yourself staring down the barrel of a gun, then either you had put yourself in that position by the moral choices you had made or God had put you in that position as part of His divine plan.

And then there was the matter of Teach's apparent bulletproofness. Twice James had fired at Teach from point-blank range. Once, a bullet barely grazed his side, and another time the bullet missed him altogether, or perhaps *passed right through him*, which sent shivers down the spines of the Miraclers whenever they thought about it. The skeptics argued (why do they always have to argue, the Miraclers complained; why can't they just accept certain things?) that no one really knew for sure where James's guns were aimed, relative to Morrison's position each time. All the witnesses who gave police reports had either taken refuge behind stacks of bricks or in nearby buildings, were injured on the ground, or were running for their lives. The shooter himself wasn't talking – literally. James Henry had not said a word to anyone since his enshovelment and arrest. As for Teach, his story remained consistent throughout his televised interviews and in his statements to investigators: he heard James's gun firing as he threw his brick and as he charged toward him with the shovel, and he saw a gun pointed at him, but, as he said in full hero-mode on *Good Morning America*, "being shot at was not my primary focus at the time."

The biggest problem for the Miraclers, within their group, was not with the message that was being sent, but with the messenger. Many people who fervently wanted to believe that Tox County had been chosen by God for divine intervention, or at least to make His divine presence felt, found themselves having a hard time squaring this with the fact that it was Teach Morrison who had been selected to carry out the holy mission. A significant rift developed between these two camps of believers. The side that was able to swallow hard and accept Teach as a divine messenger said, in effect, "They said the same thing about Jesus when he returned to Nazareth: 'Why should we believe a lowly carpenter's son?'" The other side – led by the Reverend McAllister – was aghast that good Christians could even utter the name of Teach Morrison, devil worshiper, in the same breath as Jesus.

In the weeks and months following the shooting, the subject of this debate was asked his opinion, several times daily, about everything that was swirling all around him. Teach would just smile serenely and say, using a variety of different metaphors and clichés, that he didn't have a dog in this fight, it's out of his hands, *que sera sera*, you all just fight it out amongst yourselves, why can't we all just get along?, I think everybody needs to take a chill pill, and so on. But even this equanimous attitude shown by Teach created more questions to be debated. "Have you noticed," the Teach-*cum*-Jesus crowd said, "how differently he is behaving since he came back from New York and Hollywood? The first week after the shooting, he was all over television bad-mouthing everybody who lives here and making a fool of himself, but since he came back he's like a totally different person. He's been nothing but humble and sensible and responsible in his comments and actions. Don't you see what's going on here? The man's been touched by Jesus. This proves, if we ever needed more proof, that this community has been blessed with a great miracle." Others said, simply, "No wonder the guy's chilling out and settling down – look at what he's been through."

And so, the various debates and debates-within-debates continued, and the monument continued to not be sculpted; and Teach continued living his life, but with a new maturity, noticed by everyone, but understood by none.

GRIEF EVENTUALLY DIES

SCHOOL REOPENED ONE WEEK after the shooting. Teach, of course, had spent all week on planes, in hotel rooms, and in television studios and other places he had never been and never thought he would be (such as the Oval Office). It had been a great experience, but all in all, it was good to be home, though he wasn't happy about all the hostile and threatening messages he received when he returned from New York. There were two things, apparently, that were very difficult for people to tolerate regarding the things they love – a joke and the truth.

It was hard to believe it had been only one week since the shooting. It seemed like a month. He was looking forward to seeing his students again. He imagined his classroom would be a very strange place for the foreseeable future, with a celebrity for an instructor and kids trying to deal with even more upheaval in their already heaved-up lives. Since he had been feted everywhere he went in Washington and New York and LA last week, he fully expected more of the same when he returned to school. It would make sense for a news crew to be waiting for him in the hallway, with Randy beaming for the cameras and playing up the department.

As Teach pulled into his parking spot, though, it was almost as if the shooting had never happened. Everything looked the same. Well, there was a news van parked in front of the administration building, so he prepared himself for at least one more interview. As he locked his car and walked toward the commons he experienced that strange dream-like sensation of returning to a routine after having that routine sharply disrupted for a period of time. The-same-yet-not-the-same. The campus was quieter than he expected. Much quieter. There were plenty of people moving around, but no one was saying anything. This same number of people on the commons most mornings usually made a lot of noise. He had never noticed it before, but he noticed it now that it wasn't there. Definitely-not-the-same.

Jet-lagged and running late, Teach reluctantly skipped his usual coffee in the cafeteria and headed straight to his classroom. Things seemed more-like-the-same when he entered the Adult Literacy Department, which, frankly, disappointed Teach. It wasn't as if he was expecting a marching band and the key to the city, but he certainly expected to be treated a little differently on his first day back from being a superstar. The department had been unscathed by the shooting, so apparently Randy wanted everything back to business as usual as quickly as possible.

At least Teach was accorded a hearty "Hey! Look who's back!" by the receptionist. He stopped in to see Randy, who gave Teach quite a bear hug. He thought Randy was going to cry. "Teach, I know you've been told this probably a thousand times already, but I don't think anyone can really tell you how grateful we all are for what you did. I know the president is planning to come over here personally today to thank you in person" – which was a big deal, because the president never set foot in the Adult Literacy Department – "and everyone here at the college will be forever in your debt." At this, Randy indeed did begin to tear up.

"All right, Randy, pull yourself together. El Presidente might be here any minute. . . . Am I going to have class today?"

"Sure, Teach. Business as usual. Hopefully everybody came back today."

"Okay, good. I was just afraid, what with all the distractions. . . . I didn't know if I would be teaching or hobnobbing. I've done nothing but hobnob all week. The hobnobber-in-chief."

"We'll keep the hobnobbing to a minimum, Teach, I promise." Randy smiled a red-eyed grin.

Teach walked down the hall from Randy's office wondering what to expect from his students. Probably nothing. These kids have seen and done a lot already during their young lives – it's hard to impress a GED kid.

He opened the door to his classroom and was bombarded immediately with a loud "Surprise!" from everyone. A large banner was draped across the front of the room which read WELCOME HOME TEACH. Everyone applauded and whooped. Now it was Teach's turn to strangle his tears. He hugged everyone who wanted a hug and shook Oliver and George's hands. They acted as if it was the first time anyone had shaken their hands. Maybe it was.

"Whose idea was this?" Teach marveled.

"Maria and I," Charlotte said. "I wanted to get here early and do something for you, and then Maria got here right after I did." Charlotte and Maria were beaming.

"We even a-wrote your name a-Teach," Maria said. Charlotte never called him Teach, out of respect.

Teach spent the first hour of class, up till the ten o'clock break, regaling everyone with stories about Saturday Night Live and Los Angeles and meeting the president. Nobody said anything about what he had said on the Larry Davidson show – probably because these kids would have agreed with him one hundred percent. And Charlotte would never be caught dead watching a show like that, though surely she had heard all about it. Apparently everybody had.

After everyone returned from break, they tried to settle back down into somewhat-normal. The president of the college had not shown up to shake Teach's hand – not that Teach even remembered he was supposed to. After all, Teach had just shaken the real president's hand.

Teach spent a long time working with Charlotte on some long-division problems. One bugaboo that plagued many GED students, young and old, was, strangely enough, their meticulousness and attention to detail. Those were great assets in most situations, but on a timed math test where you have to average one answer every 1.8 minutes in order to finish, such ultra-tidiness will slow you down and jeopardize your success. Charlotte insisted on forming each numeral perfectly. If she wrote a 5 that didn't have enough curl at the bottom, she would erase it and make another 5. And in doing long division, it's important, obviously, to keep your numbers lined up as they trickle down the page; but Charlotte's determination to keep her numbers in line approached OCD levels of fussiness. She understood how to work the problems, but it took her forever to do so. This put Teach in an awkward position. He didn't want to criticize her care and caution – it was much more common for students to have the opposite problem of numerical recklessness – but he tried gently to persuade her not to erase a whole row of numbers; that as long as she could read it, it was fine. "Keep in mind, Charlotte – on the GED test, all of your math work is done on scratch paper – it isn't even graded. So just try to do it as neat as you can, but as fast as you can, too."

"I know, Mr. Morrison, but I just can't stand seeing a whole row of messy numbers. It drives me crazy – and there's just no reason for it. . . . What I need to do is just make sure I make all my numbers neat the first time." Which wasn't a feasible solution, either, since then it would still take Charlotte forever just to complete one problem.

Teach always contrasted his teaching methods to Clara's across the hall. In fact, he sometimes thought his whole teaching philosophy was simply to do the opposite of whatever he had seen or heard Clara doing. All instructors have these fastidious-to-a-fault students who are never satisfied with the visual quality of their work. Teach had heard Clara more than once saying loudly to a student, "You're never going to pass your test if you can't work any faster than that," or "You're not going to be able to take that much time writing one lousy sentence – get a move on." Why wasn't he allowed to hit Clara over the head with a shovel? Teach wanted to know.

Teach next worked with Maria on her English grammar. As with anyone making the switch from *español* to English, it was the smallest of words that tripped her up. "Maria, keep in mind that in English the word *is* is spelled *i-s,* not *e-s.*"

"But, a-Mr. Teach, it's a-the same word."

"You're right, it is the same word. You say it the same and it means the same, but you have to spell it differently."

"Okay, Mr. a-Teach. I know that, but I yust a-can't remember."

As Teach talked with Maria he also noticed Jerry's hand in the air. There was nothing Teach liked better than a raised hand. Jerry – as well as Lillian – had created a bittersweet dilemma for Teach this semester. Both should have finished their GEDs by now. They were a little weak in math, but they never worked on their algebra – they chose to spend their class time doing what they loved rather than what they loathed. Jerry did little else but draw his hideous Possum character scurrying around Toxic City in its black cape, while Lillian obsessively recreated her traumatic childhood in her voluminous journals. Teach knew he should do more to goad them into taking their Math test, which he was confident they could pass (even if they weren't). Math-test-phobia was a crippling obstacle for many GEDers. As difficult as it was for him to admit, Teach grudgingly admired Clara in this one – and only one – respect: she would march students down the hall, literally, as if at gunpoint, and force them to sign up for GED tests they were terrified, but qualified, to take. But Teach had adopted a Wilsonian policy of self-determination for his students. Jerry and Lillian would take the Math test when and if they decided to. Meanwhile, he would continue to enjoy their presence in his class as two of his all-time favorite students.

After finishing up with Maria, Teach strolled over to Jerry. "Yeah, Jerry, what can I do you for?"

"I just thought of something, Teach."

"There's a first time for everything, Jerry old boy." Teach smiled, but cringed a little as well. Sarcasm didn't go over well with kids. They tended to take everything a teacher said a bit too literally. It was a bad habit Teach could never completely break himself of – that of bringing his usual smartass self into the classroom where it didn't belong.

Jerry didn't react to Teach's quip, thankfully. "I just wonder if anyone has ever thought of this. Maybe you can tell me if you've heard this before."

"Sure, Jerry. If you're plagiarizing from the greats, I'll let you know, but keep in mind what Ecclesiastes says – there is no new thing under the sun. It's getting harder and harder to have an original thought. But hey, I'm not trying to rain on your parade, my good man. Tell me what's on your mind."

"Well, have you ever thought about how there's no such thing as time? I mean, not really."

"No such thing as time. Okay, I'm with you so far. Keep going."

"I mean, you have three ways of looking at time, right? You have the past, and the present, and the future, right?" Teach nodded in agreement. "That's all there is. Something is either in the past, or in the present, or in the future, right?" Teach continued to nod. "But the thing is, the past doesn't really exist – not anymore anyway. It's just memories in your mind –"

"That's what people keep telling me, Jerry," Teach interrupted.

"So you can't say that something really exists if it's all just in your brain, right? And the future doesn't really exist, either. You know how I know that?"

"How?"

"Because we never actually get to the future. It becomes the present as soon as we get there. We can *think* about the future, but when that time actually gets here – it's just the present. Does that make sense?"

"It makes perfect sense. I think you may be on to something there."

"So there's really no future, either. And the present – I think that's what people really don't understand, Teach –"

"I know I don't."

"I mean, what exactly is the present? How much time is it? People think it's a long time, but it's not. How much time do you think the present is, Teach?"

"It seems like it's been a long time, Jerry. It seems like it might go on forever."

"But it doesn't!" Jerry was getting excited. "As soon as it exists, it's gone. As soon as it exists, Teach, it's gone. . . . Just like that–" Jerry snapped his fingers. "Just like that." He snapped his fingers again. "The present only lasts for a split-second – then it becomes the past. You see? What do they call it? A nanosecond? That's all the present is – a nanosecond."

"And I think you can go even smaller than that, too, Jerry. Smaller than a nanosecond."

"Really? But that's just it – the present just keeps getting smaller and smaller, until it's just like a nano-nano-nano-second – right, Teach? . . . So that's what I mean by time not really existing. If the present is just a little nano-nano-nano-second, or maybe even less than that, and the future never does even exist, then all we really have is the past in our brains. Do you think that's right, Teach? That the past is all we really have? That our memories are really the only things that exist? Is that possible? Can that possibly be right? That the only thing that is real is our memories? . . . Teach, are you okay? Teach? Are you okay?"

"Yeah, I'm okay, Jerry. Just my allergies acting up. I'm okay. I'm okay."

So it went for Teach, back in his natural habitat, going from table to table, dealing with each student's idiosyncrasies as humanely as possible, carrying out the imperative of his chosen profession – to teach.

The next day, half-way through Teach's class, Randy entered Teach's classroom and handed him a note which read, "Call Kate," above a phone number with an area code that made Teach's heart leap. He followed Randy out and asked him, "Do you know who this *Kate* is?"

"I don't know, Teach. I didn't ask her last name. But she said she was an old college friend. She said it wasn't urgent, so you need to wait till after class to call her back."

Teach didn't hear Randy's last sentence. "Can I use your phone to call her, Randy? As a favor? I need a little privacy. This is the girl I would have married, if things had worked out a little differently. I haven't talked to her since we graduated. . . . And she's calling from Boston – and you know how spotty our cell-phone coverage is around here."

"Okay, sure. I'm sure you have a lot of catching up to do. I'll be going to lunch anyway."

"Thanks, Randy. I owe you one." Teach headed down the hall toward Randy's office.

"Where are you going? I said after class, not now."

"Oh, okay. Sorry. I'm just a little excited to talk to this chick after all this time."

Teach walked back into his classroom, furiously scheming. "Okay, class, your attention, please. What day of the week is today?"

Maria raised her hand and said, "Tursday."

"That's right. Here's a harder question. Who knows who Thursday is named after?"

"Wednesday," Oliver said.

"No, Oliver, not what Thursday comes after – who is it named after? Who is it named for?"

"Is this another damn homework assignment?" George asked.

"No, no homework. I'm just asking if anybody knows."

Jerry, complacently, without raising his hand, said "Thor – god of thunder."

"Excellent! Five points for Mr. Speziak, our mythology expert. . . . And, as luck would have it, today is Thor's birthday."

"Thor has a birthday?" Jerry asked.

"Sure he does. Everybody has a birthday. December twenty-fifth is Jesus's, and today is the day that some parts of the world celebrate Thor's birthday. . . . It doesn't always fall on Thursday, but this year it does. That makes it even more special. And to celebrate Thor's birthday, I thought I would dismiss class early today. So you guys are free to go home. . . . And drink a toast to Thor."

"Are you serious?" said Jerry.

"Sure I am. Class dismissed. You all get on out of here, before I change my mind."

Randy's door was open. "Okay, Randy, I apologize for kicking you out of your own office, but you said I could use your phone."

"*After* class, Teach – not right now."

"I dismissed early, on account of Thor's birthday."

"What?"

"You didn't know today was Thor's birthday? Scandinavia practically shuts down all day today. It's like their Christmas."

"You didn't have my permission to do that, Teach."

"Randy, for crying out loud. I dismissed class early, for probably the first time ever, so I could call the girl I almost married, whom I haven't spoken to in eighteen years. Cut me a little slack, will you? Go ahead and treat yourself to an early lunch. Go ahead – you deserve it. . . . And shut the door behind you."

Your hands are trembling as you dial. You are dizzy.

"Hello?"

You recognize her voice immediately, with just that one word. "Cait. Cait. It's me, Tommy."

"Tommy! How are you? Thank you so much for calling me back. . . . I've been following what happened on the news. My God, you never know where these things are going to happen next."

Eighteen years melt away. "Cait. . . . It's so good to hear your voice. How are you?"

"I'm great. It's good to hear your voice, too, Tommy. I saw you on the Today *show. It looks like you're quite the hero. And you're such a natural. The camera just loves you. I died laughing when you said that you tell all your students to call you* Teach. *That is just like you. The Tommy I knew would do something exactly like that. . . . So what was that like, being interviewed on national television?"*

The feeling comes back. The feeling you always had around Cait, the feeling you haven't had since Cait. Tears are emerging from your eyes, but you don't mind. Your voice sounds normal, your tears unbetrayed. "Pretty surreal. You're trying to have a semi-normal conversation, you know, and all these bright lights are shining down on you and everything. It was less like an interview and more like a Gestapo interrogation. But it was fun being a hero for a week."

"You could have gotten yourself killed."

"Yeah, well, worse things have happened. . . . So how was Europe?"

"What? Excuse me?"

"Europe. How was Europe? You went to Europe right after we graduated."

Cait waited a moment before answering. "I didn't go on that trip, Tommy. After that horrible breakup we had, I wasn't exactly in the mood to go traipsing around Europe. I've been over there a couple times since, though. . . . I'm sorry, Tommy, I didn't know what you were talking about at first. That was such a long time ago."

"It doesn't seem like that long ago, does it? Not for me, anyway."

"So. . . . Are you married? Any kids?"

"Nope. None of the above. . . . What about you?"

"Oh yeah. Married. Two kids."

"Okay. . . . That's good. Congratulations."

"Thanks. So, you're teaching there at the community college. The Toxo-nono, whatever. I never could get that right. Are you teaching history? No, wait a minute – you said in your interview – you teach the GED."

"That's right."

"I was so thrilled to see you that I don't think I heard half of what you were saying. What exactly is the GED? I've never quite understood how that worked. I know it's for dropouts. . . . That's very noble of you to want to do that, Tommy. You've always been a very good person at heart. I've always known that about you."

You are silent. You want to say, Then why didn't you give me another chance? But you remain silent. The tears are coming faster; you don't know how much longer you can hide them from Cait.

"Well, okay, Tommy. I guess I should let you go so you can get back to your teaching –"

"No. Please, Cait, don't go. Not yet. It's been so long since I talked to you. I don't have a class right now. I can talk for as long as you want."

"Okay, well, I guess a few more minutes won't hurt. It's so good to talk to you, Tommy."

"You too, Cait. . . . I guess you're a big-shot lawyer now, right?"

"Well, I don't know about big-shot, but yes, I work out of the DA's office – in Boston. I moved back after Stanford."

"That's great. That's great, Cait. I'm very proud of you. Who's your husband? Is he a lawyer, too?" You wipe your cheeks with the side of your thumb. You regain some of your composure, but the tears refuse to stop.

"Yes. I met him at Stanford, but he liked the idea of living in Boston. He was a California beach bum growing up, but he said a little culture would do him good. . . . You said you weren't married, right? Divorced?"

"No. Plain ol' single. And I'll be that way for a while, it looks like. I think my girlfriend and I are getting ready to split up."

"Oh, I'm sorry to hear that."

"Yeah, well, it turns out, she's not Cait. . . . And the next girl I meet won't be Cait either."

There is a painful silence on both ends of the line.

"I guess I need to go now, Tommy. I hope everything works out well for you."

"Can I ask you one more question before you go, Cait?"

"Sure. What is it?"

"Do you ever think about me? At all?"

"Sure I do. Of course I do. Why do you think I looked up the number of your school and called you?"

"But you saw me on TV. . . . Did you ever think about me before that?"

"Sure. Of course I did. . . . Of course I did. . . . Okay, Tommy, you take good care of yourself, okay?"

"Do you ever miss me?" Your voice cracks.

"Tommy. . . . I need to go."

"Hey, Cait, one more thing – please. . . . Richard Nixon."

"What? Richard Nixon? What about him?"

"Cait – Richard Nixon."

"I'm sorry, Tommy, I don't understand."

"Richard Nixon. He put the fix in."

There are a couple of seconds of silence, but then Cait bursts out laughing – the laugh that causes your tears to break all their bounds. You put your hand tightly over the mouthpiece and weep uncontrollably. "Our rhyming game! Oh, Tommy. . . ."

There is silence, except for the sound of you trying desperately to contain your sobbing. Any more words, though, are impossible. "Well, I guess I really need to go now. . . . Bye, Tommy. . . . Take care."

You can't say bye. You just let the phone go dead. You put your head down and weep. You start weeping a river of grief. The same river of grief you wept standing naked in front of Cait with her blood soaking through the towel on her head, the blood you had caused to pour. The grief has not gone anywhere. It has neither abated nor changed. It is all still right here. Throughout that call all you had wanted to do was to pick up where you had left off, eighteen years ago, begging her forgiveness, telling her you were so sorry, telling her how you couldn't tell her how much you loved her. But you were so happy just to hear her voice.

So you start crying your river of grief, reliving all the pain that is still in your heart. But you've cried these tears before, the tears of self-pity, of loss, selfishly mourning everything that you lost, that you threw away, that you destroyed. These are old tears, cried and recried so many times, only more acute now, with Cait's voice still playing back in your head. The last time you had heard that voice she told you that she was okay, that it was okay for you to leave her, that she was okay, seemingly more worried about you, even then, than herself, still thinking more of you than of herself, even with her blood dripping from under the towel, even after what you had done to her.

But those tears you cried then, the same tears you're recrying now, were just tears for yourself, standing there in front of Cait and her friends just like a big baby, babbling incomprehensibly, unselfconsciously naked, just like a big baby. Thinking only of yourself and how much you have lost. Cait was right, of course, about you – you could never think for even a second about what she might be feeling. She said she had been up all night crying. And you, you stupid, stupid fool, you thought she was just crying tears of indecision, of fearfulness, of doubt, tears of sadness or self-pity – the only kind of tears that you had ever cried, even after you killed Charles. But she was crying her own river of grief, crying a river of grief all night. Have you ever cried all night about anything – even Cait? Even Charles? Her decision had already been made. She wasn't crying because she didn't know what to do. She was crying because she did know what she had to do. Sure, she cried for her own loss, the fact that she might never see you again, and sure, she cried thinking of all the joy you had shared that you would never share again. But do you really think she cried all night about herself and her own pain? That's all you would have been capable of feeling, but not Cait. Do you have any idea how much courage it took for her to do what she did? To walk away from you –

not just to lose you, but to give you up? You lost Cait, you threw her away, but would you have ever given her up? Can you even give her up now, after all this time? You didn't even have the courage to leave her room. She had to tell you to go. You were desperate to hang on to her, but no more desperate than she was to hang on to you. But yet she gave you up freely; she didn't lose you. And she had the courage to walk away from you even though she knew that you would hit her, or worse. She fully expected you to assault her, and you did. But yet, even knowing the violence that was sure to come, that she had been so fearful of, she still had the courage to walk away.

So Cait wasn't crying all night about herself and her own loss. She was grieving for you. Because she knew how much this would hurt you. She knew that you weren't man enough to take it. She knew that this might destroy you, that you might never recover from the blow you were about to receive. And she was right. She was grieving for you, because she knew that you were going to suffer even more than she was suffering.

But she suffered a lot. She loved you as much as you loved her – probably more than you loved her, simply because she was capable of a lot more love than you could ever be capable of. She wanted you in Europe with her. She wanted you in California with her. And did you ever really doubt for one second that she wanted to spend her whole life with you?

So, if you want to cry, why don't you cry for Cait for once in your life? Cry for the one person in this whole miserable affair who didn't get what she deserved. You got what you deserved. You got a life sentence of shame, guilt, and misery without parole for killing Charles, and you lost Cait because you deserved to lose her. But did Cait get what she deserved? She deserved you – but not the you she had to walk away from. She deserved the you she thought she was getting, the you she fell in love with and wanted to spend her life with. That was the you she deserved, the you she wanted. Do you think she really wanted that beach bum lawyer from California? No more than you really wanted Angie or Cheryl. So don't you dare stop crying yet, not until you've cried at least as many tears for Cait as you've cried for yourself for eighteen years.

So you continue to cry, crying tears for Cait now as well. The papers on Randy's desk are sodden, the ink running and soaking through the paper and mixing with your tears. And after you've cried for yourself, and cried for Cait, you think maybe you can stop crying now. But then something else occurs to you, something even more important than your grief, than Cait's grief.

Cait called.

Cait called you. Haven't you been waiting eighteen years for that call? That means she forgives you, doesn't it? If you can't have her back, can you at least know that she forgives you? That was all you said you wanted, eighteen years ago. You didn't give Charles a chance to forgive you. But you gave Cait her chance. You never tried to speak to her again that semester, even though there was still a month left before graduation. You went a whole month, locked away mostly, in your room, not going to the classes you had with her. Going to the cafeteria at odd hours when you knew she wouldn't be there. Walking to class in roundabout ways, when you decided to go to class, just to get out of your room. You didn't want to see her because you knew you didn't deserve to see her. If she wanted to see you, to forgive you, she knew where to find you, but you didn't want to see her unless she wanted you to see her. That was the least you could do after what you had already done. The least she deserved was to be rid of you, if that's what she wanted. And you assumed that's what she wanted. She didn't call you or come see you. You knew you had lost her, but could she, at the very least, at some point in her life, forgive you? That was the most you could ask for. Just to know that you had not hurt her in any permanent way, other than a scar on her forehead. That she was able to put your monstrous existence out of her mind and get on with her life. That was truly all you wanted that last month of school.

So wasn't this phone call confirmation of all that you had wanted?

So now the tears, dried for a couple of minutes, start up again, your head back on Randy's waterlogged desk. But these are tears of happiness, the first time you have felt honest elation since you threw Cait away. You cry the joyous tears of the forgiven, knowing finally that Cait is indeed okay, that it's okay for you to let go, to leave. It's okay, she had said. I'm okay. That's all you had ever really wanted to hear her say again. Just to make sure, one last time.

THE SPRING SEMESTER HAD BEGUN, and though it was still the dead of winter, it indeed did feel a lot like early spring. It was one of those not-really-rare but still greatly appreciated warm spells enjoyed by this part of the country almost every winter, a mid-January sneak preview of what everyone had to look forward to three months hence. And it was three months previous that Teach had been a supernova exploding into the national consciousness – the reverberations of which were still being felt. The Shoveler hullabaloo over the proposed memorial had commenced in earnest and, regarding the rather surprising possibility that Teach was a divine instrument of God, the citizens of Tox County had already divided themselves into the *you-gotta-believe* and the *you-gotta-be-kidding* camps.

Even Teach was tiring of all the attention. He could no longer tolerate how ridiculously serious everyone was about, well, *everything*. Of course there were memories of this catastrophe that had to be spoken of with hushed tones and lowered eyes. Fifty-eight seconds' worth of memories, to be precise. Teach remembered every small detail of his lifesaving rampage, his onslaught of deliverance (and for those who had been on the commons that morning, the elapsed time had slowed and expanded so that those fifty-eight seconds would always register as the longest minute of their lives); he would never forget the blonde girl walking in front of James and would never forgive himself for the solely prurient interest he had taken in her; and there was absolutely nothing else he witnessed, involving those who were lying motionless or writhing on the bloody cobblestones that he would ever in his lifetime make light of. But everything else, after the ambulances sped away, had become increasingly ridiculous. And here was the thing: the more ridiculous things became, the more seriously people took them. Sure, people prayed solemnly over the victims and foamed at the mouth over James Henry – but if you told someone who believed in magic bullets that they were not actually real, then you had a real fight on your hands.

But it wasn't only for his sake that Teach wanted this lunacy to stop. He had decided, after Cait called, to try to salvage, repair, and, hopefully, improve upon his relationship with Cheryl. He knew that she was a nervous wreck worrying about him. After he returned home from his triumphal procession through America's media empire, Teach had gotten a call from Dr. Carney, offering support and free advice about the dangers of PTSD. He suggested to Teach that it might not be a bad idea to come back in for some counseling, even if he weren't presently aware of any stressful

245

symptoms. Cheryl hoped he would take Carney's advice – yet it was Cheryl who was having trouble sleeping and who woke up startled and sweating from dreams – dreams unsymbolic, in no need of interpretation, of Teach running through gauntlets of gunfire, the action terrifying and portentous. During the days, during her planning periods, she caught herself having thought-visions of what Teach must have gone through during those fifty-eight seconds. She shuddered, her body noticeably twitching or shivering.

In one respect, life with Teach now was much better for Cheryl – he was no longer crying and yelling at her – so she was glad that Teach had gone to see Dr. Carney. It would be nice to know what all that crying had been about, Cheryl thought, but she was willing to let sleeping dogs lie, at least for now. Had he been cheating on her? Was he still cheating on her, but had gotten over whatever guilt he was feeling? And what was the deal with that blanket? Teach was such a blabbermouth with everyone else, but so tight-lipped with her. What was he hiding? One day, Cheryl hoped to have the courage to confront Teach with all her questions, but now was not the time. Not with everything else that was going on.

Despite her nightmares and her moments of terror during the day, Cheryl suspected that the source of her anxiety wasn't really what had happened on the commons that day, as horrific as it was. Sure, Teach could have been killed – but he wasn't. He survived, almost unharmed. The problem was, Cheryl still feared for his safety. It was as if those fifty-eight seconds never really ended. "These people are crazy!" she said to Dr. Whitaker. "All these crazy phone calls – he doesn't answer his phone anymore, but they still leave messages – 'It should have been you that was killed.' That's what they say, Francine! Just because he made some stupid joke on TV. . . . Or wrote some stupid article in the paper. . . . These people are crazy!"

Cheryl dreaded those nights now when Teach wanted to go out to eat – which was most nights. He always picked the most crowded restaurant. He loved all the attention. And, Cheryl had to admit, most of the people loved Teach. He made sure he had a pen with him at all times now, because he signed at least one autograph anytime they went somewhere. But she also noticed the odd stares at some of the tables. "And it only takes one nut, Francine. . . . One crazy nut is all it takes." And Cheryl was aware of something about her own behavior as well. She was always self-conscious now of how close – in physical proximity – she was to Teach. If he held her hand as they walked to their table, she found herself subtly pulling away, afraid of being too side-by-side, their arms not dangling loosely together but forming more of a taut barrier between them; if they didn't hold hands, Cheryl hung back so far from Teach you might not realize they were a couple.

246

"Well, I'm sure you're not as comfortable as Teach is with always being the center of attention," Dr. Whitaker said.

"That might be part of it, I guess. I hope that's all it is. . . . But I can't stand being so afraid all the time, Francine. . . . Teach is so oblivious to everything. . . . He's on top of the world, and I'm terrified. I'm such a coward – that's what I can't stand. . . . I should be trying to protect Teach, but instead I'm trying to get as far away from him as I can. It's horrible, Francine. . . . *I'm* horrible."

"Cheryl," Francine said sternly, straightening up and staring directly at her friend and patient. "You – are – not – horrible," she added, slowly and evenly.

"Thank you, Francine, for saying that – I hope I'm not too horrible. . . . but I feel so helpless. And Teach is just so. . . *stupid.*" Cheryl half-laughed. "He never makes the right decision – about *anything*. It was so *stupid*, what he did." Cheryl fell silent, but Francine could tell from her eyes that she had something else to say, once she figured out how she wanted to say it. Cheryl soon continued: "Everybody treats Teach like such a hero. . . . I mean, he *is* a hero – he saved so many lives. . . . God, I'm horrible, Francine! How selfish is that? I *hate* myself sometimes."

"You could have lost the person you love. You're not going to view what Teach did the same way as everybody else."

"But is that the right way to view it? I don't know –" Cheryl trailed off. "If that had been the first time Teach had ever done something really stupid like that, then maybe I would look at it differently – maybe I would say, 'Wow – that was really heroic, what he did.' But it's not the first time – and it probably won't be the last time, either." Cheryl sighed and looked around the room for a moment, before continuing. "I told you that Teach was fired from teaching middle school, right? Did I ever tell you why?" Francine nodded no. "Well, I don't think Teach has ever been able to face up to the truth. According to him, it was all because of school politics and some stupid parents who accused him of – well, it's crazy. The whole thing was crazy. But I know a couple of teachers who knew Teach when he taught sixth grade, and they've told me what really happened. One of Teach's students caught his classroom on fire – this was *actually during class.* It was horrible – honestly, I don't know how I would react in that situation, you know? I don't guess any of us knows until something like that happens to us. But Teach was just so inexperienced. We have fire drills all the time, you know, and you like to think they do some good, but I don't know. . . . Teach loved those kids, I know that much for sure. He will always bend over backwards to do whatever he can to help one of his students – even stuff he really shouldn't be doing. So I know he wasn't being selfish, or thoughtless, or neglectful – Teach just isn't like that. He just didn't know what the right thing to do was. As soon as the fire started, I'm sure he tried to get all the students out, or he yelled at them to get out. I'm sure he thought that once he yelled at them to get out, or as soon as they saw him running, they would all follow him – I've never actually talked to him about this, you know. What's the point? It happened before I knew him and it's not something he wants to talk about. But a lot of the kids just froze, and panicked – even Teach talks about how quick the room filled with smoke. So he ran outside before all his students were out. . . . And you just don't do that. You don't do that, Francine. You're taught to get all your students out first – you don't evacuate yourself until everyone else is out – at least that's what we're taught to do. But like I said, Teach was practically a brand-new teacher. And I don't even know if that would matter much in that situation. It all happened so fast, I'm sure. And I know that Teach would have run back into his classroom as soon as he saw that not all of his kids ran out with him, but the assistant principal was on the hall when it happened, so he was the one who ran in and escorted all the other kids out. And so all he saw was Teach running out of the building, with maybe half his kids following him. So the assistant principal comes outside with the rest of Teach's students and Teach is just standing there looking like a –" Cheryl suddenly started to cry. It was the first time she had talked about this to anyone. She reached for a tissue and tried to continue. "It just made Teach look like such a – like such a coward."

"Were any of the kids hurt?"

"No – thank goodness. Can you imagine? But poor Teach. I know he must have been humiliated. I don't know if he was actually fired, or if he was asked to resign – or maybe he just decided to resign, because he felt so ashamed. I don't know. But I can't help but think that this was just the same thing happening all over again – Teach being put in a really stressful situation and just not knowing what the right thing to do is. What do you think?"

"I don't know, Cheryl. I'm sorry. I can't speak to that."

"Well, I just wish he would stop being so. . . so god-damn *stupid*."

Teach, on this unseasonably warm January morning, strolls into the cafeteria before class for his usual cup of java. There is a long line at the counter, with most folks ordering the local favorite – a fried Mmmmm biscuit. He could easily use his celebrity to cut to the front of the line – all he would have to do is slap a couple of shoulders and shake a couple of hands – but he is content today to join the end of the queue.

He is behind a woman he doesn't recognize – or, at least, he doesn't recognize the back of her head. All Teach can see is a partial profile, but he estimates her age to be somewhere comfortably within his cohort. And from what he can see, she is several grades above school-marm beautiful as well. He waits patiently for her to turn around, and when she does, she recognizes Teach immediately – as everyone does now. "Well, well – all hail the conquering hero."

Teach lets loose with a loud belly laugh. "Thank you so much for that tone of sarcasm. You have no idea how much I appreciate it. . . . It's music to my ears."

"You're welcome. . . . It's not that I'm not in awe of what you did and all, Mr. Morrison –"

"Call me Teach –"

"– but don't you think it's getting kind of ridiculous?"

"Oh, absolutely. Just yesterday, an old lady came up to me and said, 'Can I please touch you? I just want to touch you.'"

"And what did you say?"

"I said, 'Are your hands clean?'"

Now it's her turn to laugh.

"And, of course, she took me utterly seriously and seemed rather offended that I would call her hygiene into question."

"Did you let her touch you?"

"No! . . . I mean, I did come up with a compromise solution. I said, 'How would you like a hug instead?' So I hugged the old battle-axe."

"That was nice of you."

"What was I supposed to do? I didn't want to be rude to the lady, but what am I supposed to say? – 'Yes, you may place your hands upon the sacred fabric.'" To demonstrate, Teach takes this opportunity to place his own hands upon the fabric covering the shoulders of this woman he has just met. "What's your name?" Teach asks, removing his hands.

"Caitlin."

"Really? . . . That's one of my all-time favorite names."

"Are you hitting on me? . . . I'll have you know, I'm a married woman." She smiles and holds out her hand, fingers splayed, to display for Teach a large diamond ring.

"Since when did that ever stop anybody? . . . But no, Caitlin, I'm not hitting on you. I'm more or less married myself – I want to see if I'm any good at it first. . . . I'm practicing marriage without a license. But no, seriously – I really do like that name. It's a long story, so you'll just have to take my word for it. . . . Do you ever go by just *Cait?*"

"Not if I can help it."

Teach laughs again. "I bet you're not from around here originally, are you? I don't detect a twang."

"Oh hell no. . . . You know what I mean. I loved what you said on Larry Davidson – about this place. . . . It's so true – unfortunately."

249

"Ain't it though. . . . So, where are you from?

"Providence."

"Rhode Island? . . . Wow. So how did you end up down here in good ol' Stinkville, USA?"

"That's a long story, too – but basically it's because you go wherever your husband goes. . . . He's one of the VPs at Amerimeat. . . . He's a potted-meat maven – a member of the potted-meat mafia, as I like to call them. So here I am – in the cornhole of America, as you would say. . . . God, Roger would have a stroke if he knew I was talking to you like this."

"Yeah, I imagine I'm no longer on their Christmas card list. . . . Are you an instructor? I don't think I've seen you in here before."

"No, just a student. . . . They actually have a really good photography program here. I've sort of taken that up as a hobby."

"Hobbies are good."

"Do you have any hobbies, besides being a hero?"

"Oh, I don't know. . . . Pissing people off, I guess. . . . That's a good hobby. It's a lot of fun – plus it's totally inexpensive."

"Yeah, unlike photography. . . . But photography is fun, too – and I do like the idea of stealing people's souls."

"Well now, there's something else I'm really good at, if you believe what people say in the paper. I can either steal your soul or save it, depending on who you talk to. . . . The jury's still out."

The line has moved steadily, so Caitlin's turn comes to order a bagel, followed by Teach's requisite coffee.

"You waited in this line just for some coffee?"

"You do what you gotta do."

"Well, I'm gonna go over to the toaster and then I need to get to class. It was nice meeting you, hero-boy." Caitlin begins to walk away.

"Do you mind if I walk with you to your class?" Caitlin hesitates for a moment and looks back at Teach as she walks toward the toaster table. "Now don't give me that look, Caitlin – I'm just enjoying talking to someone who doesn't give a crap about anything I've said or done in the past three months, that's all."

"Aren't you going to be late to your class? The GED, right?" (Everyone, it seems, now knows the basic facts of Teach's life and livelihood.)

"That's all right. I've got a good bunch of self-starters. . . . That's the great thing about a GED class – they don't even need you in there half the time."

Caitlin toasts her bagel and quickly spreads on some cream cheese as Teach slowly sips his coffee. At the cafeteria exit, Teach pushes the door open with his back and allows Caitlin to exit in front of him. He follows her out into the already-warm sunshine. "It's so nice out here," Caitlin says, looking up and around at the blue sky. "You don't get many days like this in January – especially up north. . . . Isn't this just a glorious day? Isn't life sometimes just really wonderful?"

Teach smiles. "Yes, it is."

www.ingramcontent.com/pod-product-compliance
Lightning Source LLC
Chambersburg PA
CBHW020402210626
46816CB00006BB/2086